Matched Passion

She felt a wildness within her take over, the same sort of wildness she knew was in him too. As she thought of this he came toward her, took her roughly in his arms, found her mouth with his lips, and kissed her with the same hunger that she felt in herself . . . She locked her arms around his neck and abandoned herself to him . . .

Midnight Gold

Sylvia Grieg

AVON
PUBLISHERS OF BARD, CAMELOT, DISCUS AND FLARE BOOKS

MIDNIGHT GOLD is a work of historical fiction and an original publication of Avon Books. Except for the real-life characters who did exist, the others are the product of the author's imagination, and any resemblance or similarity to actual persons, living or dead, is purely coincidental. Incidents and conversations depicted between the real and the unreal characters are completely fictitious.

AVON BOOKS
A division of
The Hearst Corporation
105 Madison Avenue
New York, New York 10016

First Avon Printing: August 1987

AVON TRADEMARK REG. U.S. PAT. OFF. AND IN OTHER COUNTRIES. MARCA REGISTRADA. HECHO EN U.S.A.

Printed in the U.S.A.

K-R 10 9 8 7 6 5 4 3 2 1

To my daughter, *Carla Luise Weber*,
who never lets me waver in the middle of a risk

and

To my sister, *Inez D. Geller*,
who is always ready to laugh and cry with me

Note to the Reader

The history of the period for MIDNIGHT GOLD is not only fascinating but rich with detail. There was so much information, at first I had no idea what to keep and what to discard. Soon I realized that if I took a few small liberties with dates, I could use the very best of the material that was available. So I did—and I hope that serious historians will understand that MIDNIGHT GOLD is, after all, pure fiction surrounded by events that happened in a slightly different sequence.

Prologue

New York, 1864

Every seat in the theater was taken by eager spectators who felt that five dollars was not too high a price to pay to see the famous Booth brothers perform together. Marielle Preston sat in her box regally, head high, shoulders straight, her long creamy neck exposed and gleaming as audience members on the ground floor craned around to see her. Her dress was of almost transparent gossamer gold and had been specially made to show off her round, perfectly formed breasts underneath the filmy silk of her bodice. Her long cape, laying casually at her side, was made of white fox fur imported from Russia. Her wild, red hair, flaming in extravagant glory, was a perfect foil for both the ornate costume she had chosen and the dazzling diamond necklace and tiara that complemented the outfit; it framed skin that was translucent, making her startlingly blue eyes with their long, dark lashes look big and extremely provocative. Her small, beautifully boned face was equipped with wide, full lips and piquant nose. She was every inch a young, glorious queen.

She tapped her fingernails lightly on the railing of the theatre box as she waited for the play to start. The man beside her noticed and was fascinated by this show of impatience. Marielle Preston was young, rich, and beautiful and, best of all, she was an actress. That, alone, was enough to fascinate Prince Grigori Aleksandrov, her companion and theatrical producer. He smiled softly at her, not realizing that she was seething inside.

The world should have been hers tonight! She had planned her New York opening on the exact night the Booths had engaged the Winter Garden and were performing *Julius Caesar* for one gala night. They were using the profits to fund a statue of Shakespeare in Central Park, the wonderful new pleasure ground that had been a wilderness only three years before. The event, with the three Booth brothers appearing on stage together for the first time, had become the talk of the town.

Luckily, when she had found out about the Booths' arrangements, she had been able to postpone her opening for another week, and wisely made arrangements of her own for one of the best boxes in the Winter Garden. She was still upset, but having dear Grigori at her side helped to quell her disappointment. Not only was he a prince—in fact, a distant relation to the Prince of Wales—and very rich, but more important, he was a true friend.

Marielle watched the play start. She had decided she would enjoy the Booths' peerless performances tonight and use whatever she could to benefit her own opening night next week. The publicity for *Julius Caesar* was the grandest New York had seen in recent years, but Marielle knew it was nothing compared to what was going to begin on the morrow for her own production, thanks to the largesse of the prince. New York would never be the same after her own lavish opening, or so she hoped with all her heart.

As the band struck up and the brothers made their entrance in Caesar's train, an ovation rocked the house. Marielle closed her eyes for a moment and pretended it was for her. The sound of an appreciative audience was music to her ears.

She forced herself to sit back and relax. She had to admit it was worth the money to see the three Booths outdo themselves, each at the top of his form: Edwin as Brutus, Junius as Cassius, and John Wilkes as Mark Antony. Edwin was nervous, Marielle noticed, which surprised her, for he was, by far, the best actor of the three brothers. As was her habit, she began to move her lips silently along with the actors on stage. She knew all their parts and mouthed the lines with her soft, full lips, not noticing that, as she did, the prince was becoming even more fascinated with her than with the actors on the stage.

It was then that she felt her pulse quicken and her heart pound dangerously in her chest, as she realized she was being watched by a man downstairs in the orchestra. He was in the fourth row and his head was turned not to the stage, but toward her box. The man was far away, though, so for an instant Marielle was not sure it was he. Finally she forced herself to look in his direction. Once she was able to stare directly into those bold, sooty grey eyes filled with storm and fire, she was sure. He was beardless, contrary to the fashion, and he had the same jutting jaw she remembered, the dark curly hair, the bold carriage of the head, the air of domination—all were the same; it was Morgan Quinn.

She breathed deeply and exhaled and as she did, his name came off her lips and Prince Aleksandrov turned toward her with a questioning look. She bit her lip, vexed at the slip of her tongue. Morgan Quinn was not a name Marielle wanted to remember. Long ago she had decided never to see him again, to stay as far away from him as she possibly could.

But the memories flooded into her head and she could not shut out his presence. He reminded her of California and of the Far West, a place as savage and uncivilized as he, where the sun shone every day and the sky was so blue it seemed like a painted theatre backdrop. He reminded her of the outdoors and horses and the smell of the earth. He sat in the dress circle in clothes that were stylish and correct, but he looked like his muscles might break through the cloth of his evening clothes if he took so much as one deep breath.

Was she really able to see all that from where she was sitting? Marielle was not sure, But she felt the magnetism of the man below and she was helpless to tear her eyes from him. And as she looked and thought about him, she had to admit to herself that what Morgan Quinn lacked in finesse he made up for in energy, determination, and imagination. She had to admit that in spite of everything, she loved him still.

She wondered if he was in New York now to try to force her to return to the West. He was a man of considerable force, but this time she would be stronger and more determined than he.

Marielle tossed her head and took a deep breath. Maybe his presence here tonight was no more than a coincidence. Maybe he would be long gone before her opening night, the theatrical event she hoped would be as momentous as the Booth brothers' performance. She did not want Morgan Quinn to be around to watch and unnerve her next week, because Marielle was going to attempt to do what had never been done before. She was going to play Hamlet, and she intended not only to be America's first female Hamlet, but the best Hamlet *ever* on any stage.

The play was perfect for her; she knew she could portray the moody volatility of the brooding Dane better than any actor since her father, the great Jeremiah Preston, and at the same time cause a sensation because she was a woman. With her wild, red hair clustering round her head, a short tunic of black silk trimmed with dark sable, black hose and a long flowing silk cloak, she would seem to her audience the very embodiment of the sorrowful young prince. She would give her admiring public proof of her courage and talent, and they would acclaim her and heap upon her the rewards of fame and fortune.

She looked down at the back of Morgan Quinn's handsome head and gave his curls a whimsical smile. She would cause a lot of raised eyebrows and surprise a lot of people within a week's time.

She wondered if there would be a look of surprise in Morgan's eyes if he was present at the theatre on the night of her triumph. Maybe she would enjoy seeing that look. Maybe she should make *sure* he was there. Maybe knowing that he'd witnessed her theatrical victory would help her rid herself of the man who had the effrontery of a devil. Then she smiled again, this time behind her silk fan, as she remembered the old saying: "The devil is no match for a clever woman."

Part I

The Tender Years

Chapter One

The young girl heaved a huge sigh of relief and leaned against the railing of the ship. It seemed to her a miracle that they were safely on board the *Andrew Jackson*, heading around Cape Horn to San Francisco. The winds were good. That meant they would sail that very day.

The girl, whose name was Marielle Preston and who was almost sixteen years old, watched in fascination as the cargo was stowed, the hatches battened down, and the officers helped aboard still in their shoregoing clothes. As the passengers shouted their last farewells and the sun started to slip behind the horizon, the clipper was off to California and the gold fields.

She leaned over the railing, letting her flaming hair blow bright and shiny in the breeze, and watched as a fussy, puffing paddle-wheel tug pulled the ship out into the harbor. There were creaks and groans as the yards moved on the masts, chirps and squeaks from the blocks as the water's roll shifted the lines in them. Marielle heard a deep hum like that of a huge harp playing; it was the wind in the rigging, and every line and stay had its own sound, according to its length and tautness.

The crew, strong and tough, working in different parts of the ship, sang chanteys as they heaved on sheets and halliards. Having a good chanteyman aboard was very important; the rhythm he set helped all hands pull together and thus, lighten the load. The rough sailors on the *Andrew Jackson* seemed to feel that their chanteyman was the best and as they sang, Marielle noted the approval in their looks and voices.

It was very romantic; it was an adventure; 1855 was going to be a good year. She and Papa were going to start a new life. She felt it in her bones. She, Marielle Preston, was different from everyone else; she was the daughter of Jeremiah Preston, a great Shakespearean actor, but also an enthusiastic tippler. Ever since Marielle could remember, it had been her duty to see that Papa arrived at the theatre on time and in a condition to perform his magic as a thespian. For, indeed, it was magic when Jeremiah Preston's magnificent voice boomed over an awed audience. One night he was Hamlet, another, Iago, another Richard III or Romeo or Richelieu.

Life in California was going to be different for the two of them, though. For one thing, Papa was not going to drink. And they were going to earn much more money than they had on the stages in New York. Hadn't old Junius Booth promised that the streets of California were paved with gold?

It had all started last New Year's Eve. Papa had finished his performance at the Park Theatre amidst happy ovations, and then talked her into accompanying him and his longtime acting partner, Sybil Darby, to a party uptown. "We are not going home, Marielle," he'd announced as soon as he'd changed from his costume into a conservative suit of black serge. "We are going to celebrate tonight. Sybil has a friend from England who also believes in consecrating the holiday season. His name is Junius Booth and he is a fine actor. I have seen his work. He is at the National Theatre— uptown." Jeremiah drew himself up more proudly. "For professional reasons, we are going. Get yourself together, daughter. Do you want Mrs. Darby to feel slighted by our inattention?"

Marielle sighed. She doubted that Mrs. Darby would feel slighted whether they went or not, but Papa was a gentleman and concerned about such things.

The celebration was at its height when their carriage arrived at the National Theatre. Introductions were made and Marielle was glad Papa took her hand proudly when he presented her to the renowned Junius Booth.

Junius Booth turned out to be an extremely short, crusty old man with bowed legs, but gallant looking. "You are ravishing, my dear," the actor said to her. "You must meet my two sons who are here tonight . . . my older son, Junius, and my younger boy, Edwin. June . . . Ted . . ." he called to two young men in different parts of the room.

Junius was a lively and sturdy young man with a vivacious wife at his side. But it was Edwin who caught Marielle's imagination: a young man several years older than she, somewhat taller than his father, but slighter and frailer. He had dark, straight hair and deep, dark eyes that looked very sad under a high forehead, eyes that seemed to hold the pain of the centuries within them. Edwin Booth smiled at her and she smiled back shyly as they were introduced. It was immediately as if she had known him for a long time.

"Please call me Ted like my family does," he said solemnly, and Marielle knew at once that she could trust him. Marielle lost track of time as they talked that evening.

Later they found their fathers, the two old actors, seated opposite each other, matching each other drink for drink as they traded theatrical stories.

It was then that young Junius, Jr., joined them and started to describe the land of gold beyond the Sierras. He wove a good story and kept his audience captivated. Marielle learned that he had recently returned from Sacramento and San Francisco where, he said, there was more money to be made in the acting profession than in the gold mines. The miners, it seemed, loved a good show and were ready to pay any price for entertainment.

His words brought an excited light to Jeremiah Preston's eyes. "Tell us exactly what you have seen, lad."

Everyone stopped to listen to June Booth's tale. "I tell you, you do not need a pick and shovel. All you need is experience in the theater. Then the gold dust is there for you to take the easy way. No need to find it and mine it. It is given to you with love and affection by the fortune hunters who found it and now have nothing on which to spend it."

Marielle and Edwin Booth exchanged looks. The room was absolutely quiet.

"I am returning to California and I'm going to manage the finest theaters there," June continued. "I have offered my father a warm invitation from the West . . . a contract he cannot refuse, it is so profitable." He looked around the room and especially at Jeremiah Preston. "And to everyone in this room, I offer a job on the legitimate stage at a finer salary than you have ever received. All you need is your own passage to the West."

Marielle saw the look that crossed Papa's face. In an instant, the golden land over the rainbow had beckoned to Papa and he'd responded with a fierceness that bordered on madness. It unnerved her completely and she felt a sickening feeling in the pit of her stomach.

"Who will be going with me besides my father?" June Booth asked of the small crowd surrounding him.

To Marielle's dismay, the first one to open his mouth was Jeremiah Preston. There was no hesitation. "Count me in," he orated in his most melodious voice, flinging one arm skyward in a dramatic gesture. "My daughter and I will be happy to leave for California immediately. And if she is willing, I invite Mrs. Sybil Darby, actress extraordinaire, to travel with us to paradise."

The actor tried to stand up, found it difficult, but finally managed. He held up his glass and made a toast. "To California," he said.

Marielle had, at first, tried to talk her father out of his bold plan, but every time he spoke of California a fire lit in his eyes, and she knew it was no use. And now, standing at the railing of the *Andrew Jackson*, she felt caught up in the plan, too. They'd be traveling around Cape Horn, by far the longest, but also the least expensive route they'd found, and it excited Marielle to think of all the exotic places she'd get to see—places she'd only read about in books. So, although life in the past had not been easy, Marielle was full of hope for the future.

She started toward the airless cabin that had been assigned to their company of three, a cabin they were most fortunate to have since the rest of the passengers, all male, had been put on the 'tween deck where they all had to live together in temporary bunks.

As she turned, her skirts brushed over the wet deck and she nearly upset a bucket being used by one of the seamen. The sailor was on his hands and knees swabbing the deck, using a porous stone about the size of a Bible. He used sand as an abrasive and water as a lubricant to scour the deck until it was white. The seaman raised his head and smiled at her, and at the same time caught the bucket deftly with one outstretched arm.

She stopped right in front of him. He was barefoot, the wooden bucket with a rope handle now back at his side. His trousers were rolled halfway to his knees with one neat patch sewn over the left knee. His dark shirt was pushed up at the sleeves to reveal sinewy forearms, and there was a jaunty red cotton kerchief tied around his sun-tanned neck. On his head, he wore a black shallow-brimmed hat from which damp, dark curls escaped onto his forehead.

Marielle stopped and her hand flew up to her face as she felt herself blush. "I'm sorry about the bucket."

"Nothing disastrous. It takes time to learn how to roll with the ship." Catching her look of embarrassment and grinning, the sailor straightened up and whipped off his hat.

Marielle saw a shock of dark, curly hair falling over an intelligent forehead ending at straight, clean, dark brows. His eyes were bold and gray with a lively sparkle, and slightly slanted, and his mouth was well-formed and sensuous. Best of all, he had a devil's smile, which at the same time made him look like a mischievous boy.

"Maybe you can show me how one rolls with the ship," she said impetuously.

"I'm sorry, miss. But I can't talk to you." The smile left his face.

"Why?"

"I'm a sailor. You're a passenger. It's not permitted." He turned from her abruptly and started to stride away.

"What's your name?" she called after him, desperately wishing he would stay. Her face glowed with the sea air and her blue eyes sparkled. Without knowing it, she made a very pretty picture standing on the deck of the ship.

Turning his face back to her for a moment, the man smiled once again, and she thought that when he smiled he was absolutely beautiful with all that dark, unruly hair and those white, even teeth. It was a real masculine beauty, much handsomer than all the elegant young actors who played with her father.

As she glanced at his rugged good looks for the last time before he disappeared, she found he stirred strange feelings within her, feelings she had never felt before. The heart within her bosom began to beat with such violence that she had to bring her hand up to still it.

She couldn't stop herself from running after him, not really knowing why, but knowing she must speak to him once more. "What is your name? Please!" she called to him when his strong back came into sight.

He turned around, and did not smile this time. "My name is Morgan Quinn." With that, he frowned and turned away from her.

When she opened the door of the cabin, she caught the sour smell of old liquor, and wondered if it came from Papa's bunk or from that of Sybil Darby. The raven-haired, buxom Mrs. Darby had been well-known in London and in New York as a fine actress, but her love of whiskey made her a bad influence on Papa, though he hardly needed Mrs. Darby to urge him to drink. Still, Jeremiah Preston and Sybil Darby made a formidable team when on the stage, and Marielle loved Papa enough to accept Sybil.

A long time ago, Papa had told Marielle about her mother, a beautiful Frenchwoman with whom Papa and every other man in New York had fallen madly in love. It was a most romantic story, the way Papa told it. But Mama had died when Marielle was two years old, and she didn't really remember her even though she tried. It was Papa she remembered, holding her in his arms and loving her and raising her.

Now there were the two Prestons and Sybil Darby. They clung to each other in desperation for survival from day to day. But more and more she was becoming the strong one of the three, the one who kept her wits about her and used all her resources to keep starvation away from the Preston doorstep.

The cabin was empty when she arrived, though it was evident that Papa and Mrs. Darby had stowed their things while Marielle lingered at the railing of the *Andrew Jackson*, and then headed off to the passengers' saloon; but for once she was glad. It meant she would be left in peace in the cabin.

The stateroom assigned to them was tiny. It contained two double-decker bunks and a washstand. When they'd first been shown the cabin, Papa had insisted that Marielle take a lower bunk. He would sleep in the bunk above her, and Mrs. Darby in the lower one on the other side of the cabin. A thin sheet of canvas was rolled down the middle each night to make Papa's presence appropriate. It was not an uncomfortable setting, but as usual, Mrs. Darby had started complaining immediately. Considering where all the other passengers slept, though, Marielle knew they were lucky to be here at all.

Marielle unpacked her meager possessions. Then she washed her face and made herself neat and tidy in front of Mrs. Darby's makeup mirror. Studying herself carefully she decided that although her dress was adequate, it was not what she would have chosen for her meeting with the sailor, Morgan Quinn. She wondered if the seaman might have mistaken her for a young lady of eighteen, but after a meticulous scrutiny, she sadly admitted to herself that it was not probable, that unfair though it was, she looked younger than her actual years, not older. She was sure that even if they bumped into each other again, he would not be impressed with her anymore than he was today. And, suddenly, she felt bereft of something, but did not know what.

Just before Marielle was to meet Papa and Mrs. Darby in the dining room, she began to feel seasick. She wondered if it was because the *Andrew Jackson* was a clipper that was known mainly

for her speed and had, during one exceptional trip, broken the
record from New York City to San Francisco by making the voyage round the Horn in eighty-nine days and four hours. But now
the ship was old and decrepit, and she was sure that no records
would be broken on this trip.

Instead of eating dinner that night, Marielle remained in her
bunk. She continued feeling wretched for almost eight days, which,
she was told, was what she could expect under the circumstances.

During her illness Papa was very tender and brought her special
bowls of simple gruel from the galley when she could not stay on
her feet for the trip to the dining saloon, but she could keep nothing down.

"You must keep up your strength, my darling. We have a long
journey ahead," Papa told her as he kissed her white forehead and
held a basin to her lips whenever she needed it.

But the weather became stormy, and Marielle continued feeling
miserable.

Finally, on the ninth day of the voyage, Marielle awoke without
that nauseated feeling in the pit of her stomach. She got out of her
berth, stood up straight for the first time in many days, and
stretched luxuriously. She was very hungry.

Papa came in to see her after breakfast in the dining room. He
brought her a bowl of oatmeal with sugar and milk, and watched
her gobble it down. "You must be well, Marielle," he said, staring at her with relief in his blue eyes.

"I feel like a new person," Marielle said, and stretched some
more.

"Get dressed, daughter. We will stroll on the deck together,"
Jeremiah said. "We will meet right outside." He left her alone to
get dressed. As he closed the cabin door, he blew a kiss in her
direction.

It looked like Jeremiah Preston and Sybil Darby were having a
good time on the ship—although the actress from England continued to complain. However, as Papa explained, the food for passengers was not so terrible, and they thrived on the fresh sea air.
In fact, Marielle had not seen her father or Sybil Darby look so
healthy for a long time.

She took out her best outfit to wear on her first real stroll on
deck. Perhaps she would catch a glimpse of Morgan Quinn. Mrs.
Darby had given her one of her old velvet gowns, from which
Marielle had fashioned an entire outfit for herself. She had cut the
chocolate velvet into a dress and a short cape and had stitched it

by hand with tiny, careful stitches, working far into the night as Jeremiah tred the boards at the Park Lane Theatre. In one of the outdoor stalls on Fulton Street, she found a pale beige lace collar and on Fourteenth Street she found a fetching beige bonnet that pulled the whole outfit together. The color looked especially attractive because it showed off her deep red hair and very fair skin.

She was glad she had gone to all the trouble when she was fully dressed and ready to leave the cabin. Papa looked at her approvingly as she came on deck, and paid her extravagant compliments on her outfit even though he had seen the dress many, many times in its original form on Sybil Darby. "You have never looked so beautiful, my precious," he said in his strong, melodious voice. "Though I think you've lost a bit of weight during your illness. We shall see to it that you put some flesh back on your bones."

Marielle listened to that voice that was saturated with the magnetism of his personality. He was in fine form this morning, not a trace of the thick speech and slurred words that came when there was a glass in his hand. On a morning like this, she was proud to be his daughter.

They took a slow stroll all around the deck, with Jeremiah checking every so often to make sure his convalescing patient wasn't getting overtired. Marielle kept watching for Morgan Quinn. She tried to move grandly, with dignity and grace, just in case he was watching her. It was only after they'd circled the deck several times that the seaman appeared.

He seemed to be moving away from a small crowd gathered at the railing of the clipper. Marielle held on to Papa's arm tightly, and as the sailor came closer she smiled prettily and held her head up high. The sudden lurch she felt in her bosom was the same as when she had first met him, nine days ago.

From the look on his face, there was no doubt he remembered her and she was grateful. She had forgotten how tall he was, but she had not forgotten how handsome he was.

"Good day, Mr. Quinn," she said, and stopped Papa in his tracks as they came face to face with the sailor.

His eyes looked cold and angry as he passed her and Papa without stopping. Against the sound of the boisterous sea, Marielle thought she heard a "Good day" in return to her greeting before he passed right by and disappeared from view.

It happened so fast that she had no time to do anything but continue on at Papa's side. Even Papa, who had no idea what had taken place, looked somewhat surprised. Morgan Quinn had been like a storm passing swiftly by. The storm was over, but Marielle still felt its effect, although she could no longer see the center of the disturbance.

They moved on toward a group gathering near the railing of the ship and found themselves in the middle of a funeral at sea. A passenger standing nearby told them one of the sailors had died, and was now going to his watery grave. He had been sewn into a canvas bag, which had been loaded down with stones and then lowered into the ocean after a brief, cursory ceremony by the captain. It was a sad and dismal group who looked on as the sea burial progressed. It was not the way Marielle pictured anyone should leave this world.

She wondered if the sea funeral had affected Morgan Quinn so strongly that he had to leave in the middle. Was the dead sailor a special buddy? Was that why he had been so abrupt with her as she passed him on her stroll around the deck? Was that why he looked so cold and angry? She shivered. She would never forget the look on his lean, strong-boned face. It was as if he were ready to fight the whole world all by himself. In that brief moment, he had looked like a wild man with a spirit that other men lacked—a spirit that, nonetheless, drew her to him. For good or for evil, she felt united with Morgan Quinn, captive to the passionate nature his stormy look had so clearly expressed.

Chapter Two

Late that afternoon Marielle found herself thinking about Seaman Morgan Quinn as she waited for Papa and Mrs. Darby to awaken from their naps so that they could go to dinner. It would be her first time in the dining saloon. She realized as, at last, Papa and Mrs. Darby readied themselves for the evening meal, that the sailor had invaded her thoughts so deeply she could not make his image disappear. She tried to compare him to men she had known in the past, men like Ted Booth, but the comparison made her head whirl—for in her past there had been no men like Morgan Quinn.

On deck, the stars in the dark sky seemed very low, and Marielle felt that if she reached out with her hand, she might be able to touch them. But it was just an illusion so, instead, she focused on the first star she had seen and made a wish.

She, Jeremiah, and Sybil had filed along the narrow companionway onto the starlit deck. As they approached the dining saloon, Morgan Quinn appeared out of the shadows. "May I have a word with you?" he whispered to Marielle, who was lagging behind her father and Mrs. Darby.

Her wish had come true.

"I need a shawl," she called out to Papa. "I'll meet you in a moment."

Thankfully, Papa and Mrs. Darby continued on without stopping. "Don't get lost, my precious one," she heard Papa say over his shoulder as he complacently took Sybil's arm and escorted her into the dining saloon.

Morgan Quinn looked around the deck before he spoke to her again. "I'm breaking the rules. Only officers may speak with the passengers . . . as I told you once before."

"Is there no way at all that we may talk at length?"

15

"I think not. But it has occurred to me that I was very rude to you this afternoon. I want to apologize."

He did not bother to explain why he had been rude, but the apology was enough.

She felt bold; perhaps it was his mere physical presence that made her so giddy. "There must be a time when we can arrange a rendezvous." She loved the word. She'd heard Mrs. Darby use it in a play.

He laughed out loud, a wonderful laugh that spread crinkles at the corners of his eyes and opened his mouth wide to reveal perfect white teeth.

She could hardly contain her pique. "That wasn't supposed to be funny."

He sobered instantly. "I'm sorry. I only meant you are so young, but your words seem older than you . . ." He stopped. "I'm making it worse. I didn't mean to . . ." He didn't try to finish the sentence, but his lips quirked upward in amusement.

"There is no need to be rude again, Mr. Quinn. I doubt if you are that many years older than I." His face was magnificent to her, every curve and plane accentuated by the shadows spilling down over his sun-bronzed features.

"What is your name?" he asked suddenly.

"Marielle Preston."

"I didn't mean to be rude twice, Miss Preston," he said. "But I'm sure you have no intention of getting me into trouble either," he finished, giving her a rakish grin.

"How long have you been a seaman?" she asked.

"This is my third and last trip. I promised my father I would give the sea a chance, and now I have. But I won't be going to sea again." His face was completely expressionless, but she could read the passions that lay beneath it. He was certainly not like the gentle Ted Booth.

"Well, then, Seaman Quinn. I do not suppose, under the circumstances, that we shall be speaking to each other again during this long voyage. I certainly don't wish to cause you any further trouble." She held her head high and started to move away.

He allowed her to pass him, then she felt his arm pull her back. His voice softened. "Perhaps I can find a way for us to meet, Miss Preston," he said, looking at her now almost tenderly. "If I cannot contact you myself, my friend, Johnnie Fox, will. He'll let you know where and when we can *rendezvous*." He smiled, that wonderful, mischievous smile that gave her the feeling they shared a secret.

"Who is this Johnnie Fox? How will I know him?"

"He is messboy aboard this vessel. He is in the dining room during most meals. It is easier for him to talk to you than for me."

With that, he put his hand forward as if for a formal handshake. Marielle extended hers. When they touched, he held her hand for what seemed a second longer than necessary. "Good night, Marielle," he said.

"Good night, Mr. Quinn," she said, trying to find her way to the dining saloon in as haughty a manner as she could. This was just in case Morgan Quinn was still watching her.

When she dared look back, she found he was no longer there at all, which not only disappointed her, but made her angry. Once she found Papa and Sybil Darby, she flounced down beside them with a pout on her soft lips and a steely look in her wide blue eyes.

"I'm glad you're here, Marielle. Where's your shawl?" Papa asked absently. "We were making festive plans for your birthday. If you approve, we'll arrange everything with the captain."

Ordinarily, the idea of a birthday celebration would have excited her, but she was still too consumed by her meeting with Morgan Quinn to get caught up in the plans.

"Whatever you wish, dear Papa," Marielle said meekly in answer to his question, and Jeremiah looked at her curiously to see why she was acting so strange.

She scanned the room to see if she could find Johnnie Fox. It was fitted with panels of beautiful wood. The mizzenmast rose through the center of the room and around the mast was the mess table, which was fitted with racks to prevent dishes from sliding off in rough weather. The swivel dining chairs were fastened to the deck to keep them from shifting. The captain and his mates ate together with Sybil Darby and the Prestons. There was a steward and a messman attending to their needs, and the food was quite good and included fresh meat, biscuits, jam, milk, and coffee.

The moment Marielle saw the round-cheeked, sturdy lad taking dishes off the mess table, she knew it must be Johnnie Fox. He was younger than the rest of the crew, yet he performed his duties with a relaxed nonchalance that belied his youth. Marielle watched him intently to see if he would acknowledge her existence, while Sybil chattered away.

"We will put on a theatrical evening the night of your birthday. Your father and I shall perform something light . . . perhaps if we're well received, we'll follow up with a pantomime. We shall set up the lounge as a theater and invite all the passengers from the 'tween deck. We'll have the captain break out some bubbly and we shall toast you. It is, after all, a grand occasion.''

"I would like to recite a poem," Marielle heard herself say.

"I don't want you performing in front of all those men. You're too young," Papa replied almost immediately.

"No. Let her. It's a good idea, Jeremiah. She can recite a lady-like poem," Sybil Darby said. "She's old enough."

"Thank you, Sybil," Marielle said politely.

"Have I nothing to say about this?" Jeremiah asked.

"A pretty little girl won't hurt us, Jeremiah," Sybil said placidly. "It will liven up our performance. I'll go and arrange everything with the captain." She got up and walked purposefully in the direction of the captain.

Papa looked disconcerted; Marielle was elated.

The days leading up to her birthday passed quickly enough. She had hoped to find a way to talk to Morgan before the night of the theatrical and invite him to watch as she recited her poem. She had chosen a piece from Thomas Campion's *Fourth Book of Airs*, one of the few poetry books in Papa's costume trunk other than the Shakespeare he always carried with him. Jeremiah and Sybil had been busy all week long setting up and rehearsing their performance, so Marielle was left to her own devices. After memorizing the poem and practicing her elocution and gestures, she explored the parts of the clipper on which she was allowed.

Once, she saw Morgan in the distance, but as she got closer he climbed quickly up a Jacob's ladder, so high she got dizzy merely looking up at him from where she stood.

In the dining saloon, she had no better luck with Morgan's friend, Johnnie Fox. Never once did he so much as glance at her, and whenever she tried to catch his eye he busied himself clearing dishes and wiping the table.

Finally, one evening, when she had given up all hope of extending Morgan a personal invitation to her celebration, she heard a male voice call to her from behind the quarterboat on the starboard side of the ship.

"Miss? I'm over here. Just turn right and walk ten steps and don't say a word . . . because someone could be watching you."

She couldn't see a soul. It all sounded very mysterious. The voice did not remind her of Quinn's; maybe it was Johnnie Fox behind the small boat.

She was right. The messboy crouched low, hidden by the boat, and beckoned to her. His round apple cheeks puffed out into a smile as she reached him, and he pulled her down to the safety of his hiding place.

"Miss Preston?" he asked, whispering conspiratorially. "My name is Johnnie Fox. I'm Morgan Quinn's friend."

"I know. I see you every day in the dining room. But you've never spoken to me. Why?"

His face broke into a grin mingled with embarrassment. "The captain is a hard man. I cannot talk to you at the mess." He paused before going on.

"Miss . . . Marielle. I have a message for you from Morgan Quinn."

"Yes!" She tried not to sound too excited.

"He says he cannot find a way to see you. It's impossible. There's no place on the ship that's safe. He doesn't want to be flogged. Or worse!"

"Of course he doesn't want to be flogged. Or worse! Tell him to come to my cabin after his watch is over. I'll tell Papa that I'm not hungry. He and Mrs. Darby will be in the dining room and no one will see Mr. Quinn. I'll leave the cabin door open. All he has to do is slip in."

Johnnie Fox looked unconvinced. "I'll tell him, Miss . . . Marielle. But I don't think he'll come."

"And why not? All I want to do is invite him to my performance tomorrow night. It's my birthday. You're invited too."

But Morgan did not come at the appointed time, and Marielle became angrier as the night became older. She started to storm around the cabin, furiously pacing back and forth in the narrow space. She felt miserable, hungry, and horribly alone.

She had almost decided to join Papa and Sybil in the passengers' lounge when the cabin door, still open a crack, the way she had left it, opened wider and she saw Quinn slip coolly and gracefully into the cabin and close the door behind him. He made no sound as he leaned against the closed door and eyed her.

His appearance was so unexpected she did not know how to react. "Why have you kept me waiting? You're insufferable," she cried, the same way she had seen Mrs. Wendell Pyne do when she had appeared with Papa last year in Baltimore. She was not quite sure she was using the word *insufferable* correctly, but it sounded right.

"If I'm insufferable, I would not be here. In fact, I'm here only because Johnnie Fox made such an issue of the matter. I believe you've made a conquest." He arched a brow and smiled at her derisively.

"I can't stay. The captain isn't lenient to those who break ship's regulations. I've seen men flogged for less."

She could see he was serious, and somehow simply looking into the depth of his sooty gray eyes made her anger fade away. She calmed down, and invited him to her birthday celebration.

"I'm sorry," he said. "But for obvious reasons, I don't see how it will be possible." With that he opened the door of the cabin, as if to leave. Marielle could feel tears collecting in the corners of her eyes—she'd so wanted him to accept her invitation. But then he bent down and picked up a parcel sitting at the foot of the door. "I came mainly to bring you a birthday present." Opening the paper it was wrapped in, he handed her an orange. It was a perfectly shaped fruit, bright in color, thick in skin.

She had not eaten an orange in months. They were scarce even in New York during the winter months. It was a great luxury.

"It's very good for scurvy," he told her, smiling again and as she accepted the extravagant gift, she felt deep remorse for her anger at him earlier.

A beam of pleasure filled her eyes and he gave her an answering smile. "Wherever did you find it?" she asked.

"You can thank Johnnie Fox. He's been known to come across the most interesting edibles. He works closely with the steward and the cooks."

"Thank you for the present. I wish you could attend my birthday celebration."

"I'm not an officer. I'm sorry."

"I'm sorry too," she said sadly without pressing the matter any further.

He was gone as quietly and quickly as he had appeared, and she was left once again with a yearning she did not understand. It was the same kind of sweet yearning she had felt the night she first saw his face. Again she felt bereft, experiencing a hunger for him that was new and frightening.

Chapter Three

Sybil Darby found the unopened bottle of spirits in her costume trunk as she probed to the very bottom to find the banjo. Marielle saw her bring forth the long dark bottle and the banjo almost simultaneously and saw the older woman's eyes open wide with delight. Marielle knew her delight was not for the banjo.

"Can you play? Perhaps this will amuse you?"

"No, not really," Marielle said as she looked worriedly at the bottle dangling like a prize from Mrs. Darby's plump hand.

"Jeremiah, see what I've found. Can you imagine forgetting it was there all along?"

Papa chuckled, danced a little jig over to Sybil, and together they capered around the crowded cabin holding the bottle between them.

"It's fitting that you found it for Marielle's birthday celebration. Let's have a taste of it, beauty," he said to Sybil.

Marielle looked away. What she thought was going to be a perfect day was not going to turn out that way at all. She knew her Papa. He and Mrs. Darby would never stop at just a taste.

Knowing there was nothing she could do about it, Marielle went out on deck and left them alone. Away from her father, whom she feared might not be in any shape to attend her birthday celebration tonight, Marielle breathed the salty sea air freely and drank in the sunshine.

As she did, she thought of her papa; there were so many contradictions to his character. He could be so irresponsible at times, and at others so warm and loving. Like that very morning.

Papa had still been asleep in his upper berth when Marielle opened her eyes. Sybil was asleep on the other side of the canvas curtain. On the washstand were two birthday presents: a pretty handkerchief trimmed with lace from Sybil and a tiny seed pearl brooch set in gold from Papa.

She immediately climbed up to his berth and woke her father. "It's beautiful, Papa. I love it," she cried gleefully, kissing him as he pretended to still be asleep.

But, finally, when he opened one eye and she knew he was pretending, she kissed him and he opened the other eye too. "It belonged to your mother. She brought it with her from Paris. I know she would have wanted you to have it."

The noise they were making awakened Sybil, who sat up and groaned, "It's too early to make so much racket," but she laughed with gratification when Marielle told her how much she loved her handkerchief.

"Today is your day, my baby," Papa had said. "We will have to see that you enjoy it right through the last minute." He swung his legs over his berth and prepared to drop down from his elevated bed.

"What are you wearing?" Marielle heard Sybil ask from her side of the room.

"It's between my burgundy wool and my chocolate velvet . . . so I guess it will be the velvet . . . and the new brooch . . . and I shall carry my new handkerchief in the cuff of my sleeve."

"Very nice, child. Let me see what I have in my costume trunk that might liven up the outfit," Sybil said. "Besides, I'm certain I have a banjo somewhere in that trunk." She moved the canvas to one side for the rest of the day, and opened her costume trunk. It had taken only a moment or two for Sybil to discover the bottle.

She did not know how long she stayed on the quarterdeck while presumably below Papa and Sybil toasted to her health, but she knew she had missed both breakfast and the noonday repast from the hunger pangs she felt. It was then that she saw Johnnie Fox coming toward her. His merry eyes danced as he walked toward her with a purposeful stride.

Since she did not want to get him into trouble, she started to retreat, but he stopped her.

"Don't go, please. I have special permission from the captain to seek you out and present to you a birthday present from myself and the rest of the good hands on the *Andrew Jackson*." He held a small wooden box, which he handed her after making his speech.

The box did not have a cover. Inside was some discarded material, and in the middle of the rags sat a small, all-white kitten. "She was born on board ship," Johnnie Fox explained as he put his hand inside the box and took the kitten out by the scruff of its neck. The crew and I thought you might like to have her. Her mother lives with us in the forecastle.''

"She's adorable. I love her,'' Marielle said, and took the kitten from the messboy. Suddenly her spirits spiraled. She felt good again and kissed the cat between its greenish yellow eyes. "I thank you. And please thank the rest of the crew.''

"It's nothing, Miss . . . Marielle. She has six brothers and sisters still down there.''

They both laughed. "I shall call her Snowball,'' she said as she gazed tenderly at the kitten.

"I must go now,'' Johnnie said.

"I know Quinn won't come to my celebration, but will you?'' Marielle asked with a trace of sadness.

"I'll be on duty so I'll definitely be there. If I may say so, Miss, Morgan Quinn would be there too, but ordinary hands don't have the same rights the officers do. You understand!'' He left her with a cheery good-bye after wishing her a happy day.

She hugged the kitten to her, talking to it and cuddling it as if it were a baby. Then she put it back in the box and went back to the stateroom.

Papa was worse than she had anticipated. She gathered he had consumed most of the bottle.

"What does this mean?'' Marielle asked Sybil. "What happens to the theatrical we had planned?''

"Everything will be fine. Just give us a few hours to rest. You will see!''

"Can I do anything?''

"Nothing, child. Oh, God, I feel rather ill. Just let us sleep. Nothing will go wrong.'' She backed up her statement by going to the washstand and standing over it ready to heave. Then she changed her mind and got into her berth. "Let me sleep for exactly one hour and then wake me. Promise?''

Marielle nodded numbly. "I promise,'' she mumbled.

With much misgiving, Marielle left them once again and took Snowball to the dining room and asked the steward for some milk.

"That's all right for now, but cats earn their keep here. Just send her below once a day and she'll come back well fed. Mice,'' he said, and laughed out loud when she hugged the kitten to her bosom with a look of horror.

She strolled the quarterdeck still feeling forlorn and talked to Snowball for what, she hoped, was more or less an hour's time, returning to the stateroom when the sun was just beginning to slip behind the horizon. Papa and Sybil were still dead to the world and from the snores emanating from Papa, Marielle knew he would be that way for a long time. She jostled Sybil in the hope she might wake, but Sybil just covered her head with her arms and turned over.

She would go to dinner by herself, she decided. She washed herself with water from the ewer on the washstand and noticed that her breasts seemed larger, that the pink nipples stood proudly erect, rising above her slender-waisted figure.

Dressing herself carefully and wearing exactly what she said she would, she combed her wild, red hair into a softly fluffed halo of shimmering fullness. After making sure that Snowball was safely asleep in her box of rags, she was ready. But before she left, she tried once more to wake Sybil.

This time, to Marielle's relief, Sybil awoke. "What time is it?"

"Almost eight o'clock."

Sybil sprang into action. Her first stratagem was to try to wake Jeremiah, who only moaned loudly at her repeated attempts. Instead, she dressed as quickly as possible, quicker than Marielle had ever seen her do.

Her second trick was to examine Marielle and then, to Marielle's dismay, cut her dress so she would look more grown-up. She did this simply by scissoring away part of the dress to form a deep vee. Clipping the new brooch at the bottom of the vee, Sybil stepped back to survey her work and frowned.

"What's wrong with me?" Marielle asked.

Sybil threw up her hands. "I made a mistake. You look younger that way, not older. Too late now. Just get out there and sing. I'll try and accompany you on the banjo."

She hustled Marielle out of the stateroom and into the passengers' saloon, ignoring Marielle's protests. "I can't sing. I have only one poem to recite," she cried, alarmed at the state of affairs and wondering if Sybil had gone completely mad.

In the passengers' lounge, every voyager on the clipper was squeezed together, practically hanging from the rafters. Word had gotten out that there was to be entertainment and that they were to see Sybil and Marielle perform. The men had been at sea for over a month, with no entertainment except for an occasional game of cards or checkers. They were ready for anything, especially if there was a female involved. Even before the entertainment started, the rough men stamped their feet and clapped their hands. That is what Marielle saw when Sybil pushed her toward the makeshift stage.

"I shall be right there with you, girl. Don't be afraid," Sybil said. "And for God's sake, don't recite. Sing."

"What shall I sing?" Marielle cried.

"Sing *anything*. Sing *everything* you know. Sing the poem, for God's sake. Look at all those men out there. We can't leave them empty-handed. Just get out there and do whatever you can."

She danced out, her red curls flying haphazardly, framing the delicate oval of her face. The velvet dress, scissored low to expose her young breasts, was molded to her body, enticing every man present with her childish charm.

For the first moment, she looked out at her audience with alarm. But then something came over her and she started. Once she did, she never stopped for a second after singing the verses of the poem she had memorized to the tune of an old lullaby she had heard Papa croon to her when she was a baby.

> *There is a garden in her face,*
> *Where roses and white lilies grow;*
> *A heav'nly paradise is that place,*
> *Wherein all pleasant fruits do flow.*
> *There cherries grow which none may buy,*
> *Till "cherry-ripe" themselves do cry.*

The room became quiet, so she sang the verse of the poem again. When she finished, the audience started cheering. She had never heard cheers like this before, not even at the theatre where Papa performed. It gave her courage and made her feel good.

Then she danced jigs, sang every song she could remember as Mrs. Darby accompanied her on the banjo, which she played with a lilt, if not musical perfection. The men kept cheering and applauding, so she did a pantomime as a last resort. After she finished each number, the men stood up and whistled and stamped their feet and threw coins at her feet. They could not get enough of the girl with the wild flaming hair and childish, high-pitched singing voice who filled the makeshift stage with her magic.

At first she did not know what to do, but Mrs. Darby nodded discreetly at her and Marielle understood that she was to continue until the coins stopped flying. She did not mind by this time. She was enjoying herself immensely.

But the best moment of all for Marielle was when she discovered that Morgan Quinn was outside the saloon and had been watching her entire performance, and that he was as mesmerized as the rest of her audience. She saw his face outlined clearly in the moonlight.

She was a great success, much more so than she could possibly realize. Apparently, though, Mrs. Darby realized it immediately, because she kept urging her on and on. When there was absolutely nothing left in her repertoire and she was soaked to the skin with her own perspiration, she sang the Campion poem, "Cherry-Ripe," once more and finished her show.

Instinctively, Marielle knew the proper moment to curtsy low and let the men know that the show was at an end. They were still cheering her when she skipped lightly out of the passengers' saloon.

As she came into contact with the cool night air, the soft wind wafted through her clothes and revived her so that the flush on her cheeks became a soft subdued pink and the flaming damp tendrils falling onto her forehead dried into feathery wisps. Without hesitation, she turned left and went directly to the spot where she knew Morgan Quinn had spent the last two hours watching her intently.

She was not surprised to find him still there, as if unconsciously he was waiting for her. Still in a state of high stimulation, Marielle saw Quinn move quietly to the stern of the clipper, looking at the sea beyond. He seemed to be deep in thought and unaware she was coming toward him. But when she approached, he turned suddenly as if he knew she had been there all along.

He did not smile at her or greet her. He just looked at her as if he were seeing her for the first time. "I have never seen anyone in the theatre do what you did tonight," he said simply.

She knew he meant it as a compliment. Before he could stop her, she threw her arms around his neck, pulled herself up along the long length of his body and put her lips to his. She was so close she could feel his muscles stirring and the sound of his breath came out in a great gasp, as if the kiss was totally unexpected. She was so close she could hear the sound of his heart beating in rhythm with her own.

It was then that Marielle Preston, just turned sixteen, discovered that desire worked two ways, and that there was as much desire in Morgan Quinn for her as there was in her for him. After she'd felt him responding, though, there was a second when she thought he was going to thrust her aside in anger; instead, he seemed to change his mind and enfolded her in his arms and kissed her as she wanted, just as she had always imagined a first kiss should be. The kiss did not last as long as she would have liked because he did finally thrust her aside with a look of disapproval that said her brazenness did not please him.

She was not angry, because how was he to know that it was her first kiss and that she wanted it to last as long as possible? How was he to know how much she had enjoyed that bittersweet melding of their lips, the way his arms held her, and the feel of his body against hers? But she forced herself to put those physical feelings out of her head almost immediately. There was something more important, as far as she was concerned. She realized she had not only taken his body by surprise, but she had surprised him emotionally, as well; he had succumbed to her with runaway passion, even if it was only momentary. For one brief, magical moment, she had the upper hand.

She smiled at him sweetly and docilely allowed herself to be held at arm's distance by Morgan Quinn. He was angry, but his anger did not frighten her now.

She left him standing there and returned to her cabin. Papa was fast asleep when she came in. She undressed by the light of the moon and climbed in bed, falling almost immediately into a deep, untroubled sleep.

Chapter Four

The next day she learned that a hand on the clipper had been flogged. Even before she made the inquiry, she knew that the man must be Quinn and that he had been seen by one of the officers in her embrace. She wanted to find him and offer him solace from his physical pain, but there was no way she could contact him without making matters worse. She dreamed of the flogging that night, and woke up crying.

Papa, remorseful once again for having been drunk, was extra kind and tried to comfort her, but to no avail. She was desolate. Weeks went by and she did not see Quinn and wondered how it was possible for a crew member to stay so well hidden from her sight in the middle of an ocean. During mealtime, she tried to make contact with Johnnie Fox, but it was as if she did not exist. He did his job around her without so much as a single sign to let her know that he was aware of her anguish.

They were rounding the Cape, or doubling it, as the old-timers said, and the weather was terrible, as it usually was in this part of the world. The food became worse as all hands were needed for more important chores than cooking, and many of the passengers became ill. Several of the men died and were given dismal sea burials, but Marielle was assured, when she asked, that these passengers had been ill before they started the voyage.

As the storms battered the clipper and the crew worked harder and longer hours, everyone's nerves became taut, and Marielle had more time to sit in the stateroom and think and become more depressed. Often she sat in the dark because the passengers were not allowed to light the oil lamps for fear they would fall and break and cause serious fire damage. This was in addition to Marielle's fear that the ship was splitting on the rocks of Cape Horn. Only

Snowball, purring contentedly on her lap, helped assuage her irrational fears during the terrible weeks when the ship made little progress toward its destination and on some occasions, in fact, lost nautical mileage to the savage winds buffeting her.

She could not help remembering she had been an enormous success her one time on the stage, though. When the money thrown in admiration at her feet was counted, it had added up to more than one complete passage. The idea of having earned so much money in so little time was a constant source of wonder to Marielle, who had, in the past, had to pinch pennies for luxuries and necessities alike because of Papa's spendthrift ways. Sybil immediately figured that if two more performances were given before the voyage was over, their three passages would be paid for free and clear.

But Papa put his foot down. When Sybil sang her praises and shoved the money belt that held the receipts of Marielle's performance in front of him, Jeremiah scoffed.

"She is as good as a heavily veined gold mine," Sybil declared.

"Save your praise for the time when she deserves it," her father said, and Marielle was hurt as she had never been hurt by Papa before. After all, he had not even seen her perform. "She has a lot to learn. It will take her a long time," Papa finished, and she had never seen him look so self-righteous.

But in her heart of hearts she knew that regardless of what Papa said, he loved her and wanted what he thought was best for her. One day, in a moment of calm after yet another storm, he looked at her peaked white little face sadly, and suggested they get a breath of fresh air.

On deck, the fresh air did make her feel somewhat better. She carried Snowball in the crook of one arm, covered from the elements by her warm cloak. Jeremiah, too, was wearing his black wool cape, as well as a large-brimmed black felt hat and his abundant French silk scarf tied in an artistic bow at his throat. Marielle looked at him and smiled. No one, anywhere, would ever mistake him for anything other than an actor.

They strolled slowly, relishing the fact that they could be outdoors at all. Even now, the sea was so high it was not easy going. But since the ship had been their home for so long, they had learned how to maneuver from one section to another as the sea swelled over the bulwarks and tried to engulf them. It was not raining or storming for the time being, and that, in itself, was a relief. Marielle put Snowball down on the wet deck and the kitten romped off, a white furry blur, happily exercising feline muscles for the first time in many weeks. The kitten cavorted in front of and in back of Marielle, racing away and returning, but always staying close enough for her to keep an eye on it.

"We will be coming to a port within the next two weeks. It's called Valparaíso, and we shall be there for several days to make some minor repairs and to take on extra supplies," Papa told her. "Maybe we can buy you a pretty shawl or a summer dress."

Nodding absently, she linked arms with Papa and they moved majestically around the deck.

"I did not mean to be cross with you the other day," Papa went on. "I only meant that one has to work long and hard to be ready for the stage. I am sure you were very good, but . . . you will have to work and refine your art. It is very rare that one can perform for the first time and become a star without having paid one's dues. You have to practice, practice, practice and work, work, work. The money is the last thing you must think about."

"Yes, Papa."

Silence took over as they continued to stroll, as it sometimes did between the two Prestons. Each one was deep in thought; nevertheless, Marielle felt better than she had in days. Papa was only trying to help her in her chosen career; he was not saying she lacked talent.

As they strolled toward the bow of the ship, Marielle saw Snowball climbing the spray rail and then sprinting spiritedly out on the cathead, a large beam of wood near the bow of the ship to which the anchor was fastened.

"Snowball! Come back!" she shouted against the noise of the sea pounding the side of the ship.

Instead, a big wave hit the side, and the kitten became wet and disoriented and started to claw its way in the wrong direction, toward the sea instead of away from it, all the time meowing piteously.

Without waiting to think twice, Marielle unlinked her arm from Jeremiah's and quickly climbed the wooden beam toward Snowball. "Don't move, Snowball. I'm coming for you."

Marielle moved on all fours toward her pet but the kitten, more frightened than ever by the high wind and breaking waves, backed away and then leaped high over the spray rail onto the outer side of the cathead, which jutted out over the ocean.

"Please, Snowball, stop!" Marielle continued to edge toward her on her hands and knees. She heard Papa's strong voice in back of her screaming against the sound of the wind.

"Come back. You'll fall, Marielle. Let the cat be. She will return on her own." Along with the thunderous strength of Jeremiah's vocal chords, there was an echo of panic that made his voice sound foggy and far off. "Marielle, you are in great danger," Papa shouted.

She was so close to Snowball it would have been foolish to turn back. One foot more and the kitten would be in her grasp. Unfortunately, Marielle slipped sideways and went halfway over the cathead; she hung on by hugging the broad beam of wood protruding high over the sea. It was then that she looked down and saw the ocean below.

The distance between her and the waterline seemed like leagues. She began to feel dizzy and tried to look back up, and as she did she saw Papa, and with him, a sailor in his foul weather gear. The sailor wore an oilskin slicker and boots, and a sou'wester pulled down low at the back of his head to keep out rain and sea water. He had been working high in the rigging, had seen Marielle start to crawl onto the cathead, and had swung down from his high perch and prepared to rescue her.

"Hold on, little one," he called, and Marielle recognized Quinn's voice. Somehow it calmed her, and although she had felt panic quiver through her only a moment before, she was now able to hold on for dear life, sure he would rescue her.

He climbed toward her and just when she thought that a waft of wind would blow her away before he could save her, he grabbed on to her waist.

"Don't forget Snowball," she shouted, and he laughed into the wind, but she saw him put his arm out and grab the kitten with one hand as he held on to her waist with the other. Then she saw him tuck the bedraggled kitten into his oilskin.

By the time he had Marielle back on deck and in the arms of her father, she was soaking wet too. She felt faint as he put the kitten safely into her arms; and as she looked into his eyes with grateful acknowledgment that she owed him her life, her legs crumbled. He picked her up and held her, while Papa hovered anxiously, but uselessly, at his side.

"Thank you, sir!" Jeremiah said to Quinn with a surprising amount of humility in his voice. "You have saved my daughter's life and I shall never forget you. I shall see that you are rewarded properly."

"That will not be necessary, sir," Quinn replied.

"I am forever in your debt." Papa said, and there were tears in his eyes.

Now that Marielle was out of harm's way, Papa was being very dramatic, and Marielle, feeling safe and secure in Quinn's arms, wondered how he felt saving her life after having been flogged earlier because of her.

But Morgan made no mention of this as he carried her back to the stateroom and deposited her gently on her berth, the kitten still in her arms. When he prepared to leave, Papa was adamant that he stay, even for a short while.

"I must not, sir," Quinn said uncomfortably.

"Well then, my boy, you may be sure, the captain will hear of your heroism, and when we stop at Valparaíso, you will take supper with my daughter and myself on shore," Papa said with authority.

Marielle, lying on her bunk, held her breath as she waited for Quinn's answer.

"If there is shore leave, I shall be happy to accept," Quinn said, and Marielle let out her breath with a sweet sigh of happiness.

Now that she was feeling better, she took note of Morgan Quinn in a slightly different way, taking in things she might not ordinarily have noticed. She noticed that his clear, gray eyes fastened on her whenever he was not speaking or looking at her father. In fact, it seemed difficult for him to tear his gaze away from her.

He stood there in his oilskin, a tall man with a beautiful face under his sou'wester, who, she could feel, knew she meant danger to him. He wanted no part of that danger and she could not blame him. But he was so handsome, and he had been so brave that no matter what she saw in his eyes, she wanted him to be part of her life. If he did not wish it, she would have to find a way to change his mind.

It was while she looked at him and silently admired his courage that the plan took shape in her head. The plan was simple. Somehow, very soon, he was the man who would make her, Marielle Preston, future famous thespian and adored stage address, a real woman. He was the one to be the first to make love to her, and that would be his reward for saving her life, for having been flogged because of her, for being able to make her feel differently than anyone else ever made her feel. The tumult racing through her told her that she would never find another man so exciting. And— he had saved her life. She wanted impetuously to give herself to him so that he would know how much she appreciated his valor.

Papa gushed on and on in his most oratorical way so that Quinn could not leave without seeming rude. As Papa paid homage to the sailor who saved his daughter's life, Marielle quietly memorized every facet of Quinn's face and plotted the occasion of her journey into womanhood. There was nothing Morgan Quinn had to say about this. It was her decision—which is why it felt to Marielle so perfectly right.

Chapter Five

The weather became warmer and sunnier as they sailed into the Pacific Ocean, approaching Valparaíso. The cooks went back to cooking instead of working on deck, so the food improved somewhat. There was a terrible shortage of water though, and everyone waited eagerly for the new supplies of food and water they would pick up in the Chilean port.

When at last they arrived, the weary voyagers found Valparaíso a small, cheerful city on a steep hill. It was filled with little white houses roofed in red tile; the sun reflected the whiteness of the walls, making them seem drenched with a startling sunniness.

The ship was scheduled to be in port for four days. The waterfront in the harbor of Valparaíso was crowded with enterprising natives waiting to greet the *Andrew Jackson*. There were some whose business it was to sell, some who wanted to buy, and some in the business of pleasure.

Marielle was surprised to see girls who looked hardly any older than she waiting for the seamen who waved and shouted at them from the ship. The men had not seen any woman other than Marielle and Sybil since they had boarded the clipper in the harbor of New York.

There were also American businessmen and their families living in Valparaíso, and they, too, were on the wharf, seemingly as brisk and animated as the native population. It was a happy scene, and Marielle was glad she could get down on the wharf and stretch her sea legs on ground that did not sway.

Papa had kept his word and talked to the captain about Morgan Quinn. When the captain was informed by Jeremiah of Quinn's heroism, he dryly informed him that Quinn was free to come and go as he wished when on shore leave. If Papa wished to take Morgan Quinn to dinner, it was perfectly permissible.

When Jeremiah announced that they were going to have dinner at the best hotel in town and that Quinn had consented to join them, Marielle was delirious with joy.

Papa was in an expansive mood these days and prescribed fun and frolic and sightseeing each day they were in the city. And it was gold from Sybil's moneybelt that paid for everything, gold that Marielle had earned on her one night on the ship's stage. But, of course, Papa did not notice where the money came from, and Marielle could find no fault with the way Sybil handled the large amount of cash. It left Marielle free to think of other things.

The first thing the three of them did while on land was to go shopping. Papa insisted that the two ladies each purchase a summer dress that would keep them cool and pretty in Valparaíso and on board ship; there would be warm weather for the rest of the voyage.

Sybil found herself a dress first. It was an attractive sprigged muslin in beige, apple green, and rose. When Marielle's turn came, she chose a magnificent dress that cost more than any frock she had ever owned. It was sheer white cotton with long leg-of-mutton sleeves and white lace trim on the high collar and on the hem of the skirt. Down the middle of the dress were tiny tucks sewn with pale pink silk thread to form small pink stitches with rosebuds embroidered in between. It was the prettiest dress she had ever seen, and Sybil, full of enthusiasm and admiration, insisted that Marielle buy a matching white, lace-trimmed parasol and a pale pink leghorn hat. Marielle felt like a vision in white and pale pink, but in the back of her head she felt herself thinking she must earn more stage money before the ship docked in San Francisco. She felt beautiful and rich in her new costume, and vowed that there would be many more dresses like this—if all it took was a few songs in front of an audience to make money. But, it was not until she saw Quinn's look of admiration that evening that she was absolutely sure that the dress she had chosen was as much a success as she had hoped.

They all sat in the hotel dining room, serviced by a waiter with a droopy mustache and a red sash draped around his waist. Quinn had arrived a bit late; his watch was over but his replacement had not shown immediately; he made up for it by wearing his best shore-leave clothes. Marielle thought he looked very handsome even though he did not seem to own the starched linen she expected at dinner. Still, his bleached white muslin shirt was clean and pressed and fitted him perfectly, and his grey wool trousers had a crease in them and were tucked neatly into freshly greased cowskin boots, and his dark gray neck scarf was of China silk. His jacket was of buckskin, but because it was too warm for comfort, he wore it only until he greeted them and was seated. Then he removed it, as did several men at other tables. Obviously, it was not a formal dining room, even though many of the Yankee traders at their own tables kept their serge jackets on during the entire meal, the way it was done where they came from.

Marielle sat quietly, her enormous eyes on Quinn, hoping that Papa and Mrs. Darby would not notice that she could not stop staring at the handsome sailor. She needn't have worried because they were oblivious to her, chatting at each other, waving at other passengers who were also dining at the hotel. But Quinn did notice, and smiled at her. "You look beautiful tonight," he said, almost under his breath.

"It's my new dress." She fluffed a sleeve and smoothed a nonexistent wrinkle on the bodice.

Quinn shook his head. "It isn't the dress . . . it's you . . . I have never seen anyone lovelier than you . . ." His voice was so low that Papa and Mrs. Darby never heard him. "I cannot get enough of looking at you."

And now he stared at her in just the same way as she stared at him. They sat an interminably long time, just looking at each other, watching each other like two people in a dream.

At last Marielle broke the silence. "Is California beautiful?" There were so many questions she would have liked to ask, but this was simply the first one that occurred to her.

"Yes. But not as beautiful as you." His hand reached out to touch hers and then withdrew quickly as if he had forgotten his manners. But she looked at him with such longing, he could not resist, and his hand reached out for hers once more.

The feeling that charged through both of them as their hands touched was incredible. It was romance. Silent romance. No words, no kisses were necessary. The touch of their fingers and the look in their eyes was enough.

She turned a tender shade of pink, and he seemed to like that. He bent toward her and asked, "Will you be going to school in California?"

"Oh, no," she said. "I'm an actress. Have you already forgotten my performance on board ship?"

At that moment, Papa interrupted, asking Quinn to tell them something of his life. He was, he told them, returning from his third and last voyage around the world. Before that he had been in school for several years in the east. His father had been an Irish sea captain and his mother, still alive, was a native Californian who had sailed with her husband when they married. Morgan was born in the port of Yerba Buena, a small settlement that eventually became San Francisco.

After many voyages, though, the captain's wife became ill and could not recover at sea. So it was decided that she should remain in California while Morgan's father, Captain Patrick Quinn, continued on the high seas. He bought a large ranch with hundreds of acres of land and installed his wife and son there. He returned after two more voyages. The third trip out was to be his last before retiring from the sea, but only served to settle him at the bottom of the Indian Ocean, and not on the land in California as he had planned. Carmel Quinn, by now recovered from her illness, got married a second time, to a gentleman from the Basque country between France and Spain. The man's name was Pagonne and Carmel bore him a son, too, Morgan's half brother, who was three years younger than Morgan. Señor Pagonne died soon afterward, and Carmel Quinn Pagonne expanded the ranch and made it pay. Morgan was returning to California to continue in the family ranching business with his mother and his half brother.

"My father hoped that I'd take to the sea," Quinn told them. "I have tried to love the sea the same way he did, but my mother loves the land, and I take after her. But at least I have fulfilled my pledge to my father."

"Very admirable," Jeremiah said, clapping Quinn on the back with a hearty thump. "I like a man who fulfills his obligations."

"How long have you been a sailor?" Mrs. Darby wanted to know.

"I promised only that I would go to sea three times—long voyages of at least one year each. I have been around the world; I have touched the shores of India, seen the wild continent of Africa . . ."

"Oh, do tell us all about that," Sybil enthused.

And Morgan launched into a description of the boisterous parts of Africa as they all sat, captivated by his tales.

It was not until the table was cleared of the remains of their dinner that Marielle realized it had grown late. She had been so fascinated with Quinn's stories, the time had passed all too swiftly and now he was preparing to leave. Regretfully!

"You must not go yet, my boy," Jeremiah said as he urged the sailor to stay. "Why don't you come with Mrs. Darby and myself and see the city. It is our last night on shore and before long it will be time for Marielle to retire. We will take her back to the ship, and afterwards you can show Sybil and myself some interesting sights."

Marielle gave her father a look that could kill. Suddenly the beautiful, new dress was unimportant. She felt very young and distressed.

"I am sorry, sir," Quinn said to Jeremiah. "But I have made other plans for later this evening. It was my intention to meet some of my comrades after our dinner."

"I understand," Papa said knowingly, and Marielle was almost sure he winked at Quinn. "In that case, Sybil and I will leave you. When Marielle is back on board we will return for one last evening in this beautiful city. We all thank you for saving Marielle's life and for being our guest tonight." He turned to his daughter. "Say good night to Mr. Quinn, dear child."

"Perhaps I may have the honor of escorting your daughter back to the *Andrew Jackson* since I am going in that direction."

Marielle's head jerked up and the first thing she saw was the gleaming light in Morgan's eyes. It was almost as if he'd read her thoughts and come to her rescue.

"You have my permission, sir!" Papa said, and he got up at the same time as Sybil. "I know I need not worry about my daughter's safety with you accompanying her." He turned to Marielle. "Mrs. Darby and I will meet you back at the ship at a later hour, my dear."

Marielle hoped that the look on her face did not seem as wildly enthusiastic as she felt. She could not have plotted for a better outcome if she'd tried.

Chapter Six

They talked but little on the way back to the ship, due to the commotion in the streets. But for Marielle the air was charged with a fire that left her breathless. She watched him with shy side glances every now and then and tried to keep in step with his long, far-reaching strides.

Just before they reached the ship, a light rain began to fall. On the street nearest the harbor, they passed a red-tiled, white house all lit up. From the inside, Marielle could hear the merry laughter of women and the jovial sound of men speaking in many different languages. She looked over her shoulder as she passed, and paused, trying to see the activity; Marielle felt Quinn turn her back toward the ship.

"That's not for you to see," he said, but she saw him cast a lingering look in the direction of the house and she felt that he would have preferred to be there instead of with her.

"You think I don't know what that is," she said, listening to the high-pitched screeches and masculine shouts of laughter.

"Never mind. We're almost on board," he said, and took her hand and led her along.

There was more silence between them after that until she felt impelled to speak. "Do you really think I'm beautiful, like you said tonight?"

He did not answer immediately. "Yes," he said finally.

"Then why are you so cold to me now?"

He sighed out loud and did not bother to answer, but when the rain became heavier he took off his buckskin jacket and put it around her shoulders.

They managed to get to the ship and into the cabin before they became too wet. It was very dark and the rain outside fell more heavily than it had all evening. They both tried to find the unlit oil lamp.

While Quinn busied himself with the lamp, Marielle decided it was now or never. Feeling uncommonly uneasy and nervous, Marielle approached Quinn and planted herself very close to him in the dark room. "Will I never see you again now that we are back on board?" She took the buckskin jacket from her shoulders as she talked and handed it back to him.

"It's just as well, little one."

Marielle was very conscious of his closeness. It was quiet on the ship. Except for a few men on duty, everyone was enjoying the excitement of life on land. She wanted him to put his arms around her but, instead, she heard the clatter of the oil lamp falling to the floor and a "Damn" from Quinn.

The closer she leaned toward him in the darkness, the sharper was the wave of pleasure his nearness aroused in her. For an instant, she felt frightened, but then she touched him with her body and the wave of desire that went through her drove all fear away. It was right, she decided, whether he thought so or not. Yet as she leaned toward him she did not know whether it was the right thing to do, as she'd never before tried to seduce a man. Somehow, though, she didn't imagine that it could be so very difficult.

But Quinn backed away. Quickly finding the oil lamp on the floor, he lit it expertly. By the light of the lamp, Marielle could see one corner of his mouth twitching, and the dimple on that side of his face deepened. Then she saw the other side twitch and she was sure. He was holding back laughter.

It was hardly the response she'd expected. His mirth filled her with anger. She stamped her foot, an immature gesture, she knew. But she couldn't help herself. She'd offered herself to him—a gift surely any man would accept—and he'd simply laughed in her face!

"I chose to become a woman tonight. And it was you I chose to make me one . . . because I love you, Morgan Quinn." She had not known she was about to say those words, but now that she had, she was glad.

Suddenly he stopped looking as if he were going to laugh; in fact, his expression was now utterly serious. He leaned against the cabin door and sighed; his eyes, which had been downcast before, began slowly traveling upward, taking in every inch of her form— the billowing white folds of her dress, her slender waist, her perfectly formed erect breasts, the lushness of her lips. When they finally fastened on her rich blue eyes, he shook his head and said,

"Little one, you cannot know what you're asking . . . what it could mean. . . ."

"Oh," she gasped, "I know that being here puts you in danger. But we've been careful—"

"It isn't that," he interrupted. "God knows, looking at you now, I think I'd brave the wrath of a hundred captains to be here." His voice was heavy and low as he went on. "But sweetheart, you don't really know me—my plans, my expectations. I don't want to hurt you, but you will be if you don't stop me right now . . ."

While he spoke she tried to arrange her face so that she would seem irresistible to him. She could not tell if she succeeded because she could not get to the mirror to check, but suddenly his face took on a different look and he pulled her toward him, his eyes hardening.

"Damn," he said to no one in particular as she found herself against the length of his hard body. His mouth found hers and covered it with a wild kiss.

Frightened at the change in him, she opened her lips to protest, and gasped when she felt his tongue push past her teeth and start to explore. Her heart lurched in her chest and suddenly she was absolutely certain that this was right, and moved even closer so that she could feel the strength of his body through the many layers of her clothes.

She did not know what was supposed to come next and glanced at Quinn's face to see how he felt. It looked like he felt the same way she did; one thing for sure, he was no longer amused.

His arms went around her tighter, as if he had no will of his own, enveloping her in the cloak of his maleness, his sinewy strength pressing her soft body against his muscular one. The bliss was such that she wanted him to continue kissing her forever.

"You'd better stop me now," he said again. His face belied his words; she did not think he *could* stop now if she'd asked him to.

But he surprised her. His character was stronger than she thought and, unexpectedly, she felt him thrust her aside.

"Little minx," he whispered, and his voice was not bitter, but confounded as he pulled himself away from her.

Why? She looked up at him, hurt and astonished. Didn't he want her after all? Her huge, innocent blue eyes tried to understand what was behind his intent gray ones. She wanted to touch him, but she did not know where to start; she chose his hair, which the wind had blown into a mass of dark curly softness. As she touched the ringlets, he pulled her back to him with a groan. She felt his steely body with all its exquisite ridges, and fitted her own softness against it, in an all-consuming need to become one.

"Sweetheart," she heard him murmur between kisses, and smiled to herself because, without knowing it, Quinn's voice had changed from firm and definite denial to a tone of tenderness. But he made one last effort to stay in control of the situation—and of himself.

"I am a sane man, and I think that this better not happen. Also, I think it's quite possible that you're not in complete possession of your senses tonight," he said quietly.

In answer, she took the lead and kissed him. "That is my answer, Morgan Quinn," she whispered in between filling herself with the taste of him on her tongue. "Do what you have to do . . . please." She rubbed closer to him, her hungry body telling him she was completely serious.

"There is no turning back," Quinn said, as if in answer to her physical command, and there was a hint of sadness in his voice. But he did not let her go.

At last, he'd complied with her wishes. His body had made the decision first, and now his mind seemed to be giving his body permission to go ahead. And suddenly, she was frightened. One part of her was already his; she could not have stopped what was happening if her very life depended on it. But another part said she was giving him too much control over her, and she was not sure she would always be as happy about this as she was at this moment.

Morgan moaned softly as he came even closer. Without saying another word, he led her to her narrow berth and unbuttoned her dress and opened the top, allowing his hands to caress her white breasts. He lingered over the tautness of the pale pink tips that hardened to his touch until she thought that the sensation was more than she could bear. Then, when she was certain she could stand it no longer, he put his lips first over one pink tip and then the other, and kissed them as she urged him on with a sweet fever that grew sharper with each touch.

"You are more beautiful than I could possibly have imagined," he whispered.

Tentatively, without a plan of any sort, as if she were in the throes of something much more complex than she understood, her hands started to roam over the muscles of his body, first slowly and carefully, then heatedly, trying to feel as much of him as the tips of her fingers could. It was bliss, even before he pulled the skirt of her dress up.

She tried to help him, but he pushed her hands aside and did it himself—with a tenderness and thoroughness that enhanced the strange sensations surfacing from the depths of her body. When he finished undressing her, Marielle felt herself blush as she watched him undress and saw him for the first time. He was beautiful, and waves of desire came over her as she watched him turn back to her with the same kind of craving in his face.

Even now, he looked at her nudity with reluctance, as if he were trying to stop her from giving herself to him. His eyes burned into hers. "Do you still want to go through with this? I think you are too young."

And without saying a word in answer, she moved into his arms as if she had always been there and as if she belonged. There was no way, she was sure, he could stop himself from surrounding her body with his own.

They stayed together in that way until he became more and more aroused as he explored her body with his lips and his hands. She became bolder and tried to explore him in a similar way. The more intense her emotions as his fingers continued to explore, the more she became awed at the feelings spilling out between them.

"When does it happen?" she whispered. "When are you going to make me a real woman?" She looked into his eyes with love and innocence.

He groaned as she said this and very tenderly spread her long, pale legs as she strained toward him and then, breathing unevenly, he entered her with another deeply sensuous groan that captured the way she felt too.

As he pushed into her, she pushed with him and her eyes opened wide at the pain she did not expect. But it was a pain she did not mind as long as he remained inside her, and she threw her arms tightly around him and pulled him closer and closer as he went deeper. The pain became secondary to the passionate rhythm that fused them into one. He put his mouth over hers and as they clung together it was as if their bodies were melded into one. As his strong hands held her to him and positioned her to move exactly the way he wanted, she unexpectedly started to feel contractions spread through her, starting from the inside of her thighs and working slowing upward all the way through the most intimate parts of her body past her belly and into her breasts. He pressed her closer to him by putting his hands under her and bearing down so that he went deeper and deeper, and as he did, lightninglike tremors raced through her body until she thought they would never stop. It was as if her mind and her heart and her body had all teamed together with those of Quinn.

After a long time, when it was all over and she lay in Quinn's arms in a daze of joy and fatigue, her eyes half-closed, she felt him kiss her disheveled hair, then stroke it away from her face. "I think you'll be sorry tomorrow," he said with a touch of regret.

She opened her eyes languorously and touched his face with her fingertips, outlining his flawless features. "Never," she said. For at last, although she was sure she did not look any different, she felt like a woman.

She fell asleep almost immediately afterwards, lulled by the sound of the rain and the warmth of his arms.

It was a lazy, luxurious sleep that lasted for more than twelve hours. When she awoke in her berth, the clipper had sailed and Quinn was no longer at her side. Sybil and Papa were asleep in their respective bunks and, as she got up, she smiled at her sleeping father, then climbed up to where he was, and gave him a kiss on his crumpled whiskers.

Dressing quickly, she slipped out of the cabin to find Quinn. She looked everywhere, but could not find him. Tired of searching, she leaned against the rail and looked out over the greenish waters; suddenly she heard the crackling voice of Johnnie Fox from behind a lifeboat. Peering around to make certain they were not being watched, she crouched down beside him.

"Where is he?" Marielle asked.

"He said to tell you good-bye, Miss . . . Marielle."

Startled at his words, she put her arm out and touched Johnnie's shoulder. "What do you mean, Johnnie Fox? Who said good-bye?"

"Quinn!"

"Why?" Her voice became high-pitched and childish with fear.

"He's jumped ship, Miss. He's not on board."

She looked at him in astonishment. "That is impossible."

"It's true! Morgan Quinn jumped ship. He had to."

"But why?" she cried, her face becoming very pale.

"It was necessary. He was seen coming out of your cabin by the first officer. The Captain was sure to make an example of him. After all, it was not his first offense on this voyage."

She looked at the sturdy messboy mutely, begging him with her eyes to say that his words were a bad joke, that Quinn would pop up from behind some clever hiding place and laugh uproariously at her torment. But all the time she waited, she knew that Johnnie Fox was telling her the truth, that Morgan Quinn, with the warm loving body and the gentle but insistent lips and the raw animal attraction, had quit the ship and was somewhere in the city of Valparaíso at the same time as she was sailing toward San Francisco.

She sat down on the wooden deck and put her head on the lifeboat as Johnnie Fox stared at her sadly. She realized how small were the chances that she would ever see the man she loved again. Her tears came then, heavy and scalding hot on her smooth pale cheeks.

Part II

The Upward Climb

Chapter Seven

There were many entertainers who came West to take advantage of the gold being lifted from the ground. These men and women plied their way up and down the Sacramento River and its tributaries, the American and Feather. Gold miners, they found, were extremely generous, and the rivers got them where they wanted to go safely and rapidly.

The Prestons had been moving up and down the Sacramento for almost a year now, and Marielle was the mainstay of their act; Papa could not perform the way he used to. He seemed to grow more frail every day, and his bouts with the bottle lasted longer than they ever had in the past. The theaters they performed in were usually nothing more than paper shacks. Sometimes, they performed on an outdoor stage surrounded by oil lamps. As usual, they always needed money.

They had met with setbacks from almost the moment of their arrival in California, which had been delayed due to their long trip around the Horn. On their disembarkation, they'd found that the Booths had finished their tour. So, full of hope and optimism, they had gone at the theatrical business on their own, and because of Marielle's youth and beauty, had done rather well at first. Theater impresarios took one look at Marielle, asked her to sing and dance, and were happy to set up a show around her. There were few young female entertainers in California, and even fewer of Marielle's caliber. But Marielle made the new California moguls understand they had to take Jeremiah Preston and Sybil Darby too—that is, if they wanted Marielle's fresh beauty and innovative talent. They did.

This week they were on their way to some small town, a mining camp really, and it did not matter whether it was Bidwell's Bar,

Spanish Bar, Grass Valley, Rich Bar, or Red Bluff, the northern-most terminus of traffic on the American River. They were all the same.

Marielle was usually the one to choose their campsite, but today it was Sybil who had found them their spot, set in a majestic location that seemed perfect in every way. There was even a shallow cave overlooking an embankment that would afford them a bit of privacy.

Marielle had become used to waiting for Papa in strange places while he scouted around and generally wound up occupying a stool at the nearest bar. Sybil and she would set up a crude camp and bathe, wash clothes, and cook, and then wait. Sometimes Marielle would have to go in search of him. Eventually, she always found him, sleeping it off in some nearby mining town.

Unfortunately, Sybil now drank almost as heavily as Papa; the two of them had grown extremely close. But where drink had made Sybil stouter, it had weakened and emaciated Jeremiah. His once-bright blue eyes were watery and distant, and there was stubble on his chin instead of the neatly trimmed beard of the past. Occasionally he was as jaunty as ever, and then he would recite his Shakespeare as beautifully as when he had been a young man. But those good days were rare.

But Papa and Sybil were Marielle's only family, so she stood up for them at any cost. Marielle did not mind. She loved Papa too much to deny him her strength, and after all they'd been through together, she'd found she had deep affection for Sybil, too.

But within her, Marielle harbored a secret sadness, and it had nothing to do with Papa's and Sybil's drinking. She could never forget Morgan Quinn, and she had no one with whom to talk it out. She found herself thinking of him more often than she cared, and it was no good trying to wipe him from her memory. Since she had met the seaman, she had never been able to think of another man in the same way.

With men who showed a predilection for her, Marielle was aloof; somehow, though, her very haughtiness made the interested ones want her more. In fact, the more disdain she displayed, the more excitement she aroused in them. To her, it was very simple. She was not going to let herself fall in love a second time. She would let the gentlemen who admired her play their desperate game, but she never singled out any man, young or old. She treated them all alike, with a fascinating coldness that drove them wild with desire.

But to most, Marielle noted with relief, she was considered still a mere girl, although she was almost seventeen. Looking younger than her years helped keep her out of trouble.

The sun was still high in the sky as she and Sybil set about pitching camp that day. They laid out their belongings on the bank of a stream, under a tree. Once they'd finished, they had only to wait for Papa to return from one of his expeditions. The broad, bluish green stream rolled calmly past the tree, and for the first time in days, Marielle felt she could settle back and breathe easy.

Sliding down to the edge of the stream, she stuck her toes into the water, luxuriating in a pleasurable moment of shock as her toes parted the inviting coolness of the stream. She stuck both feet in and gasped. Sybil, right next to her, groaned as she slipped her own feet, swollen and blue-veined, into the water up to her ankles.

Enjoying the solace of the comforting stream, Marielle took a mirror from her makeup box and studied herself. Somehow, despite the hard life, she had developed into a very presentable young lady. Her hair was a rich, burnished red, flamboyant, alive, and heavy with natural curls that never stayed put. Her face was small and pale, but, her paleness only accentuated the intensity of her large blue eyes.

She waded out of the water, put away her mirror, and nimbly climbed up the embankment to examine the mouth of the cave. It was dark and dank inside and on the ground outside, there was the blood of some animal. Marielle had no desire to explore the possibility of any privacy it offered. Instead, she skirted the entrance and used the nearby underbrush as a place in which to get undressed for her bath.

"I'm going in now," she called to Sybil, who was still at the stream, washing her legs.

"Go ahead. When you're finished I'll take a full bath," Sybil said. She got out of the water and went back to the campsite under the tree, scarcely glancing over at Marielle as she ran toward the cool water.

Seating herself against the tree, Sybil rummaged around in her reticule and brought out a revolver, which she tested by cocking the hammer, squinting, and making sure it was loaded. It was only recently that she kept a gun handy for occasions when she and Marielle were without the protection of a male. Putting the weapon on the ground next to her, Sybil closed her eyes as she relaxed against the tree.

Marielle looked at her and smiled. The revolver made Sybil feel protected, but Marielle did not think that Sybil would be able to use it effectively if it became necessary. Making her way to the edge of the stream, Marielle jumped in. The water felt fresh, and she enjoyed the small balmy breeze that started to waft over her body as she floated indolently.

She looked toward Sybil to see just how impatient Sybil was to take her turn in the stream, and found that the older woman had fallen sound asleep. It was a magical day, and Marielle floated languorously, her wet hair a mass of brilliant red spread out on the surface of the azure stream, allowing herself to think of anything that came into her head. She was not surprised that what came to her first was a picture of Morgan Quinn, tall and dashing.

Annoyed at herself, since she'd resolved to forget him, Marielle closed her eyes tightly and tried to squeeze Quinn from her mind. Instead, an agitating fantasy of Quinn touching her pervaded her inner being and seemed to be so real that she brushed the pink tips of her breasts with her hands as if to remove the touch of a phantom lover. She knew she was creating Quinn out of a figment of her imagination, but the sensations her phantom lover aroused in her were so true to life that she had to open her eyes to make sure she was alone.

She closed her eyes a second time and Quinn's chiseled face loomed over hers. Then she gave in and let herself imagine the rest of him, his body as naked as hers, his arms capturing her and holding her tight.

The physical sensations coursing through her evoked emotions that had been dormant since she last saw him. He had left an indelible mark on her psyche. She felt her body shudder and gave herself up to the wildness within her. Afterwards, she wrenched herself back to reality and the still of the afternoon.

To put herself in a different mood, Marielle took a bar of sweet-scented soap and washed her hair, scrubbing her scalp and sudsing the long unruly mass of red curls. After soaping the rest of her body, she rinsed off the suds from both her body and her hair, drying herself with a rough towel that had lain in the hot sun. Feeling wonderfully clean and terribly hungry, Marielle no longer dreaded the hours of waiting ahead.

She dressed slowly. She still owned the white cotton dress she had purchased a long time ago in Valparaíso, but it no longer felt crisp and new. But it was clean and pressed, and she viewed it with nostalgia. She dried her hair in the fresh afternoon air and combed through it. Then she went to the tree, bent over, and wakened Sybil with a gentle touch. Sybil sat up with a start and a loud groan, and shook her head to clear her senses.

Suddenly, they both heard a sound from inside the cave. The noise reverberated like a trumpet from hell and both women turned toward the mouth of the cavern. Even as they looked, a creature came to the entrance from somewhere deep in the cave, stood upon his hind legs, and surveyed them. Almost simultaneously, they both realized that what was in front of them was a savage old grizzly whose intentions were clearly murderous.

Chapter Eight

It did not take Marielle long to determine that the animal, stomping angrily at the mouth of the cave, was a killer—she could see he was wounded and in pain, which made him all the fiercer. There was a large flap of flesh torn over one of his eyes, and his blood dripped down onto the dry earth in front of the entrance. Marielle had never seen an animal so big.

"We must be still as sticks," Marielle heard herself saying above the bear's roars, and glanced sideways at Sybil, who was frozen with fear.

The bear stopped his wild growling and dug deeply and viciously into the earth in front of him. Buckets of earth flew behind, and occasionally a huge stone was torn out of the ground and hurled with one paw at Marielle and Sybil. Once he stopped digging, he rose high on hind feet and looked around. He sniffed the air and got down on all fours again. Marielle watched him, holding her breath, and saw him turn his head up toward the top of the cave. There stood Papa, a keg of whiskey in his arms, too confused to move. The bear lunged upward and with one immense arm sent Papa sprawling in the mound of soft earth he had just dug up. The keg of spirits rolled to one side and broke, the whiskey forming an odorous puddle.

Papa lay still, his eyes closed, his face the color of parchment except for several long, red lacerations where the bear had clawed him. Then the animal backed slightly into the cave, still facing the three Prestons. His red eyes looked out at them as he charged once more. Abruptly poor Papa, lying prone on the ground, was flung even further across the thicket next to the cave. The grizzly heaved a noisy victory whoop.

Marielle rushed to Papa's side. As she got closer, the sight of his blood became appalling. He had a deep wound in his scalp. Marielle screamed, but the bear took no notice. Instead, it began to lick at the puddle of whiskey. Marielle felt she could stay at Papa's side while the bear was busy at the puddle.

Cradling Papa in her arms, Marielle turned toward Sybil. "Use the gun, Sybil," she shouted at the paralyzed woman.

Sybil looked back at her in a daze, clearly not understanding what Marielle was saying.

"You must shoot him or he will kill us all." She wished she could be closer and do it herself, but there was no way she could get to the gun without passing the grizzly.

It seemed ages before Sybil came to her senses and pointed the gun toward the bear. Marielle watched as she cocked the hammer and fired. Under different circumstances, the look on Sybil's face as she saw the bullet hit the bear in the neck would have been funny. The creature, already mortally wounded, pitched to its fore-feet, gnashing and pawing at its neck. But the bullet seemed only to enflame the beast's anger even more. Three more times Sybil fired, but only grazed the monster.

Once again the bear rose to its full height and now, having been attracted to Sybil by the gunshots, lumbered rapidly to her and attacked. But even as the bear bit into her shoulder, laying bare the bone, his foot slipped on the embankment and the immense animal tottered backwards, away from the mortally wounded woman.

Marielle cradled Papa even closer in her arms and looked on in horror. A moment later she rallied, ripped off her petticoat, and tried to staunch the bloody flow coming fast and furiously from Papa's wounds.

Just then, a band of riders thundered into the campsite. The men surrounded the area. There must have been close to a dozen of them, each dressed in fancy leather, seated on tall, splendid horses that did not buck or rear at the terrible sounds coming from the grizzly.

Marielle was torn between leaving her father and getting over to Sybil. The decision was taken away from her when one of the men indicated that she was not to move from where she was.

One of them, definitely the leader of the entire group, was about twenty years of age, a little over medium height, slenderly but gracefully built. He had deep olive skin and black, burning eyes, and a neat black mustache framed by long, glossy, black hair that hung over his shoulders. He shouted orders to his men, half in

Spanish and half in English, and several of them surrounded the wounded bear.

He then rode over to Marielle and Papa, and introduced himself very politely. His name was Joaquín Murieta. "Do not be afraid of all the blood. More times than not, it looks much worse than it really is."

Marielle looked down at Papa's unconscious form and kissed his pale cheek. "Is my father dead?" she asked the *vaquero* leader.

The man swung off his horse, put his finger on a vein on Papa's neck, and held it there for a moment. "No," the man said, and swung back onto his horse.

One of the riders approached the bear even more closely and swung his *reata*, lassoing the grizzly. Unfortunately, the *reata* caught the enraged bear around the neck instead of the required forefeet, and the bear caught hold of the lasso and nearly killed the horse and the rider before he could cut his *reata* free.

The rider was immediately rescued by his friends before the grizzly could harm him, but not before the grizzly had tired out the horseman. Suddenly there was a loud whirring sound, and the *reata* of a second rider caught the astonished monster by one forefoot. The coil of another *reata* made another circle, and the bear was caught by the other forefoot, as well. With terrible growls, the grizzly tottered around until both the *reatas* tripped him and he fell heavily on his back, where he struggled desperately.

Marielle's large blue eyes followed the straight back of one of the men, his broad shoulders square and upright. The back of his fancy leather jacket glistened with perspiration. As he lifted his arm to move the *reata* into position, Marielle could not help noticing his narrow waist and the long, muscled contours of his thighs. She could not make her eyes leave the man's figure as he and three others dispatched the helpless grizzly with their lances.

When the bear was dead, the man laughed and she thought she recognized the sound of his voice. His dark curly hair was plastered to the sides of his well-shaped head; his hat had slipped off his head and hung on the back of his neck by its leather tie. Even as the man turned, Marielle felt helpless to wrench her gaze away. It was a face she had been waiting to see for a long time. When he turned toward her, she gasped. It was the face of Morgan Quinn, the same Morgan Quinn whom she had not seen since the fateful night aboard the *Andrew Jackson*.

The impression did not last more than a second before she knew the man was not Quinn. But he could have been a twin, or brother, he looked so much like the man she could not forget. The stranger came closer to her and she was absolute in her certainty that he was not Morgan. His hair had begun to dry in the same wild tangle of dark curls that she remembered Quinn had; his eyes were the same gray as Quinn's, but this man did not look at her with the same directness—rather there was a self-centered quality in those eyes. Nor was he as well-proportioned; he was more muscular and his stance expressed an arrogance much more aggressive than Quinn's easy assurance. She saw all this and wondered if all men in this wild country looked this way.

When the stranger finally finished with the bear, he rode to her side. His grin was so reminiscent of Quinn's, Marielle caught her breath and her hand flew up to her breasts as she tried to control her violently beating heart. He reined his horse to a stop inches away from her and swung off his saddle gracefully.

"Is that your father?" he asked as he came toward her.

He tipped her face upward, his fingers pressed under her chin, and studied her upturned face with curiosity.

"Yes," she said. "He is dying, isn't he?"

"No. He'll pull through. He will be very popular with the ladies after this." His mouth became wide and sensual, and his teeth showed straight and white as his lips widened into a grin that was almost the same as Morgan Quinn's. "A chawed up man is very much admired in this part of the world."

She continued to look into his face in astonishment. "Who are you? What's your name?" She had to know. Was it possible he was Quinn's kinsman, the brother Quinn had talked about in Valparaíso?

His grin became even wider. "I can't tell you, ma'am. I'm not supposed to be here with my friends. My maw would tan my hide if she knew I was fighting ba'rs." He turned and started speaking in Spanish to his friends, who all looked at Marielle and laughed good-naturedly.

"Are you making fun of me?"

He stopped laughing. His English became perfect. "I'm sorry, Miss, if I upset you. But I meant no discourtesy."

She smiled tentatively at him and continued to stare. These men—and especially the dark stranger before her—seemed surprisingly kind and respectful for *vaqueros*. She had heard of the Murieta gang, read newspaper articles about how they killed and raped, raided and plundered as their sturdy horses took them from one town to another. If these men were the same gang she had read about, Marielle wondered about the accuracy of all the accounts. She didn't know what to think except that they had saved her life and Papa's too, and if they said that Papa was not going to die, she believed them.

Joaquín Murieta came over with the man who was second in command, a large, rugged Californio with a fierce face. He told her his name was Manuel Garcia, but everyone called him Three-Fingered Jack. He held up his left hand and showed her why, chuckling loudly at her instant look of sympathy.

Someone else, whom everyone called Claudio, led her away, after telling her that Papa's wounds would be attended to. He had seen people with much worse wounds recover, or so he claimed. They were getting a doctor, but they knew what to do until he arrived. However, there was nothing they could do for the lady near the tree. She was dead. They were sorry. Marielle felt a great sadness. She wondered if what she had felt for Sybil these past years was love.

Papa passed in and out of consciousness. Whenever he came to for a short period of time, he tried to talk to Marielle, but he was not able to make much sense. At last, the doctor arrived, tired and dusty, looking like he needed attention himself. Dr. Fayette Clappe had come by mule, and his animal had nearly suffered a misstep on the narrow trail the doctor had taken to save time. But he examined Papa immediately and cleaned and dressed Papa's wounds as Marielle watched anxiously. Every once in a while the doctor shook his head, but then he would remember that Marielle was close, and would smile at her reassuringly.

While Dr. Clappe worked on Jeremiah, the *vaqueros* set about digging Sybil Darby a grave close to a peaceful young pine tree, with a wooden cross to commemorate the spot. The men, holding their hats in their hands, respectfully stood looking down at their boots while Marielle recited a short sad poem. She wished she knew some formal tribute for Sybil's funeral, but she did not, so she ended the service with the words, "Sybil Preston was a fine actress. She gave joy to the world."

By that time Dr. Clappe had finished with Papa and had washed up; he came over to the fire the *vaqueros* had built and sat next to Marielle. "Your father will live . . . but . . . ." He looked very sad. "Maybe, if you brought him to Rich Bar for a few days, I could look after him. My wife, Louise, could keep you company while I attend your father."

"Will it make a difference to Papa's recovery?" Marielle asked with a frown.

"Not really, I guess. Only his strength and will to live can make a difference at this point."

"Then I thank you, Dr. Clappe, but I must get to Sacramento and find work as soon as possible. Afterwards, when Papa is stronger, I will take him to San Francisco and then back home to New York. I have been promised work in Sacramento and in San Francisco. We need the money. In fact, I don't know how I'm going to pay you."

She looked up and saw the handsome *vaquero* who looked like Morgan Quinn listening with interest to her story. She felt embarrassed. There was no need for everyone to know how very poor the Prestons had become. She turned away, pretending she had not seen him, and focused again on the doctor.

The doctor looked at Marielle with compassion. "You don't have to worry about my fees. I'm sure that if you can pay someday, you will."

Marielle gave him a message to take into Rich Bar to explain why the Prestons would not be fulfilling their obligations there. "Of course they will understand," the doctor assured her. "A young girl almost losing her father. I think you are very brave."

As the good doctor spoke Marielle realized how her world had changed in just a few moments. Never would she see Sybil again. Sybil, with her brassy, loud voice, her flouncing bright skirts, her careless love of life, her crude remarks and bad advice, her constant complaining, and her loyalty and love for Jeremiah. Most of all, she would miss Sybil's ability to survive, something Marielle had taken for granted after all their time together.

Marielle watched the fire burn peacefully as the evening turned into night, and pondered her future. The doctor had left to return home before dark. He would come back and see Jeremiah again in a couple of days. Looking up, Marielle found the *vaquero* who looked like Quinn watching her. When he saw her returning his gaze, he gracefully picked himself up from the ground, came to her side, and seated himself next to her. Again she was taken with how much he resembled Morgan Quinn. They sat quietly, and neither one said a word until the man broke the silence.

"Is it true you will be settling in Sacramento?" he asked politely.

"I've been promised work at the Sacramento Theatre. I'm an actress," she said, and she looked at him with a sweet smile that did not hide the pride she felt for her chosen vocation.

"You are more beautiful than I ever thought a woman could be," he said pensively.

Marielle was startled. His words were so like the words Morgan Quinn had once uttered.

"Thank you," she whispered.

The man looked at her with undisguised fascination. "I'll come to Sacramento and see you perform. I promise you."

"That is after Papa is better and can travel."

"Of course. And I will find you no matter where you are," the man said. He looked around to see whether they were alone, and continued. "I don't want you to be offended, but I would like to give you a present. Will you accept a gift from me?"

"I don't think so. I don't know you, and you won't tell me who you are."

"Someday you *will* know me. I can assure you of that. Won't you accept a token of my esteem?" He pulled out a small suede poke and handed it to her.

Marielle started to push the bag away, but the man would not allow it. He took her hand, put the poke directly into it, and closed her fingers around it. "If you must return it, you can in Sacramento, but not now. I'm very anxious to see you sing and dance."

"I am an actress—who also sings and dances," she said, knowing somehow that she had to make sure he understood she took her profession very seriously.

"I can't stay here with you. I must leave. I have business elsewhere. But my friends will treat you well and see that you reach your destination safely."

"Thank you," Marielle said, and watched him as he walked to his saddled horse, untied its tethers, and slowly led it away from the camp. As he topped the embankment, he looked back at Marielle with a hungry look that made her feel uncomfortable until he turned his face away and led the horse out of sight.

It was only when she could no longer see his face that she looked inside the suede bag. It was filled with gold nuggets, enough to keep her and Papa fed and housed for more than a month in a good boarding house in Sacramento.

Chapter Nine

In fifteen days, and with constant care from Marielle, Papa was able to walk about. They had stayed and camped on the embankment. The kind, mustachioed highwayman who had told her his name was Joaquín Murieta, and who returned periodically with Dr. Clappe, gallantly ordered two of his men to accompany Marielle and Jeremiah to Sacramento when they were ready. Marielle never saw the stranger who looked like Morgan Quinn again. Every time Joaquín returned, he had Dr. Clappe in tow, and he rode with Three-Fingered Jack, Joaquín Valenzuela, and Pedro Gonzalez. The stranger who had given her a bag of gold nuggets seemed to have disappeared from the face of the earth.

They made a bed for Jeremiah to repose in on the trip to Sacramento and Jeremiah slept much of the way; Marielle administered to his every need as they traveled. The trip was uneventful and the two Californio escorts, under strict orders from their leader, were silent guardian angels, polite and helpful in every way. When Marielle and Jeremiah were installed in a boarding house of her choosing, they disappeared with their wooden cart after a solemn farewell. Marielle would have liked to have paid them; she offered them gold from the poke given her by their fellow *vaquero*, but they laughed and refused to take it.

In about six weeks' time Papa seemed himself again. But there was now a strangeness in him. He was distant and his thinking was confused. He could not remember his Shakespearean lines at all, and when told about what had happened to Sybil, he remained unmoved, as if he'd forgotten her completely or as if the violent scene at the cave had been mercifully blotted out. Surprisingly enough, the first person he asked for after regaining his senses was

Morgan Quinn, the man he was sure had now rescued his daughter twice from death's door.

It didn't take Marielle long to acquaint herself with the town. Sacramento City was younger and smaller than San Francisco. The miners who poured into it daily were tough and dirty and lonely. The city was filled with rutted streets and most of the makeshift hotels and rooming houses were infested with bedbugs.

Marielle was lucky and found a rooming house that promised clean sheets every two weeks and two complete meals every day. It was expensive, and Marielle realized she couldn't have managed without the bag of gold nuggets the stranger had given her. As much as she hated to take and use money that wasn't her own, she thanked him silently each time she doled out a nugget for their immediate needs. She'd find a way to pay him back someday.

Mrs. Harriet Sweeney, a lively widow who owned the boarding house, promised Marielle she would keep an eye on Jeremiah if Marielle found work, and her ten-year-old son, Brendon, looked with admiration into Marielle's eyes and vowed he would run errands for her. She was ready to resume her theatrical career on her own.

As unkempt and uncivilized as the city was, there were several theaters. One of them was a dingy old building on a back street called the Sacramento Theatre. Marielle had met the manager, a loud-mouthed fellow named Ben Baker, once before, and he had told her that he could always find her something to do in the acting profession. The man, outspoken and calculating, but with a beam of a smile, boasted he had a knack for finding good actors. She would visit Ben Baker. She would take any position in the theater he had available, anything to earn more money so that Papa could recover at leisure and never go hungry while he was doing it. The gold nuggets in the poke were being used up at a most alarming rate. In less than a month, she would be penniless once again.

She dressed in her best dress to go see Ben Baker. It was a soft, plum-colored muslin with a fitted bodice, matching buttons fastening up the center front, and a small beige lace collar at the throat. The skirt was decorated with ribbon ruching just above the hem that matched the ruching on her bonnet. She had brushed her unruly hair into a center part and drew it back loosely to a round chignon at the nape of her neck. The bonnet was small, and she wore it back on the head to show her face and hairline. Her footwear consisted of white stockings and black kid boots. She wanted Ben Baker to see how stylish she was. It was the one outfit she kept for special occasions, and this was going to be a very important day in her life.

It was sunny but cool when she set out, a perfect day for getting on with her business. It would be a long time before Papa would appear on the stage, if, indeed, he ever did again. She told herself she would see that he had everything he wanted, and if that included a daily ration of spirits she would see that he had that too.

Ben Baker turned out to be younger than she remembered when she had last encountered him. After he led her into his shabby office, he extended his hand in a friendly way. Marielle remembered that he was called Uncle Ben by most of the thespians he hired.

"Do you remember me, Uncle Ben?" Marielle asked boldly as she extended her gloved hand to his outstretched one.

"Of course I remember you," he said, but by the blank look on his face Marielle was sure he was only fibbing to make her feel good.

After several moments of polite and useless conversation, Marielle got to the point. "I need work, Uncle Ben," she said. She recounted the story of what had happened to Jeremiah and Sybil, telling her tale with simplicity. When she was finished she felt she had stirred the manager's emotions.

Ben opened his coat and loosened his tie. "I am sorry," he said. "I wish I could help you. I really do remember you now. I remember saying to myself, 'Jeremiah Preston's little girl is going to be a great actress. She already is a great beauty.' But I've just turned the theater over to Mrs. Catherine Sinclair, and she is readying *Hamlet* for her first production. Mr. Edwin Booth has returned to California for several months, and he'll be Mrs. Sinclair's *Hamlet*, as far as I know. I have no information other than that. I've a signed contract with Mrs. Sinclair, so there's nothing I can do to get you work in this theater." He looked geniunely sad at not being able to help Marielle, and she felt that he would have if he could. Obviously, she had come to Sacramento at the wrong time.

"Where is Mrs. Sinclair staying? And where is Mr. Edwin Booth? Ted is an old friend of mine." She was grasping at straws, she knew, but she felt that she simply had to locate the two of them.

Getting up, Marielle straightened her gloves and adjusted the ribbon on her bonnet as she waited for an answer. But before Ben could reply, a woman entered the office whom Uncle Ben introduced as Mrs. Sinclair.

Marielle's first impression was that Mrs. Catherine Sinclair was a charming and fastidious woman. She was also beautiful. It was common knowledge that Edwin Forrest, the great Shakespearean actor, had sued her for divorce on the grounds of adultery. After the divorce, she had taken her maiden name back, and now not only acted but was a theater manager as well. Ben Baker was happy to make the introductions.

"I know your father well," Mrs. Sinclair told Marielle. "In fact, I have seen him perform many times in New York. You must give him my best regards."

Marielle and Ben looked at each other sadly, and Marielle told her story once again.

"I'm really sorry there has been such havoc in your life, my child," Mrs. Sinclair said softly.

Marielle regarded her gravely, wondering if she had the courage to ask her for work. Mrs. Sinclair's dress was beautiful, Marielle thought, and she wished she could afford to have a similar one. She stared with open-eyed admiration at the older woman, who smiled back at her with a little lift of her upper lip that was beguiling. I'll ask her for work, Marielle speculated uneasily. What can she do except, at the worst, refuse me?

"I would like to play Ophelia to Mr. Edwin Booth's Hamlet," Marielle heard herself say.

"Oh?" Mrs. Sinclair said, obviously taken by surprise.

"I know all the lines," Marielle said, "even Hamlet's."

"Oh?" Mrs. Sinclair said again. "And next year you intend to be old enough to play Lady Macbeth?"

"No. Not next year. But soon," Marielle said, and gave Mrs. Sinclair and Ben Baker an enchantingly dimpled smile.

"The miners know the popular dramas almost by heart; they can finish lines from Shakespeare before they're spoken. They're well versed in the theater."

"I am well versed in what they like. I will not disappoint them," Marielle said.

"They often toss actors who displease into blankets. They throw vegetables. They shoot at them until they leave town."

"I've been performing for some time now, ever since Papa, Sybil, and I arrived in California. We've played every city, town, and mining camp in this part of the world."

"I see," Mrs. Sinclair said thoughtfully.

"I've seen her perform," Ben Baker said as he turned to Catherine Sinclair. Marielle thought she detected a gleam in his eyes.

He was up to something. As far as she knew, he had seen her sing and dance one night. He had never seen her perform Shakespeare because she never had. "I will find some sort of work for you in one of the other theaters. Perhaps another company needs a young, beautiful Ophelia."

"I would prefer to play Ophelia opposite Ted Booth," Marielle insisted politely.

"Would you indeed?" Mrs. Sinclair said.

"Who is using my name in vain?" Edwin Booth boomed as he entered the small office.

Marielle looked up in surprise. She had not seen him since the party in New York two years ago that had so dramatically changed her life. Today he looked much older, mature and full of confidence. She wondered if as much had happened to him as had happened to her. She wondered if he would remember her.

She needn't have been afraid. After the first pleasant shock of having a beautiful young girl thrust herself into his arms, Ted's face showed happy recognition. He kissed her soundly on both cheeks, hugged her with sincere delight, and then held her at arm's length to examine the change in her that time had wrought.

"You are just about grown-up," he said. "And such an intriguing-looking young lady." He turned her this way and that way and finally sat her down in her seat again. "Don't move. Now that I've found you I want to have a long, long talk. Don't disappear on me the way you did last time."

Marielle nodded happily. She watched him greet Mrs. Sinclair and then Ben Baker, whom he knew from his last trip to California.

"Uncle Ben, you old so-and-so," he said, and glanced hastily at the ladies. "I hear we've got your old theater for the time being. What're you going to do while we're selling out every night?"

"Funny thing that you asked," Ben said jovially. "An idea just came to me. What would you say if I told you that I know the most beautiful Ophelia in the whole world? Not only that, she could be the youngest most beautiful Juliet on the American stage ever."

"I'd say I must have her for my Hamlet. I would also say that my Romeo needs that Juliet."

Uncle Ben took Ted by the arm and brought him directly in front of Marielle's chair. Pointing at her, he said, "There is your Ophelia! There is your Juliet!" He paused a moment for the effect "What do you think?"

Catherine Sinclair rose to her feet before Booth could reply. "Just a minute, now. We haven't even seen the young lady's work!"

"There's no need for that," Edwin Booth said quickly. "She comes from theatrical stock. And just look at her, my dear Mrs. Sinclair. She is perfect, is she not?"

Mrs. Sinclair scrutinized her intently and then smiled. "Yes, I suppose she is striking—with all that glorious red hair of hers."

"And I shall coach her in the part," Edwin went on excitedly. Marielle was holding her breath.

Uncle Ben said to Mrs. Sinclair, "We can work something out, I'm sure. Why don't we discuss this over dinner tonight?" He looked at Edwin Booth, who nodded. Mrs. Sinclair still seemed not entirely convinced.

"I know you must have other business, dear Marielle," Uncle Ben said as he took her firmly by the arm and steered her toward the door. Then he said in her ear, "I will see you tomorrow." He looked her straight in the eyes. "The part is yours if you want it. Of course, there will be a percentage of your salary for me. Right?"

"But of course," Marielle whispered with as much dignity as she could muster, and swept into the hallway with a backward smile at Catherine Sinclair and a sideways glance at Ted from under her long lashes. Smiling and looking unconcerned was one of the most difficult things she ever had to do. There seemed to be more acting in real life than on the stage.

She knew Uncle Ben would come through, no matter how he had to do it. She would tred the boards as Ophelia opposite Edwin Booth as her Hamlet. She also knew she would not embarrass Ted. She would be worthy of him. She had memorized every line of *Hamlet* when she was a little girl and had listened to Papa and had mouthed the words along with him. Mrs. Sinclair's production was sure to attract full houses. *Hamlet* and *Romeo and Juliet* were the miners' two favorite plays.

Marielle smiled widely as the sun outside the dark theater struck her full in the face. She knew that today was the start of something momentous for her.

Chapter Ten

Ted Booth worked her regularly up to twenty hours a day for two weeks before opening night. Marielle, who knew all the lines, still thought she would fall apart all during the rehearsals, she was so tired. But she learned a lot and was grateful to her dear friend and mentor, who always treated her with so much kindness and gentleness.

Most of the time she felt more child than actress as Edwin Booth molded her performance to fit his own. He knew what he was doing; he was extraordinary when it came to the littlest detail, but he was a hard taskmaster. Very rarely did she question his judgment. He would not have it, and if she so much as raised an eyebrow at an interpretation, he immediately made sure that whether she understood or not, she was to do it his way. She was a quick study. She learned it his way. Often she thought of asking Papa's advice, but he seemed to belong to a different world these days, to have forgotten that his whole life had once revolved around the theatre. Now there was nothing he enjoyed more than spending several days out in a close-by mining camp, his feet in a cold stream, panning for gold that he never found. Papa was content. That was all that mattered. His panning kept him occupied while Marielle worked with a man whom she knew would, one day, be America's most important Shakespearean actor.

Mrs. Sinclair was not only a fine figure of a woman, but she was calculating and bright. When she was assured of six weeks of brisk lucrative business at the theater, she acquiesced charmingly to Ben Baker's and Edwin Booth's demands for Marielle as Ophelia and Juliet. She, in turn, contented herself with the roles of Gertrude, Portia, and Lady Macbeth, and it looked like a happy working relationship for the entire company.

Marielle put her career into the hands of Ted Booth and Ben Baker, and felt this stroke of luck was just the beginning of her success. She was a very lucky girl in many ways. Ben Baker had arranged an excellent contract with Mrs. Sinclair, and although he received a healthy percentage, Marielle would be able to support Papa nicely for the time being.

When she returned to the boarding house late at night after rehearsals were finished, Marielle always found a hefty sandwich, freshly baked cookies, and creamy milk waiting for her, set out by Harriet Sweeney. And the care the two Sweeneys gave Jeremiah while Marielle was at the theater was exceptional. Mrs. Sweeney would lead Papa to the dining table and see that he ate the food she put in front of him. When Papa drank too much, her son, Brendon, saw to it that Papa was undressed and safely put to bed. It was an ideal arrangement.

The day before *Hamlet* was to open, Marielle got home later than usual to find that Papa had not returned from the mining camp he'd set off for that morning. It was not unusual. Sometimes he stayed for several days. By why today? Tired and cold because the fires in the house were banked, Marielle wished Papa had not chosen to stay away at this particular time.

Hating to wake Mrs. Sweeney or Brendon, Marielle sat munching her chicken sandwich and wondering if she should go directly to bed or knock discreetly on Mrs. Sweeney's bedroom door and ask if she had heard from Papa.

She was also worried about the success of her first performance with the eminent Edwin Booth. She wanted to be brilliant, to be loved by the entire audience, and, finally, to be acclaimed. She needed it desperately. If only she could discuss this with Papa. He would understand and advise her. The once-talented Jeremiah Preston would not only know how she felt, but would have felt that way himself at an early stage in his career. But Papa was not around and she felt alone and depressed. If only tomorrow was over and done with!

Then, suddenly, she started to cry. She cried and nibbled at the sandwich simultaneously until it became wet with her tears. At last she wiped her wet cheeks and blew her nose into her handkerchief. It was stupid, she decided, to feel this way. She needed only to be bold to make the public know her and love her. She would be a success. *She was her father's daughter*, and she wanted the whole world to know it. She had talent. Feeling better, Marielle left the cold kitchen and went to bed.

In the morning, long after the other boarders left for the day, Marielle ate breakfast and drank cups of strong coffee. "You will find Papa for me and see that he is suitably dressed and at the theatre at a reasonable time?" There was an anxious expression on her face as she talked to Brendon.

She had arranged for three good tickets to be set aside at the box office in Papa's name. Ostensibly, Jeremiah would escort Harriet and Brendon Sweeney to the theatre. What it really amounted to was that the good landlady and her young son would see that Papa arrived on time and in good condition.

It would be Brendon's first experience inside a theatre, and the snub-nosed boy was filled with excitement. When Marielle told Brendon she was an actress, he immediately put her upon a pedestal and, this morning as usual, he gazed at her with eyes full of puppy love.

"Don't you fret, ma'am," Brendon said. "I will find Mr. Preston and see that he gets to the theatre early. You think only about your actin' job, ma'am."

"Mr. Preston will be at the theatre in time," Mrs. Sweeney said as she came into the kitchen. "Don't you go spoilin' your feelings, lass. There's nothing for you to be worrying about. You do what you have to do today, and rest your mind about your father. You leave him to the Sweeneys."

Harriet Sweeney's faith in herself rubbed off on Marielle and she began to look forward to the opening night performance. They were opening with *Hamlet*, and if all went well according to plan, they would do *Romeo and Juliet* the following night. That afternoon there would be several hours of last minute dress rehearsal and then the show would go on. Marielle would not return to the boarding-house before curtain time.

When she arrived at the theatre she found that most of the company were already assembled except for Ted Booth and Catherine Sinclair. Ben Baker stopped by shortly afterwards, kissed her lightly on the forehead for courage, and told her he knew she would be wonderful. He would be sitting out front and rooting for her.

"Go out front and take a lookee," Uncle Ben said just before he left her.

"In a minute," Marielle said as she finished unpacking the jars of makeup she would use later on.

When she went out to the front, Uncle Ben, his spectacles perched high on his round cheeks, beamed at her from the door-way.

"Lookee, lookee, lookee," he kept saying, and chuckled with glee as Marielle glanced up at the huge poster pasted on the front of the theatre. He slapped his knee as he saw her eyes take on a look of astonishment.

Her name was stretched across the front of the poster, about half the size of those of Edwin Booth and Catherine Sinclair. Marielle could have wept for joy, except that she started to get a sick feeling in the pit of her stomach. It was called opening night jitters and every thespian felt it, she had been told. But would she get over it the way everyone else did before curtain time?

Later, Edwin Booth gave an opening night speech to the company, then met with Marielle, checked her costume, showed her the peephole from which every actor looked at the audience before the audience saw him, and told her not to be surprised if she got so sick she vomited before the performance started. The moment he left her cubicle, Marielle threw up into the slop pail. She felt a little better after that, but still her stomach felt fluttery.

Mrs. Sinclair appeared shortly thereafter, looking very cool, calm, and under control. Her gray silk dress was beautifully tailored and seemed to complement the rest of her exquisite accessories.

"You will be a wonderful Ophelia," Catherine Sinclair told Marielle graciously. "Don't be afraid to spread your wings and fly. Tonight will be the most extraordinary night you will ever have in the theatre. It's your first as a star."

After Mrs. Sinclair had gone, Marielle did her makeup slowly, using her face as a canvas, her jars as a palette. She had seen Jeremiah and Sybil do this night after night, and it was a ritual she intended to incorporate into her life on the stage. The moment she was satisfied with the paint and powder that changed her from Marielle to Ophelia, she hurried to the peephole to see if Papa and the Sweeneys were already in the theatre.

The theatre was already half-full. But Papa was not out front, nor was there any sign of Mrs. Sweeney or Brendon. What she did see, however, was a new arrival coming down the aisle—one of the most beautiful women she had ever seen in her entire life.

The woman, seemingly ageless, was surrounded by adoring escorts. It was small wonder. She was the most feminine woman in the theater, yet she was dressed in a strange suit that looked like a man's. The beautiful lady's shirt front was lacy and her coat and trousers were velvet and beautifully tailored. She wore natty boots and a black hat, which she was in the process of removing. In her hand was a handsome riding whip. Never had Marielle seen such an unusual-looking and elegant person.

"Who is she?" Marielle asked one of the actors waiting to use the peephole.

Marielle gave up her place. The actor looked through the peephole and turned back to Marielle. "Good heavens! That's Lola Montez."

"It seems to me I read about her once when we lived in New York. But I was so little, I don't really remember."

The actor gave Marielle a gossipy, complacent smile. "My dear, Lola Montez used to be the mistress of King Ludwig I of Bavaria. I've heard she's never gotten over the feeling of power that was hers when she lived with him. Except now she's in California and there is no Ludwig for her to manipulate."

"Really?"

"Really. She's an adventuress. I'd give a week's wages to know what she's up to in these parts."

"She's so beautiful. I've never seen anyone who looked like that, not even in the theatre."

"You just go back to your mirror, little one. You're beautiful, too. She just knows exactly what to do with her beauty."

Marielle smiled and made her way across the bustling stage back to her cubicle.

She put her head down on her dressing-table. She was really beginning to be very distraught about Papa, and together with the squeamish flutterings inside her stomach, she wondered if she dared even try to make her Shakespearean debut. Her mouth had gone dry and she was thirsty, but was afraid to drink fully; so she simply moistened her lips.

Forlornly she lifted her head, took a deep breath from the very bottom of her lungs, and went back to the peephole at the side of the velvet curtain. As she peeked out, her breath came out in a sigh of vast relief and the knot in her stomach eased slightly. Seated in the front row of the audience, looking carefully groomed and dapper, was Papa. He had on his best suit, his hair had been cut and slicked back, and someone had given him a proper shave. Best of all, he looked to be sober and was perusing his one-page playbill attentively. Harriet and Brendon Sweeney sat by his side.

When Marielle saw Papa, safe, sound, and sober in his front row seat, she felt as if a great weight had been lifted from her shoulders. He was there to see her debut as a full-fledged serious actress. Only tonight, she was no longer the little girl who sang, danced, and giggled her way into the hearts of her audience. Tonight she would perform as a professional. And his presence gave her the courage to face the challenge.

She moved away from the peephole, but somehow, she found herself unexpectedly turning back for one more look. It was then that she saw them.

There were three people sitting toward the front, on the far side. They must have been among the last to enter the packed theatre because she had not seen them earlier. One was a middle-aged woman dressed in expensive but sedate forest green velvet; she was flanked by two young men. Marielle stopped breathing and held on to the old, dusty curtain as she looked once more to make sure. There could be no doubt whatsoever. It was Morgan sitting to one side of the woman, and the attraction she felt for him seemed to be as strong as ever. His face drew her gaze like a magnet. Only after a minute of drinking in the sight of Quinn did she notice that the man on the woman's other side was the stranger who had helped kill the grizzly and who had given her the poke of gold nuggets.

Marielle's heart was hammering in her bosom when Edwin Booth stepped to her side, took her gently by the arm and said, "It is time."

Marielle could not speak. She simply nodded, took her place, and prepared to make her entrance.

Chapter Eleven

Afterwards Marielle remembered nothing of the three hours of her first *Hamlet* except that she played it to Morgan Quinn as if he were sitting alone in the theater and as if his approval meant the difference between her life and death. But although Marielle played to one man, she still *became* Ophelia, and the audience knew it.

When it was all over they stood up together, almost as if on cue, and cheered and clapped. Marielle, from her marked spot on the stage, saw no one but Quinn. Someone thrust a bouquet of flowers into her arms and she bent down and put her nose into the blossoms. She had never seen a curtain call like this in all her days backstage with Papa.

She felt Ted Booth's hand in hers and they both bowed in unison, then threw kisses. The applause went on for five solid minutes. Marielle was happier than she had ever been in her entire life.

As the ovation thundered on, her gaze went to Quinn again. He was helping the dignified lady next to him leave her seat. The stranger's back was to her also, and the two men, both almost the same height, but still taller than most of the men in the room, made an impressive pair. Quinn was conservatively dressed in evening clothes with a starched white shirt, while the stranger looked as flamboyant as he had when Marielle saw him last. His fawn-colored suede coat and matching trousers looked expensive, though, and very dashing.

When at last the curtain rang down, Marielle found herself being swept along by Edwin Booth to his dressing room. The cubicle was minuscule in comparison to what a famous actor expected in New York, but Ted held court there nonetheless, and in his kindly way kept Marielle at his side while receiving well-wishers and friends.

Papa and Harriet Sweeney, with Brendon trailing behind them, were the first to reach Marielle after the performance. Brendon shyly remained behind his mother, but there was an awe-stricken, love-sick look on his freckled face. Papa hugged Marielle tightly, his face wet with tears of love and pride.

As the little room filled with well-wishers, Papa leaned over and whispered to Marielle, "I'll see that Mrs. Sweeney and Brendon get safely home. Then I'll return for you. What a lofty night for you, my girl. There's no reason for you to hurry back to the boarding house."

Ted Booth overheard Jeremiah's words. "You are welcome to return, sir, but please return to the Golden Eagle Hotel. We intend to move our celebration over to the suite of rooms Miss Lola Montez has reserved for us. Please allow Marielle to be part of the company celebration. She deserves it."

"I consider that an honor, sir." Papa turned to Mrs. Sweeney, took her arm as if she were a duchess, and exited the crowded room as if he were the star of the evening. Marielle looked after him fondly. She had not seen him in such complete control for a long time.

But she did not see Morgan and his party, though she'd been half hoping he would show up backstage to congratulate her. And finally she slipped into her dressing cubicle and changed into her good plum-colored outfit. When she returned to Ted's dressing room, she saw that Catherine Sinclair was there.

Mrs. Sinclair embraced Marielle as if she'd never doubted her abilities. "You are a leading lady now, Miss Preston," she said, "and once you are a leading lady in my company, you are a very important personage, indeed."

"Yes, ma'am."

"You are going to become famous, I am sure. Do you understand what I am saying to you?"

"I hope so, Mrs. Sinclair."

"Good! Then I must say this too, child. You now have the responsibility of getting yourself another outfit. This muslin you wear all the time is awful."

Marielle opened her mouth to tell Catherine Sinclair that it was her best dress, but before she could speak the room went silent as the beautiful Lola Montez and her retinue entered. Again, Marielle could not keep her eyes off her. Lola Montez's beauty was a wild sort of comeliness. Her cheekbones were more prominent than Marielle had ever seen on a recognized beauty, her eyes were very dark and soft, her hair pitch black, and her skin smooth and olive. Marielle thought her easily the most glamorous woman in the room, though she remembered that some said her beauty far exceeded her talent, that she was not as good a dancer as her reputation made it seem.

Lola swept in, men on both sides of her, and moved directly to Edwin Booth, who obviously was a friend from the past. Marielle was fascinated.

"You've done it again, Teddy. And I hate you for being so good." Lola struck him playfully on the arm with her riding whip, speaking softly in some sort of combination French and Spanish accent. They embraced and chatted casually until Ted looked past her shoulder and beckoned to Marielle.

As she moved to Ted's side, Marielle wished she had the sophistication of both Lola Montez and Catherine Sinclair. Mrs. Sinclair was notorious; Lola Montez was scandalous. They collected men and behaved as if they were the only women in the world. She wanted to be like those two ladies, both so beautiful in their own ways, both so rich and famous.

Marielle stepped close to Ted, looked shyly into Lola Montez's face, and was immediately put at ease by the friendliness she saw in the other woman's eyes.

"I congratulate you, my dear. Oh, to be young enough to be a convincing Ophelia. Am I to understand you're to be Juliet tomorrow evening?"

"Yes, Miss Montez," Marielle said.

"Call me Countess. All my friends do."

"Thank you, Countess."

"You're coming with us, little Shakespeare girl," Lola Montez said, and clapped her hands high over her head even though she already had the attention of all the guests in the cubicle. "The Golden Eagle Hotel! The Countess will hold court there for the distinguished company of dedicated actors who performed at the Sacramento Theatre tonight."

And before she knew it, Marielle found herself moving alongside Lola with Edwin Booth on the other side of the hostess. When they reached the street, Marielle tried to catch a glimpse of Quinn, hoping he had come to the back to pay his respects. But there was no sign of his party. She felt a twinge of deep disappointment. He had not cared enough to come and talk with her, even for one brief moment.

* * *

The suite turned out to be two upper rooms of the hotel, hastily opened up into one. The bedroom furniture in the front room had been replaced with two stained horsehair sofas, badly in need of recovering. A bar had been set up on the other side and there was champagne in tin buckets full of ice, waiting to be snatched up by the thirsty guests. For many who preferred it, there was whiskey and rum. For the teetotalers, there was icy lemonade. The walls of the suite were stained with brown rain spots; the windows were dusty and without curtains. But the moment Lola Montez walked in, the place took on an air of glamour. Marielle wondered why the atmosphere was suddenly so exquisite simply because the elegant ex-mistress of the King of Bavaria had walked into the dismal suite.

Other than knowing the company players and the Countess, Marielle recognized no one except Ben Baker, who appeared shortly after the guests had made themselves comfortable. Uncle Ben kissed her, congratulated her, and moved on to chat with others. Once again she felt left out of things; but suddenly, some of the young men broke through their own initial shyness at seeing Marielle close up, their theatre girl in the flesh, their fantasy in street clothes, and they swarmed around her. One, a youmg man straight from the diggings with a blue and black checked flannel shirt and red suspenders holding up his trousers, asked her if she wanted something to drink. Another, in a suit that could easily pass muster at any brokerage house in New York, danced attendance on her the moment he found that "Miss Ophelia" could smile. Soon there were three or four men surrounding her, and she found herself studiously copying Lola Montez, circulating around the room, smiling at everyone, and laughing gaily.

She saw Papa return alone after having escorted the Sweeneys home, and she hurried toward him, happy that he was with her and looking so fit. She kissed him and took his arm, hanging on to him proudly so he could not get away from her.

"Did you want something to drink, Papa?" she asked cautiously.

"Nothing for me tonight, dear child."

Marielle looked at him gratefully. "Thank you, Papa!"

He smiled thinly. "I can only promise you this for now."

"Now is good enough for me."

At that precise moment, Marielle became aware of the three people standing at the open door to the Countess's suite. They entered the room as if they owned it, and made their way to their hostess. Marielle could not keep her eyes off them as they exchanged pleasantries and introductions with the Countess.

Papa noticed her look, glanced in the direction of the three people, and raised a hand in greeting as his face lit up. "Do you see whom I see? Come with me, my darling. There is our good friend, Morgan Quinn."

Reluctantly, but with heart pounding, she allowed herself to be dragged over to the group. Lola Montez put one arm around Papa and the other around Marielle and made the introductions in her own bewitching way so that everyone stopped what they were doing and watched. "Dear Jeremiah and Marielle, I want you to meet Mr. Morgan Quinn—an old friend—his mother, Mrs. Carmel Quinn Pagonne, and his brother, Rio Pagonne."

Morgan's face was expressionless, while Rio could hardly contain his pleasure as he beamed at Marielle. Carmel's countenance was an expressionless as Morgan's; still Marielle found herself fascinated by her.

Morgan's mother was diminutive and fragile, except for her face, which contained the same strength Marielle saw in her two sons. If she had met this woman anywhere in the world, Marielle felt she would know that Carmel was the mother, and these two handsome men were of her flesh and blood. Together they appeared a mighty family, close and tightly knit.

Marielle gave her hand first to Mrs. Pagonne, who looked her over frostily as she acknowledged the introduction. The woman's eyes met hers and then penetrated deeply into the innermost recesses of Marielle's thoughts, as if she could read how Marielle felt by merely looking into her clear, blue eyes.

Rio, whose turn was next, was obviously in high spirits. "You see. I told you I would come and see you act. That I would find you, wherever you were." He turned to his mother. "Look at her. Isn't she as beautiful as I said?" He turned back to Marielle. "I told my ma I found an enchanting damsel in distress in the wilderness, and I don't think she believed me."

"Rio!" his mother exclaimed in a low but imperious voice.

"Sorry, Mother," Rio said, but his mischievous grin showed that he felt sorry about nothing.

When she got to Morgan, Marielle gave him her hand gravely, trying to contain the tumultuous emotions she was feeling at seeing him again. As their hands met, the same startling sensation she had felt the last time they had touched shot through her. Looking up at him, she saw a muscle twitch in his cheek.

"Hello again," he said, and smiled for the first time that night.

She tried not to be flustered by his smile.

"Mr. Quinn?" she said, and quite deliberately she looked him full in the face.

For a long moment they stood, drawn to each other as if they were completely alone in the crowded suite of celebrants. It is not finished, Marielle thought as she stood there, miserably trying to collect her wits, and he knows it as well as I do. And as his hand continued to hold hers, she tried to break away with a hard tug from her small wrist. It didn't work.

"I want to talk to you," he said in a self-possessed way, as if she had not tried to break his hold.

"No. We can't." Instinct told her to resist this man who'd played havoc with her heart once before.

"I don't mean now. I mean soon. When we can be alone."

"No . . . there's nothing to talk about. It was a long time ago."

"We're not finished," he said in a whisper, as if he were reading her thoughts.

When she caught a sharp look from Carmel, who was only a short distance away, she managed to wrench her hand out of his. There were fires inside her, banked temporarily, but ready to burst into flame, and it would not do to lose control in front of Quinn's mother.

Quinn continued to smile, calmly, with an arrogant assurance that made her tremble. She turned her face away, afraid he might see what she was thinking. She knew she could not afford to let this man enter her life again; his love was too consuming, his nature at once too passionate and mysterious. She'd been a vulnerable little girl when she'd abandoned herself to him before—but now she was a woman, and an actress, and this was the night of her triumph; she intended to control herself and triumph over her need for him as well.

"We have been finished for a long time," she said very softly, and left him to turn and smile sweetly at Rio, whom she saw approaching with a glass of lemonade.

Chapter Twelve

The company of actors was delighted with the success of their venture. But Marielle was tired, her nerves strung to the breaking point. Work was her only salvation. Work . . . work . . . work, she thought. Go through the motions. Forget who you are. Forget Morgan Quinn. Forget everything but the hours on stage. Please the audience. Please Mrs. Sinclair. Please your colleagues. Please Papa. Please Edwin Booth. Please Ben Baker. Close your mind and drift through the weeks until the contract is finished. Only life on the stage counted.

She played Ophelia one night and Juliet the next, six nights a week. The seats were always sold out in advance for *Hamlet* and *Romeo and Juliet*. The people of Sacramento City continued to return, many of them attending the productions several times a week. The miners, coming down from their diggings for a single night of enjoyment, found it difficult to buy a ticket. Edwin Booth and the rest of the cast were given raises in salary, and that included Marielle. Much of Marielle's salary raise went to Ben Baker, but she still felt she was doing well.

It was Rio who came to the theater every single night, not Quinn. Rio always purchased a seat in the first row and sat watching the entire production intently. One time only he was with someone else. From her peephole, Marielle saw Joaquín Murieta seated next to Quinn's brother. The alleged bandit sat politely through the play and mirrored Rio's intense interest in her performance. He never came a second time.

At the end of the evening, Rio clapped louder than anyone else, yelled "bravo" when Marielle made her bow, whistled and stomped and showed up immediately afterwards backstage. Marielle vowed to remain aloof from this enigmatic man, not only because he was Quinn's brother, but because he, too, could be trouble she did not need.

Nevertheless, every night he would knock politely on the door of Marielle's cubicle and leave a small poke of gold nuggets on the doorstep, disappearing before she could stop him. He never made a move to talk to her or see her in person, though.

Already she had a small cache of pokes all neatly stacked and locked away in her dressing table drawer. She planned to return the gifts to Rio, but she did not know how. She was afraid to tell anyone what was happening. She was afraid to try to find him. Most of all, she was afraid the gold was part of Rio's ill-gotten gains as part of the Murieta gang. She wanted no contact with Rio Pagonne. Marielle still found it difficult to believe she had seen Murieta seated so sedately in a front row amidst a houseful of theatregoers when there were wanted posters with his likeness pasted all over the city. But, because he seemd so conservative and unthreatening, no one in the audience looked at him twice. It was Rio who caught the glances of the crowd, especially the women. His bold, good-looking face with its ready and slightly crooked grin held a kind of crazy charm, and his darting, dark gray eyes seemed to see through the object of his interest. Like his brother, he dwarfed the rest of the men in the audience, and that included the slender, unprepossessing Joaquín Murieta.

Marielle wished he did not look so much like Quinn, but she was glad to note that he was not in the least bit moody, like his older brother. Still, there was that self-centered look about Rio she had noticed the first time she saw him. And his eyes could turn instantly cold and distant.

Though Rio made Marielle uneasy, she had to admit that she was also secretly charmed with his gallantry. Regardless of the fact that she knew he was a bandit, on a certain level Rio delighted her because he was so obviously a romantic. She was sure that Quinn did not have an ounce of romance in his soul.

The night before closing, Marielle looked through the peephole moments before the first act but could not find Rio's face. It surprised her, and she felt a momentary pang of disappointment. Instead, in a seat in the last row sat a tense and obviously unhappy Morgan Quinn. Even from on stage, Marielle could see the ill temper on his handsome face.

Despite her prior resolve, she felt her heart leap in abandon and was glad that tonight she was playing Juliet. Quinn had not seen her in this love story as yet, and she knew she would outdo herself because he was here. She looked at him once again before she gave herself up to the difficult role that demanded so much of her.

During Romeo's long speeches, Marielle found her thoughts wandering to Quinn and that indefinable tension between them. What was that strange excitement that burned so strongly between the two? And why couldn't she suppress it as she desired? Why had she not felt this way when Rio sat up front every night? Could only Quinn do this to her? After all, wasn't Rio as tall and as handsome as Morgan Quinn?

But there was no room for bitterness in her heart tonight. Quinn's moody countenance would not daunt her. Her audience would see her as her best Juliet ever, and as the tragedy progressed, she was certain she was giving the performance of a lifetime. She was proud that Quinn would see her as the beautiful heroine, the girl who was ready to give her life for love.

Now, on stage, she became Juliet, her cobalt velvet gown hugging her beautiful shoulders, shimmering pearls worked into the lushness of her red hair. Yet although she was Juliet, lost in the throes of love and tragedy, one very small corner of her mind wondered why Quinn had come to this particular performance and why Rio had not, and what would happen after the curtain came down. Would Quinn come backstage to see her, and if he did, what would he say?

When the performance was over and she had changed into her street clothes, the man whom she could not seem to forget appeared. He knocked on the door of the cubicle, a loud, rhythmic knock that spoke of strength and impatience. When she did not answer the door immediately, he knocked again. When at last she opened the door, he stood before her relaxed and under control. He actually gave her a smile as she ushered him into the room. Her heart pounded so hard against her rib cage, she found it difficult to breathe, much less to smile back.

He looked like a man with a purpose. His jaw, after the smile faded from his face, was tight and square and there was a glint of stubbornness in his steely gray eyes. His broad shoulders, pulled back straight and proud, seemed to wait for a time when they could assert their muscular strength. The expensive dark broadcloth covering the smooth, rippling muscles of his forearms was taut and tailored.

Once he was inside the dressing room, Marielle closed the door behind him. Whatever they discussed tonight was a private matter, although the walls were so thin it seemed futile to try to keep any conversation clandestine. When the door was closed, there was no room for both of them to move around. He filled the cubicle, and had to stoop because of his height.

He definitely didn't have the look of the stagedoor johnny; instead, he surveyed her from top to toe, and then waited for an indecently long interval before he spoke. "I came to see you about my brother."

Her heart sank. "What about him?" she asked frostily. "Is something wrong? I mean, why isn't he here himself?"

"He won't be coming to see you anymore. Not tonight. Not tomorrow night. Not ever."

She looked him over coldly. "And why not?"

"We have decided that it would not be to his advantage for him to continue seeing you."

"I see. And are you aware that he merely came to see a performance, that I've never had words with him since the opening night party?" She was cold with anger and did not mind that he saw how she felt.

"I am aware that he has been giving you presents. Gold nuggets. Worth a great deal."

She was furious! He had no right! Rushing to her dressing table, she unlocked the drawer and pulled it open. It was more than half full, stacked neatly with the small suede bags that Rio had left at her door. "Is this what you're so anxious about?"

He didn't answer. Instead, his eyes went to the bags of gold and then accusingly back to her face.

"Well! Why don't you take it? That's what you're here for, isn't it? But I want you to know I didn't ask for anything. In fact, I don't want his gold. But I do want you to know one thing. That gold was given freely and without strings. One of these bags was left outside my door every night. Your brother never stayed to find out whether I would accept his gifts or not."

He didn't look as if he believed her.

She became angrier. "Take it, I tell you. My only crime was not knowing what to do with it. Now I know. Take it all away this very instant."

"I didn't come to take back what was given you. I came to tell you to stay away from my brother."

"What did you say? I don't think I heard you right."

"You heard me right. Stay away from Rio."

He turned away from her almost as if he could not bear to look at her face. But she fooled him. She dashed around to his other side and forced him to look straight into her blue eyes. She was sure that if he could see the anger, he could also see the hurt. She wanted him to know exactly how she felt.

His face hardened, but his steely gray eyes grew sad. "I didn't think you would turn into a . . ."

There was no time to finish the sentence. She slapped him so hard and so fast that the palm of her hand became red immediately and began to sting from the blow.

"Get out," she said icily.

"You have me at a disadvantage," he said, putting his hand to his face. "You're more beautiful than I've ever seen you. Your skin is like fine porcelain and I refuse to mar it by striking back. But don't test me again." He took his hand away from his face and touched her, and shook his head in wonder at the softness. "I don't deserve such disfavor from you. If only you knew the strange circumstances in which I find myself."

"But I don't know."

"And I'm at a loss for words . . . the right words to tell you that I'm not at liberty to discuss certain matters with you."

"You've already made an impression—without words," she whispered, and turned away.

"Rio's not like you and me," Morgan said hoarsely.

"Of course not. He's a much nicer person. Therefore I don't deserve him. Or he doesn't deserve to be burdened with me. Is that it?"

He looked at her in astonishment, but did not answer.

"Let's not bandy words about anymore. I'm beginning to like Rio better every single minute I talk to you. He has a monster of a brother to deal with . . . so just get out and take the gold with you."

"It's not the gold, I tell you. It's something else entirely."

There was cold contempt in her voice. "What else?"

"I cannot say."

"Naturally. I didn't think you could."

"It's not something that concerns you or that you need to worry about. I really wish I could explain . . ."

"Just like you explained the night you disappeared on the *Andrew Jackson*? I was just a little girl, Quinn. Oh, how I needed you." Then she gasped as she realized what she had said. He was a dangerous man; he made her do and say things she had no intention of doing or saying.

"A little girl indeed! You look like a fragile waif, but you're strong as a forest vine," he said ruefully, rubbing the side of his face she had slapped. "Like a tenacious vine that spreads its roots deep into the earth. You've wrapped yourself around my heart and I cannot tear you loose, much as I would like to."

She hadn't expected him to say that. She felt a wildness within her take over, the same sort of wildness she knew was in him too; and as she thought of this he came toward her, took her roughly in his arms, found her mouth with his lips, and kissed her with the same hunger that she felt in herself. He savored her mouth, forcing her soft rosebud lips open. They quivered for only an instant before opening to him. She locked her arms around his neck and abandoned herself to him, recklessly returning his kisses.

She tried to think herself back in time, to the night on board the *Andrew Jackson*, to the very moment Morgan Quinn's lips touched hers for the first time. The thought made her breath catch in her throat and she became terrified of the feeling, yet she wanted to extend it forever. But there was no use in going back; going forward was the only way. Her own passion matched his. In that moment, Marielle knew she was lost. There was nothing she could do except accept and give in to his needs. Hungrily he continued to kiss her, sending the blood racing through her body until it left her weak-kneed and wobbly.

His lips presented pleasure she could not resist, made her feel faint with delight. All she could think of was that his touch inflamed her. She kissed him back and allowed him to enfold her in his strong embrace and wished with all her might that it would never end. She could feel his hard body pressed against her soft one as his lips moved rapidly over her cheek and down her neck. Anything—and everything—was what she would have offered up to him if he would only ask. She was lost, enmeshed—more and more what Morgan Quinn wanted and needed and less and less herself. And still he held her so tightly she could scarcely breathe. She wanted peace between them and wondered if it could ever be. But he seemed to inflame her with madness—and still he did not ask or say the words she wanted to hear.

"Marielle," he breathed, "I wish I could give you what you want. What you need. But I have other obligations. It would be too difficult for you to be part of my life at the present. But how I wish it were different. I really wish . . ." Again he trailed off as if he were a million miles from her.

She stiffened and pulled away from his embrace. There could never be love and peace between them. Only passion. And passion alone was never satisfactory for long. It was all clear to her now. It was as if an invisible curtain had descended between them. *"There are no explanations. Am I right, Mr. Quinn?"*

He released her, stood stock still for a second before he started pacing the tiny cubicle. Every now and then he looked at her with longing. But he had made up his mind. *"There are none."* His voice was controlled, even if his emotions were not.

"I am not surprised." The anger she felt earlier returned. "Get out. And take your brother's gold. I don't want that kind of money anyway. I think I know how he gets it."

Quinn's face went pale. "I have no idea what you're talking about. That gold was dug up by Rio just as it could have been dug up by any other miner at his diggings."

"Really?" She could not help being sarcastic.

"You can keep the gold. But, goddammit, stay away from Rio."

Superhuman strength coursed through her body along with a thundering rage. She managed to lift the drawer out of the dresser and heave it toward him.

"No need to worry on my account. Your precious brother is safe from me. *Take your gold,"* she screamed, pointing at the shattered drawer and gold nuggets lying on the floor. *"I never want to see you or your brother again."*

"Don't be so hasty about giving back the gold. It adds up to a tidy sum. I have found from experience that actresses usually are only too happy to accept gifts from admirers. Why don't you keep this as a token of Rio's esteem. He would never have given you such a gift if he didn't feel you deserved it."

"Oh . . . oh . . . oh . . . ." was all Marielle could scream in indignation. But before she could give full vent to her fury, he turned sharply on his heels and left the cubicle without a backward glance. He closed the door with such force the decrepit thing flew open again. Marielle could not resist watching as he stalked away. She saw Ted Booth pass by, quirk an eyebrow, and ask, "Are you all right, Marielle?"

She nodded her head mutely, not daring to speak, and Ted passed her cubicle, waving good-bye as he left the theatre for the night. Marielle was left standing, breathing hard, her face pale and full of wrath, her hand to her heart to still the clamor within. Around her lay the terrible gold nuggets, attesting to the drama they had innocently inspired.

* * *

The next night, closing night for the company at the Sacramento Theatre, Marielle was not sure she could survive the three grueling hours of the tragedy, but she looked at herself in the mirror and told herself that she had survived much worse. The next day she was free. It was the only thing that kept her from burying her head in her arms and having the kind of cry she had been needing for a long time.

Marielle was sitting at her dressing table when Ted Booth arrived. After letting him in, she went back to her jars and brushes. Ted bent over her as she applied her paints. "Marielle, let's talk after the show tonight. I have an offer to make that may interest you. At least you must listen."

Marielle kissed him lightly on the cheek, then shook her head. "I'm tired, Ted. Can we meet tomorrow, or anytime other than tonight?"

"There's some sort of celebration afterwards, I'm told. Will you be there? Your father is invited, of course."

Marielle turned back to her mirror and picked up a lip brush. She looked at Edwin Booth in the glass as she worked on her face. "I don't think so, Ted. It's been a long six weeks for me. All I want to do is sleep for the next twenty-four hours."

"Well, my dear, then let's talk over lunch tomorrow. I think you'll be very interested in my proposition." He left her, giving her a shy smile, always solicitous of her moods when she was off the stage.

Shortly afterward, in costume and stage makeup, Marielle made her way to the peephole out front. She knew it might be a long time before her next engagement anywhere. As she looked through the small, round hole, idly scanning the crowded theater, she saw Rio walking down the middle aisle to his usual seat in the front row. He looked unusually handsome in a rather soberly styled dark suit. His ruffled white shirtfront sported a cravat of bright red silk with a brilliant gold stickpin in the form of a golden raven. He was so close to the peephole when he was seated, that she could see the stones that formed the eyes of the raven. They were two large diamonds.

Marielle had never expected to see either of the two brothers again. But maybe Rio being here tonight was a good omen, she thought. It would give her the chance to return his gold.

Rio's gifts had been on her mind ever since Quinn's hasty departure the night before. She had slept badly last night, worrying how to return the bounty without having to contact any member of the Quinn family. Now it was settled. Since Rio was already in the theater, she would send him a note so that he would not leave without coming backstage.

When the play ended, there was a last standing ovation for the entire cast. Marielle stood beside Edwin Booth, feeling, like many of the other thespians, tears slide down her face as the curtain at last came down.

By the time she got to her dressing cubicle, Rio Pagonne was already there, leaning against the door. "Please come in," Marielle said. She opened the door and ushered him in.

Rio looked around the tiny room with interest. "I always wanted to see what an actress's dressing room looked like."

"This is it. Not exactly what you expected?"

"Not exactly. But it's fine." He moved to the dressing table, looked into the mirror and tried to flatten his unruly hair. He picked up a jar of white grease paint, sniffing at it curiously before he put it down. Then he picked up several of the makeup brushes and examined them with great interest before putting them back carefully in the exact spot from which he had taken them. He, like Quinn, had to stoop in the low-ceilinged cubicle.

Marielle went to her dressing tablee and opened the drawer. "Here is all that gold you left me. I can't keep it."

He looked surprised. "Why not?"

"Because it's not proper. In fact, I want to pay you back for the gold I did keep the first time we met. And, another thing. Do you expect me to believe you didn't know your brother was coming here last night?"

"Don't worry about my brother. And don't worry about anything else. Everything will be good and proper when you are mine."

Marielle gasped. "When I am yours?"

"I told Morgan. I told him that I plan to marry you. That I must have you." The words were said plainly enough, without a trace of guile. He was being completely candid. "I told my mother too."

"When did you see your brother last?" she asked when she finally found she could speak.

He hesitated just enough to give her a hint that all was not right. "The night before last."

"And why didn't you come to see me perform?"

"There was a little trouble in the family." Rio looked away from her. "I didn't stay at the ranch. I stayed at Joaquín's camp."

"You may as well tell me. Was the trouble over me?"

He smiled at her, that same little crooked smile that she'd seen on Quinn's face. "It's okay. They'll come 'round. Nothing to worry about. They'll love you like I do. Just give them time."

"Your family would never accept me, Rio." She looked very sad. "I have no intention of thwarting your mother or your older brother. You'll just have to forget me. Take the gold and go."

"I'll win Ma over. And as for Morgan . . ." His face grew dark. "He may be older, but I can take care of him."

Marielle sank into the one small chair in the dressing room. "I'm leaving Sacramento, Rio. I have no idea where Papa and I will be next. What you have in mind can't be. I'm sorry."

"Yes it can. I'll find you. Wherever you are. What I have in mind is to marry you. So that you will be mine forever."

"Rio, you're embarrassing me. Please take back the gold and let things be."

"The gold is for all those doodads you women have to buy for a proper . . . what do you call it? Trousseau?"

"Rio, I can't even get all this gold out of my dressing room, much less go carrying it around while I shop for dainties. Take it away. Please!"

He slapped his forehead. "Of course not. I'll take the gold to the assayers and change it into paper money for you. I'll get you a bank draft. It should come to about ten thousand."

Marielle looked up at him in surprise.

"You'll be able to buy the right kind of finery for our wedding," he continued. "And if you need more . . ."

She sighed.

Then, on bended knee, he implored her to marry him. "I want you for my wife. Doesn't that mean anything to you? I love you. I adore you. What can I do to make you say yes?"

She did not doubt his sincerity—in fact, it made her smile. Suddenly he seemed like a big, lovable giant and she liked him. She liked him a lot.

"You are a romantic and I like that. But you're also the most impractical person I've ever come across."

"You mean about the gold? You just don't know. We have lots of gold. No matter what I give you, it won't hurt our supply. We have a mountain of gold."

"Who is this 'we' you're talking about? Do you mean Joaquín Murieta?"

He laughed, took her in his arms and before she could protest, he kissed her. To her surprise, she found his lips warm and soft and able to fill her with a dizzying desire not altogether unlike what she felt for his brother.

The closeness of his body felt natural as she surrendered to his kiss. A little thrill went through her as she became aware that another man could do to her what she thought was reserved only for Morgan Quinn. Somehow, the knowledge made her feel stronger.

His arms tightened about her and his voice was low and hoarse in her ear. "We'll wait till we're married for the rest. I known how important it is to a woman." He drew away regretfully.

"Why is Joaquín Murieta giving you all this gold?" she asked when she'd caught her breath.

Rio laughed heartily. "Little you know. Joaquín had nothing to do with our gold. 'We' means Mother, Morgan, and I."

Marielle looked at him skeptically. "Where is all this gold, Rio, that you claim you have?"

Rio lowered his voice and then leaned over her mysteriously. "Since you're going to be part of the family," he whispered into her ear, "I don't see anything wrong in telling you. We own a mountain. It's on our ranch. The mountain is pure gold. We have the gold stacked underground. Ma says we can buy the whole state of California if we want. We're rich. Didn't Morgan tell you?"

Chapter Thirteen

She sat in the middle of her bed wearing her warm, cozy night-gown, her hair freshly brushed and hanging down her back almost to her waist, examining Rio's golden stickpin. The two diamond eyes of the raven glowed at her by the light of the candle she had lit the moment she was able to get into her room and close the door behind her. The stickpin was a beautifully hand-worked piece of jewelry, fashioned by a clever artisan; it must have cost a pretty penny. But what did money mean to a man who owned a mountain of gold?

Marielle didn't know whether to believe Rio's story or not. It was not a likely tale. It was ridiculous. But all indications led to the fact that perhaps he was telling the truth. And now the unusual stickpin was hers. Rio had forced her to accept it in exchange for taking the golden nuggets away.

Now she stashed the stickpin beneath her pillow and went to check on Papa. He was fast asleep when she entered his room, his frail hands and arms outside the coverlet veined with myriad little blue lines. His broken, dirty nails proved he was no longer an actor, but a miner—though in the six weeks Marielle had worked with Catherine Sinclair's company, Jeremiah Preston had dug up exactly three dollars' worth of gold. Even at that, he had used up more strength than he had to spare, and Marielle was afraid for him. He seemed to be forgetting more and more of their past life as each day went by. She had no idea what to do. The Sacramento City doctor, recommended by Dr. Clappe, told her that Papa was fail-ing.

She kissed her father on the forehead, then returned to her bed, where she drifted into an uneasy sleep, awakening once to find the golden pin no longer beneath her pillow, but digging into her flesh. Rolling out of bed sleepily, she took the pin and fastened it into the collar of her plum muslin dress hanging ready for her business date tomorrow with Ted Booth.

While she floated restlessly in and out of slumber, she dreamed of Quinn and the stance she knew he would take over Rio's announcement concerning her. She knew she was having a nightmare, but found herself caught up in the fierceness of the hate Quinn and Rio felt for each other.

By twelve noon, still groggy for want of more sleep, Marielle was seated opposite Edwin Booth at a small table in the dining room of the Orleans Hotel. Edwin Booth had ordered for both of them and Marielle, out of respect for him, took a bite of the flapjacks with molasses and bacon that was placed before her. But it was the coffee that she needed more than anything. She drained her cup and was glad to see the waiter hurrying toward her with a full pot of the steaming brew.

"I'll be in San Francisco for one week," Ted Booth told her as he sipped his coffee. He opened a small silver flask that he had taken from his hip pocket and poured a shot of brandy into his cup.

Marielle was surprised. She had never seen Ted drink in the daytime before, only after his performance was over.

"Then I'm going back to New York," the actor continued. "I've some lucrative offers in good theatres. All sorts of doors are opening for me."

Marielle waited, not knowing what to expect.

"There may be similiar opportunities for you. I know I can arrange for your acceptance in one or another of the better companies. If you're interested in returning to New York, of course."

Her eyes opened wide and she caught hold of his hand. "Ted. How can you ask? Am I interested? I want that more than anything. You know how I feel about my career."

"Good. Are you signed for anything further with Ben Baker?"

"No. I'm free to go whenever I like. And for personal reasons, I think it would be best for me to leave California," she added, thinking of the Quinn family and the problems they brought her. "And, Ted, I am ready for New York. I really am."

Suddenly she thought of something. "What about Jeremiah? Will I be able to bring him with me?" She looked at Ted pleadingly.

He hesitated. "Naturally there is no reason why you can't, except we both know he will never work in a theater again. However, I know how well you care for him and I'm sure, with luck, you can earn more than enough to continue supporting him."

"Thank you, Ted. I'm overwhelmed." Her eyes misted with tears of gratitude; once more Ted Booth had thought of her in a loving, generous way.

"Before you make any decisions though, think about the journey. We'll be going by way of Panama. It's a more arduous journey than around the Horn, although it's considerably shorter. Men much younger than your father have succumbed before they reached their destinations."

Marielle nodded gravely.

Booth looked at her with sympathy. "Remember, dear child, you're still very young. This is only the first opportunity of many that will come your way. I keep remembering my own father. Do you remember Junius, Senior? He died on the ship he was taking back to an engagement in New York. I received a very nice letter from the doctor on board ship. He said Junius died in his sleep. He didn't suffer. Just died from fragility and general bad health."

"I'm very sorry to hear of his death. But I am glad he didn't suffer."

"I know how much Jeremiah means to you. I want you to come to New York, dear child, but, I also know you must give some thought to your father's health. Whatever you decide, I will understand and try to help."

"How long do I have to make a decision?"

"Nine days at the most. Two days while I'm here. Seven days in San Francisco. I'll sail from there. If you can, I would prefer to know one way or another before I leave Sacramento City. So that's only two days. You think you can make up your mind that fast?"

"If Papa can travel, it's yes, yes. Yes! I can tell you that right now."

Booth smiled at her enthusiasm and sipped his coffee.

"I'll go see Dr. Lyons this afternoon. He's the one with an office in town. We'll see what he says. I'm so excited, Ted."

"And so am I. I want to tell you a secret. There is a young lady back East. We are not betrothed as yet." His face lit up when he spoke of the lady he intended to wed some day. "Her name is Mary Devlin. I intend to get to know her better and to ask for her hand in marriage. You will love her, Marielle. She is an actress, like you. A few years older than you. Just right for me. I have great hopes she will love me as much as I love her."

"How wonderful!" Marielle leaned over the table and kissed him on the cheek. "I truly wish you the best of everything. You deserve great happiness."

"Thank you," Booth said simply, his usually sad, dark eyes temporarily bright with thoughts of his faraway love.

After they finished their talk, Marielle left him at the table after promising to give him her decision as soon as she made it.

At the doctor's office, which was in a rickety wooden building that was also used for storing grain, Marielle had to wait until Dr. Lyons returned from delivering a baby. Once there, dusty from the trip back to town, he settled Marielle into a chair and talked with her while he washed the journey's grime from his face and hands. "Am I to understand you want to take Jeremiah back to New York?"

"Yes, doctor."

"How you goin' to take him, girl? Fly?"

Marielle smiled. "We'll go the shortest way possible. Chagres. Gorgona Pass. Panama. If we're lucky, we could be in New York in less than eight weeks."

"If you're lucky. If you're not, I 'spect Jeremiah'll be dead."

"What's wrong with him, doctor? What's really wrong?"

"Everything, girl. It would be easier to ask me what's not wrong with him."

"Then you don't think my father can withstand the rigors of the trip back to New York?"

"I think he doesn't have much time, Miss Preston, and a trip like that will only hasten the inevitable." The doctor sat down heavily and looked at Marielle quizzically. "You love him, girl?"

"Yes. I love him, doctor. I love my father more than anything in the world. What shall I do?"

"You do what you have to do, girl." He sighed loudly. "I can't tell you. But I think he might just up and die before he gets to New York. But if you don't go, he may up and die anyway. So you see, you have a difficult decision to make."

"Thank you, Dr. Lyons," Marielle said as she got up from her chair and prepared to leave. "You may not know it. But you have been more helpful than you think."

Back at the hotel, Ted Booth received Marielle immediately upon being summoned by the desk clerk. He was clearly surprised to see her back so soon, but when she told him she had made a definite decision he politely escorted her to the dining room once again.

They were settled into their chairs, and although Ted waited expectantly, Marielle found it difficult to start. Still, she knew she was doing the right thing for both herself and for Papa. She finally found her voice. "I wanted you to know as soon as possible, Ted. I will not be going to New York with you." She offered no further explanation, but from the look on Ted's face she thought he understood.

"I'm sorry," he said at once.

"It's Papa," she whispered.

"How long?" Ted asked sympathetically.

"Not too long one way or another. It doesn't look good."

"I understand."

"Will we ever see each other again?"

"Absolutely. You can't get rid of a Booth just like that." He gave her that wonderfully melancholy smile.

It made her cry. Strong Marielle Preston. She hated herself, but she couldn't help it. "I want to go back to New York with you, Ted."

Booth sat opposite her without touching her and looked into her unhappy eyes and gave her a long, shrewd look. "We will meet again, Marielle Preston. No doubt about that. It's not good-bye, Marielle. It's only farewell. I will see you next in New York."

Marielle cried on softly, holding a handkerchief up to her face so that anyone coming into the dining room would not see her tears. Luckily at that hour the room was almost empty.

Booth patted the hand he was holding awkwardly. "I have an idea. Lola Montez is in Sacramento City for a short visit. Why don't I talk with her? She mentioned, the last time I saw her, that she would like to invite you to be her guest in Grass Valley. Perhaps we can arrange for you and Jeremiah to be paying guests for a few weeks. The weather there is much better than here in Sacramento—and it is not a long or difficult trip. Jeremiah might benefit, and you can nurse him into better health without being bored to death. One is never, never bored when in the company of Lola Montez."

Marielle looked up, her tear-stained face taking on a look of hope. "Do you think you can arrange it, Ted? Fresh air, good food, and rest. Maybe Papa will get better."

"Of course he will, dear child. I'll arrange it today. Oh, another thing. When my brother John comes to San Francisco I want you to get there and see him perform. And then I want you to promise to go backstage and introduce yourself. I have mentioned your name to him in several of my letters.''

''Is he really coming out West?''

''He wrote me that he signed for a ten-week engagement.''

''I promise,'' Marielle said.

''You will like him very much, dear Marielle. He is very handsome and a fine actor.''

''Are you trying to be matchmaker, Ted Booth?'' Marielle's eyes started to twinkle as the tears dried.

Ted chuckled in a deep melodious way. ''You are very beautiful, child. You'll be pursued by many. Why not a young, handsome Booth?''

They both laughed, and Marielle's mood lifted. She left the hotel feeling a lot better than when she had arrived. For the rest of her visit, Ted had kept her smiling with tales of his large family. He also convinced her that there was hope for Papa. And he was right, she felt. A few weeks rest would do them both good. It would give her time to get her life in order, and Jeremiah a chance to regain some of his physical strength. And then she would see.

When she arrived at the boarding house, she found that Papa was out on a panning trip but was expected momentarily. Marielle told Harriet Sweeney about her new plans immediately. Mrs. Sweeney nodded her head in agreement at the undertaking, but was sad about losing her best boarders.

When Brendon came into the house and was told the news, his face fell and he looked like he was about to cry. ''You're my favorite actress,'' he mumbled, and turned red. He said it as if he had been going to the theatre all his life and had seen hundreds of productions and had chosen her as his idol from among many leading ladies.

Marielle kissed him on the forehead, remembering how Ted Booth had made her feel better earlier in the day. ''It's not goodbye, Brendon. It's only farewell.''

It was not long afterwards that Marielle heard a horse and buggy draw up in front of the boarding house. Minutes later, Harriet Sweeney came to tell her she had a visitor.

''It's that crazy lady. The one who did that spider dance last year at the Sacramento Theatre. Before you came. The one who drinks champagne every day and is always surrounded by men. Lola Montez.'' Mrs. Sweeney's eyes were round with surprise, her hands fiddling nervously with the apron strings that held her apron tightly around her shapeless middle.

"I'll see her in the parlor," Marielle said, a bit surprised herself to see how fast Edwin Booth worked. "Don't be nervous. She's very nice."

"Is she now? She's got two menfolk in tow, both lookin' all the world like idiots. Both madly in love by the looks on their silly faces. I swear it. As if one suitor isn't enough."

"I'll be right there, Mrs. Sweeney." Marielle patted her hair into place and looked at herself in the mirror. She was still wearing the plum muslin Mrs. Sinclair had commented on. She had to admit that, like Mrs. Sweeney, she too was just a little bit nervous.

As Marielle entered the parlor, the Countess turned and put down the Sweeney family Bible, whose pages she had been turning as she waited. She wore a pink dress, beautifully fashioned to her fabulous figure, and an elaborate pink bonnet with black ribbons on it. The lady looked absolutely gorgeous. She was smoking a thin, brown cigarette. Marielle had never seen a woman smoke publicly before.

Lola swept up to Marielle, embraced her warmly, and looked her up and down with shrewd eyes. "You, poor, poor child. Teddy Booth has told Lola everything and she commiserates deeply. You and your dear *dad-dee* will be guests at my house. Lola says it is her pleasure." Her eyes automatically went to the stickpin Marielle was wearing on the collar of her dress. "That is a very beautiful pin." She gave Marielle an odd look. "It is very exceptional. You must value it deeply."

Marielle opened her mouth to answer, but the Countess didn't give her the chance. The lady continued on in her soft accented voice, "You understand that Grass Valley is not big. But the mountain air is delicious, the vegetation is green and very beautiful, and your father will breathe the healthiest of air into those tired little lungs of his. My house is nothing but a log cabin, but there is plenty of room for both you and your dear *dad-dee*, and we even have a neighboring child you can play with."

Suddenly she frowned. "Well, not exactly. You're several years older than she, but she's sweet and lovable and you'll like her. We live a very simple life in Grass Valley. I give parties only on Wednesday evenings. You are old enough to enjoy them. Poor Lotta is too young. Many of the men who come are very rich and illustrious. Unfortunately," she added, bending toward Marielle with a conspiratorial air, "there are very few women in the vicinity, and it is difficult to find women friends. The territory absolutely cries out for more females. But what's a woman to do? Now you will be there, and at least Lola will have you and you will have Lola, and we will both have many, many interesting men surrounding us. Lola insists you come back with her this very night.''

Marielle knew the Countess had no intention of letting her make a choice. But she did not mind. She liked the woman regardless of the fact that she was different from anyone Marielle had ever met. Lola Montez had such confidence in herself, such boldness of spirit, such dash and such beauty, Marielle felt powerless to resist her. She wanted to be just like her, in fact. If Lola wanted her and Jeremiah to be her guests in Grass Valley, Marielle was happy to comply with the lady's wishes. It was Marielle's wish too.

"Thank you, Countess," was all that Marielle could get in before Lola began again.

"Remember one thing, pretty girl. You are not, nor will you ever be a *wild girl*. I do not approve of them. Do you know the kind I am talking about? I am an aristocrat, and so are you."

"Yes, ma'am," Marielle said.

"And," the Countess said, "the best men are those who have lived hard and dangerously."

"Yes, ma'am," Marielle said meekly.

"And women are very scarce, so you are at a premium."

"Yes, ma'am," Marielle said again.

"And never forget, dear Marielle," the Countess said with a kindly smile that made her face even more beautiful. "I have seen you perform. You have great promise. But so far, Lola Montez is the only woman who has ever given a special dancing performance in the old Alta Hall where the reserved seats in the first row commanded sixty-five dollars a ticket. Sixty-five dollars for one ticket in a ramshackle theater in Grass Valley, and every seat was bought with golden money dug out of the ground. So Lola hopes you will listen and learn from her."

"Yes, ma'am."

"Well, why are you dawdling, Miss Marielle Preston? Find your dear *dad-dee* and get your belongings together. We leave for Grass Valley straightaway."

Chapter Fourteen

Grass Valley was a sunny town sheltered by gentle slopes covered with purple wildflowers. The town was full of optimism and vitality even though there were no more than three thousand five hundred inhabitants, of whom less than three hundred were women. The little mining town was set in extraordinarily beautiful California terrain and had several small wooden theatres, many large saloons, and a school. One enterprising widow had even opened a dancing school and earned her living giving lessons not only to children, but to any miner who wanted to learn the latest steps. The citizens were a mixed group, coming from every corner of the earth and speaking almost every language. Everyone tolerated everyone else, and most of the citizens were planning on remaining there for the rest of their lives. More than one hundred mines were being worked more or less successfully in a radius of seven miles, so the region was fairly well-to-do.

Marielle relaxed and enjoyed the sloping hills, the dark green pine trees so tall she had to crane her neck to see their tops, and the cold mountain streams with their fresh, sweet water. Since wildflowers grew everywhere in abundance, Marielle was constantly hugging a huge bunch of colorful blooms to her bosom as she walked along the mountain paths.

Papa perked up immediately and made friends among the miners, many of whom invited him to join them working their mines. He had his supplies and a hazy dream that perhaps he would find gold yet. Marielle saw that he took a lunch basket along with his mining equipment and let him be. When he came back each night, his eyes were clearer and there was better color in his face.

Lola's log cabin was a four-bedroom cottage on Mill Street, with happily flowered wallpaper, cheery curtains in all the windows, comfortable furniture, Chinese wool rugs, and an indoor bathroom. Marielle had never lived in such luxury before, and life was a daily whirl of excitement in the Countess's establishment.

The lady who once was the paramour of a king was generous to one and all and spent money freely, wantonly, as if there were no tomorrow. When Marielle protested that she would prefer to pay for herself and Papa, Lola gave her dirty looks and acted hurt for hours afterwards. The only way Marielle could win her approval once again was to accept the next gift offered her. Only then did Lola smile and forgive her.

Small, elegant dinner parties were given continually in the Mill Street house, but Lola had become more famous for her delightful Wednesday night soirees, to which some of the richest and most brilliant men in California came.

The dark-haired beauty had given Marielle three of her own beautiful dresses. After accepting them reluctantly, Marielle fitted them to her measurements and wore them whenever Lola had guests. Lola had also given her a lovely English-style riding habit, which supposedly did not fit Lola; but Marielle knew that was merely a ploy to make her accept it, which she ultimately did. She ended up wearing it almost every day after that, since the famous Miss Montez also insisted on teaching her houseguest how to ride.

Next Lola invited over the little neighbor girl she had told Marielle about. Lotta Crabtree was several months past seven and a pretty, precocious child. Both girls liked each other from the very first moment they were introduced. Lotta wore a little riding habit very similar to Marielle's and obviously she, too, had been taught to ride by Lola, who was an expert equestrian. They went riding on two sturdy horses from the stables nearby.

"I'm going to be an actress when I grow up. I sing and dance now. Are you a famous actress?" Lotta asked as they urged their horses to a gentle slope. Lotta had been very impressed on meeting Marielle to find that her new friend had played Juliet and Ophelia, and to see that Marielle had red hair like her own. But where Marielle's hair was a deep, fiery, burnished red, Lotta's fat little sausage curls were light reddish blonde.

"I'm not famous. But I will be."

"Are we going to be friends forever? Even when we're in different parts of the world?"

"I expect so," Marielle told the lovable little girl.

"We'll help each other become famous," Lotta said, and galloped away on her horse, giggling as she turned her head and saw that she would win the race she started.

Several hours later, after a picnic lunch, the two girls headed back to the stables. It was Wednesday and Lotta was obliged to go home because she was too young to stay for the soiree that night.

It was the third Wednesday in a row that Marielle would be attending her hostess's soiree. She had enjoyed the first two events and tried to make Lola and Papa proud of her. Papa was able to make a brief appearance at each one, and had behaved charmingly, though he had retired early. This evening, Marielle watched as the guests started to ride up to the cottage on Mill Street shortly after sundown.

One bedroom was set aside so that the riders, especially those who came from long distances, could clean up and change to more formal attire for the evening ahead. Almost all of Lola's Wednesday night guests were men.

There was melodeon music played by the organist of the First Episcopalian Church of Grass Valley, caviar imported from faraway Russia for Lola's visitors, and cases of French champagne. The cook made sure there was enough good finger food to satisfy everyone from the most absent-minded poet to the roughest miner. Every man, to the end, tried his best to act like a gentleman.

Tonight, Marielle wore a pale yellow silk dress, one of the three Lola had insisted on giving her. It set off her red hair dramatically and gave her an aura of sophistication, she felt. Lola was expecting more guests than usual. Several ships had anchored recently in San Francisco and had brought some famous newspapermen into the region. People were constantly coming and going between San Francisco and Grass Valley, and tonight there would be a banker who was thinking of setting up a bank somewhere in the region and a historian who was planning a book on California. Kirke Adler, a handsome German baron, was one of the guests of honor this evening, as well as John W. Mackay, who was fast becoming famous as the Bonanza King.

The usual regulars were coming, of course, the ones whom Marielle had met the last two Wednesday evenings. And, as the Countess pointed out, there were always the surprises.

Soon Lola's salon became filled with the sound of male laughter and clinking glasses, as well as the good smell of different blends of tobacco. Every man had something of interest to say, and if he didn't, it was no reason to keep his mouth shut. There was something about the West that made men express themselves in extravagant terms—especially when they talked about California, and they never seemed able to stop, always insisting that everything in this wild new land was the oldest, the biggest, the richest, and the most wonderful in the entire world. When they talked about themselves, they made themselves sound ten feet tall, faultless, cocksure male specimens; and when they all came together in the Grass Valley salon of Lola Montez, the room exploded in good will and joviality.

Tonight Johnny Southwick, who made a fortune from his Empire Mine, was at the soiree. Marielle had heard the rumor that it was Johnny Southwick's money that had paid for Lola's ornate swan bed with the silken canopy that played such a key role in the decor of her private bedroom suite.

It was while Marielle sat modestly sipping from a champagne glass filled with lemonade, that she heard Johnny discussing politics with Stephen Massatt, the poet and composer. Marielle learned that Californians were talking about the possibility of a war sometime in the future that would involve the North and the South, started because of the South's slavery-based economy.

"I tell you," Johnny Southwick said as he puffed on an important-looking cigar, "it's coming. There's no stoppin' it."

"Not by a long shot is it coming," Stephen Massett answered. "We're not going to have a civil war now or anytime."

"I'll take bets on that, sir," Johnny replied. "And I'll take bets that when it comes—and it will—California will side with the North, and Oregon, right on California's border, will side with the South. You want to make a small wager?"

Marielle sat quietly, the glass forgotten in her hand, listening to the two men. The conversation was fascinating, but surely war was unlikely, she thought to herself. A civil war meant brother against brother, maybe even father against son. No, a war between the states was too bizarre an idea to even contemplate.

Papa came over and sat down next to her. He had a gentle smile on his ravaged face and he seemed content enough. The fire that used to be inside him was extinguished; he was no longer opinionated, no longer needed to be the center of attention at a gathering like this. Tonight, as usual, he would slip out of the room for his bed. Afterwards, Marielle would look in on him to make sure he didn't need anything, that indeed he was sound asleep.

"Stay until after I've sung my songs, Papa. The Countess has asked me to entertain."

"Naturally, little princess. I would be very unhappy if I missed hearing your sweet voice or seeing your dear face as you sing."

Papa left to get himself a small shot of the spirits she knew he needed so desperately to keep up an ordinary appearance for any length of time. When he returned, she gave him a little kiss, and he smiled sweetly at her.

"I shall sit on the veranda, on the steps. We'll leave the door open. That way I can watch you and feel the cool night breeze and see every single thing you do."

"Okay, Papa. You know I love you, Papa?"

"Yes. And I love you too, sweet person. You know that?"

She nodded solemnly as he took his drink out to the veranda and settled himself at the foot of one of the stately white pillars that Lola had insisted be built at the same time she had the veranda added to the cottage. Marielle watched him fondly, a sense of peace settling over her as she again took note of his childish sense of resignation to life in general. She felt sorry for him, but at the same time she envied him his contentment.

Lola found her and took her by the hand and led her to the melodeon, a small keyboard organ in which the tones were produced by drawing air through a metal reed by means of a bellows operated by pedals.

After clapping her hands to get everyone's attention, Lola announced that the entertainment would start. The men found seats if they could; if not they leaned politely against walls, their glasses still in their hands while they waited expectantly for Marielle to begin.

Marielle, one hand posed lightly on the melodeon, the other on her side smoothing the folds of her beautiful pale yellow silk dress, felt all eyes turn upon her; no one touched the drinks in their hands nor dared to whisper as she sang, and on every man's face Marielle could see complete veneration.

During one song, she looked out the open front door into the darkness beyond, and saw Papa's outline, seated where she had left him. There was the outline of another man sitting next to him, and Marielle wondered as she sang who he was. She appreciated the kindness of this person who sat outside with Jeremiah instead of trying to crowd around her inside. She finished her singing to wild cheering; she was tired but pleased she had done well. It was now time for Lola to do her provocative spider dance, and the men regrouped themselves, ready for a long-awaited Wednesday night treat.

It was difficult for Marielle to extricate herself from the fierce group of admirers who encircled her. At last though, she was able to. As she came out the front door onto the veranda, Papa stood up in the dark and the man he was with stood up too. Marielle did not need to see his face to know that it was Morgan Quinn. She felt it simply by the quickening of her heartbeat and the jolt that swept through her body and made her furious with herself. She had hardly expected to see him here, at one of Lola Montez's exclusive Wednesday night soirees.

She could not see his face but she heard his voice greet her quietly. She wanted to turn around and leave immediately, flee back into the cottage filled with callers who made their veneration openly felt. She did not need another confrontation with this man. But Papa was so pleased that she had joined them, she felt she had to stay, though she wasn't able to make small talk with Quinn so close beside her in the dark. She finally found her voice and told Papa that she had to return to watch Lola's performance.

"I'll accompany you inside, Miss Preston," Quinn said. "It would be impolite for me not to watch Miss Montez dance." Not seeming to need any further permission, he took Marielle by the arm and turned to Papa. "Are you ready to come inside, Jeremiah?"

Papa nodded happily, unaware of the tension between the two. He was still under the illusion that Quinn had saved Marielle's life twice and clung to the younger man as the protector of his daughter.

When they got inside, where every lamp was lit and the entire house was ablaze with light, Marielle saw that Quinn had ridden hard in order to be present at the cottage. His clothes were dusty, although it looked like he had brushed them very recently and very quickly. A black hat with a wide brim and low crown was removed when he entered the house. His black leather jacket and matching leather vest swung open to reveal a wool shirt and narrow silk ribbon tie. In the middle of the tie was a stickpin exactly the same as the one that was sitting in Marielle's special tea tin, which she used as a jewelry box. Marielle stared at it as fascinated as she had been the first time she had seen its duplicate on the cravat of Quinn's brother. The stickpin was the only adornment on Quinn; the rest of his clothes were somber and understated, and yet he stood out among the other men regardless of the fact that they were much more formally dressed. He wore no guns, the way other men who rode fast and traveled far did.

Frankly, though, it did not seem to matter what he wore or what he said or did. She could not keep her eyes off him, exactly the same as the men who could not help gaping at her. Suddenly she thought she knew how they felt.

Marielle and Quinn stood quietly in the rear of the room, his hand still on her upper arm, searing her flesh with his touch. She was slightly in back of him and could not help looking at his profile and the back of his head, studying the dark ringlets curling onto his neck as he watched Lola dance. The look she saw on his profile was one of great admiration for the dancer, and Marielle felt a twinge of jealousy. When Lola was finished with her performance, Quinn took his hand from Marielle's arm and clapped enthusiastically. She tried to compose herself and did, but not before Quinn turned his head and saw the jealous look on her face. She was surprised he smiled at her anyway, and because she was not sure why he smiled, she jerked her arm away when he took it once again.

After Lola's sensational performance Marielle tried to escape to her room. It was not easy being within the same four walls as Quinn, not easy watching the special friendliness with which the Countess treated him. Or so it seemed to Marielle. Was it only her imagination, or did she see more than just a friendly glint in the notorious enchantress's sparkling dark eyes? And if she did see evidence of a possible alliance, why did it matter so much? Why should it be of so much concern?

At that moment she heard Johnny Southwick tell a group surrounding Lola that a baby bear, certainly not more than a couple of weeks old, had been captured early that day after its mother was killed. Even now, the cub was at old Mr. Hardwick's general store, where his fate would be decided tomorrow.

"I must have him," Lola cried to the group. "What a perfect pet he will make."

"That's not the sort of pet I would want myself," Stephen Massatt said. "Too much trouble. What're you going to do with him when he gets to be full grown?"

"We'll worry about that when the time comes. But we must get a party together and rescue that darling baby before someone decides to dispose of him the way they did his mother," Lola insisted.

"I'll buy him for you tomorow," Johnny Southwick said generously.

"Tonight. It must be tonight, *mon amis*. Who is game to come along?" Lola became her most enchanting self and cajoled her guests until before long everyone in the room had put down his glass and was ready to head off to the store.

"Are you not coming?" Lola asked Marielle as she saw her young friend detach herself from the rest of the guests.

Marielle did not have to think before she answered. "Jeremiah is asleep. But I think I will stay anyway. In case he wakes up and needs me." She was fully aware that Papa never woke up once he was asleep, but she did not want to make an issue about her fear of bears. She felt it was not the time to explain to Lola that it would be fine with her if she never saw another bear.

"Well, suit yourself, *ma petite*," Lola said, looking not too happy with Marielle's decision. "The servants will turn out the lamps when they leave for the night. If you can't sleep, I have a box of books in my bedroom that just arrived from London. Try *Jane Eyre* or *Wuthering Heights*. Seems that a couple of sisters, Charlotte and Emily Brontë, have become the rage of the literary world. The poor dears had to wait for years before they could use their own names. Before that they had to use male pseudonyms. One of them, Charlotte, I think, died recently. You're a romantic, my dear. You'll love them." She ran off with the crowd of men at her heels, all with different ideas about how to rear and train a baby bear. Marielle was left in the house as the servants cleared up, turned off lamps, and prepared to withdraw.

Marielle retired to her room, happy to be alone, but irked when she recalled that Quinn was one of the large group who could not resist the Countess and had gone off to acquire her a new pet.

She supposed it was ungrateful of her not to have gone along, but she had wanted so badly to distance herself from Morgan Quinn. She was glad she was alone in the house. The fire in the huge marble fireplace was banked. The house was still and serene. There was a calmness in the air that was never there when the flamboyant Lola was home.

Marielle brushed her hair and made herself ready for bed after first peeking in on Papa and finding him safely sound asleep. As she prepared to get into bed, she thought about the new books Lola had told her about. She loved books and they were so hard to come by in California. She decided to try one of the Brontë books that Lola had recommended.

In her nightgown and bare feet, Marielle made her way in the dark toward Lola's bedroom suite. She had been inside the resplendent room only once before, when the Countess had given her a tour of the house on the first day she became the houseguest of the captivating woman who, at one time, had shared a bedroom with a king.

Aside from the silk-canopied bed built in the shape of a swan, the room featured fine wood paneling framing delicate Empire wallpaper. The carpet matched the pale color of the bed, and had come from Munich along with the lace curtains. All the furniture in the room was gold-leafed, including the huge ornate mirror.

There was a moon out, which enabled Marielle to find a candle on a small table near the bed. When the candle was lit, it shed an eerie light on the pale silken coverlets of Lola's resting place. Finding the books without any trouble, she took *Jane Eyre* and *Wuthering Heights* from the box and sat on the bed, leafing through the pages to see which one she would read first. Both were beautifully illustrated with pen and ink drawings, and the covers were meticulously bound in fine leather. Since she could not make up her mind, she decided to take both books with her.

Putting out the candle with a bejeweled candle snuffer, Marielle was ready to start back to her room when she thought she heard the sound of muffled footsteps outside the bedroom door. They sounded like a man's footseps. She knew Papa was sound asleep in his room at the other end of the house, and as far as she knew she and Papa were alone in the cottage. Stopping short of the door, she held her breath, feeling very much alone in the big room, and waited for the footfalls to pass. It seemed that the sounds stopped in front of Lola's bedroom door, but then they started up again, became louder than before, and passed through the house. Soon the night was hushed once again, so still she wondered if she had imagined the noises. She waited, holding on to the doorknob, but she heard nothing more. Perhaps it was the houseboy who had returned on some errand and then left again.

Finally, she slid the door open, hoping it would not creak. The hinges were well-oiled and not a squeak came forth as she tiptoed out, edging her way back toward her own bedroom, holding her two borrowed books under one arm.

She passed through the parlor, making her way through the huge room in order to get to the other side of the cottage, where her bedroom was situated. Suddenly, halfway through, she stopped and became intensely alert. She felt, or somehow knew, that there was someone else in the parlor besides herself. She could plainly hear breathing. Her first reaction was to hold her own breath. Then when she let go, her own breath came out in wild jerks as she ran to where she knew there was a candle. It seemed forever before she could get to the spot, and when she did she could not see it. She bent over and found the candlestick holder and remembered there was a cache of wooden matches close by. She found them with her hand, struck a match, and lit the candle with quivering fingers. When her eyes grew accustomed to the added light, she looked around more with curiosity than with real fear.

At first it seemed the room was empty, but when she looked again among the outlandish shadows formed by the light of the one candle and the moonlight, she saw a man in a big high-backed chair, sitting calmly, his eyes watching her with an amused gleam as she obviously tried to calm her shaking self. It was the surprise of finding someone in the dark room that startled her more than anything else and, of course, the fact that it was Morgan Quinn facing her from the depths of the mysterious shadows.

"Why are you here?" Marielle demanded.

"I might ask you the same question." His observant gray eyes held a speculative glint.

"I am a guest of the Countess of Landsfeld, Lola Montez," she said, using her hostess's full title and drawing herself up in her most haughty way.

He brooded for a long moment. "So am I," he said quietly.

"You? Why you when there are all those others?"

He threw back his head and laughed. "The others," he punctuated his words in the same way she had seconds before, "took all the rooms in town. There was nothing available and I've come a long way. Besides, I have business with your Countess."

"I don't believe you."

He smiled that special crooked smile, and the shadows made his healthy white teeth gleam even brighter. "It's true. I will be here till she and I have finished our business. A day or so. Depending, of course, on the lady's whims. And, since you are here too, I would like to talk to you also. In fact, we can do that right now. Shall we light a lamp?"

"No. I don't want to talk to you," she said, enraged that he was so logical and businesslike so late at night. She looked at the two books still under her arm and if she hadn't respected books so much she knew she might have thrown them at him.

She stood before him, momentarily at a loss to know how to handle this unexpected meeting. For some strange reason, her gaze went to the golden raven stickpin in Quinn's ribbon tie. He noticed immediately. "Do you fancy it?" he asked.

Marielle flushed, furious with herself. "I have the twin to it," she heard herself say with as much dignity as she could.

"I know," Quinn said politely. "I heard. Would you like this one too?"

Marielle gave him an entirely withering look. "You have a macabre sense of humor, Mr. Quinn. I do not appreciate it."

"My brother told me that you forced him to take back the gold he gave you as a gift."

She waited, illogically hoping the subject would somehow get dismissed.

"I wanted to apologize for my incorrect presumption of your guilt."

"That's all you wanted to talk about with me?"

"Mostly."

He had surprised her once again. She'd assumed him to be the sort of man who didn't apologize. But now he seemed to want to make amends. "All right," she said, and she could not keep her dimples from showing on her ivory cheeks.

His smile returned too as he took off his stickpin and stretched out his hand to her.

Her eyes opened wide in astonishment, then suddenly she decided this was some sort of test. So instead of accepting the tempting double, she threw both books at him; one of them missed the mark, but the other grazed his knee.

"My God," he said, getting out of the chair swiftly. "You are not an actress. You're a pugilist." He was no longer amused or polite. Coming toward her, he looked dark and dangerous. Her experience told her that when he looked like that she had a formidable opponent on her hands.

As he came closer, she was truly frightened and backed away. She had gone too far throwing the books at him. He continued forward and she stopped when she reached the wall, powerless to move further. In an instant he was as close as he could get without pulling her into his arms. The moonlight chose this moment to accentuate his remarkable good looks, the lean, well-muscled outline of his noble head, his well-built torso, the perfect shape and proportion of each part of his body. How desperately she wanted to touch his face; how she had to hold herself back from keeping her hands off his hair, his broad shoulders, his narrow waist, every part of him. It horrified her to think that every time she saw him she felt that very same way, even after all the cruel things he'd said in her dressing room in Sacramento. And suddenly, as if he felt the same way about her, he pulled her into his arms—it was as if she had begged him to take her and he could not resist the plea—and she forgot everything except his magnificent body pressed to hers. All she wanted was for the sensations that broke over her to continue forever.

Marielle pulled him even closer, her lips close to his. "Just hold me, Quinn," she heard herself whispering, and was shocked. She'd tried her hardest to resist this man, but it was no use.

Quinn picked her up in his arms without ceremony, as if she weighed nothing, and carried her to the first bedroom he could find; it was on Lola's swan bed that he deposited her. She made no objection and she was no longer shocked.

Chapter Fifteen

It was just as she'd always seen it in those dreams of him she could not obliterate. His arms went around her with the fierceness of his desire. Those strong arms were not a dream; they were flesh and blood and very real; now they were cajoling her body into a state of wanton anticipation. She'd waited for this for over a year. It was a long time to wait to be transported to paradise.

She sat totally still as he removed her chaste, white nightdress and, by moonlight, she saw him studying her body as he undressed in front of her. Not a word needed to be said by either one. Marielle marveled at each part of him exposed as he undressed. He was magnificent.

Finally, when he was close beside her and she could feel his breath as if it were her own, she raised her trembling fingers to memorize the chiseled planes of his face. At the same time she felt his hands move deliberately over her body and return over and over again to her round white breasts. Then he bent over her, tenderly caressing each pink nipple with his sensuous lips. She felt great pleasure within her, and it grew stronger and stronger as he brought his hips toward her in one languorous motion, slowly closing in on the deep, burnished velvet triangle between her thighs, taking her to a world where only love was important. She felt the fullness spreading up through her thighs and moved closer to him so that every part of her could touch some part of him.

He seemed to understand her great need for the most intimate of touches. His powerful hands moved down to the smallness of her waist and onto the tender curve of her belly as he slowly pulled himself down to the lower part of her body. When his lips left the swollen little nipples and his probing tongue advanced into the deep depression in the middle of her flat belly, she cried out, the cry of

109

a woman in ecstasy giving up all to receive the hot moist touch of her man, the lover who understands her body so well he can avail himself of it like a connoisseur.

His touch was strong and knowing and she trembled as her desire rose to heights she did not know were possible. She was drowning with the need to be one with him. At that moment he stopped what he was doing, took her in his arms, and still in complete control, looked down at her warm and flushed body. He sighed deeply after he pushed the mass of her disheveled red curls away from her face.

"You are as beautiful as I've always remembered you. If you've changed at all it is only to have become more beautiful." Whatever she had not yet surrendered, she surrendered now.

His mouth probed hers and she tasted her own amatory juices on his lips until his mouth left hers and found all the most delicate, flowery petals of her flesh and moistened them with his tongue as she lay in a spell of rapture. And then when the very core of her cried out to be taken, he eased her thighs open and entered the warm dampness so eager to receive him, clasping her even closer after placing a small pillow under the sweet rounds of her buttocks.

He started the rhythm of his thrusts slowly, watching her closely, working up to a crescendo, thrusting deeper and deeper as Marielle clung to him and adjusted her body to fit exactly the way it should to his every movement, exactly the way his body directed hers, exactly as if they were one. The moment became theirs together, passion coursed between them until a final thunder of jubilation raced through her, stormier and more ecstatic than she had ever known. She heard her own cry once again, and cry of a woman on whom her man's magic had been performed. She was as madly in love with Morgan Quinn as she had been on shipboard, oh so long ago.

They stayed together for a long time in a silence broken only by their own breathing and the sound of some night animal far in the distance.

Much, much later, but sooner than Marielle wished, Quinn left the huge bed, lit one of the lamps and looked at a small clock Lola kept near her bedside.

"I'm not sorry this happened," Quinn said as he returned to the side of the bed and looked down at Marielle, his eyes showing his appreciation of her beauty. "But, unfortunately, it's the wrong time and the wrong place."

"I'm glad it happened," Marielle said.

"We don't have the right."

"Why?" she asked desperately.

He shook his head and remained silent.

"Why?" She tried to read the look in Quinn's eyes as a shadow passed over his face.

"I didn't realize we were in this room. I think we'd better leave," he said ruefully, adroitly changing the subject. "That crowd is bound to return sooner or later."

Marielle stretched her body sensuously like a cat and purred a deep sigh of contentment. She tried to pull Quinn back into the big bed but he was much too big for her to budge. "How do you know where we are? Have you ever been in this bed before?"

"This bed is famous," Quinn said dryly.

"You haven't answered my question."

"It's none of your business," he said, but Marielle noted a strange tenderness in his voice. He scooped her naked body up with one strong arm and draped her over one shoulder as she unsuccessfully tried to stifle a laugh that turned into a shriek. Before she could protest any further, he bent down gracefully, still holding onto Marielle, picked up his clothes with his other hand, and strode through the door in the direction of the other side of the cottage.

"Which one is yours?" he asked as he came to the guest bedrooms.

Marielle pointed and he carried her into the room, dumped her unceremoniously onto her own bed, and sat himself on the edge as he started to get dressed.

Marielle slipped under the warm feather quilt and sat up, watching him quietly. "Are you leaving me again?" she asked.

"You want me to stay tonight—under the circumstances?"

"Yes," she said stubbornly. "It's important to me."

"It'll mean we have to get up very early, before anybody else does."

She nodded her head.

He smiled at her wickedly, and started to pull off his clothes once again as she held out her arms to him.

She woke in Quinn's arms as the sun came through the lacy curtains, throwing rays of strong yellow light onto her face. She could not imagine what time it was, but she knew it was very late. Looking around, she could not find a clock in her bedroom.

Quinn was still asleep, holding her closely, his bare muscled arms entwining her so that she could not escape unless she awakened him. She lay there, snug and comfortable, still wishing they need not have to part. But they were in someone else's house . . . in fact, the house of the notorious Lola Montez, who firmly believed that every man was put on this earth to make *her* happy.

The door to her bedroom opened, and the very person Marielle was thinking about entered the room and stood at the foot of the bed looking at Marielle and Quinn, who was still sound asleep. Lola looked very beautiful and serious in a pale gray dress with a white collar. She had one eyebrow raised quizzically and she was holding Marielle's nightdress balled up in her hand. "I found this in my bed when I came home, *ma petite*," she said in her soft strange accent.

The Countess waited for the message to sink in, then she let the nightdress fall to the floor. "I will see you and my other guest," she said pointing at Quinn, "at lunch, I presume. Breakfast has been over for many hours."

Marielle got the distinct impression that Lola Montez was not pleased with her.

She was spared from the wrath of her hostess just before lunchtime when Lotta Crabtree arrived with her mother to fetch Marielle for the afternoon. Marielle had forgotten the appointment she had made with the Crabtrees days before, and she welcomed them so enthusiastically that they eyed her with suspicion. Papa had left early that morning for some diggings close by, she learned, so the house was to be empty, except, that is, for Lola and Quinn, who could conduct business all afternoon at their leisure without interruptions from anyone. Marielle was not sure she was pleased with the situation but there was little she could do about it.

It was difficult to concentrate on the happy chatter coming from the Crabtrees when she kept wondering what kind of business Quinn had with the glamorous Lola. Both Crabtrees stopped to take a look at Lola's new pet, which was tethered in the back yard. Marielle refused to go with them. She did not want to become friends with the baby bear, whom Lola had named Major.

Afterwards, they went to the dressmaker's, where a costume was being made for Lotta and where Marielle was able to buy a very practical black skirt that some entertainer passing through had ordered but never picked up. Then there was Lotta's dancing lesson. After much cajoling from Mary Ann Crabtree, Lotta's mother, who was a practical-minded lady who ran a boarding house, helped support a large, indolent family, and directed little Lotta's career as an entertainer, Marielle joined in and learned the Highland fling from Grass Valley's dancing instructor.

Later they went to the local hotel for a treat of hot cocoa. Lotta never once stopped chattering. It took Marielle's mind off the fact that she had committed a serious faux pas in forcing a reluctant Quinn into staying in her room all night. What had she tried to prove anyway? What was this great need in her that made her act the way she did? Jeremiah Preston had taught her good manners, even if he had not taught her other things.

As the long and uneventful afternoon started to come to an end, Marielle decided she was fortunate that the Crabtrees had come along when they did. They had saved her from having to face both Lola and Quinn at the same time. She knew Lola could be very impressive at the height of her anger. Perhaps Lola had cooled off by now, though.

But before they were finished with the spicy cocoa that was laced with cinnamon, Mary Ann Crabtree gave Marielle something more to think about. "I've been playing with an idea," Lotta's mother said. "It's about you and Lotta forming an act. A sister act. You both look enough alike. I think we could make some good money."

"Oh, goody," Lotta cried, jumping up and down and nearly upsetting her cocoa. "We'll pretend we're *really* sisters."

Marielle was surprised and pleased. It was a very good idea and she promised Mary Ann she would discuss it with Papa. She preferred being an actress, but when money became scarce—and she was sure it would be soon enough—a sister act with an adorable seven-year-old might be very lucrative.

When Lotta and Mary Ann brought her back to the cottage in their little wagonette, Marielle was glad to see that Papa was back from the diggings and that Lola and Quinn were not around. It would give her a chance to rehearse how she would apologize to Lola and to figure out what to do about Quinn. She desperately needed to see Quinn again to find out whether last night had meant anything to him, whether it had altered their stormy relationship at all.

She went to her room to make herself presentable. As she settled down in front of her mirror, the maid knocked on her door and handed her a note, which she said was from her mistress.

Marielle opened it. Lola explained in the note that she would be away several days on important business but that Marielle and Jeremiah should continue to make themselves at home until she returned. At that time, Lola made clear in the note, it would be best for Marielle and herself to have a *nice* talk about all that had been going on. The lady was generous even now. Only a very unusual person would handle such a touchy situation the way Lola Montez did. Marielle was impressed and vowed to let Lola know how she felt. She had learned a great deal from the way the Countess of Landsfeld conducted herself.

Later, when she met Papa for a quick light supper before retiring for the night, he told her he had a message for her, but he had lost it somewhere.

"From whom, Papa?" she asked patiently.

"From young Mr. Quinn," he answered.

"All right, Papa. Let's go at this slowly. You mean Morgan Quinn?"

"But of course, my sweet one. Who else?"

"Good. We'll go on from there. You must try to remember. Where were you when he gave this message to you?"

They reconstructed the incident as best they could and finally came to the conclusion that the message was in the form of a letter

"Try very hard, Papa," Marielle urged him desperately. But no matter what she did, she could not get Papa to remember where he had left the white envelope that he said Morgan had given him for Marielle just before he left with the Countess late that afternoon.

Marielle combed the house as best she could and even asked the maid to help, but no one had seen the envelope. Papa seemed unsettled that he had lost something that his precious daughter wanted very much, and Marielle tried to make him feel better.

"We'll go on a picnic tomorrow, Papa," she said. "How would you like that?"

His face became sad. "I want to go to my diggings. I found a new place I must try. For us, you know. Gold."

"Good. We'll take the picnic with us to the diggings. We'll take your pans and I'll pan with you. We'll have fun and perhaps we'll find lots of gold. Won't that be nice, Papa?"

The sadness left his face and he smiled vacantly at her and said, "Pans. We'll take the pans with us tomorrow." He led his daughter to his panning equipment, ready and waiting to be packed on his mule the next day. Inside one of the pans was Quinn's letter, exactly where Papa had put it when Quinn first gave it to him.

Marielle grabbed the letter, rewarded Papa with a big hug and kiss, and dashed into her room. She closed the door quickly, leaning on it, almost breathless, unable to wait to open the envelope a moment longer. She took out the one sheet of paper inside. The first thing she saw was that at the bottom of the letter Quinn had pinned the gold raven stickpin that she had refused the night before.

The letter was written in a large strong hand; its every word cut open Marielle's heart.

Dear Marielle,

By tomorrow my heart will quicken when I hear your name and my body will ache to touch yours. But today, I am still strong enough to be true to the obligations that life has thrust upon me and which make it impossible to offer you the safety and permanence of my name. If it is any consolation, I offer you the permanence of my love. May we meet again under different circumstances.

Sincerely,
Morgan Quinn

She read and reread it, but the message made no more sense than when she'd read it the first time.

But she refused to cry. As it was, she had cried far too often for this man who had no intention of including her in his life. No matter how intimate they had been, he did not need her. It was only her body that he'd wanted after all.

She pulled the stickpin out of the missive and placed it in the tea tin in which she kept its twin. After further reflection, she folded the letter, put it back in the envelope, and put it into the tin alongside the two stickpins.

She lay awake all that long night, dismally gazing at the colorful tin, which she had placed close to her bedside.

Chapter Sixteen

She wanted desperately to sleep, but Papa refused to stop knocking on her door until she gave up and called for him to enter. He said it was a beautiful day and time for him to go panning. Did she still want to go with him? The cook was preparing a basket of food.

Pulling the pillow she had used to bury herself from off her head, she opened her eyes. "Give me a few minutes, Papa, and we'll be on our way." Throwing aside the bedclothes, Marielle slid out of bed and hastily began her toilet.

Long before she was clearheaded, and while she was still yawning, she found herself on a horse, riding toward the diggings with Jeremiah and his mule in tow. The picnic basket was at her side, covered with a freshly laundered red and white checked tablecloth. Her hair was plaited into one thick braid falling down her back and she wore her oldest dress, a thick wool shawl around her shoulders, and a wide-brimmed hat covering her head. She was glad there hadn't been enough time to look in the mirror. She knew the hours of anguishing over Quinn late last night had taken their toll on her face.

When they reached their destination and settled down at the spot Jeremiah had told her about, he took out his equipment and started working while Marielle found a tree under which she stretched out to take a nap. Occasional black clouds loomed through the sparse branches of the tree and dimmed the clearness of the sky before they moved past. The rainy season would soon begin. Marielle dozed.

When she woke a couple of hours later, the clouds were gone and the sky was dazzling blue. She saw Papa down a ways, standing in the middle of the stream.

116

"This is good panning, child," he called to her when he saw she'd opened her eyes. "And maybe today we'll get lucky." Papa was forever optimistic when it came to panning for gold.

Marielle lay back again, her arms stretched behind her head, and gazed at the blue sky, which now contained lazy little white clouds moving slowly toward the east from between the branches of the tree. It was good to do nothing.

She did not know how much time had gone by when her eyes opened suddenly as her ears caught the jubilant sounds of Jeremiah whooping and then splashing through the muddy water toward her.

"Hoo, girl. Look what I found." He slapped his damp knees and hopped around on his long, skinny legs, holding one of his pans high in the air.

"What is it, Papa?" Marielle asked, sitting up and rubbing her eyes.

"Gold, girl. Gold! Two of the biggest nuggets you've ever seen."

Hopping out of the water and making for the spot under the tree, Papa carried the pan, hollering all the time he sprinted toward Marielle. "By God, the gold nuggets in this pan are almost pure. It's incredible. They're worth a small fortune, I'll wager."

For some unknown reason, Marielle looked straight up to a small hill behind him. Seated there, overlooking the stream where Papa had been working and surrounded by the yellow poppies that clothed the hills in the richest profusion, sat Rio Pagonne, looking down at the two Prestons with interest. Near him was a strong pony tethered to a bush. When Marielle looked up and saw him, he waved at her cheerily and got up.

"What did you find, old man?" Rio shouted down to Jeremiah.

"Come and see for yourself what I washed up," he called gleefully. Papa didn't seem to realize that he had met Rio previously, and treated him as he would any friendly stranger passing through.

Rio untethered his pony and started toward them, his eyes full of amusement, a crazy light shining out of them and, suddenly, Marielle knew that it had been Rio who had, somehow, planted the two gold nuggets that Papa had found. How he did it without arousing Papa's suspicion, she did not know, but her bright blue eyes narrowed as she waited for Rio and his pony to cross the stream to her side.

"Is it really gold?" Rio asked, the amused glint in his eyes becoming stronger. He greeted Marielle with a formal and polite handshake that seemed out of place in this wilderness.

"I saw you throw gold nuggets into the stream. Just before you reached us," Marielle whispered to him angrily.

He gave her a wide, innocent stare. "Me, ma'am?"

"Yes you, you big oaf. You've got them stashed in your pockets."

He slapped his knee and started to holler and hoot just like Jeremiah. "Gold! Ain't it excitin', old man?" He ran back and forth across the stream, arousing Papa to greater heights of craziness. The water flew, and they were in danger of becoming soaked to the skin as they dashed around haphazardly.

Marielle didn't know whether to laugh or to cry. "Go away. That's the meanest thing I ever saw. He'll be looking for gold on this spot forever."

She watched as Rio surreptitiously dropped even more nuggets into the stream until the pockets of his vest were empty. Papa was too busy with his metal pans to notice. Then Rio came toward her, shook himself off like a wet animal spewing water everywhere, and threw himself down under the tree with his arms outstretched, trying to dry off.

"I'll bet you find lots more'n that stuff," he called to Papa. "It looks like your lucky day."

Jeremiah waved at him and went happily back to his equipment. "You're more than welcome to give it a go, young man."

"No, thanks," Rio called back, and turned to Marielle with a laugh. "Did you tell your Papa we're getting married?"

"No. Go away."

"I told my family. My mother and my brother know I've got plans. I tell them every day. So they won't forget. Or think I'll ever forget you."

"What do they say?" She remembered being with Quinn only last night. Cryptic Morgan Quinn! Inexplicable but unforgettable. Brother to a man who loved her enough to want to marry her. Her feelings went out to Rio, who offered her the most any man could offer a woman. "What did your brother say when you told him?"

"Morgan isn't happy. I can't make out his feelings. I don't know whether he thinks you're not good enough for me, or I'm not good enough for you."

"Oh?" She tried to keep her face expressionless.

"It doesn't matter. Believe me. Once Ma gets used to the idea, Morgan will come around too. When he gets to know you, he'll love you just as I do."

"Listen, I'm not sure I want to talk to you, much less even think about marrying you. Why are you trying to make a fool of my father?"

"I'm not. What's wrong with him finding a few pieces of gold? Look at him." He turned in the direction of Jeremiah, who was in the middle of the stream, happily panning gold nuggets. "It makes him feel good."

"It's cruel."

"Cruel? To make him feel good? The alternative is for him to feel bad. You want that?"

Shaking her head in mock despair, Marielle flopped down on the ground next to Rio. "I don't know what I'm going to do with you. I never know what to expect."

"You're going to love me and marry me. That's what you're going to do. And you can expect a lot of love from me in return."

"Rio . . . please!"

"Say, do you know how beautiful you are even with that danged miserable-looking hat?" He bent toward her as if to kiss her.

She backed away, without getting up. There was too much of Quinn in him. She felt it; she could almost smell it. If he was not as disturbing a man as Morgan Quinn, he came very close.

He did not attempt to make good the kiss after she moved away from him. Instead, he smiled that crooked little Quinn family smile, almost as if he were glad she was saving herself for him.

She could not resist him. Sighing, her sense of humor surfaced and she laughed. "Since I've just refused to share a kiss with you, why don't you share our picnic lunch?"

He joined her laughter. "Thank you, ma'am. It is my pleasure. Perhaps you'll be kind to this poor fellow and give him the kiss for dessert."

"Rio . . ."

He grinned happily and looked up at the sky. "Rain . . ." he said in a very positive way, but Marielle laid out the checked tablecloth and the substantial lunch the cook had prepared.

"It won't dare rain before we've eaten this good food," she said, setting a small pail of frothy milk in the center of the tablecloth to help hold it down.

There was cold fried chicken, German potato salad, pinto bean salad made with onions, garlic, and fresh parsley, and freshly baked sourdough bread.

"You must stop and eat, Papa," Marielle called to her father. Just as she was about to give up and go get him, a horse and rider came splashing from downstream to their picnic clearing. When Jeremiah saw who it was, he waded across the stream and up to the embankment to join the new arrival.

"Judge Walsh. Just the man I've been thinking about lately."

"Well, howdy," the judge said as he recognized Jeremiah. "You get lucky today?"

"Sure did, Judge," Jeremiah said as he shook the judge's hand heartily; then he introduced him to Marielle.

"I see you got lucky too, you scalawag, having lunch with such a beautiful lady," the judge said to Rio, whom he obviously had known for a long time. "Looks like a fine meal that the mosquitoes will get at if you people ain't going to dig in." He looked longingly at the food and Marielle immediately invited him to stay and eat with them.

Jeremiah, it seemed, had met Judge Walsh while he was panning, and the two men appeared to be fast friends. Judge James Walsh was a sun-tanned, smile-wrinkled man with prematurely white hair, a neat white beard, and cheery faded blue eyes. He couldn't have been much more than forty, but looked at least ten years older than that. When he had been a very young man, he and his father had come to the region to build sawmills a few miles out of town. As they finished, the group of workers were attacked by Indians. The judge's father was killed with a poisoned arrow, as was everyone else in the group except young Jimmy Walsh, who fought his way to safety with only a knife. After alerting the other settlers in the district, he became their leader and drove the attacking savages away. From that day on, he was hero to the citizens of Grass Valley.

Rio Pagonne and Judge Walsh did more than justice to the food, to make up for Papa's lack of appetite. After the meal was over, the judge took out a cigar and a flask of brandy, and Rio rolled himself a cigarillo with brown paper. His hands were quick and practiced, and the cigarillo was perfectly formed when finished. They sat contentedly around the tablecloth, under the tree.

She was glad that Judge Walsh had found them. Papa was so pleased to see his friend. After everything had been put away and the judge was preparing to leave, Jeremiah, pan in hand and ready to resume his work, said, "Judge, can I call on you next week? I have some business I'd like to transact."

"Why, of course, man. How can I be of service to you?"

Jeremiah looked around. "I don't want to discuss it now. But it's a legal document I want you to draw up for me. I want it to be foolproof. It's very important to me."

"I'm at your service, when you need me, friend."

"Then I'll see you soon," Papa said, and took himself back to the middle of the stream.

Marielle was sure it had something to do with the gold he had found and made a mental note to tell her father the truth about how it had come to be in the riverbed the very next day. She watched as the judge left with Rio right behind him.

"Take your Papa home," Rio urged just before he started the journey to the Quinn ranch, which he said was a hard six hours' ride away. "Look at the sky. It's going to rain bad and it'll get dark and raw. You'd better start back now. And you tell your Papa about you and me," he said. "We'll make arrangements next time I'm able to come your way. And if you haven't told your Papa by then, I'm going to get down on one knee and ask for your hand myself."

Marielle looked at him sharply. "This meeting was not an accident, right?"

"I was coming to town to see you anyway," he said, and gave her a charming smile as he rode away. "You must tell your father. It's only proper," he called as he left.

She watched him ride away and grow smaller and smaller in the distance. He looked so much like his half brother, yet they were so unlike in character. Rio was a much more lovable man, she decided, despite his bizarre practical jokes.

Halfway home, the rain started. All the streams and gullies filled and overflowed quickly, and it was difficult to ride through the mud. Both she and Papa were soaked to the marrow of their bones by the time they got back to the cottage. Even after they got inside, Marielle was freezing and was sure she had caught a cold. Papa was shivering and shaking and had started to develop a racking cough.

Marielle put him to bed immediately and had the houseboy bring several hot bricks to place under the coverlets. His cough got worse and he refused to eat or drink anything besides brandy-laced tea.

Trying to find Lola, Marielle learned that her hostess had not as yet returned from her business trip with Quinn. She had no time to be angry or jealous. All her time was spent trying to make Papa comfortable. She was not successful. He wheezed and coughed and could hardly breathe. His condition worsened so quickly that she became truly frightened for her father's life. The poor man had a wretched time trying to breathe during the night, and even turned blue a number of times.

Early the next morning, Marielle sent for Dr. Lyons. Never had she seen Papa as sick as he was now. The doctor arrived almost immediately, took one look at Papa, and made a diagnosis. Papa had pneumonia; the prognosis was grim, especially since the patient had been in a weakened condition to start with. Under no circumstances, Dr. Lyons instructed Marielle, was Jeremiah to be moved. Immediate bed rest was mandatory.

It was as Dr. Lyons was outlining the rest of the treatment, which consisted mainly of quinine doses, that Lola arrived back at the cottage. Amidst the flamboyant sound of horses' hooves, carriage wheels, her own accented chatter, and the loud voices of admiring men vying to be close to the popular lady, Lola Montez found her home had become a hospital and that her elderly guest was fighting off the specter of death.

Chapter Seventeen

Lola came back from her business trip without Morgan Quinn, and Marielle did not wonder why for long. The glamorous charmer had a new man in her life, who promised to be very special.

The man was Augustus Noel Follin; he was tall, handsome, and sensitive-looking, with a wife and two children back in Cincinnati. He had fallen madly in love with Lola now though, and it was rumored that the two were talking of going to Australia together, where Lola had offers to perform.

Fortunately, the unusual woman showed great compassion for Jeremiah when she learned how sick he was. She showed even more sympathy for Marielle and seemed to have forgotten about the talk they were supposed to have had when she returned. Each day she waited for Lola to bring up the subject, but Lola did not do so. "I have a very bad memory," Lola said when Marielle thought she'd better bring up the subject herself. They never mentioned Quinn's name again.

Papa proved to be a difficult patient. He wouldn't follow the doctor's orders; instead, he kept getting out of bed and practically crawling either to the window to see if Judge Walsh was on his way or in the direction of Lola's wine cellar. Marielle had to keep an eye on him every moment of the day, and he was wearing her out. He kept calling for his friend, and only when Marielle finally gave Papa her word that Judge Walsh would be visiting within two or three days when he returned from Nevada City, did her father settle down.

The course of Papa's illness was straightforward: Chills, high fever, pain in his chest, a terrible cough. He lay in bed, looking wraithlike and wizened, like an old man who was ready to die. The sight of him drove Marielle to sit up all night at his bedside, although there was not much she could do.

Sometimes as she kept her lonely vigil, she would take out the letter Quinn had left her and reread it. Oddly enough, she did not want the hurt he had caused to go away. On the contrary, she wanted to remember it forever, so that she would never let herself be hurt like that again. The letter was beginning to look old and faded, even though it had been written only a couple of weeks before.

Finally, one day when Marielle was ready to collapse, Judge Walsh arrived back from Nevada City and immediately came to call on his friend. Papa perked up at once, and even sat up in bed. He gave strict orders not to be disturbed, and Marielle suddenly found herself banished from the sickroom. He and the judge were closeted in Jeremiah's bedroom for several long hours.

When the judge finally emerged from the bedroom, Marielle heard him say, "I'll be back tomorrow, Jeremiah, and I'll have what you want all ready for you. I'll also bring those witnesses. It's going to be foolproof, just as you wish. I promise you. So hang in there, good friend."

She could not imagine what he was talking about and was extremely frustrated when he refused to tell her. "He's my father and a very sick man. What's he up to? Maybe he's not in his right mind."

"He's in his right mind, I assure you. I never saw a man more in possession of his senses than Jeremiah Preston."

Marielle gave up and went to tend her father, who seemed a little better since the judge's visit. And that was all that really mattered. If Judge James Walsh's "business" could do this for her father, she was with him one hundred percent of the way.

The next day, a rainy one, the judge came back as promised with a long, legal-looking paper and two witnesses, who seemed more interested in seeing the inside of Lola's house than in the document at hand. Again, Marielle was forbidden by Papa to enter the sickroom until all business was over and done with.

"I think I'd better ride over to *you-know-where* myself and deliver a copy of this in person," the judge winked. Another copy was put in an envelope to be opened by Marielle only after her father's death. A third copy was to be filed at the county seat.

"Thank you, my friend," Jeremiah said, and collapsed back onto the bed as Marielle rushed into the room.

Dr. Lyons arrived soon after and administered a short draught of opium to Jeremiah so that his respiration would slow down and he would not choke to death.

"I'm not ready to go," Jeremiah cried dramatically before the draught had time to take effect.

"You're not going to die yet, you old reprobate. You're just going to feel a little better and have a good night's sleep. Just don't go thinking it's a cure," the doctor replied.

Marielle breathed a long sigh of relief that she was going to be able to sleep an entire night. The next morning both nurse and patient felt much better. He even told her, rather craftily, she thought, that he didn't need a twenty-four hour nurse and that he would be a lot happier if she took care of herself and just let him be for a while so he could enjoy his illness.

"I don't need you watching me with that woebegone look on your pale, sad little face. Go out and get some fresh air, ride over to Lotta's and visit with her. It'll do you good. I'll be just fine," he said.

"You must be getting better, you're becoming so ornery," Marielle said as she kissed him and fluffed his pillows. "I'll go if you eat something first."

She fed him a bowl of hot gruel and a dose of quinine and closed the door behind him reluctantly. But he looked sleepy and content, and she felt less apprehensive than she had for the last few days.

Discovering Lola ready to leave for the Crabtree boarding house to pick up her Mr. Follin for lunch in town, Marielle saddled up a horse and decided to ride alongside her buggy.

When they reached the boarding house, Mary Ann Crabtree greeted Marielle and Lola, and with a prim look on her face, presented them with a current issue of the *Grass Valley Telegraph*. Henry Shipley, the editor of the newspaper, was the only man in Grass Valley who did not get along with the Countess of Landsfeld. Lola scanned the newspaper and softly, in a hushed accented tone, read the lead article before handing the newspaper over to Marielle. The byline was Henry Shipley. The article told about Joaquín Murieta's latest exploits. A gold shipment meant for a bank in San Francisco had been confiscated by his gang. Two of the security guards riding shotgun had been cut down by Murieta's men, the article said. The gold was taken and every man in the gang escaped. There were no clues as to the whereabouts of Murieta and his confederates.

The gold is in the form of nuggets,'' Marielle continued where Lola had left off, reading out loud to everyone present. ''A reward of one thousand dollars is offered for information leading to the recovery of the gold, plus one thousand dollars for the head of Joaquín.''

Marielle's first reaction was to think of Rio. Had he been with Murieta, and was that where the gold he had salted into the stream for Papa to find had come from? It made sense to her, certainly more sense than the story of a mountain of gold on the Quinn ranch. But, of course, there was no proof. Making haphazard assumptions about where Rio got his seemingly endless supply of gold was unfair. After all, the gold he had left her after each performance in Sacramento was given before this particular crime was committed.

Her thoughts were interrupted when Mary Ann took the newspaper and turned to the second page. She pointed to another article. ''For a tiny little place in the universe, Grass Valley has its share of excitement,'' Mary Ann said. It seemed, she explained, that somewhere in the vicinity of Grass Valley an underground railway for runaway slaves had been formed and was operating, if not openly, at least in efficient secrecy. This was against the law, the article stated further, because although California was a free state, a law enacted in 1851 provided that slaves brought in from other states could be reclaimed and returned to their owners.

Lola became fascinated with the article and asked permission to take that page of the newspaper with her. Mrs. Crabtree took a pair of scissors and neatly cut it out for her. The Countess left with the article and Mr. Follin and headed for the center of town.

By the time Marielle returned to the cottage, there was a softly pounding rainstorm, cold and penetrating, promising to muddy up the trails and roadways within the next few hours. Marielle was glad to be indoors once again, and went to her room immediately to change her clothes. She did not want to bring the chilling wetness into the sickroom.

After changing into her black wool skirt and a clean, if rather old, white shirtwaist, she went to the kitchen, where the cook helped her prepare a tray of delicious creamy potato soup with bacon bits, cornbread, and hot tea.

She carried the tray to Papa's room, set it down, and knocked gently on the door. But he did not answer, and after several more knocks, Marielle opened the door, picked up the tray, and walked in. Papa was not in bed; in fact, he wasn't in the room.

She was filled with an unnatural foreboding. In a stiff mechanical way, she walked out of the sickroom and opened each door of each room she passed, checking for her father. She even searched Lola's bedroom, which she had promised herself she would never enter again for any reason.

Where was Papa? The question made her body grow cold with fear. She flew to Lola's wine cellar on the other side of the kitchen. If he was not there, she could not imagine where else she could look.

The wine cellar was large, dark, and very cold. Marielle lit a lamp and searched everywhere, behind wine racks and under long wooden tables. Papa was not there.

Marielle raced back to the kitchen. None of the household staff had seen him for the last several hours, they reported. They were gathered in the kitchen, hushed with concern. Jeremiah Preston was a very sick man. How had he gotten out of the house and where had he gone in his condition?

Suddenly, Marielle looked out the kitchen window, which faced the back of the house. Through the mist, she saw Major, the bear cub that had become Lola's pet. Near him lay a sodden bundle of what looked like rags.

A loud gasp escaped her throat as she hurtled out the back door into the yard. The ground was extremely soft and soggy, and her shoes sank in the ooze. Without thinking, she slipped out of the shoes and ran in her stockinged feet to where Major was tethered.

As she got closer, she saw that, just as she thought, someone was lying on the ground close to the bear. Then she saw the bear cub pick up an almost empty bottle of spirits and drink from it as if it were a baby bottle.

She felt herself flying in slow motion over the mud, her feet making footprints in the ground. When she reached the bundle of wet, shivering rags, she saw that it was Papa, lying there drunk and half dead. In one of his hands, held closely to his chest as if he were cuddling a baby, was another empty bottle. The bear cub had not touched him in any way.

As she stood in the spongy mire, sinking almost to her ankles, Papa opened one eye, recognized her, and moaned in a low, hoarse, unrecognizable voice. It was a cry for help, or perhaps a cry of embarrassment.

With the servants' help, it did not take Marielle long to get Papa back to the sickroom. The maid was sent to fetch Dr. Lyons, and

Lola's houseboy helped strip the hapless man and make him comfortable.

There was no time to think, only to do. She brought a huge slop pail to the side of the sickbed, lifted Papa up to a sitting position, stuck her finger down his throat and made him vomit. She kept at him until he was empty and she was crying with fatigue. Papa had become unconscious but would not stop shivering. Marielle put hot bricks in the bed and wrapped him in Lola's feather quilts.

Dr. Lyons arrived and shook his head sadly when Marielle told him what had happened. "We'll know within twenty-four hours. If he survives for that long, he has a chance," Dr. Lyons advised her. He complimented her on her choice of action in making Papa vomit out the poisons in his body and dosed him up with quinine. Papa vomited again. His poor wracked body could not hold the important drug. Dr. Lyons dosed him with opium, and Papa became quiet.

Marielle changed into clean, dry clothes once again before she began her vigil at Papa's bedside. Dr. Lyons had left after saying he would return in the morning. There was nothing more he could do at the moment.

Toward evening, Papa opened his eyes and smiled at Marielle. "I love you, dear child," he whispered.

Marielle looked at him with alarm.

"Don't worry, my darling. You're safe. I don't want to die, but I've left you in good hands."

"Papa," Marielle cried, crossing to his side and taking his hand in hers.

He closed his eyes as he squeezed her hand. Then his hand went lax and his head lolled to one side.

Marielle sat still as a mouse. She did not cry. After a while, she became chilled and automatically pulled a shawl around her shoulders. Finally she kissed Papa, left him, and told the servants that he was dead.

Slipping into the parlor, she sat at the front window and looked out. She was alone now. Papa was gone. Granted, he hadn't been a safe harbor in her life these last few years, but she had loved him nonetheless and had depended on him simply being around. She reached up and touched her cheek to find it wet with tears. She hadn't even known she was crying!

It was still raining and soon it would be dawn. Streaks of light began to break through the darkness. One of the servants brought her a cup of steaming black coffee and she drank it gratefully.

It was then that she saw Morgan Quinn riding toward the house. He was riding fast, dressed for the weather in a long oilskin that covered a heavy sheepskin coat. Rivulets of water fell from his hat onto the oilskin and then onto his horse. Steam came from the horse's nostrils as he galloped rapidly toward his destination, and the clippity-clop of its hooves sounded through the quiet of the night outside.

Marielle watched as Quinn reined in his horse at Lola's hitching posts in front of the house and tethered him; he shook himself off before taking long, swift strides onto the veranda. After shedding the oilskin and cleaning the heavy mud from his boots, he knocked on the front door with impatience. The houseboy let him in.

He found Marielle soon enough. By the time he entered the parlor, though, she had made sure there were no tears on her face. Her fragile features were calm.

"I must see your father at once," he said quietly. When she didn't answer, he looked at her strangely. "I must talk with him. I've ridden all night. Would you please tell him I'm here. It's of the utmost importance."

Chapter Eighteen

She was not sure why she was wearing black. Papa would not have liked to see her in that somber color, but Lola had been kind one more time when she donated the funeral outfit, and Marielle had been too distraught to object. She donned it simply because everyone expected it of her.

Everyone, that is, except Quinn, who looked sadly at the beautiful black suit and said, "I hope you will not be wearing that dress for any length of time. You are too young to embrace death so publicly."

She felt like the color of her dress, though, in a mood so black she thought she might never recover to enjoy the sunshine again. Her beloved Papa was gone. Not only that, but before he'd gone, he'd managed, with the best of intentions, to ruin her life. The legal paper presented to her after his funeral by Judge Walsh was a blow second only to the death itself.

"It's foolproof," the judge told her as she read Papa's last will and testament, and learned how her father had planned she'd live until she attained the age of twenty-one.

She had, as yet, not celebrated her eighteenth birthday, though it was due in several months. That meant that for every single day of more than three long years Morgan Quinn would be her legal guardian. He had complete control over her. She could do nothing without his consent. According to Papa's will, he was her defender, her protector, her caretaker, her surrogate father. She was his ward, and had absolutely no rights of her own.

Marielle had seen Quinn in bad humor before, but now he was positively cold with rage.

"Let's forget the whole thing," she said when she learned of his unhappiness with the legal document Papa had foisted upon

given her that had a high neckline. Promptly at seven, she joined Carmel Quinn-Pagonne downstairs. The woman solemnly handed her a tiny crystal of aperitif as they sat down at a long mahogany table in the dark, elegant dining room, which could easily hold fifty people for dinner, but which now seated only two.

Like her eldest son, Carmel did not smile very much. But the slender woman, dressed in somber brown wool, impressed Marielle and reminded her somehow of an independent brown bird, perched on the vast estate, protecting the nest and watching over her young. Marielle knew she was a lot taller than the diminutive Carmel, but she was awed by the strength and determination she saw in the face of this tiny mother of two giant men.

"My son has gone to San Francisco at my request," Carmel said in a soft voice that required Marielle to listen attentively. "I have sent him to fetch a special tutor for you. I have been given to understand that your education has been rather sketchy."

Marielle couldn't contain herself. "That's ridiculous. I can read. I know my Shakespeare. I've read many popular novels and plays. I have a quite acceptable hand when writing, and I know my numbers. That is considerably more than most people in these parts. I thank you—but it really won't be necessary."

"I have sent Morgan for a very particular reason. I have learned that Mrs. Penelope Watson, a recent widow and daughter of an old friend of mine, needs work. Her husband and baby son both died recently as a result of a tragic accident. She was spared, but has lost all her worldly possessions along with her husband and son. She has advertised her services. I saw the notice and wrote her a letter. She comes with the highest recommendations. I was not thinking of an ordinary schoolroom education. I was thinking of foreign languages and drawing room manners."

"No, thank you. You need not bother."

Carmel did not reply. She cut the meat on her plate daintily.

"I am nearly eighteen years old and expect to be treated accordingly."

"Are you so ungrateful, young lady, that you cannot accept the bounty we offer you?" This was said softly and sweetly.

"It's absurd. I'm an actress, not a wayward child."

"Penelope Watson needs a post. She is a very proud woman. She would never come as a permanent guest. You are a perfect excuse for me to bring her here. And from our conversation just now, I would say you do need a few lessons in good manners."

Hurt to the quick, Marielle looked up from her plate. "I really should not be made to suffer so that Mrs. Watson has a position."

"Penny Watson has always been a fine daughter to her mother, a good wife to her husband, a loving mother to the poor baby that perished. Also, I understand from portraits I have seen that she is very beautiful." She hesitated, then smiled that wonderfully crooked smile, the same one that Morgan and Rio shared. "I would not be unhappy if Morgan fell in love with Penelope." She continued smiling at Marielle from her seat at the head of the long table.

"Or Rio? Have you forgotten Rio?" Marielle could not help the hint of sarcasm in her voice.

"Rio seems to be in love already," Carmel said dryly.

Marielle bent over her plate and forced some of the splendid dinner down her throat. It was veal, cooked delicately by Hu Ming's son, who was a master chef. She was not sure she would be able to swallow, but she found it was easier to waste time cutting bits of veal than to carry on a comfortable conversation with Carmel. It was not that Carmel was impolite or inhospitable, it was only that she was the most contained woman Marielle had ever met. Obviously she loved her sons, but the rest of the world did not live in her heart.

At one time toward the end of the meal, Marielle asked, "What may I call you, ma'am? Mrs. Quinn or Mrs. Pagonne?"

"Since it was Mr. Quinn who purchased the land for this ranch and started the work we hope to finish, and since Mr. Quinn was the father of my firstborn, I prefer to be called by that name. Mr. Pagonne was part of my life for only two years before he died." She was silent after that and finished her supper slowly and methodically.

The interminable meal came to an end eventually. Even if she had not been as tired as she was from the long trip, she would not have enjoyed Carmel's cold-blooded words and hints about her matchmaking endeavors for Morgan and Penny Watson, though to give the lady credit, she could not possibly have any knowledge of Marielle's relationship with her oldest son.

Marielle returned to her room, went straight to the lamp, and lit it. The room seemed as cavernous as ever, and the lamplight sent spectral shadows dancing into the far corners. She went to the fireplace and lit the fire, and as the flames brightened the semidarkness, she turned to her bed for the first time since she had entered the room. There, looking very comfortable, was Rio, stretched out full-length on her bed. He was fully clothed, and that included his boots, spurs, and a gunbelt containing a pistol on each side. He had a finger to his lips warning her to be silent just as she was about to let out a loud scream.

She held back the scream, walked straight up to him, and silently pulled him off the bed with all her strength. She was angry and made no pretense of being civil. In a loud whisper, she told him how she felt; she also tried to push him out the door of the room. He stood tall, laughing silently and enjoying her anger, then he sank into the one large easy chair in the bedroom. His long legs stretched out as he claimed the chair and made himself comfortable.

"You're sure a jumpy gal. All I want to do is take you somewhere. Show you something important. Something you should see."

"What?" she asked suspiciously.

"It takes showing. It has to do with those gold nuggets I tried to give you back in Sacramento."

"Why can't it wait till tomorrow? I just got here."

"It's got to be tonight. Morgan's gone to the city. Ma will go to bed soon. So it's now or never." Suddenly the laughter left his impassioned face and he started to move closer to her. She drew back. Still, she was intrigued. Maybe Rio would take her to see his mountain of gold.

"I don't like it. But—okay," she said swiftly.

"It's more'n an hour away. Riding hard, that is! More'n an hour coming back." There was a dangerous glint in his eyes.

"How do I know you'll bring me back? That you're not tricking me to get me alone?"

"I'll bring you back. I swear."

"How can I trust you? Here you are in my room. A lady's room, where you don't belong. No. There's no trusting you. You're probably a rake, just like your brother."

"No, ma'am. You can trust me," he said quietly and in utter earnest. "You're going to be my wife. I won't take advantage. Not of you." He settled deeper into the chair, looking like he planned to stay.

Every one of her instincts told her not to trust him, but she couldn't resist the lure of seeing the Quinns' secret mountain of gold, or at least finding out whether it really did exist. Besides, she didn't know how else to get Rio out of her room.

"How did you get in here in the first place?"

He took a key out of his pocket. It was the large iron key that she had seen earlier in the door. "You left the key in the lock. Anyone could get in. You're very trusting."

"Give me the key and I'll go with you," she said, vowing never to let the key out of her sight again.

He handed her the key and politely turned his back as she changed her clothes for the trip.

It seemed longer than an hour's ride. He had given her one of Carmel's heavy sheepskin jackets, which fitted perfectly, and which she was happy to be wearing, in the cold night. Around her head and neck she had wrapped a plaid woolen scarf, and over that she wore one of Rio's flat-brimmed hats. She sat on her horse stiffly as it was led by Rio, who rode ahead of her. Everytime she opened her mouth, her breath came out in wisps of steam that wafted into the cold air. She was sorry she had committed herself to the journey. After the long trip with Quinn, she was already bone tired.

After a while, they started to ascend a steep trail that took them upwards into mountainous terrain. In the darkness of the night, she saw the ghostly outlines of trees, which looked to her like gargoyles in repose. The track became more narrow and finally there seemed to be no trail at all. Rio pushed back foliage which, like magic, sprang away as they moved forward to reveal a hidden path. When they passed, the foliage sprang back to hide the path behind them once again.

Rio turned around. "There's no way you'd find this by yourself. You'd get so lost you'd never come back." He seemed to get some sort of satisfaction from telling her this and frightening her. Shivering, she followed him. Rio stopped and dismounted. He helped her off her horse solicitously and tethered both animals carefully.

Then he shook the bottom branches of a huge, dark tree standing like a guard right in front of them. Without warning, the entire tree, trunk and foliage, swung to the left as if it were on some giant pivoting wheel, revealing a cavelike opening in the mountain in front of them. On the ground inside the opening were several lanterns. Rio took two, lit them, and handed one to Marielle.

He moved forward into the bowels of the cave, with Marielle so close behind him she could hear him breathe as he moved. For the first hundred yards, the opening was so low they both had to stoop to continue on. But soon, unexpectedly, they were able to stand upright, and by the light from the two lanterns, Marielle could see that the cave's ceiling now soared to a lofty pinnacle.

"Over here!" Rio said, and took her hand. A moment later she heard his voice, far in the distance, echoing, "Over here! Over here! Over here!"

He led her farther in until there, before them, stacked neatly was the gold Rio had told her about.

If the mountain in which she found herself was a golden one, the gold had been taken from its veins by humans. Much of the dust and nuggets had been pressed into small gold bars, tidily squared with a gold press, and now sat in naked stacks as if ready for distribution.

Marielle had never seen such a sight and swung the lantern closer to get her fill. Pokes of gold nuggets, bags of gold dust, bare stacks of gold bars: they faced her in quantities that challenged the imagination. She stood motionless, staring for a long time.

Then she swung the lantern closer to Rio's face. He was gaping at her, and on the features of his visage she could make out a look of sheer but perverse joy at the attention his outrageous disclosure was getting.

Could anyone, ever, spend all that golden money? Without thinking, she grabbed his hand and held it tightly as she continued to gaze upon the extraordinary sight.

"You believe me now?" he said triumphantly.

"I'm not sure I believe what I see," she whispered, and automatically tightened her grip on his hand. She could not stop herself. She squeezed his hand so hard, she was sure that if it were not so big and strong, it would surely be broken.

He removed his hand from her grasp gently and put his arm around her. The comfort of his physical presence made the dreamlike quality of her discovery a little more real. She stared at the gold, turned and stared at him, and turned back to the gold.

Then she heard his voice. Low. Vibrant. An echo of Morgan Quinn's voice. "You see all that gold?" he said. "That mountain of bullion belongs to this ranch. And it can be yours. I'll give it all to you, if you will only marry me."

Chapter Nineteen

The sight of all that gold became a constant reminder to Marielle of her own state of poverty. But, strangely enough, instead of wanting to own it, she began to feel that it was a threat to happiness. Was Carmel Quinn happy? Was Rio Pagonne happy? Was Morgan Quinn happy?

"You thought I was fibbin', didn't you?" Rio had said while they rode back to the ranch late that night.

"Whose gold is it really, Rio?" she was able to whisper finally.

"It's Double Raven gold just like I told you. It belongs to Ma, Morgan, and me. You'll marry me now, won't you?"

She refused to answer his question. Instead she asked him one of her own. "How did you get it out of the ground? You'd need lots of workers for that."

"Indians. Blood brothers. Somewhere way in the past. Ma's connections and Morgan's doings. The Indians had no need of gold. We paid them with goods we imported on ships that came around the Horn. We sent gold going in one direction and received goods when the ships returned. Finally we owned the ships. We paid everyone well. That included the Indians. When the gold was taken out of the ground and the job was finished, they left. No one else knows. Morgan says if anyone finds out, the place will be overrun with squatters. Fightin' to find more. There ain't no more. But they'll ruin the ranch. It's happened to lots of other ranches in California."

Now, days later, she was still amazed that there really was all that gold on the Double Raven Ranch and that the family had managed to keep it a secret. She wished it had remained a secret.

Carmel had urged her to explore the countryside close to the estate, but it was Rio who appeared like magic to show her around.

The first week she was there, he showed her all the places in which he had played as a boy and taught her where to find water when there was no water to be seen by the human eye. He also taught her how to use a *reata*, and kept at her until she became proficient enough to lasso the huge, friendly sheepdog named Barker, who stood graciously by and played cow until Marielle was successful.

Another day, they took a picnic with them and stayed away all afternoon. The valley was filled with sunshine and flowers, and Marielle found herself enjoying Rio's company. In fact, she could not remember the last time she had enjoyed herself as much. Rio was like a happy little boy who would not let his latest toy out of his sight, and was full of amusing ranch lore she had never heard as a city girl.

When they sat down to eat, the food was plentiful and delicious. There was cold roast beef and hard-boiled eggs with crusty sourdough bread and a small crock of creamy butter. There were oranges for dessert, along with a carrot cake filled with fat, juicy raisins, and good strong coffee and fresh milk. Every hour had been perfect, and Marielle was content and tired. The fresh air and outdoor living were new to her, but she liked them and promised herself to learn as much as she could about ranch life.

They started back to the house, riding leisurely. Rio had picked a huge bunch of wild blossoms for Marielle's room after she told him how much she loved flowers. It was then that she remembered that they had forgotten the picnic basket with the leftover food and utensils.

"I'll go back," Rio said. "It'll take just a few minutes. Hope the bugs ain't got into things."

Marielle leaned back contentedly under the shade of a tree and waited for him. When some time had elapsed and he had not returned, she decided to look for him. She had almost reached the picnic site when she heard gun shots. She started to run toward the sounds, even though she knew it would be foolish to try to help Rio if he was in serious trouble. She carried no weapons. But she continued on. As she got closer to the spot, she saw Rio's graceful back half-bent as he held a gun in each hand. He was shooting continuously at a dim figure which seemed to be dancing in front of the picnic tree.

When she got closer, almost fully behind Rio's half-crouched form, she saw that the man under the tree was black, and almost middle-aged; his clothes were tattered, and his feet bare. Rio kept shooting directly into the dust at his feet, as the man hopped up and down in a wildly, hysterical dance.

"You bastard, you keep on dancin' or you gonna die as sure as your skin is black."

"Yas, massuh," the man howled.

"Rio! Stop! What are you doing?" Marielle screamed as she reached his side.

He glanced sideways at her, his look, dark and intense. "That's a runaway slave. He thinks he's a free man here. He ain't, s'far as I'm concerned. Somebody, somewhere, owns him."

"Stop it! Leave him alone. He isn't hurting you."

Rio lowered his guns. "What difference is it to you? He was stealin' our picnic basket."

"He's hungry. Let him have it."

"Why?"

"Because we don't need it and he does."

"He's on our property."

"He probably doesn't know that. Leave him be, Rio. Please!"

She rushed closer to him and pulled at his sleeve, looking pleadingly at his face. "For me, Rio!" She screamed so loudly the black man stopped dancing and looked at her with curiosity.

Rio gazed at her with narrowed eyes. Then he put his guns back in his holsters. "Take off fast, boy," he yelled at the terrified man. "If I see you again, I swear, boy, you're dead."

The man took a long look at Marielle as if he were memorizing her face, shot Rio a guarded glance, and then ran.

Marielle shuddered. When he was out of sight, Rio turned to her. "Why are you so hot under the collar? Who cares about some runaway? We don't need that kind of trouble on this ranch."

She remembered the article in the newspaper in Grass Valley. "Rio, the man had no weapons and was not harming you. He was hungry."

"Okay, okay. I did what you said." With that he swept her up on his horse as if she weighed nothing and they rode back to the spot where she had tethered her animal.

When they got there, the horse was gone. Rio was furious. "You sure this is where you left him?"

"Yes. You were with me. This is where we stopped."

"Well, guess what? Your runaway ran away with your horse."

"He needed it more than I do," Marielle said. "Besides, we don't know for sure he did it."

They rode back in silence, Marielle behind him, hanging on to his waist. She did not know what he was thinking, but she was sick over what had just happened. She had seen Rio become cruel and ugly so suddenly and unexpectedly that it took her breath away. Now he turned around and smiled at her, and there was no trace of brutality in his face—in fact, there was now that aura of lovable sweetness about him that she was beginning to like. If she had not witnessed the sudden change in him, she would not have believed it possible.

When they got back to the house, she would have to make it very plain that she had no intentions of ever becoming his bride. Instead, she had no opportunity to talk to him alone. She found a visitor had been waiting for her all afternoon. It was Junius Booth, Jr.

June Booth wanted her to go to San Francisco. He had a job for her. She could play Ophelia and Juliet opposite John Wilkes Booth, June and Ted Booth's younger brother, who was arriving in San Francisco the following week with a twelve-week contract at one of San Francisco's finest theaters. John Wilkes was in need of a leading lady, and Marielle had been highly recommended to him by Ted.

"Will I take the job?" Marielle cried. "Of course! Thank you so much, June. How could you think otherwise?"

Junius looked around the large, cold, formal parlor. "Ben Baker told me you got yourself a rich guardian."

"I'm an actress, June. I've been waiting for something like this to happen. I'll tell Mrs. Quinn. Then I'll pack. You'll stay for supper, won't you?"

Junius Booth nodded happily

Carmel was as gracious as she could possibly be to Junius Booth. At seven o'clock, Marielle and June arrived at the dinner table to find Carmel already there, elegant in subdued gray wool and strands of exquisite pearls. Rio arrived very shortly after in fresh clothes, looking very handsome.

During dinner, Marielle told them about the new developments in her career and why Junius had ridden the long distance to tell her about this extraordinary opportunity. Carmel listened quietly; Rio whooped with pleasure as he listened to her story, slapped his knee, and would have been even more jubilant if a look from his mother hadn't quieted him. He raised his glass in a toast. "To the greatest actress in the world. If I can see you one time on the stage in San Francisco, I can die happy.'' He turned to Carmel. ''What do you say, Mother?''

Carmel turned to Marielle. ''It is not for me to say. Morgan is your legal guardian, and he will see to your best interests, I'm sure.''

''But I would like to leave in the morning with Mr. Booth. It's only for twelve weeks and I promise to return as soon as the engagement is over.''

''I'm sure all this can wait another day or two. Morgan is expected back momentarily and if you are to go to San Francisco, I am sure he will attend to your safe journey,'' Carmel continued calmly.

Marielle wanted to tell the older woman that she would be going to San Francisco regardless of what Quinn said, but she kept her mouth closed.

When the evening was over, Marielle promised to breakfast with Junius, who had to leave very early the next day. She planned to have a long, private talk with Carmel later that night. Since Carmel did not particularly care whether Marielle stayed or left the ranch, Marielle planned to convince her that she would be able to pay Mary Ann Crabtree as a chaperone. Mary Ann was in San Francisco with Lotta and always seemed to need extra money.

Junius retired first. Marielle was left with Carmel and Rio in the parlor when they all heard the unmistakable sound of horses and wagons approaching.

Quinn returned to the ranch laden with gifts. The family gathered outside to greet him and catch the first glimpse of the highly recommended widow who would be the newest member of the household. As he stepped down from the carriage, his handsome face was outlined in the moonlight. Marielle's heart beat rapidly as he turned and helped the new tutor from the wagon.

The lady's hair was the color of honey. Her eyes were soft pools of dark chocolate, and her complexion was peaches and cream. She was just a little taller than Carmel Quinn, a great beauty, but also the possessor of an icy hauteur.

The two wagons behind the carriage were neatly packed with merchandise purchased in San Francisco. Apparently, Quinn had asked Penelope to buy Marielle everything a proper young lady would need for several seasons. That included not only books and teaching supplies, but an extensive wardrobe composed of the most expensive clothes Marielle had ever owned.

Unfortunately, Penelope's taste tended toward the drab. There were somber plaids from Scotland, dark woolens and pale linens from Ireland, navy serges, and houndstooth checks from England. Marielle's new undergarments were white cotton, serviceable and well-made, but totally unlike the colorful French silk unmentionables she had been shown by Lola Montez. In fact, everything looked exactly like the clothes Penelope Watson wore herself.

Only one of the frocks gladdened Marielle's heart. It was a sophisticated rose pink in a self-patterned silk, and quite fashionable. Marielle felt she could wear the dress happily to any worthy occasion and be proud of being seen in public. Above all, it was not drab—the way all the others were.

"This one is beautiful. Where did you find it?" Marielle asked. It was the only costume she would have chosen herself. "It's going to be my favorite."

Penelope sniffed delicately. Her perfect nose went up into the air. "I did not choose that gown. That was the one Mr. Quinn chose before I convinced him he did not know enough about what proper, well-bred girls wore. After all, one of the subjects I intend to teach will be decorum, and appearance is a very good place to begin." She smiled at Marielle as she sedately walked out of the room.

Marielle stuck her tongue out as she watched Penelope's netted chignon and stiff upper back move away from her.

Penelope turned back as if she knew exactly what Marielle had done. "You see what I mean. It will not do you good to be sassy, young lady. Impudence can never replace proper deportment," she said softly, and gave her student a cool stare.

Marielle decided she was not going to like Penelope Watson. For one thing, Mrs. Watson had asked Marielle to call her Miss Penelope; Marielle acquiesced sullenly. But the worst insult had come the morning after Mrs. Watson's arrival. Quinn, his mother, and Junius Booth had closeted themselves in the library to discuss Marielle's future in San Francisco. Although Penelope Watson had been invited to the conference, Marielle had not been asked to join them. She resented the meeting for many reasons, but most of all because it did not include her. They were planning her future and did not think she was worthy of consultation. When they emerged more than an hour later, Miss Penelope was smiling sweetly, but Quinn wore his most forbidding countenance, and Junius Booth looked grim.

Teeth gritted, the famous Booth brother, who was a theatrical manager besides an actor, made his way to where Marielle waited alone, and took her gently in his arms. "I'm sorry, dear girl. But *that man* will not give his permission."

Marielle's heart sank. "I will run away and join you in San Francisco," she whispered to him.

June shook his head. "T'would be for naught, dear girl. I cannot take the responsibility. *That man* is made of steel, and has too much power, even as far as San Francisco. Have you any idea how rich this family is? Their holdings in the shipping trade alone could finance every theater in New York for years and years. He would come and spirit you away before opening night. He as much as said so. He doesn't want you on the stage." June scratched his head sadly. "I cannot chance the ruin of my own little brother's debut. I am truly sorry."

After June Booth left the ranch, Marielle cornered a reluctant Quinn and insisted on a private conversation with him. As she fumed, he led her into the library and closed the door behind them.

"I have been an entertainer for almost two years. It's what I want to do the rest of my life. Why do you feel the need to thwart me in my desire to further my career?"

He scrutinized her as he spoke. "I am only doing what your father instructed me to do. I did not ask to be made your guardian, but now that I am, I shall fulfill my duties the way I see fit."

"What's wrong with my going to San Francisco for a few weeks? I can return to the ranch after the engagement is over."

Quinn did not answer, but he smiled. His face lost its formidableness, although his eyes retained a speculative awareness that made Marielle feel uncomfortable.

"You don't trust me," he said finally, and grinned when she had given up all hope that he would speak again, much less smile. Too quickly his expression returned to soberness. "You must trust me. Your life will be happier—and easier."

"Sure! If I do everything you say. Sure! If I behave like an obedient little girl till I'm old enough to be a grandmother," she fumed. She scowled and bit her lower lip.

"Instruction with Miss Penelope starts tomorrow morning at six. I expect you to show the proper amount of respect for your new teacher," he announced as he concluded the interview.

"I do not awaken with the chickens. I am an actress," she said as she got up angrily.

"And you are very dramatic. But your day will start at six o'clock. Perhaps tomorrow will be a good time for you to start changing your bad habits. Miss Penelope wishes to begin her duties as soon as possible."

"I shall soon be eighteen years old."

"So you keep reminding me, but I wish you would act your age. A few lessons in language and deportment can only help. It'll be good for you."

"I don't need schooling. I want to work on the stage."

"I'm sorry. For now that's impossible. Miss Penelope will be reporting to me about your progress. And you, in turn, will hear from me. It will be to your advantage to take these new arrangements seriously."

"We shall see about that!" Marielle said, and turned on her heel as she left him standing at his desk looking stern and relentless. Inside, however, she felt hopeless. He seemed to have the upper hand and there was very little she could do.

As she walked down the long hallway to the staircase to get to her room, a long sinewy arm reached out and pulled her into a shadowed alcove. It was Rio, who had been waiting for her.

"I heard everything. I was right outside the French window." He turned around to see if Quinn was in the corridor. "I swear he's always been a skunk. He won't change his ways." He stroked her hair gently and sympathy filled his eyes. "I hate him too," he said, and his voice took on the same hardness she had heard when he talked about the old negro whom they had discovered on the ranch. "Someday, we won't be bothered with my older brother anymore."

She started sobbing, letting out all the misery within her. Rio continued to stroke her hair as she leaned against him. It felt good to be stroked and petted.

"I'll take care of you. No matter what, I'll take good care of you. I'll see he isn't mean or cruel to you." Rio put his arms around her and pulled her close to him.

He was the only one in the house who cared about how she felt. A forlorn feeling came over her, and she moved even closer as Rio continued to hold and comfort her. She missed Papa so much. She even missed Sybil. She loathed Morgan Quinn, who was frustrating her at every turn of her life.

"We can go away from here and get married," Rio murmured into her ear. "When we come back, *if* we come back, we'll be married. Nobody will dare order us around then."

"We can't run from Morgan Quinn. He'll find us no matter where we go," she sobbed bitterly.

Rio's visage took on a sly tinge. "I know a place he knows nothing about."

"There is no such place."

"I tell you there is. I got me good pals there. He can't get in there. Besides, my buddies are always aching for a low-down ruckus. Brings joy to their dirty dog hearts."

Marielle drew away. She sniffled and wiped her nose on a handkerchief she pulled from the pocket of her dress. She remembered Rio's friends had their faces on wanted posters. "There can be no running away with you, Rio, much less a marriage."

"What do you mean?"

"Exactly what I said."

"But why?"

Marielle turned away.

"Why?" Rio asked again, this time in a louder voice. His arms closed around her once more as he looked down into her tear-stained face. "Haven't I got enough gold for you? I can give you everything you ever wanted in life. And that includes hot love and sweet talk. . . ."

She had to tell him the truth. Somehow, she had to make him understand what she felt inside. He was a kind, lovable man. He deserved it. "I have such good feelings for you. I like being with you. But . . ." she tried to choose her words very carefully. "I'm in love with Quinn," Marielle confided. "Like you, I think I hate him too. But when I give it a lot of thought, I realize that what it is I really hate *is* loving him. Still, I cannot stop."

Suddenly he looked confused.

"You want my brother? You don't want me?"

"I wish it were the other way around. Life would be a lot easier. There are times when you are so much like him that I want to touch you, to be close to you. But it is Quinn I'm aching for. I don't understand it and I'm sorry, Rio. I'm truly sorry."

She saw his face change as she finished the sentence and fear bubbled up in her chest. Before she could say another word, Rio turned toward her and grabbed her throat. His long fingers began to press. A demonlike grin appeared on his face and his shiny, gray eyes became slits riveted to her enormous blue ones.

"We will change all that," Rio said, without removing his grip on her throat. "Your feelings for me will mellow. I will deal with Morgan. He will never make you unhappy again, I promise you. He will never bother you again, I swear. I will take care of everything." As he spoke, his eyes glassed over and became so brilliant that they frightened her more than his fingers on her neck.

Then suddenly he released her and his expression changed. It was as if he did not know what he had done. Backing away, she mouthed the words, "Don't touch me!"

He looked at her with confusion on his face and tried to come closer once again. The palms of Marielle's hands shot out as she held him at bay. His face became distressed; his eyes filled with suffering. "Don't be afraid of me. I will never, never harm you again." There was torment in his voice.

A cry of dismay escaped from Marielle as the blood pounded painfully through her throat. She spun around and ran toward her room, turning only once along the long corridor to see Rio standing still, bewildered, looking after her anxiously.

"Marielle. I love you. He doesn't. He'll hurt you. He plans to marry Miss Penelope," she heard him say hoarsely.

When she reached the door of her bedroom and safety, she pushed it open and turned back one last time to see if he were following her. Rio had not moved. He was rooted to the floor, watching her with a sweet, loving expression on his face. It was a look of love and devotion. It was a look that clearly showed he idolized her, and it frightened her.

Chapter Twenty

From Penelope Watson's arrival onward, Marielle's day started at dawn. As the weeks passed, Marielle's instructress became ruthless when it came to work. In spite of herself, Marielle couldn't help but expose her intelligence, and Miss Penelope decided that Marielle Preston had a brain and was going to use it whether she wanted to or not.

She was taught French, Latin, and Greek and the finer points of deportment. "Well-bred young ladies are able to meet every social occasion," Miss Penelope said in her soft but firm voice.

Late every Saturday afternoon, Quinn received a report on Marielle's progress. Afterwards, he discussed it privately with her in the library. It became a weekly ritual that Marielle dreaded at first, but later began to perversely enjoy.

When she was alone with Quinn, she made it a point to be sassy, to undermine the little that was good about Miss Penelope's report, and to emphasize that any of the bad was more than true. It gave her great pleasure to frustrate Quinn at every turn, and to disallow him the privilege of playing the role of surrogate father. Eventually the Saturday afternoon sessions became her major joy in life, her one big opportunity each week to thwart Morgan Quinn.

One Saturday when Marielle arrived for her weekly session with Quinn, she noted that Hu Ming had set up a tea tray in the library where they met. Perhaps Miss Penelope had given her a good report for a change? But it hardly seemed likely. Marielle sighed as she helped herself to an earthenware mug of China tea and crusty bread and butter.

Quinn waited until she finished her tea before he picked up the report and started the conference. He had been watching her eat her bread and butter, and when she put down the end of the crust, she licked her fingers indelicately, baiting him with her bad manners. She wondered what Quinn was thinking as he watched her licking her fingers. He did not say a word, but looked on as she purposely allowed the butter to smear the corners of her lips. "I know you want me. Why don't you admit it and be done with it?" she said, then chewed another mouthful of bread and butter.

"I will admit no such thing. Do you know what you look like at this moment?"

"Yes." She continued chewing and smiled innocently at him. Of course he was not able to admit that he wanted her. He was Morgan Quinn, a man who never admitted anything that might make him seem weak.

She finished chewing, wiped her mouth, and pointed at Miss Penelope's report. There was nothing more to say. She had her moment, but no longer relished it. Folding her hands neatly in her lap, she kept her mouth tightly shut and waited for the onslaught.

"Miss Penelope tells me that she is not pleased with your efforts. She says you are very bright, but have a deep contempt for anything she tries to teach you."

Marielle took a deep breath and waited for the rest.

"Miss Penelope says you are a lazy student. That makes me very unhappy. I would like you to apply yourself to your education with more eagerness."

"Why? You don't really care about how I feel."

It was Quinn's turn to wait. When she did not continue, he got up from his desk and paced back and forth in front of her as he weighed his words. Marielle watched his long legs in fascination. His lean body was taut, ready to spring, but his face was controlled. "You will no doubt someday need everything Miss Penelope is teaching. The Double Raven will not always be your entire universe."

Marielle's voice was bitter when she answered him. "So you are getting me ready for the time when you can dispose of me? I knew you would eventually let me know about that. Furthermore, if you must know, I don't fancy Latin and Greek. I don't like memorizing and conjugating silly verbs all day long."

"You will thank me for it one day."

"No. I think not. You can't tell me what I need to know or what I'll thank you for."

"Yes I can."

"Rio has asked me to marry him. I think I will accept his offer. He will be kinder to me than you are."

His face became even graver than before and his gray eyes turned cold with anger. "I will not give my permission. And Rio is not a kind man."

"That's exactly what he says about you, sir. And so do I."

Quinn stopped pacing and scrutinized her face as he stood over her. "Look at me!"

She forced herself to lift her chin resolutely and look into those angry, widely spaced gray eyes that showed no sympathy. She tried to tell herself that the thick dark lashes fringing those eyes could not influence her in any way. But his magnetism held her, and her heart gave that familiar thud and began to pound until she thought it would break through her chest.

Then suddenly, unaccountably, he grinned with that wonderful crooked smile of his and the anger went out of his eyes. "I am not as cruel as you think. I am only pledged to your well-being until you are twenty-one."

The gentleness in his tone took her completely by surprise. She began to speak but then saw he had dismissed her by going to the half-open French window and turning his back on her. What a maddeningly changeable man was Morgan Quinn!

Days disappeared into weeks as six mornings out of every seven, Marielle fought the battle of the lecture hall unsuccessfully. Sunday, however, was her day of rest. Languidly, Marielle allowed herself the luxury of staying in bed till noon. Penelope Watson was one member of the household who did not luxuriate in Sundays. She awakened early and rode off to church alone. After the first couple of Sundays she had done this, Carmel found out about her lonely rides. She insisted Quinn escort the beautiful widow to services in the pretty little church in the village.

Sometimes, the couple did not return until late in the afternoon. Marielle resented their absence from the ranch and their being together, but she could not make herself resent it enough to get up and go to church with them.

Rio told her, rather gleefully, she thought, that the only reason that he and Marielle were not forced to attend church by Carmel, and that Carmel didn't attend herself, was because of the *courtship*. Morgan Quinn and Penny Watson were using those precious moments to get to know each other better. Carmel not only approved, she aided and abetted the pair, according to Rio.

So for Marielle, Sunday fast became a day to mope and watch after Quinn and Miss Penelope. Except for meals, Marielle would spend the day in her room if the weather was bad. When it was fair, she walked alone through the beautiful grounds of the Double Raven or rode out into the hills.

One Sunday Marielle returned from one of her long lonely rides sneezing, and it soon became clear that she'd caught a chill. Rio noticed something was wrong and tried to divert her by telling her about an upcoming bull-and-bear fight. Since this was a bear Rio had caught, he especially wanted Marielle to see it. It was not too often that the neighborhood was privileged with a truly important fight by a huge, fierce grizzly that belonged to Rio Pagonne.

"I'll stay home. I have no wish to be a witness to this barbarism you call sport," Marielle told Rio.

His face fell, and he was about to retort when Carmel put down her coffee cup. "Morgan and Penelope are gone for the day. Rio is going into town and I'm going with him. I think it best if you come with us," Carmel said.

Rio smiled charmingly at his mother and threw up his arms helplessly at Marielle as Carmel rose from the table.

The town had built a special arena to contain the performing beasts and a raised platform for the women and children. Many of the men stayed on horseback outside the ring, although they had the option to join the women on the platform if they so wished.

Marielle was surprised to find that on this occasion most everybody from the neighborhood was present. Many of the townfolk had been to church and now were ready and eager for the noise and thrills of a community spectacle. Nothing seemed to satisfy their appetites for excitement better than to see the unleashing of a grizzly against a bull. The crowd gathered, made bets, and took refreshments from picnic baskets.

Marielle felt a bad headache coming on. When she saw Penelope Watson being escorted toward them by old Harry Arkin, who was the preacher in the little church that had been built only recently, she waved half-heartedly, and the preacher and Penelope started toward her. Quinn was conspicuously absent from Penelope's side, which made Marielle wonder if he, like she, disapproved of the sport.

It was not that she had any great love for grizzlies, especially after what one had done to Papa and Sybil, but Marielle felt that no animal should be subjected to the terrible indignities that these two beasts would go through today before they died.

Much to her surprise, Marielle learned from the talk around her
that California legislature had made provision for licensing bear-
and-bull fights, imposing a tax of twenty dollars per exhibition,
payable into the local county treasury. It was legal.

When she saw the full-grown bear, Marielle shuddered, remembering her past ordeal. The bear was large and weighed over twelve
hundred pounds. He floundered around the ring the best he could,
hampered as he was by the long *reata* around his hind leg so that
he could not escape. The other end was tied to a bull's front leg.

The bull was a beautiful animal, a dark purple color marked with
white. His horns were regular and sharp, and his coat was smooth
and glossy. He stood for a moment and surveyed the bear, the ring,
and the crowd of people.

The bull advanced slowly as though taking aim and finally
charged straight at the target with all the speed and fury he could
muster. The spectators, from a safe distance, shouted excitedly.

The grizzly crouched and, as the horns smashed against his own
ribs, sank his teeth into his opponent's sensitive nose, swung his
arms over and behind his head, and squeezed mightily. The bull,
suffering intense pain, bellowed horribly and could not gore him.
Marielle turned her gaze away.

The fight continued for almost an hour. Marielle was the only
one who turned around, went to the back of the platform, and was
sick. She wiped her face with a handkerchief and started to return
to her seat when, suddenly, she became even more violently ill.
She waited, wiped her clammy face as best she could, and stumbled back to her seat next to Carmel. Carmel looked over at her
but said nothing.

Before the end, the bear, with its entrails dragging, ripped off
the tongue, the ears, and much of the lower jaw of the bull. At
last the battle ended in triumph for the bear. The bull lay dead, and
one of the men in charge shot the grizzly.

Marielle refused to watch the beasts being dragged out of the
arena. She looked over at Carmel and found the woman as impas-
sive as ever. Penelope was looking down at the Bible in her lap
with a tight expression on her lips. Feeling the fight had been a
disgusting spectacle, Marielle firmly believed that anyone who
attended it did so because of curiosity and a depraved lust for the
sordid and sensational. It was cruel and senseless, and Marielle
wondered how parents could bring their own small children to witness such a repugnant theatrical.

The audience clapped, shouted, and stamped their feet exactly as if they were in a theatre. The applause and shouts of delight told Marielle that the townspeople were having a good time. People began paying off betting debts, and some of the men were given mugs of rum by the womenfolk. Rio, after a cheery wave in their direction, took off on horseback with Paco, the ranch foreman, and other cronies.

Marielle began to feel even more sick than she had during the fight. She did not think she could get up if she tried. Finally, Carmel put her hand over hers. Marielle looked up, then saw why. In the distance, Quinn rode swiftly toward them. It took his horse only a few minutes to reach their side, but she saw his face, hard and angry, look around for his brother. When he could not find him, he glared reproachfully at his mother and Penelope.

"I'll take all of you home. Right now . . ." he said to Penelope when she was about to object. His face was a chiseled mask of disapproval.

Carmel's eyes went back to being completely inscrutable as she stood up. Penelope, a pinched look on her face, sidled up to Carmel. Marielle tried to stand, faltered, and swayed as Quinn caught her in his arms. She hardly remembered the trip back to the ranch except that she was in Morgan Quinn's arms for the entire journey.

She was ill for over a week. The daily lecture hall routine stopped, and there was a steady stream of "nurses" at her bedside.

Carmel cared for her silently, and with large doses of bad-tasting medicines. Miss Penelope nursed her by sitting at her bedside and reading long, dull passages from her Bible, which made Marielle's head ache. Hu Ming brought her soups from his homeland, which he said would cure her. He cajoled her into trying them. They were delicious and uncommon to the palate, but it was difficult for Marielle to swallow more than a few spoonfuls at a time.

Rio came to visit every single day with bunches of wildflowers in his hands. Carmel did not let him stay long, but he was cheery and kept Marielle awake with household gossip and Double Raven activities.

And Quinn, too, came to see her, though usually late at night. She would be dozing lightly when he arrived. Somehow she could feel his presence and would waken to find him sitting at her bedside. He always sat in a chair close to the fireplace, facing her bed but far enough away so that his face was illuminated from the embers of the glowing fire, a shadowy figure who sat very quietly.

At times, she would find a look of concern on his face when he thought she was not watching him.

He said the most ordinary things, but they meant a lot to Marielle. It was the way he said them. "How are you feeling today?" he would ask her, or, "Are you warm enough?" Simple words, but still, they made her feel happy. His quiet strength seemed to flow into her.

On the evening she felt well enough to sit up in bed for the first time in a week, Quinn visited her earlier than usual in order to find her awake. She looked very pale and small sitting in the middle of the huge four-poster. Her white cotton nightdress with the eyelet embroidery around the high neck and long full sleeves only made her look smaller, like a delicate child who'd been given the privilege of using a grown-up's oversize bed. Her long hair had been brushed by one of the servant girls and shimmered in the light from the fire.

"You're getting better," Quinn said quietly. He made the statement unemotionally, although he looked pleased. "If you continue to improve, how would you like a holiday from the ranch?"

She waited to see what he had in mind.

"Perhaps we can go to Sacramento City."

Still she said nothing.

"How about if I reserve an entire floor of the new hotel there. I hear it's just finished and very luxurious. I can also arrange for theater tickets," he said and stopped. When she did not answer, he asked, "How does that sound?"

"Who's *we*?" she asked politely.

"The family . . ." He paused, thought for a bit and continued. ". . . and Miss Penelope."

"Oh? Am I considered part of the family?"

"Of course you are."

"And is she?"

He hesitated. "Yes . . . she is. Don't be difficult, Marielle. We can celebrate your birthday. You can go shopping, if you want."

She was surprised he remembered her birthday. He had been present once before on her birthday—on the *Andrew Jackson* on the way to San Francisco by way of the Horn. It seemed such a long time ago. Two years.

"What do we need Miss Penelope for?" She heard her own voice sound childish and small. "I'm sick and tired of Miss Penelope. I see her every single day."

Quinn's voice was calm but there was a dangerous glint in his eyes. "Miss Penelope lives in this house now, just the way you do. You should consider her part of the family too."

So that was what he had on his mind. He was preparing her for the time when he would announce his engagement to the widow. Everything Rio told her was true. Quinn was going to make Penelope Watson his bride.

She sat up straighter in bed and felt the anger flow through her. She was not going to be compliant and mild-mannered in the light of this new information. "Do whatever you please," she blurted. "You will do it anyway."

"Is this the sweet-tempered Marielle Preston I've been visiting all week long? The frail, delicate Miss Preston?" He did not wait for her to reply. "No, this is more like the Marielle Preston of old. You must be recovering faster than I suspected," he said with a lift of one eyebrow. "I thought the news about a trip to Sacramento would cheer you up."

She turned on her side so that her back was to him and pulled the coverlets over her head. She stayed under as long as she could, and then came up for air.

He was still sitting in his chair watching her, a little smile flickering around his lips.

"Why don't you and I go to Sacramento alone? Without the family," she asked in as bold a manner as she could muster.

At first she thought he was considering her proposal, he looked at her with such curiosity. Then he laughed—a wonderful laugh.

"That wasn't supposed to be funny," she said, but weakly.

He laughed some more, stepped over to the big bed and sat on the edge that was the farthest from where she was propped against the pillows. "You seem to have a deep contempt for reality. That may be because you were brought up in the world of the theatre. And that's too bad. I am a realistic man."

"I don't particularly care what you are. And you don't understand me at all."

"I understand you are a willful whelp and if you weren't in the sickbed, I would turn you over my knee."

"Never!" she said haughtily. "My father never did, and neither will you."

"Don't be too sure," he said darkly, but turned away and returned to his armchair.

How could she allow him to make such a fool of her? She had to fight back. It was important for him to find out she was a person with spirit, not like the insipid Penelope Watson.

What did Miss Penelope have that she didn't have? Dimly, Marielle tried to think of the older woman's advantages: Well, the lady was beautiful, and good breeding showed in every one of her quiet movements. Was that enough to make her the future Mrs. Morgan Quinn? Yet, in his own words, Quinn had all but confirmed it, and when she'd offered herself to him, alone in a Sacramento hotel room, he had laughed.

Then a thought came to her and a peal of merry laughter escaped her own soft lips. It was the first time she had laughed since she had become ill. If Quinn was her legal guardian and the substitute for her father, it would be absolutely above suspicion for them to go anywhere in the world alone together. The thought was delicious, but she knew better than to tell him. Instead, she became so cheerful that he looked at her with apprehension.

They all went to Sacramento City together. The three women rode in one of the family carriages. The valises went on ahead in an open buckboard. The two brothers rode alongside the ladies' carriage for protection. Letters had been sent in advance to the new hotel, and Quinn had actually ridden into the city to make sure everything was as it should be. When he returned, he reported that an entire floor of six bedrooms and a large, double-sized sitting room had been reserved for the party. The new hotel was as fine an establishment as the most expensive hotel in San Francisco. When asked who the sixth bedroom was for, Quinn smiled and said, "Perhaps for the purchases to be made by the ladies of the manor."

Rio clapped his hands as he poured forth suggestions for the three nights and four days to be spent in the big city. On the night of Marielle's birthday, there was to be a dinner party at the hotel in her honor. It could not be a surprise, of course, but one of the two dining rooms had been reserved for the occasion and there was to be an orchestra for dancing after dinner.

The other two evenings had been set aside for the theatre. John Wilkes Booth had finished his San Francisco engagement and, according to the newspapers, would be in Sacramento at the same time as the Quinn party. An entire box had already been reserved for his opening night appearance. On the second night they were going to see Mrs. Catherine Sinclair's company.

Marielle was astonished to see how much Sacramento had grown since the last time she had seen it. It was now a very respectable city; the streets were cleaner and the citizens looked more prosperous. The city had just recently become the capital of the state, and an imposing structure was being built at the cost of three hundred thousand dollars. The building would serve as the official capital of California. The just-finished hotel in which the Quinn party made its headquarters had every modern convenience imaginable.

When the bustle and to-do about getting settled ended and they were entrenched on the top floor of the hotel, Quinn came to see Marielle in her room.

He seemed embarrassed as he handed her five crisp one-hundred-dollar bills. "I don't want you to think this is your birthday present from the family. This is just something extra from me to you for you to spend in any way you choose."

Marielle had never seen bills so large. She gaped at them stupidly, and as Quinn held them out, she backed away.

He mistook her astonishment for pride. "I know giving money to someone is bad taste," he said with a certain amount of shyness. "But I've recently been told that I have very bad taste in women's fripperies. So instead of my buying you something that you would hate, I thought you might buy something for yourself." He grinned sheepishly and pressed the bills into her hand.

She remembered the rose pink dress he had chosen for her in San Francisco, which she'd brought along. It proved he had marvelous taste, far better than Penelope Watson's!

"It's a lot of money," she said uncertainly.

"Please! If your father were giving it to you, you would not hesitate to accept it. Am I right?"

She giggled at the thought, knowing her father would never have handed this much money over to her. When she saw the hurt in his face, she became grave. "I'll show you what I've spent it on."

"You don't have to."

She nodded. "I do. If you were my father, I would want to show you."

Miss Penelope interrupted their talk by sticking her head through the open door of Marielle's room. She was dressed for shopping. Marielle wondered if Quinn had been as generous to his soon-to-be fiancée as he had been to her.

Did Morgan or Marielle wish to accompany her on her jaunt to the shopping district, Penelope wanted to know. Marielle felt that her name had been added simply because Penelope had no other choice.

Quinn declined the invitation on the grounds he had business in Sacramento City that could not be avoided. Marielle declined, saying she wished to have breakfast and poke around the hotel for a while. Then both Quinn and Penelope left her to her own devices, for which she was thankful.

Never had she had so much money to spend on herself. After a quick breakfast, which she hardly touched because of the excitement in the pit of her stomach, she asked the day manager at the desk for directions to the finest couturiere, then hailed a carriage and gave the driver the address.

A Madame Benét greeted her at the door of a studio that was nearly empty of furniture. The couturiere was of indeterminate age and was dressed in a fashionable but simple dark gown. A younger helper, who seemed also to be French, sat idly at a long, empty sewing table. A large folding screen for fittings stood at one side of the room. Bolts of many-hued materials were stacked one on top the other almost to the ceiling. A large mirror dominated another wall, in front of which stood several dressmaker's dummies, draped with cloth.

Marielle quickly explained what she had in mind; she wanted the most beautiful party dress that was ever created. "Can you do it for me?" she asked the French dressmaker.

"*Naturellement,*" she said in a heavy French accent. "When will you need this fabulous party dress?"

"This afternoon," Marielle said.

The couturiere threw up her hands. "Impossible. It takes weeks to make a fine dress. Besides, I am returning to France. I, Francine Benét, used to work for the House of Worth in Paris. I was appreciated there. Here, you Americans are not ready for me."

"I am ready for you," Marielle said calmly.

"But it is impossible, I tell you. There is much work involved. Have you never been fitted for a dress before, young lady?"

"No," Marielle said. "But I have money." She held out a crisp one-hundred-dollar bill.

"Not enough," the woman said contemptuously. "Besides, there is no time to even cut, much less sew, a fine garment such as you describe."

Marielle took out a second hundred-dollar-bill and put it next to the first one.

Madame Benét contemplated the two bills for a long time. "Do you like white?" she asked.

"What are you thinking?" Marielle wanted to know.

"I have a white wedding gown made from layers of the finest lace and silk. It's finished. But I lost my client before the wedding."

"Did the bride die?"

"*Mon Dieu, non!* She ran off with a miner who arrived in Sacramento City from his diggings with suitcases filled with gold."

"Show me the dress," Marielle said with authority.

Madame Benét went behind a screen and rolled out a dressmaker's dummy with the most beautiful white lace dress Marielle had ever seen.

Six hours later, the dress hung in Marielle's room at the hotel. Madame Benét had cut the long sleeves off and made small caps that fell over Marielle's smooth, round arms. The neck was changed completely, again by the magic of Madame Benét's shears. It was now low and at the base of its deep décolletage was a garnet and gold brooch. The waist fitted tightly around Marielle's tiny middle, and the hemline had been let out to accommodate Marielle's height.

Marielle spent the entire time with Madame Benét and her helper, and made herself useful as they sewed and talked. She left only to get a boxed lunch so that they need not stop for food. Afterwards, when the dress was perfect, she went out with the dressmaker, and together they purchased accessories: Elbow-length white kid gloves and white kid slippers, a white silk reticule, and garnet eardrops that matched the brooch. Marielle's final purchase was a white fox capelet that covered her about the shoulders.

When she looked at herself in the mirror, she saw an extraordinarily enchanting young lady, beautifully gowned. She sparkled with happiness. It was worth it every penny she'd spent. After everyone had seen her at her eighteenth birthday party, no one would ever think of her as a child again.

She thanked Madame Benét and kissed her on the cheek. "Don't go back to Paris. Stick it out here. We need you more than you know," she told the ingenious dressmaker.

She hid everything in the armoire of her hotel room until the night of her birthday dinner. She knew she would look beautiful for the celebration. But not only that, she would be so clever and so scintillating that every man in the room would want to possess her. And of all the men present, it would be Quinn who would want her the most.

Chapter Twenty-one

That night they went to see John Wilkes Booth play the lead in a new melodrama called *The Marble Heart*. He turned out to be a nervous, inconsistent actor who resembled his brother, Edwin, but who was much handsomer. He, like Ted, was of small stature, but his facial features were even and smooth, and he had thick, dark, wavy hair, glorious sad eyes of intense brown, and a jet black mustache.

For the auspicious opening, Marielle sat proudly in the elegant box that Quinn had reserved for the family. After the performance was over and the applause had died down, the Quinn group went backstage to visit with the youngest Booth. It was theatrical tradition, Marielle informed the Quinns gravely.

When he was introduced to Marielle, John Wilkes Booth made a deep, sweeping bow and kissed her fingers tenderly. He acted as if he had known her all his life, but he was very different from her dear Ted, and even more different from the businesslike June Booth, both of whom she considered family. Instinctively, Marielle could see that John was ambitious, determined to become a star.

"Teddy has mentioned you often and with great affection," he told her. "In fact, it was I who insisted that June visit you and try and coerce you into playing Ophelia and Juliet with me in San Francisco."

Marielle opened her mouth to tell him why she hadn't been able to oblige him, but saw the frown on Quinn's face. She held her tongue and told John Wilkes that she hoped there would be other splendid opportunities for both of them.

On an impulse, she invited him to her dinner party the day after tomorrow. At first, he looked disappointed. "I have a performance to give." Then he brightened. "But it will be my honor to attend after the performance is over. May I?"

"I am the one who will be honored," Marielle murmured.

The next evening, after watching Mrs. Sinclair play Desdemona in *Othello*, Marielle extended an invitation to the actress to attend her birthday party, as well. Like John Wilkes Booth, Catherine Sinclair accepted.

Sooner than she wished, Quinn said it was time they return to the hotel. Since Mrs. Sinclair had opened a bottle of champagne for her guests, and everybody was partying, Marielle was sad that they had to leave, but she kept silent and went along with his wishes.

As the carriage brought them to the hotel, Quinn jumped out and ran ahead to the front desk before the ladies could alight. By the time they were in the large, handsome lobby of the hotel, Quinn had returned though, leading them upstairs to their sitting room. As he was about to reach the door, Marielle heard the tinkling peals of childish laughter. When the door was thrown open, Lotta Crabtree flung herself into Marielle's arms as her mother stood behind her and beamed.

Marielle's arms went around the little girl, and she swept her up, hugging and kissing her with delight. Then she spun her around and they both laughed and hugged and kissed each other again. After she had greeted Mary Ann Crabtree affectionately, she went back to Lotta and the two danced around the room, laughing and giggling over nothing but the joy of finding each other again.

The surprise, according to Mary Ann, was from Quinn, who had contacted them in San Francisco and arranged everything. He was paying all expenses for the Crabtrees' entire stay in Sacramento, and had paid for their round-trip stagecoach fare, as well.

Marielle was overcome with bliss as everyone talked at once. She made her way to Quinn, who was alone by the fireplace stoking the fire. "Thank you," she whispered in his ear. "It's above and beyond anything I expected, and I'm very happy you did it." Her eyes were shiny with tears of joy.

Quinn bent over her, tall and handsome, and just a little bit forbidding in his austere evening clothes. He kissed her lightly on the forehead. "I am pleased I did well. I wasn't sure what would make you happy. But perhaps I am beginning to understand your character after all."

* * *

Since all the people for whom she felt love and esteem were coming to the party, Marielle became more nervous as the hour for the big event approached. It was the same feeling she experienced moments before a performance as the curtain was ready to go up.

The white lace party dress was perfect. She decided to wear her hair long and falling loosely down her back. An hour before it was time to meet everyone in the sitting room, she was ready. She put on her white kid gloves, adjusted her garnet necklace and eardrops, put a mirror and a handkerchief into her lace reticule, and sat in front of her vanity table mirror to study the effect. The capelet waited for her on the bed. Marielle sat quietly and hardly dared to breathe. She was afraid the beauty she saw in the mirror would disappear, and the young girl with the chaotic red hair would take her place.

Lotta Crabtree was the first to knock on Marielle's door. The little girl wore a short, fluffy, pale pink dress and white stockings with little, black dancing slippers. Her pale red corkscrew curls jumped up and down deliciously every time she moved her head. Her freckles covered the tip of her tiny nose and were sprinkled liberally over her round cheeks. Her pert little face never stopped smiling. Mary Ann Crabtree followed her into the room shortly afterwards. She looked festive in a metal blue taffeta dress. When they had finished complimenting Marielle on her dress, they left her to join the others in the sitting room.

The next person to come and see her was Quinn. When she opened the door and stood before him, his eyes told her she had made a wise choice.

"You look like an alabaster princess in a fairy tale," he said softly. "I have never seen you look more dazzling—and more feminine." His eyes drank in her sparkle. Suddenly she saw herself the way he did, and felt more beautiful than ever.

Quinn, too, looked more handsome than she had ever seen him. For the occasion, he was dressed in a new three-piece suit of dove gray. The color brought out the gray in his eyes and made them seem even brighter than usual. A white, highly starched, ruffled shirt poked out of his matching dove gray waistcoat, and his highly polished black boots hugged his long, muscular legs up to his knees.

Involuntarily, the thumping in her heart started up. She tried to stop it, sure he heard its every thud.

At that moment Rio popped his head through the open doorway of the room, then stepped inside to see for himself how Marielle looked. Wearing new evening clothes with ruffled white linen, Rio was as handsome as his brother, but, somehow, even with the new dark suit, still flamboyant. "You are absolutely gorgeous. Let's go and show them what we got hidden out there at the Double Raven."

The light-hearted mood changed as Penelope stopped by the open door. She took one look at Marielle, and then pursed her lips. "I'm afraid the dress will not do at all," she said quietly.

The two men next to her, so tall and broad-shouldered that they seemed to fill the entire room, stood silently by, a look of astonishment on their faces.

"The neck is much too low for decency. It is absolutely unsuitable for a well-bred young lady," she said, addressing Quinn and not the others. She turned back to Marielle. "I'm sorry, my dear, but you'll have to change."

"I have nothing else. And there's nothing wrong with it," Marielle said, aghast at the thought of not wearing the new frock.

"Only that it shows everything God gave you to anyone who wants to see. It is utterly indecent."

"Wait a minute . . ." Quinn cut in.

Penelope smiled coolly at him. "You employed me yourself to make her a properly brought-up young lady. Please, Morgan, let me do my job."

Quinn looked very unhappy. He paced up and down the small room. Suddenly, he stopped. One of his eyebrows lifted, and Marielle thought she saw a flicker of mischief in his eyes. "Put on that fur thing," he said to her, pointing at her capelet.

She took the little white fur and covered her shoulders with it. Quinn and Rio smiled broadly.

Marielle held her breath.

Penelope gave Marielle a sharp look and turned to Quinn. "Well . . . I suppose . . ." she said, giving her consent begrudgingly.

"Then it's settled. Let's go," Quinn said.

As they left for the sitting room, Rio gave forth a hearty guffaw and even Quinn could not hide a smile.

* * *

The dinner was a huge success. There was croustade of oysters to start, followed by Cape Cod duck with apple-onion stuffing. An unusual green salad with a mild dressing was served after the main course in order to clear the palate, and for dessert there was a delicious coffee mousse. Champagne was served all during the meal, with toasts from everybody. During dinner a four-piece orchestra played in the background. Afterwards there would be dancing, but first Marielle was to open her gifts: a string of creamy graduated pearls with earrings to match from Carmel, an elaborately worked saddle with hand tooling and silver from Rio, an impressive leather Bible presented by Miss Penelope, and a new make-up box, compliments of the Crabtrees.

At last, Quinn said his gift for her was ready to be presented. "But it's outside," he told her, and led her to the window of the dining room. In the street she saw nothing but a horse hitched to a post. It was a glorious horse with a long-flowing silver mane and tail. Then she understood. The animal was hers.

She ran outside and threw her arms around the horse's neck. It was an Arabian Palomino, a very rare type of horse. The mare was perfect not only in conformation, but in color. She was golden. She had the prominent dark eyes and the underlying dark skin of the Arabian, and the breed's graceful body lines as well. Her head was wedge-shaped, wide at the forehead and tapering to a muzzle so fine the creature could have sipped water from a fine China teacup. She was a spectacular golden creature with the sheen of a brand new copper coin, not quite as bright as Marielle's hair, but almost. Marielle loved the animal the moment she set eyes on her and decided instantly to name her Lady.

It was really a joint present from everyone on the Double Raven, Quinn told her. She now owned one of the rarest horses in California. She could do anything she wished with the horse, including breeding her. In the meantime, she would have to learn how to treat and handle the magnificent animal.

As they returned to the private dining room, which had been cleared for dancing, Marielle saw Catherine Sinclair and John Wilkes Booth, in separate carriages, arriving from their respective theatres. For an escort, Mrs. Sinclair had her leading man, Henry Sedley, in tow.

At that moment the orchestra started up, and Marielle found Rio standing next to her. Unexpectedly he bent down, unpinned the frog closing holding the fur capelet together, and pulled it from her shoulders. "It's too hot, beauty, to dance in your fur." He grinned and then disappeared in the crowd to deposit the capelet on a chair. Marielle looked after him gratefully and before she could even catch her breath she was swept up into the arms of Quinn for the first dance. He looked down at her shining face and held her closer. "You look very beautiful."

The music was very romantic. Marielle danced around the room in Quinn's arms as if in a dream. Morgan Quinn! Quinn, the man whose face she kissed and whose body she held in every one of her most vivid fantasies. She wanted to tell him that tonight was theirs.

Henry Sedley cut in and she returned to reality. She was sorry to lose Quinn's firm body moving her gracefully around so she did not have to think or act or do anything but float like a white flower on a pool moving toward the shade of contentment. But the moment would return. She would make it return at the right time.

Rio returned without her fur capelet and cut in on Henry Sedley. Carmel's second son danced better than any other man in the room, including his older brother. Marielle whirled around in his arms, feeling like a weightless madonna in her glittering white dress. She saw him look down at the open expanse of her breasts and grin. Her hand flew to her bosom, but he grinned even more. She gave up, and gave him her hand back so they could continue their whirls around the room.

Next John Wilkes Booth cut in. Although he was short, he was agile and strong, and she enjoyed dancing with him. "Ted mentioned that you were a beauty, but he did not say you were an angel from heaven."

She was just as tall as he, and it was difficult not to find her face very close to his. He took advantage of her position and held her even closer. "We must work together as soon as possible. We'll sell out everywhere we play. Consider the advantages and let me know. I can arrange a long tour if you can escape your keepers." He glanced in the general direction of Morgan and Rio, then turned back and gave her a flashing smile.

She tried to pull away again, but he continued to twirl her around the room even when one number ended and another began. Rio cut in and she relaxed. But Rio was not amused with John Wilkes. As his face filled with anger, Marielle tried to placate him. "Rio. He doesn't mean any harm. He's just that way. Some actors are not as nice as others."

"Just say the word," he told her, "and I'll take him outside and finish him off." By the look on his face, he meant it.

"Don't do anything rash and spoil my birthday, Rio. Please. Besides I'm thirsty from all this dancing. Will you please get me some fruit punch? I'll wait here for you and catch my breath." She gave him her most beseeching smile.

"If you say so," he replied, and went in search of liquid refreshment. When he returned with the punch, his anger was over and his face smooth and carefree. "I know a secret that I can tell you, if you'll give me a loving smile."

"Really? What is it?" She gave him a smile, dimpling prettily as she did.

"Come with me . . . but be quiet or we'll be found out." He took her by the elbow and led her outside.

In a corner, hidden by the darkness of the night, stood Quinn and Penelope talking softly. They were so absorbed in what the other was saying, they never noticed Rio and Marielle. After several more minutes of animated but hushed talk, Miss Penelope pulled herself up on her tiptoes, put her arms around Quinn, and kissed him.

Marielle turned away before she could see whether Quinn kissed Miss Penelope back.

Rio led her away, a grin on his face. "Worthwhile sight, don't you think? They're getting ready for the big day. Maybe I should be kissing you." He tried to pull her to him, but she pushed him away huffily. "You touch me, Riordan Pagonne, and I'll tell your mother."

"No you won't," he said slyly. "But I'll wait. You're the only gal who's worth it."

Just before midnight, a large birthday cake was wheeled in from the hotel kitchen. It had eighteen candles on it. Marielle made her wish and cut the first slice.

Afterwards, at the insistence of the crowd, Lotta and she sang together. Lotta was only too happy to pull Marielle up to the orchestra and perform the little act they had once put together just for fun. But Marielle could think only of the kiss she had recently witnessed, and found it difficult to perform. Still, the trouper in her came out, and after the first song she began to have fun.

The audience was enchanted. John Wilkes, especially, did not take his eyes off Marielle and made it plain that he was smitten. Rio, as usual, seemed hypnotized by her talents. Even Morgan and Penelope, standing side by side, watched with interest.

To end the entertainment, Marielle performed solo. She sang the little poem by Thomas Campion with which she had made her theatrical debut on the *Andrew Jackson*.

> *There is a garden in her face,*
> *Where roses and white lilies grow;*
> *A heav'nly paradise is that place,*
> *Wherein all pleasant fruits do flow.*
> *There cherries grow which none may buy,*
> *Till "cherry-ripe" themselves do cry.*

Her honeyed singing voice rose above the music as she sang. The room was utterly quiet when she was finished. The orchestra stopped playing. Then everyone began to applaud, including the musicians and waiters.

Marielle stood quietly with her head bowed and accepted the homage. From under her dark lashes, she sought Quinn's approval. He stood slightly apart from Miss Penelope, his face white and tense and unhappy. He was the only person in the room not applauding.

But he remembered. Marielle was absolutely certain, as she looked into those stark, intense eyes, that he clearly recognized her song from long ago.

Chapter Twenty-two

The birthday party was over. The guests had left. Mary Ann had taken little Lotta up to bed, and the family gathered together before retiring for the night. The next day they would return to the Double Raven.

Everyone had finished saying good night to each other. When it was Quinn's turn to say good night to Marielle, he kissed her lightly on the forehead the same way he had earlier in the evening and said, "I hope you enjoyed your party." He sounded very sad.

"It was the second-best birthday party I ever had," she said softly, referring to the birthday on board the ship.

His tender expression told her he understood, but he turned away and left her nevertheless.

After a formal good night, Rio whispered to her. "Don't go to bed. I have another surprise for you. Things are about to pop, believe you me."

Before Marielle could finish the words, "What are you talking about?" he was gone with a wink and one finger over his lips.

She wondered what Rio was up to. Knowing him, it had to be mischief of some kind; nevertheless, back in her room, she changed into her travel dress instead of her nightclothes. Her blood was still racing from the evening's excitement.

About an hour after everyone had retired, Rio tapped on Marielle's door. She opened it cautiously and let him in. He had changed his clothes and was dressed for the outdoors.

"I couldn't get your horse for you. It's already on its way to the ranch. We'll have to ride together on mine. Are you ready?"

"Where are we going?"

"Ssshh!"

"I want to know, Rio. Before we leave this room."

"They're eloping tonight. They've gone off with each other."

Marielle's eyes opened wide. "Morgan and Penelope?"

"Who do you think?"

Marielle's stomach did a somersault; it was not a good feeling. "Why are you telling me? It's really none of my business. Or yours." She tried not to show the deep hurt inside her.

"Because I thought, *maybe*, just *maybe*, you'd have enough interest in our family to want to be part of something like an elopement. Besides, I think we ought to see how it's done. For when we elope."

"We're not eloping, Rio."

"Well . . . *maybe* yes . . . *maybe* no. But we'll be going to Morgan's wedding if you can get a move on."

She let him talk her into it. Why? Was it merely morbid curiosity . . . or was there something wrong with her to let one man hurt her so much? She could not think straight; she allowed Rio to handle everything and followed him out of the hotel and into the cold, where his horse was saddled and waiting.

"We'll catch up quick. They took a two-seater." He swung onto the saddle with speed and grace, and lifted Marielle up behind him. She held on while he rode off into the cold night, her body becoming numb from the chill in the air, and her heart even more numb from the pain of losing Quinn to another woman. Didn't they know he was hers? That he belonged to her?

Every now and then Rio dismounted and found the trail of the two-seater. He had no problem tracking them. The pair were so intent on talking as the two-seater sped along, they never noticed they were being followed very closely. Marielle half wished Rio would lose them. It did not seem right to be spying on lovers about to be wed.

Very soon they arrived at their destination: a large, ramshackle house built on a stiltlike platform in a secluded area not too far from the outskirts of Sacramento.

From a distance, Marielle saw Quinn secure the two-seater to a hitching post close to the house. There were other tethered horses, another two-seater, and a buckboard, as well. Quinn helped Miss Penelope down, and together they ran into the lighted house.

After securing his own horse under a distant tree, Rio crept up to the house with Marielle in tow. They had to circle the building in order to see into the kitchen, where a large group of men were talking. Some were standing and some were seated around a rickety kitchen table when Quinn and Miss Penelope arrived. She was the only woman present. Some of the men wore dark business suits, now dusty from their ride from town; others were dressed in work-clothes or riding gear. One of the men was black, young and muscularly built. He was wearing a large-patterned checked suit. The gathering did not look to Marielle like a wedding party.

A grizzled old man with faded blue eyes and faded blue overalls made a big pot of coffee and brought it to the kitchen table along with several tin mugs. Everyone settled down as best they could, although many had to continue standing. Miss Penelope was given the best seat in the room because she was a lady, and Quinn sat on a spindle-legged chair next to her. At the last moment, an older black man entered the room and sidled close to the window through which Marielle and Rio were spying. It was the same man whom Rio nearly killed on the day of their picnic. Marielle felt him tense up beside her as he recognized the man. They continued to crouch almost under the back of the old, white-haired black man, and listened to the conversation.

"There is no question that runaway Negro slaves should find safety here in California. Not only that, we must fight to end all slavery everywhere," Quinn said. He got up from his chair and paced back and forth in the small space allowed him.

"How do you propose to do that, Mr. Quinn?" one of the men in a business suit asked.

"No one can do that alone, sir," Morgan replied. "But I know exactly how we can begin our work."

"We're listening," a friendly voice said.

"We've got to make contact with the antislavery coalition back East."

"Ha!" a loud voice interrupted.

Quinn gave the man a sharp look. "We're not the only ones who know what's going to happen very soon. Just as there is going to be a civil war between the states, there are people already preparing for the fight."

"There's this Kansas fellow. What's his name? John Brown, I think," a cattleman said.

"There are many good people, not just Brown," Quinn said.

So that was it. Listening carefully to his words, Marielle suddenly realized how intensely committed to the abolitionist movement Quinn was.

Then everyone started talking at once, about what to do with the thousands of desperadoes who were for seceding from the Union. The men grew more animated as they talked.

Miss Penelope spoke up with her usual soft but authoritative voice. Everyone else stopped talking. "Let us not get away from the subject at hand, gentlemen."

"I believe the lady wants to tell us that we had better unite this community and do all we can, or we shall soon not have a country for which to unite," another man said thoughtfully.

"Aye, aye," the group said as a whole.

"Well, we can start by sending petitions to the legislature. We can see that there are editorials in all the California newspapers to sway the readers. We can send antislavery representatives to Washington. They can lobby for our cause, corner anyone and everyone who will listen." Miss Penelope finished her impassioned little speech and fell silent.

Everyone was silent too. Then the grizzled old man who had made the coffee spoke up. "Don't this take lots of money?"

Morgan faced the group, a serious expression on his face. "My family is united one hundred percent behind the cause of antislavery. I have spoken to my mother, and I am happy to announce that the Double Raven pledges one hundred thousand dollars—in gold— and our time and efforts and the time and efforts of everyone on our ranch."

"Bravo!" Miss Penelope said, and turned in her chair to give Quinn a loving look.

A series of "Ayes," followed from all present, and others started to pledge money or time and effort, or both.

"And any Negro escaping from bondage to the State of California is welcome to come and stay on my family's property until he is properly settled."

"We'll pass the word along and extend the underground railway to the Double Raven," the young black man in the plaid suit said.

Outside, Rio literally got up from his crouched position and looked straight into the window at his brother. So intent were the people in the room, that nobody noticed there was a stranger outside.

Rio shook with anger and took his fist and banged it into a tree. Grabbing Marielle's arm, he pulled her away from the house. "The bastard," he kept muttering from between clenched teeth. "The bastard . . . giving away Double Raven gold to help slaves! He never once asked me. I'm part of the family too. All that gold . . ." His face became stormier as he muttered.

Secretly, Marielle was pleased with the events of the night. The idea of slavery was repugnant to her. And it looked like Morgan and Miss Penelope would not be getting married—at least not tonight. That thought pleased her more than anything until she saw the dangerous look on Rio's face. It was the same look he had when he tried to kill the old black man.

She shivered as he pulled her along back to his horse, all the time muttering into the wind. "They ain't eloping. I expected them to be deep in some soft bed by now. Then you and me could 'a done the same," he said with bitterness as he reached the animal tethered under the tree.

He stopped and looked down at Marielle coldly. She tried to face him squarely as he held on tightly to her wrist. "But we can do it anyway. We ain't going back to the hotel. We'll elope." He scratched his chin and thought out his plans. "In fact, that's a real fine idea. We'll elope. And I know exactly where."

"I'm not going anywhere with you," Marielle whispered. "You will please take me back to the hotel immediately."

"We'll be going in a different direction," he said, the heat of anger growing in his face.

"Get on," he motioned, and didn't wait but pulled her onto the horse. "We're going to get some best men and get ourselves married."

"I refuse to go with you."

"Stop yammering. You ain't got no choice." He took hold and held both her wrists in his big hand cruelly as he adjusted her securely on the horse in front of him.

She turned around and tried to pummel him with her fists. If she could escape and get to the old house before they rode too far away, Quinn would not permit his brother to get away with carrying her off to some godforsaken place and forcing her to marry him. But when Rio took out his *reata* and threatened to bind her hands and feet so she couldn't move, she promised she would not try to escape.

"You got one more chance," Rio said darkly. "Otherwise you get trussed up good like a heifer ready for branding. And if you're thinking you might get word somehow to Morgan, you're wrong."

She turned around and looked at him, then became quiet. His eyes were wild, his face set in hard lines. This was the Rio Pagonne who frightened her. This was a man no one could penetrate. It was as if a wall had risen between them. He was a man in turmoil; his reason was terrifyingly distorted.

Instead of turning back to Sacramento, Rio rode off in a different direction. For a while it seemed as if they were heading back to the ranch, but at one fork in the road, Rio turned and they started up toward a summit, going west toward the faraway Pacific Ocean.

It was nearing sunrise, but instead of seeing dawn break, as they reached the summit of the ridge, they were enveloped in a thick fog and driving rain that soon wet them to the skin. Marielle's teeth chattered even though Rio's body shielded her partially from the raw, cold wind. Around her rose cathedrallike sugar pines.

They rode all day long, stopping only once when Rio found a suitable stream. He reined in his horse and helped Marielle onto the ground. Then he threw his leg over the pommel of his saddle and searched the stream with an experienced eye. Finally he found what he wanted, a tiny, rosy stain at the edge of the stream in a secluded spot near some rocks. He pointed it out to Marielle, took a tin cup from his saddlebag and went to the bubbling spot that sang and murmured and gurgled. As he dipped his cup into the red mineral stain, a tiny fountain welled up through a round hole in the rock. He scooped up some water and held it out to Marielle to drink. It was the most delicious sparkling soda water she had ever tasted.

After her thirst was quenched, she looked up in surprise. Rio was smiling at her, that wonderfully crooked smile that all the members of his family could use to such advantage when they wanted. The smoldering look of danger was gone. Once again, he was sweet and childish and adoring.

Opening his saddlebags once again, he pulled out two thick pieces of dried beef jerky. After handing her one of the awful-looking pieces, he refilled the tin cup and sat down to enjoy his meal. Marielle chewed monotonously on her dried strip of meat and watched him warily.

After their brief respite by the stream, they rode on again. Around dusk Rio at last broke the silence. "We're just about there," he said, and spurred his horse on.

Coming out of the fir forest, the first thing that Marielle saw was an elevated, dry slope, hidden on all sides by trees. In open space, fenced off by fir poles, was a campsite. There was a spring on one side of it, and tents and makeshift frameworks with saddle blankets tacked on to them to give privacy. Horses and mules were corralled near the spring, and most of the tents had fires burning in front of them.

Rio rode in to shouts of greetings from the men and women outside their tents. Everybody seemed to know him. He rode straight to the largest tent in the camp and lowered Marielle to the ground after swinging down from his saddle.

Marielle began to recognize familiar faces, faces she had not seen in a long time. At that moment, a man stepped out of the tent. He had shoulder-length black straight hair and olive skin; he wore fancy suede trousers with silver down the outside of each trouser leg. She remembered vividly how she had read that the price on the man's head had been raised because he was accused of every robbery and murder in the northern part of California. Marielle recognized him immediately. It was the infamous bandit, Joaquín Murieta.

Chapter Twenty-three

Joaquín Murieta was a sentimental man filled with the love of old-fashioned romance. Marielle was not able to discover whether he was accused unjustly of murder and mayhem or not, but in her presence she never saw him in anything but a mild-mannered mood, gallant and courteous. He made her feel welcome at once, especially after Rio disclosed they were eloping. Marielle held her tongue. The look Rio gave her was enough for her to know there would be serious trouble if she tried to betray him.

Of course, what she really wanted to do was to throw herself on Joaquín's mercy and explain that she was here against her will, that Rio frightened her and was the last man in the world she intended to wed. But she realized that Joaquín and Rio were old friends, and that the bandit would side with him no matter what. So instead, she decided to bide her time and wait for an opportunity to either talk some sense into Rio or escape.

Joaquín sent one of his men to the closest town to bring back a friendly padre. In the meantime, Marielle would bunk with Rosita, Joaquín's lady, in a special tent they would put up that very day, which would contain the wedding bed for the married couple.

Rosita was a fiery-looking but sweet-natured eighteen-year-old with long, thick, curly black hair and beautifully smooth olive skin. She was very much in love with Joaquín, regardless of the price on his head.

Rosita told Marielle that she used to attend *fandangos* in different towns with only a girlfriend as companion. Joaquín would join her later in the evening, disguised as one of the townspeople, and they would dance the night away without anybody recognizing her lover as the notorious highwayman for whom posses were looking. Somehow she seemed to know her love affair would end in trag-

177

edy, but she was prepared. No matter what happened, Joaquín would always be in her heart. Marielle was impressed.

As the tent was being constructed and a bed with a mattress of clean-smelling balsam leaves was assembled, Marielle began to feel panicky. What would happen after the padre arrived? The entire camp was looking forward to the diversion of a wedding. To them, true love and romance came second only to highway robbery.

Soon Rio disappeared into another part of the camp with the rest of the men to sit in front of a roaring fire, drink rum, and tell stories that made them laugh loudly and remember others even more ribald.

Because the two girls were left alone to their own devices, Marielle wondered if she could confide in Rosita. But as Rosita chattered only of her great love for Joaquín and how wonderful it would be for Marielle and Rio, Marielle decided not to try to tell her the truth. How could she ever make this sweet, simple girl understand her own complex life and feelings and the intricate patterns of behavior that had led up to this particular moment. She couldn't really understand it herself. When Rio was himself, at his best, like right now, Marielle was not afraid of him—but under any circumstances she did not understand him; nor did she love him; nor did she want to marry him. It was his brother she wanted.

She also did not know where he had brought her. The camp seemed to be on a summit and was one that Joaquín Murieta and his men obviously used often as a base of operations. But where was it located? She was sure it was far from any known town that had a sheriff and a jail and a posse. She realized hopelessly that there was no way she could escape without a horse, and without someone who could lead her out of the maze of the forest. It was impossible. There would have to be some other way. Rosita loaned her a change of clothes, but before she could clean up and don the fresh garments, she fell asleep on the bed of sweet-smelling balsam leaves.

She did not know if Rosita spent the entire night next to her, but when she awoke in the morning Rosita was already up and dressed. After a bath in the stream, which was so icy Marielle could not stay in for more than a few seconds, she donned the clothes Rosita had given her the night before. The white low-cut blouse was full and pretty, and the sprigged calico skirt was a bright red glow of color against the backdrop of dark green trees.

For breakfast, there were thick slices of bacon and hot saucy beans and tortillas. The men fed the animals first; the women fed the men and cleaned up afterwards. There seemed to be full equality between the sexes, maybe because women were at such a premium that when they came into the camp they were treated with the greatest respect. Rosita, as befitting Joaquín's lady, was never assigned mess duty, Marielle was told by the proud girl. The women were considered so precious, the men took most of the workloads upon themselves.

Rio visited his bride-to-be after breakfast was finished. She tried to reason with him since he was in good humor.

"I will be missed by the family. They will come looking for me."

"Not necessarily. You see, they'll be missing me too. And they'll know we ran off together."

"They won't know anything of the sort, Rio. They'll come after us," she said, and hoped it was true. "Why don't we go back, please?"

"No!" Rio declared emphatically. "They don't care a cuss where we went. I left a note telling everybody we're eloping. If they look, they'll be looking in all the wrong places. That's why I brought you here," he said complacently.

"It's against the law, Rio. I'm not of legal age. Your brother will never give his consent."

"It'll be too late. You'll not be a virgin after the hitching," he reasoned. "It'll be too darn late for Morgan Quinn to make rules and regulations. You'll be mine."

Marielle turned away. He was not going to change his mind. She decided there and then that as a last resort, she would plead with the man of cloth when he came into camp. Surely a padre, no matter what denomination he was, would not stoop to marry someone who did not wish to make the vows.

In the meantime, she heard Joaquín give orders to butcher a fat calf for roasting, and she saw the women start to prepare for a feast. There was festivity in the air, and romance.

In the evening, just as dusk descended over the thickets of firs and pines surrounding the encampment, the padre arrived on a mule, guided by one of Joaquín's men.

The padre was a large-boned, square-faced man with a dark bushy beard. With his black clothes and wide-brimmed hat, he looked more like a bandit than a man of the cloth. He turned out to be Joaquín's second cousin. Marielle was not sure he would respond when the time came for her to refuse the solemn affirmation of the wedding vows.

Rio, Joaquín, and the padre decided to hold the wedding there and then. There was no time for reflection or talk. Rosita gave her a pretty, white muslin dress with bits of white satin ribbon sewn around the bottom of the skirt and insisted she put it on immediately. Marielle had no choice but to do as she was told.

Rio bathed in the icy stream, and quickly dressed in one of Joaquín's fancy silver-trimmed bolero suits. The outfit was too tight around his shoulders and too short at his ankles, but the groom did not notice and, somehow, managed to look dashingly handsome.

The padre was in a hurry to get the ceremony out of the way. He smelled the wonderful aroma of roasting beef on a spit being turned by one of the men. There was also a keg of rum set up on a wooden crate, just asking to be opened.

Everyone gathered in a large circle with the padre holding his missal and Rio and Marielle in front of him. Joaquín and Rosita stood together behind the bridal couple. They held hands and smiled happily at each other as if they were the ones who were to be joined in holy matrimony.

Marielle began to shiver. There was not a soul in the crowd whom she could call a true friend although everyone was smiling. These were Rio's buddies and were gathered, primarily, to see that their friend got married and was happy.

The ceremony started, and the padre raced along. He talked so fast that there were times Marielle could not understand him at all.

When it was Marielle's turn to respond she squared her small shoulders, straightened her spine, and felt her face drain of all color. Looking directly into the padre's eyes, she said in a small but clear voice, "No! I do *not* wish to get married at this time."

There were loud gasps from the crowd of onlookers and some of the women muttered darkly. But on the whole, her statement created a silence that was thick with layers of wonder. Never had these people heard a bride refuse the vows at this point in the ceremony.

Rio stood stolidly at her side and looked blankly at her face as if he did not understand what was happening.

The padre broke the heavy silence. "Now is hardly the time to become maidenly and bashful. Of course every girl wants to get married."

He continued on with the ceremony as if she had said, "I do," and raced to the finish in record time. He congratulated the couple hastily and started toward the food.

An instant later, as the circle of wedding guests dispersed uncertainly, there was a volley of rifle shots from behind the shadowed fir thickets. The shots came from all four directions, scattering the guests who retreated haphazardly into tents and under buckboards and toward any shelter they could find.

Rio grabbed Marielle and pulled her to the relative safety of a rock formation near the tent that had been set up for them as a honeymoon nest. Then he rolled smoothly into a crouching position and pulled out his gun. The air continued to resound with shots coming from invisible rifles outside the compound. Whoever was laying siege to the camp could see everything by the light of the campfires.

Soon, one by one, the fires were put out by men daring enough to dash out into the line of whizzing bullets. Only one fire remained, the blaze under the roasting calf. Marielle saw Joaquín bravely run the gauntlet and smother the entire calf, coals, and flames with a large blanket. The attackers surrounding the camp continued to shoot at him until he put out the last flicker from the embers and disappeared into the blackness of the night.

When the camp was completely dark, the rifle shots ceased. No one moved for a long time. Rio and Marielle remained crouched behind the rock formation, but heard others creeping around trying to find better hiding places.

"Do you think it's Quinn, coming to bring us back to the ranch?" Marielle asked in a whisper.

Rio laughed a bitter laugh. "T'ain't likely. Too many of them out there." He seemed to be taking the attack in stride, and was at the moment most concerned with keeping Marielle safe from harm. There was no rancor in him as far as the disastrous wedding ceremony was concerned.

Was she or wasn't she married to Rio? She wondered briefly about her marital status as Rio moved over the ground stealthily trying to see outside the dark compound. He did not have to wait long for what he apparently expected.

After the bullets had stopped flying and a deathly silence filled the encampment, a voice from the outside could be heard. It came upon them suddenly, without warning.

"Joaquín Murieta. We have you surrounded," it began. "This is Captain Harry Love. I have a warrant for the arrest of Joaquín Murieta, Manuel Garcia, also known as Three-Fingered Jack, Billy Reis, Claudio Bell, and Joaquín Valenzuela." The speaker paused and then continued. "I have a posse of more'n a hundred mounted rangers and sworn-in deputies. You can't escape."

The disembodied voice floating through the air stopped.

Rio rolled over the dusty ground back to Marielle. "We'll have to stay a while. They don't want us. But it's two to one, and we can't leave Joaquín in the lurch."

"You think your brother is out there? Maybe he's one of the sworn-in deputies?"

"No. Morgan does things on his own. If he found us, he'd be all alone." He looked down at her and stroked her face awkwardly. "We'll get out. But not now. Joaquín needs every gun. You just do like I say and hide from them bullets and you'll be okay."

She could not answer; she could not think. Outside, the wild bullets started again from all directions as if on signal from Captain Love. There were so many and they came so fast that they created bedlam inside the camp. The men did not dare to even light a cigarillo because of the light it would cause. They returned the bullets with bullets of their own, cussing in Spanish and English at not being able to see their target. The noise was deafening but, so far, no one had died.

"Joaquín is wasting bullets," Marielle heard Rio say as one ripped past them and bounced off a rock. She did not know whether the bullet had come from the posse or accidentally from somewhere inside the compound.

After a while, the shots stopped on both sides and again there was that deadly silence that was worse than the din of the fight.

It was the coldest part of the night. Rio raised himself to lean against the rock. As the silence continued, Marielle, still in her thin muslin wedding dress, moved closer to him for warmth. Although he was not dressed for the weather either, he simply did not feel the cold.

She shivered and moved closer still, and Rio took off the fancy bolero jacket he was wearing and put it around her shoulders. She gave him a small smile of gratitude, which she knew he could not see in the dark.

Joaquín and the padre found their way to Rio and Marielle's hiding place. Marielle could not see them, but she could feel their presence and faintly see their outlines against the inky blackness of the rock.

"Once there's light, they'll be coming in. Fast and furiouslike," Rio said to them.

"I already told the men not to waste bullets on what they can't see. We got plenty of food to hold out with for a long time, but they got more ammunition."

"They'll rush us in the morning, first thing. Ain't no such thing as holding out. There's too many of them bastards."

"Maybe," Joaquín said. He sounded worried. "Listen. I brought the padre over for a different reason. My *relative* wants to tell you something." His voice was contemptuous as he used the word "relative."

"Yeh?" Rio asked. "What?"

There was silence from the padre.

"You tell him, you good-for-nothing. Quick." Joaquín's usually soft voice took on a hard quality in the dark.

The voice of the padre came through the blackness. "There was a woman . . ." He trailed off and then continued after spitting a long stream of tobacco juice into the night. "Well . . . lots of women . . . anyway, some important church people got themselves involved . . . to make a long story short, I was defrocked. Six months ago, to be exact."

"You'll have to do it again, *hermano*. I'm sorry. I didn't know," Joaquín said, addressing Rio.

Marielle could not keep from smiling to herself in the dark.

Rio let loose a string of wild oaths.

"That means there was *no* wedding?" Marielle asked.

"There was a wedding ceremony, all right. But there was no legal marriage."

"Thank you for letting me know," Marielle said.

"We can do it again some other time soon," Joaquín suggested. "With a padre who is not also a scoundrel."

"We'll do it again," Rio muttered in a disappointed voice.

Marielle did not answer. She heard Joaquín and the padre raise themselves from the ground and move quietly away.

It seemed like she sat for hours against the rock. She was stiff with cold. Her teeth refused to stop chattering. Rio, at her side, calmly took short naps, awakening every now and then and going right back to sleep when he saw that nothing was happening. She could not understand how he could sleep under the dangerous circumstances.

Dawn started to break. A soft early morning light filtered onto the camp. Soon she would be able to see clearly. Several of the horses neighed. Rio awoke in a flash. Then there was the sound of guns, the roar of men swearing and women screaming. The cacophony continued for more than two minutes.

With a whoop of defiance, Rio emptied his Colt six-shooter into the forest of firs. Marielle did not know whether his aim was true, but she heard swearing from beyond the fir trees. Then it was all over.

Quiet settled again over the camp. The troops surrounding the clearing were waiting for broad daylight. Two of the shots from Captain Harry Love's men had hit their marks though, and Marielle could see two men being dragged aside, bleeding and groaning with pain. There would be much death when the sun rose. Love and his Mounted Rangers and deputies were determined to bring the Murieta gang to justice.

She heard a sound behind the rock formation and turned her head. In the pale light she saw a man crawling toward her. He was wearing the long, sheepskin overcoat Marielle recognized. It trailed through the dirt on the ground as he crawled. Stealthily he moved toward Rio and herself. It was Quinn. She knew it even before she could see his face clearly.

She tried to crawl toward him, but he motioned her to stop. She waited where she was until he reached her side. Rio, too, saw his brother. He was not unhappy, and clapped Quinn on the back silently as he reached their sides.

"How'd you get in, man?" Rio asked him.

"The important thing is to get out. Before it gets too light. I think we can do it," Quinn whispered. "I have an extra horse and mule out there."

"Seems like you think of everything. Except one thing. I ain't going. Gotta stick by Joaquín. He's my buddy," Rio said with a stubborn set to his mouth.

"You'll hang with your buddy," Quinn said quietly.

"They'll never get him."

"They will this time. You haven't seen what I've seen outside this camp. Joaquín Murieta is a dead man. They won't give him a fair trial. They won't even give him a chance. They want his blood."

"I ain't leaving him." Rio continued to be stubborn.

"You're putting her life in danger," Quinn said. He pointed at Marielle.

"She'll be all right with me."

"I'm taking her out. If the sun doesn't come up too fast." Quinn's voice was so quiet, Marielle could barely hear it.

Rio reflected for a long time and turned to Marielle. "You want to go with him? He's as mean as a rattlesnake and even more deadly when he strikes—in fact, you'll be in more danger with him than if you stay here."

"There are no decisions for *her* to make. She's going with me," Quinn said. There was a hard glitter in his steely gray eyes.

There was no mistaking the authority in his statement. Marielle's heart hammered wildly in her chest and she moved slowly toward him, away from Rio. Quinn took her cold, little hand in his warm one and settled her temporarily in a safe spot. Then he turned to his brother with concern in his face. "I still say you should come with us. I don't want to see you hang—or be shot down."

Rio turned his eyes on his brother and there was a twinkling flicker of fun in their depths. "I'll catch up with you."

"We'll be traveling fast," Quinn warned.

"It's all right. I'll track you down."

Quinn did not say anything more. He motioned for Marielle to crawl close to him as they started to make their way out of the camp on their hands and knees in order to keep hidden. In just a little while it would be broad daylight, and then the war would begin in earnest. It was now or never.

"I'll leave you a horse. Under the big sugar pine, west of here. About half a mile," Quinn said to Rio. Marielle looked back only once. Rio had turned away from them and was reloading his revolver.

Even as they made their way out of the camp, the bloodshed started. Men shouted orders at each other; some scrambled to new hiding places; a woman's sobs could be clearly heard through the confusion. And all the time there was the shattering noise of rifles as bullets ripped through the air.

Just as Quinn reached back for Marielle to help her through the hidden opening he had made in the fence, she turned and saw the Rangers jumping their horses over the stakes of fir poles, smack into the middle of Murieta's campsite. She froze in terror until Quinn pulled her through the yawning gap and into the forest. He waited patiently while she recovered, shielding her with his body from the mayhem around them. It was a gruesome sight. Murieta's men had become living targets for the well-aimed guns of Harry Love's Rangers. Terrible oaths were mingled with screams of pain. Marielle thought of Rio and a sob escaped her lips. He was doomed.

Silently, they made their way on foot to the horses and the mule, about half a mile away. All the time, Marielle thought someone would try to stop them—if not Captain Love and his Mounted Rangers, then Joaquín Murieta and his fleeing gang members. But no one came, and the noise of men dying echoed in her ears.

Marielle realized that Rio had let her go with Quinn without a struggle because he knew that if she stayed behind she would most likely die.

She found she did not harbor any antipathy toward Rio. On the contrary, she felt great concern for his well-being. He was too troubled a man for her to fathom. He frightened her often; but there was something about him. Inside her was a feeling toward him that she had never felt before. The feeling was maternal—almost as if she wanted to protect him from himself.

And then she wondered what Carmel would do when she was told the news about her youngest son.

Chapter Twenty-four

There were two horses and a mule with a small pack waiting for them exactly where Quinn had told Rio they would be. He untethered his horse and the mule and fastened a *reata* between the two animals so the mule could not wander off by itself.

"You take the mule. It'll be easier riding. I'll lead you out. The second horse stays for Rio. If he gets out, he'll need it more than we do."

"It's cold," Marielle said, hugging her arms to her body as Quinn sat her on the mule.

Quinn opened the pack and took out Carmel's sheepskin jacket. "I figured you'd be cold."

He looked her over critically and shook his head. "Take off that bolero and use it as a head covering. It's going to get colder yet."

She obeyed quietly. It did help to keep her head warm. She wondered how silly she looked to him but she could not tell. He was busy moving them out of the area as quickly and quietly as possible. Marielle had no idea where Quinn was taking her, but it was not important. It was away from the battle.

Several hours afterwards, it began to drizzle and the day grew dark. Quinn told her they were heading toward the Double Raven. At first the drizzle did not seem to matter except that it got colder and the ground got softer, and the animals moved along more slowly as the mud became deeper. But the drizzle soon turned to heavy rain, and the day grew so dark they could not see in front of them. The muddy trail grew hard to follow, and as Quinn led them along they seemed to ride aimlessly. It looked very much like they were lost.

Marielle was afraid it would snow. She had heard terrible stories about people dying of starvation in these very parts, and even freezing to death in deep snowdrifts.

Instead, the heavy rain turned into a downpour. It rained so hard that Marielle's jacket and Quinn's long, trailing, sheepskin overcoat were soaked through almost immediately. It was as if they had stepped into a raging river, except the river poured down from the black skies.

Quinn's wide-brimmed leather hat was added protection for him, but Marielle's bolero became heavy with the rain and weighed her down. She was surrounded by a solid sheet of rain and as time went by found it difficult to see Quinn although he was directly in front of her.

He turned around, and from the height of his horse he had to shout down at her in order to be heard through the sounds of the storm. "I think I know a cabin not too far. If I'm on the right trail, I'll find it soon."

She pointed to the bolero on her head and he saw her dilemma at once, and shouted for her to take the accursed object off. It was completely waterlogged. Pulling off a heavy wool muffler he wore inside the overcoat, he handed it to her. Before she could throw the bolero aside and don the muffler, it became wringing wet and was of no use. She draped it on the neck of the mule to use at a later time. Quinn's inner clothes were drenched too, from opening the sheepskin coat. They continued on without comment, no longer even trying to keep dry. The important thing was to find the cabin.

Tree limbs fell as they rode by, cracking down with frightening force. She wondered if there would be lightning. She had been afraid of lightning ever since she was a little girl. She felt small and unimportant as the elements whipped around her and tried to separate her from Quinn. He looked back at her again and secured the *reata* more tightly.

They had been riding all day and Marielle wondered if they had made any headway. All the trees looked the same to her. She could not understand how Quinn, or anyone for that matter, could find his way in a forest like this.

But just as she thought they were desperately lost and would never find the cabin, if it had ever existed at all, Quinn led her into a clearing. Through the storm, Marielle could faintly make out a crudely built structure ahead of them.

As they got closer, she saw that the cabin was so nondescript she might have missed it altogether if she hadn't been looking for it. Yet there it was, only twenty feet ahead. Quinn, on foot now, led his horse and the mule up to the door of their sanctuary.

The cabin had not been used in a long time by anyone. When Quinn tried to open the door, it stuck. He thrust a muddy boot up, aimed at the middle of the door. It opened readily. Nobody had bothered to put a lock on it. Inside, everything was neat but dusty.

Moments after they passed the threshold of the cabin, the storm burst in all its fury. The rain fell even harder than before, thundering on the roof so loudly that Marielle thought it would come right through. The wind was even louder and fiercer than during their ride. It was dark, and Quinn took a lantern from the pack he brought inside with him and tried to light it. But it didn't work. He found a candle and lit it. The lantern would have to dry before it became useful.

He checked the windows first. They were small but did not let the rain in. Then he double-checked the door, went to the hearth and started a fire. It was not easy. The fireplace had not been used in a long time.

The cabin contained a rough bed, a small wooden table, and one chair in front of the fireplace. One wall was stacked up to the ceiling with firewood. There were cooking utensils, but no food. Miraculously, an uncracked looking glass hung on one of the walls. Quinn opened his pack and removed tins of sardines and hard biscuits and coffee.

Marielle stood in the center of the room and dripped rain onto the floor, and shivered.

Quinn looked at her impatiently as he removed his own sodden overcoat and placed it close to the hearth. "Take off the jacket and put it next to mine. It'll dry eventually. When the fire really gets going."

She did as she was told. Even after she removed the jacket she was dripping wet. Her thin muslin dress was soaked though and stuck to her body like a wet, limp rag. The fire was beginning to warm the room, but she could not keep her teeth from chattering.

They both looked up at the same time as it started to hail. The noise on the roof of the cabin was ferocious. When Marielle looked out the window, she saw why. The hailstones were as large as hens' eggs, icily transparent, and pounding down on the roughly hewn beams so that she was sure it would be destroyed if the storm continued for any length of time. The sounds were sharper and louder than the rifle shots they had left behind.

Quinn seemed satisfied though. "We'll be okay here. It's not luxurious, but it'll do," he said as he drew two heavy wool blankets from the pack. They were slightly damp, but had fared well considering what they had gone through. He threw one at Marielle. "Get your clothes off and put them near the fire. I'm sorry it didn't occur to me you'd be needing a change. I didn't think." He did pull out an almost dry flannel shirt and a pair or trousers for himself.

She looked at him in alarm, shivering even more despite the fire in the hearth. The water continued to drip down her onto the floor. She reflected on whether to follow his instructions or not.

He sat down on the edge of the bed to pull off his muddy boots and saw the rain dripping off his own clothes dampening the bed. Getting up quickly, he moved across the room to the one chair. "You'll catch a cold if you don't dry off," he said matter-of-factly as he passed her. Stopping, he looked at her shivering body and chattering teeth. She looked like a waif who had just been fished out of the ocean.

He stopped at her side and put his hands on her wet hair, running his fingers through the soaking silken strands that fell down her back in wild disarray. "You need a comb," he commented wryly.

Then without being able to stop himself, his hands went down her back until they reached the indentation of her small waist where her long length of hair ended. She shuddered suddenly, but not because of the cold in the room. The part of her body his hands had touched felt fiery hot. She drew away slowly.

"Don't be afraid," he said softly. We'll be fine now that we're here. You look so forlorn and bedraggled . . ." He drew her closer without finishing the sentence.

The wetness of his clothes emphasized the ridges of his muscles as they pressed into her, but the buttons on his shirt dug into her soft breasts, and made her body feel tender and vulnerable; it almost hurt. Still she found herself wanting more of the sweet discomfort.

She could not stop shivering, and his warmth enveloped her regardless of the wetness that went with it. Since she was soaking wet too, the materials of their clothes rubbed against each other as water dripped to form an ever bigger puddle at their feet. The smell of outdoors was still upon him and mingled with the scent that was peculiarly his own. It was a peaceful and comforting feeling which, somehow, distressed her more because she knew it would not last.

She tried to will herself to push him away. All the time she found her hands moving toward the back of his neck until they clasped, her fingers entwined, above the collar of his wet shirt.

Instead of breaking away from him, she drew him closer and moved her parted tender lips up to his. It was an exquisite madness she could not deny herself.

He had no choice but to draw her closer, and as he did her body felt his. The hard muscular leanness became a hard wall of tangible strength against which she could relax and withdraw from the peril of the outside world. She wanted to get closer still, to meld into him, if that were possible.

She wanted safety. But as he held her, his lips claimed hers so urgently she could scarcely breathe through the embrace. What they were doing was dangerous because before he was finished he would reject her once again, she was sure.

The tension between them marked the beginning of a game that destroyed her every time they played. Each tried to master his own needs. He wanted her as much as she wanted him, she felt, but he was stronger, and cast reluctantly in the role of her guardian. She, just as reluctantly, played the role of his ward. But the game would continue as long as he felt pledged to substitute for her father. She wondered how it was possible *not* to remind him by some word or deed that a dying man had changed the course of his life for the next few years.

She wiped all thoughts from her head, and abandoned herself to his touch. He was like a wild, forceful fury to which she clung in reckless yielding. But even as he tried to deny his own feelings for her by thrusting her aside, she heard a great intake of breath and saw a look of intense desire overwhelm the features of his handsome face.

She would not let the game take over again. She made her way back to his side quickly, before he could gain control. But he turned away immediately, and when he turned back she saw his face had changed and taken on the look of granite she knew so well.

She trembled, came even closer and dared to look into those angry gray eyes fringed with dark lashes. She did not like what she saw. All warmth had fled from those eyes, which were fast becoming glacial.

"Do you think I've rescued you from the arms of my brother in order to have you for myself?" he asked.

"I didn't ask for any help from you."

"I noticed. Those men are wanted throughout the entire State of California. They are bandits. Criminals."

"Does that go for your brother too?" She looked at him and tried to judge just how angry he was with her.

"Don't talk about my brother. I have nothing more to say about that. Besides, I didn't think you'd be so unhappy you'd run off with him." He backed away from her as if to escape the wiles of a wanton lady of the streets. At the same time, he was very angry.

"I did not run off with Rio."

"What do you call what I just got you out of? I can't go through life getting you out of trouble. You sure were happy to see me back there. Whether you realized it or not. What happened? Did you change your mind about Rio after you spent some time with him?"

"You insufferable cad. Are you implying that anything happened between Rio and myself?"

He lifted a dark eyebrow and gave her a sardonic smile. He did not need to ask; the look implied all.

She was just as angry as he. "Why don't you ask me what happened? I just might tell you." For some perverse reason, she wanted to get him angrier than he already was.

"I'm not going to ask you anything. If you want to run off with every man who crooks his little finger at you, it is going to make *my* life very difficult. The fact is, I am very disappointed in you. But I'll just have to work harder to keep you at home in the future."

"And what if I really and truly loved Rio and really and truly wanted to marry him? How long do you think you could stop me?"

He looked sad and tired. "Only till you're twenty-one and know your own mind. Rio cannot make you a good husband."

"Don't be too sure!"

"I will not make any further comment on the subject, nor will I give my consent, and you cannot marry without it. You can't do anything without my permission. When will you learn? I'm tired of fighting with you." He took the blanket she was still holding in her hand and put it around her shoulders over the thin dress that was beginning to dry. Then he stepped back and looked at the effect and smiled briefly, that wonderful smile of his which, unfortunately, always ended too soon. Then he sought the chair by the fire, and after settling down, looked her over again.

"What about Miss Penelope?" she demanded waspishly.

"What about Miss Penelope?"

"She is in love with you. Rio says you are to marry her."

"Do you believe everything Rio tells you?"

"He has never lied to me," she said, thinking of the story about the gold which she did not believe at first.

"Again I tell you, I will not make any comment. The subject of Miss Penelope . . . is closed. She is your tutor, and it is none of your business what goes on between your tutor and your guardian." His face was dark with anger.

"Why do you hate me so much?" she whispered.

"I don't hate you." But now, for one second, it seemed that if he didn't hate her, at least he was bored.

She approached the chair on which he sat, staring moodily into the fire. She knelt down in front of him, suddenly becoming dizzy with desire for him to touch her. She twined her arms around him.

"I love you, Morgan," she said very softly. "But you're so mean to me. You treat me as if I was a piece of fine furniture or a thoroughbred horse. You're so ready to spend a lot of money to protect your investment. *Take care of Marielle*, but never show her any kindness or compassion." She gave him soft, small little kisses he did not have to time to reject.

"You're so beautiful," he sighed, letting his gaze linger longingly over her as the blanket covering the thin muslin dress fell to the floor. "And you're so wrong about so many things."

He took her gently in his arms and cradled her body to his. She shivered from his touch, not from the cold. But he did not know, and picked up the blanket and covered her as she sat cuddled in his lap.

She moved her body as close to his as she dared. She needed his arms around her, needed his touch so desperately.

He smiled down at her. "You are so beautiful and such a miscreant girl, or woman, or whatever it is that is in between." But, at least, he did not push her away this time. Instead, he picked her up in his strong arms and placed her tenderly on the hard bed after first spreading the blanket over the old mattress. She was afraid to let go of him, afraid he would disappear or revert to rejection. But he sat down next to her, removed her arms from around his neck and still did not push her away.

He kissed her, at first tenderly—fondling her body as his lips claimed hers and deftly removing the still damp muslin dress at the same time. She was left in her white cotton chemise. He gravely removed the simple, chaste garment, examined its virginal simplicity with amusement, and hung it near the fire to dry.

Her eyes closed as he dried the last of the raindrops from her face and her body with one edge of the blanket. She could feel his light touch, carefully drying her and making her comfortable and warm before he removed his own damp clothes and lowered himself onto the bed with her.

"Is this what you want, little Marielle? What you crave?" she heard him whisper as his hands and lips sought her nakedness.

Luxurious wantonness crept through her body as his hands searched and found all the little secret parts of her she was always surprised he knew so much about. Her mind was not as sure of his motives as she was of his hands, nevertheless she simply let go and determined to accept the madness of the moment. If this was the last time they made love, at least she would always remember what it was like.

She opened her beautiful, blue eyes so she could see everything, know everything he did. She stretched her arms around his hard muscles and returned his mounting passion, straining against him as her hands sought to find the places on his body that would make him feel the same way she did.

The pace of his lovemaking changed. He became a pulsing, perfect specimen of maleness, able to fire her to dizzying heights as her body accepted all the different delights he offered her.

"I love you, Marielle," he whispered into her ear before his lips sought her white breasts with their little, hard, pink nipples. "I love you," he whispered as his lips bent to her belly, the delicate inner sides of her thighs, and the bud of dark rose inside the red triangle of down that opened with delight to his fingers and flowered to the touch of his moist mouth.

"I cannot wait too long, my love," he murmured. "We will do it again, later." His muscular thighs caressed open her slender legs and he entered her deeply and settled her body so that she fit into his.

She moaned softly and gave herself up to the ecstasy of letting go and becoming one with him. The feeling that swept through her entire being was unmistakable, the end result of the mysterious wonder that only two people who give their bodies completely to one another can share. He held her tightly and let her wrap herself in the pleasure he was giving her, and shared it with her in a storm of tingling release. They were one. She closed her eyes and hoped it would never end.

Afterwards, she lay quietly and lovingly, naked in his arms, the heat from the fire keeping them both warm as she basked in the glow of his tenderness.

"You have the ability to set me on fire," he told her as he kissed her slowly on her graceful neck. "I battle with myself each and every night so that I don't tear down your bedroom door. I cannot sleep. I stay awake all night, pacing the floor of my room. But it's no use. When I finally fall asleep, I dream of you. I am a man obsessed.''

He kissed her eyes as he looked at her longingly, and talked some more. ''Marielle . . .'' the way he said her name made it sound like music. ''I cannot go on this way. I am afraid of the consequences. I will have to send you away. I will send you to a good finishing school. I promise you it'll be the finest school in the East. Only until you're twenty-one. I absolutely cannot have you staying in the house so close to me. Especially not after this. It's wrong. I'm your guardian. You are my ward.''

She half got up into a sitting position. ''What?'' she said stupidly. Through it all she realized that he was doing exactly the same thing he had done before. He was rejecting her. Their impassioned meetings melded them together for a short time, but always ended on this same note of rejection. How dare he tell her this minutes after he made love to her? And why? Why did he want her and then not want her? Why did he yearn for her and then thrust her aside? Why did he lust for her and then refuse to sate his seething loins?

With an angry toss of her head, Marielle sprang at him from her sitting position, meaning to give him a piece of her mind. Instead, she found herself using her small, balled-up fists in a fit of fury against the one person whom she wanted to love her unconditionally, and to keep her at his side forever. He was going to send her away after tonight? After saying he loved her? After admitting she drove him crazy?

She hit him as hard as she could with her fist, and as he turned on the bed and ducked, the fist connected with his eye; he let out a loud oath as he grabbed her hands and pinned them behind her. They faced each other, so close their heartbeats were one, and gazed at each other with fury throbbing painfully between them.

Marielle could tell that his left eye would soon start to discolor, and suddenly it seemed hilarious that she, half his size, could wound him so badly as to mark him for at least a week or two. Actually she wanted to cry, but she would not give him that satisfaction, so she allowed herself to laugh instead.

''What's so funny?'' His white teeth flashed and gritted together as he asked the question.

Through the pain of her hurt, Marielle laughed harder and his grip became more cruel.

"It's your eye. I've given you a black eye." She pulled him out of bed and over to the looking glass hanging on the wall.

He examined the eye with interest and turned back to her. She stood naked next to him, wondering how badly his wound hurt.

He smiled wryly. "You don't look too great either," he said. "Like a drowned mouse."

The smile left his face as his gaze roamed down her nude body and drank in her beauty. Without thinking, he gathered her into his arms. Without needing to think, she entered his embrace. She felt the hardness of his body. His face was very close to hers. He made love to her again, in front of the fireplace. Sweetly, powerfully, slowly. Beautifully. The glow from the hearth played over their already flushed bodies.

She smiled every time she looked at his blackening eye and kissed it tenderly. He savored her body over and over again and helped her taste a delicious feast of delicate physical delights that she did not know existed.

The storm continued outside, and inside he stacked more wood on the hearth and taught her that his body could be induced to supply a diversity of carnal pleasure if she used it as he used hers. She was the perfect student, clever and willing and unafraid. She discovered she had as much female strength as he had male potency. Physically, she decided, they were a perfect match. He confirmed it over and over again without needing to say a word.

The storm continued for twenty-four hours, and while it lasted there was no way to continue on to the Double Raven. Quinn braved the outdoors only long enough to feed the horse and the mule; when he returned he simply put more wood on the fire and closed the door tight against the raving elements. They stayed in the snug cabin, eating sardines from the tins he carried with him, munching on dry biscuits, and drinking black coffee that he made in a kettle hanging on the hearth. Breakfast and dinner were exactly the same and tasted delicious.

Every moment was paradise to Marielle—except for the thought that hurtled through every one of their tumultuous encounters: he was going to send her away to school when they returned to the ranch. She would not see him for a long, long time.

What would happen then? She'd be in some terrible finishing school, and he would marry the determined Penelope Watson and forget all about her. It all seemed clear to her and marred the otherwise perfect moments. If and when he allowed her to return to the ranch, it would be Rio who would be waiting to marry her, not Morgan. That is, if Rio were still alive by then.

But the rain continued on, and Quinn and she were alone, and when he took her in his arms for another journey into joys that made her blood boil and her heart pound, she knew she was ready to give up all for him and the great pleasure they felt together.

The following day, in the late afternoon, the storm ceased and the rain died down to a dim drizzle once again. Quinn looked at her seriously. "By tomorrow morning we should be able to start back to the ranch," he said.

Marielle nodded her head unhappily. She understood what that meant. She understood they had only one more night together before it was all over. What she could not understand was why such happiness must end.

Shortly afterwards, as she lay in his arms, their limbs mingled and their skin touching, she brought up the subject. "But if you love me so madly—and I love you the same way—why do we have a problem? Surely you can give permission for me to marry *you*. Why have you never offered to marry me yourself?"

"I've told you long ago," he said, kissing the tip of her nose. "I am not at liberty to marry you—or anyone else. I have obligations that must be fulfilled first. Before I settle on my future, I must settle more important matters. I don't know how long I will be able to remain on the ranch. Or if I'll ever return. It is a big property. My mother is getting old. Rio is not willing . . . or capable," he added reluctantly.

"Does it have anything to do with your *special* cause? Your antislavery cause? That war you think will come about?"

"What do you know about that?" he asked, suddenly moving apart from her like a wary animal.

"I was outside the window at the farmhouse near Sacramento. I heard everything."

His face set in hard lines as he backed off the bed. "You've been spying on me?"

"I also know about the gold. Rio showed me where it is. I hate it. It's causing you and Rio to destroy each other."

"What you have done is malicious as well as dangerous. And Rio had no right to put your life in jeopardy. But you are to blame more than he. You should never have consented to run away with him."

"I would do it again," she said fiercely. Obviously he did not believe her story that she had *not* run away with Rio. "At least Rio doesn't treat me like a wicked child."

"Rio is not like you and me. Rio is different. And Rio wants you for himself. You must not be taken in by Rio. He can be a dangerous man when provoked."

She remembered the incident she had never told Quinn about. When Rio had almost choked her to death. Her hand flew to her throat. She did not need Rio Pagonne, and she did not need Morgan Quinn.

"I promise you. I will run away again. And next time there will be no need for Rio to come with me. I am an actress and I intend to work on the stage. I will be as rich as you. And I will be more renowned."

"That's another thing," he said angrily, stalking her as if she were trying to escape that very moment. "You will have to forget the stage while I am your guardian. It is not what I have in mind for you. I am determined you are going to grow up with the best advantages in spite of your efforts to do otherwise."

"I will never forget the stage," she cried. "My father was an actor all his life, my mother was on the stage, and I intend to follow in their footsteps." She went to the chair near the fire, grandly swept their dry clothes off onto the floor, and picked up her chemise and dress.

She turned back to him willfully. "I shall not go to some fancy Eastern school of your choice. In fact, I'm sure, it won't even be of your choice. It'll be Miss Penelope's choice. No! I shall go to San Francisco and resume my theatrical career. You are a hateful man who wants to make sure I'm unhappy."

"You really have gone too far." He scooped her up as she screeched in anger, sat down on the chair and turned her over on his knee and whacked her on her round, little backside with his open palm. It happened so fast she had no time to yelp until after it was over.

She screamed and tried to squirm away, but he held her down with one strong arm as he whacked her several times more.

"How can anyone so beautiful be so *impudent*?" He punctuated the word by bringing his hand down on her buttocks again.

She screeched at the top of her lungs. It was not the pain, although she certainly felt it. It was the ultimate insult to her dignity. It wasn't until after he stopped that she really began to feel the sting spreading over her bare buttocks.

"Don't you dare ever touch me again," she sputtered, and felt hot tears escaping down her face onto the floor.

He turned her around and set her upright. His eyes narrowed as he watched her take her chemise off the floor and then collapse, mortified, onto the bed with her face in the pillow. In a matter of minutes, the pillow was damp with her tears.

She tried to sit up but her buttocks stung too much so she stood up, put on the chemise and turned face down again. The tears continued to come as Quinn sat in the chair and watched her.

"I don't think I've really hurt you," he said, but he did not sound as certain as he usually did. "Maybe only your dignity."

When she turned her head to give him a hateful look, he returned it with an arrogant one of his own.

She got off the bed once again, made her way past him with haughty disdain, and picked the dress off the floor. She put it on. When she walked over to the window and looked out, she saw an antelope and a deer grazing at the edge of the clearing.

"We can start right now for the ranch as far as I'm concerned," she said in a surly little voice.

"We'll have to wait till morning. It will be dark soon. The ground will be drier by then."

They ate their dinner of sardines and biscuits in silence. Marielle stood as she ate; Quinn kept his eyes on her. The air crackled with tension.

Two hours passed and they had still not spoken to each other. After she watched him clean up the remains of dinner, feed the horse and mule, and pack their gear for an early start in the morning, she turned her back on him and went to bed without a word.

He sat by the fire for a long time but, finally, as the embers began to die slowly, he put some more wood onto the hearth and slid into the bed beside her. She turned her back on him, and moaned softly but dramatically when her buttocks touched the blanket. She felt him wince in the dark.

"I cannot make you out," he whispered. "What happens inside that beautiful head of yours?" She did not bother to answer.

Tentatively, very lovingly and very tenderly, he took her in his arms. She did not protest, but lay quietly in the warmth of his embrace, spoon fashion, facing the wall next to the bed.

"While you are away, I will find some sort of practical solution to your dilemma. It is not insurmountable. It is merely time I am asking for. There's going to be a war between the North and the

South. I know it, and I want you in a safe place. In the North. Perhaps New York. There are excellent schools there.''

She did not say anything. What was there to say?

"I have to do what I believe in. It may be years before I come back to the ranch. I don't know how long the war will last. If I survive, we can go on from there. I will know you are safe—and you will be older.''

She turned slightly to hear him better as he whispered.

"Believe me, it is for the best. Even now, while we are waiting, I cannot stay on at the ranch and have you there. Not the way things are between us. At the same time, I cannot leave the ranch and abandon you. I cannot trust your safety to Rio.''

She turned again until she faced him. He closed his arms around her more tightly and sought her lips with his own. He kissed her soft mouth, her eyes, her cheeks; he nibbled at her ear and under her chin, and then his lips went back to hers, more urgently now, harder, more demanding.

She put her arms around his neck as her breasts with their hard little nipples pressed into his chest through the sheer cotton of her chemise. She let her mouth join his in complete surrender to his tongue, felt the mounting pressure of his sinewy muscles. She knew his body as well as he knew hers.

It was not easy. She forced her mind away from the havoc he was playing with her emotions, brought her knee up, and hit him in the groin with all her might.

He let go of her, turned away and groaned loudly in pain. Then she heard the oaths as he left the bed to her alone.

She turned on her back and faced the wall so that the smile she knew was on her face was well hidden. She was avenged.

Then, before she knew what was happening, he hurtled himself back onto the bed and turned her around, spreadeagled, so that she was facing him once more. He kneeled over her, looking down at her, imprisoning her hands so she could not fight back. His eyes were full of anger and distrust.

"I have been too kind to you. I have been much too patient with you. I even believed your wild story about not running away with Rio," he said quietly, but there was great fury behind the even way he spoke. "But tonight I will treat you the way you have asked to be treated and see if you like it,'' and he ripped off the cotton chemise and threw it so that it landed in the fireplace on top of the fire.

His fingers that could be so gentle became lengths of steel-coiled strength as he made love to her by taking and not giving. He took her as if he were the devil and she his helpless disciple meant for his erotic pleasure. Over and over he drove into her as at first she tried to resist; then when she found that he was too strong, she tried to pretend it was not happening.

She tried to force her mind elsewhere so that all he could use of her was a warm empty shell, but her body trembled even as it tried to withdraw from his savage passion. His onslaught continued with relentless fury and she gave up and lay back and allowed him to do with her what he wanted.

And then the ecstasy of surrender flowed through her and she shuddered as she found herself pressing closely to him, letting herself go into a world where there was nothing but passion. He took her with him into his realm of steaming physical fury and gave her a taste of tumultuous frenzy that left her limp and exhausted, unable to move, but ready for whatever more he offered.

He took her again and again until he was as weary as she, and when he was drained of all rage and had no strength left, he took her in his arms and fell asleep next to her.

She was more tired than she had ever been in her life, but she did not fall asleep immediately. Without knowing it, in his sleep, he kissed her wet brow as she listened to the night noises outside the cabin. Finally, she drifted off into slumber to the short, snarling barks of a pack of coyotes far away in the forest.

Just before dawn, she awakened as she felt Quinn's body tense up next to hers. He was already awake; she felt him stiffen and hold his breath. His hand, the one that was closest to her, pressed down on hers silently, as if to keep her quiet and unmoving. She lay back, and held her breath the same way he did.

They were not alone.

Her eyes moved past Quinn. Sitting on the chair near the almost dead embers of the fire was Rio. His long legs poked out onto the hearth as he warmed his feet. His hat was perched at a crazy angle so that part of the brim fell over one eye. In his hands, he held his Colt. The noise that had awakened them was Rio loading his revolver.

Chapter Twenty-five

Fear swept through her. She did not want to think about what would happen between the brothers.

"Goddamit, Rio. What are you going to do with that gun?" Quinn did not move a muscle as he spoke.

"Plain as the nose on your face. I'm gonna kill you." Rio pointed the gun at his brother's heart.

"Why'd you want to do a thing like that? What for?"

Rio leaned back in the chair and laughed insolently, his eyes filled with the sort of amusement that could not hide the hate he felt toward his half brother. "I plain don't like you, Morgan," he sneered. "Besides, you shouldn't have done it," he said gesturing with the gun to Marielle's naked form.

"Done what, man?"

"Bedded her. I was going to make her my bride. The right way. I was gonna marry her. Make her my little virgin bride. Now it's too late. She's yours. You never gave me a chance to do the right thing by her, you bastard. You just took her for yourself. Like everything else. Like the gold you've been giving away without asking me." His eyes narrowed. "I'm gonna kill you for sure."

"It's not the way you think," Quinn said quietly.

"It sure looks it to me," Rio said.

Quinn's face was beginning to get that stony, closed look that Marielle knew well. "If you're going to use the gun, Rio, use it."

Rio coldly cocked his revolver.

At the same time, Quinn rolled out of bed and went into a flying tackle across the length of the room.

It was a strange sight. The two huge men, one naked, and one dressed for the outdoors, filled the cabin so that it seemed very tiny in comparison to what it had been just minutes before.

They took stock of each other. Rio hit Quinn over the head with the gun; Quinn lunged for the weapon with one hand as his other fist crashed into Rio's jaw.

As they fought, Marielle found her dress and slipped into it quickly. They never noticed. They looked like they were going to kill each other. There was nothing she could do, they moved around the room so fast.

One of them—Marielle never knew which one—sent the gun spinning across the room, almost at her feet. She bent down automatically and picked it up and pointed it at both of them. Neither one stopped what they were doing. They continued with their fist-icuffs, until in a moment of inspiration, she turned the gun away from them and pulled the trigger; the bullet made a round hole in the door of the cabin. The noise stopped. She pointed the gun at both of them.

"Stop fighting this very instant," she shouted. They looked at her with a mixture of surprise and impatience.

"Hand it over," Rio said, but she noticed he did not step any closer to where she was.

"I will not."

Quinn took a step closer. "Get back," she said, waving the gun wildly at him.

He looked at her face and then at the gun in her hand, and stepped back without a word.

"I'm glad you're here, Rio. I'm glad you got away," she said, still holding the gun with authority.

"They got Joaquín," he said.

"Is he dead?"

"I don't know. I couldn't tell. They got Three-Fingered Jack too. They got almost everybody before it was over. I was lucky."

While Rio told his story, Quinn pulled on this clothes. Marielle kept the gun pointed at both of them.

"Give me my gun," Rio said very suddenly. "I don't want to have to take it from you."

"Go away, Rio," she said. "While you can. Don't test me."

Instead, he looked at the gun and laughed. "You ain't gonna shoot that off," he declared and turned and threw himself on his brother.

Of course, he was right. She had no intention of shooting either man.

But the momentary interruption gave Quinn a chance to draw back his arm and let all the strength in his fist explode into Rio's gut. Rio went down with a howl, dragging Quinn with him. The fight started again in earnest until Rio's head hit the edge of the fireplace.

Marielle screamed and rushed to his side. He lay very still, a trickle of blood staining the floor at the edge of the hearth where his head rested.

Quinn examined the wound, picked up his brother in his arms and placed him on the bed. "He'll be fine in a little while. It'll give us a chance to get a good start. Bring his gun with you."

Marielle was shocked. "But he as much as said he's going to kill you. Are you going to leave him here?"

"He's my brother," Quinn said softly. "What do you expect me to do right now? He can find his own way home after his headache goes away."

"He's going to try to harm you."

"Maybe," Quinn said, and looked very sad. "I'll just have to take my chances for the time being. He's *family.*"

He gathered their gear, threw her the sheepskin jacket, and stalked out the door.

She would have much preferred to be far away—on some stage in San Francisco—anywhere else but with either one of the two men who caused so much trouble in her life. She gave one last look at the inert one on the bed, then covered him with one of the blankets and followed Quinn out the door. She made sure she had Rio's gun with her.

When they got back to the Double Raven, Marielle saw that life at the ranch had gone on as if nothing had happened. But she felt as if she was the pariah of the family; she was an outcast whom nobody considered important enough to consult about anything, even her own future.

Once again there were conferences to which she was not invited. Morgan, Carmel, and Miss Penelope decided her destiny without allowing her to protest in any way. She would go away to school in the East.

Miss Cosgrove's School for Girls had a fine reputation, and no one was known to ever run away from there. Arrangements were quickly made by mail for the new term.

Quinn stayed as far away from her as he could. More often than not, he was absent from dinner, and if he happened to find himself at home at seven o'clock, he ate quickly and excused himself immediately afterwards. Every time Marielle saw him, she noticed his black eye changing color. One day the discolorations had faded away completely.

As far as she was concerned, she was persona non grata at the Double Raven. Miss Penelope treated her with open contempt while they sat opposite each other at the dinner table. Carmel was as vague and distant as always and hardly noticed Marielle was there at all. Her only friend was Hu Ming and her Arabian palomino, Lady, whom she loved and rode and groomed every day. The weather was perfect for riding. It had not rained since she had returned to the ranch with her guardian.

In her lonely bedroom, Marielle took out the two diamond stickpins and examined them sadly; she started to wear them in an effort to understand what it was about the ranch and the people on it that made her feel so forsaken. Occasionally, she would look at the white lace birthday dress that had been brought back from Sacramento along with the rest of her things. There would be no opportunity to wear it again. She packed it away in tissue paper.

It wasn't fair. She was being sent to a place where she would be virtually as much a prisoner as she was here. She would be there for several years along with a lot of dull young ladies far less experienced than she. She detested the thought. She hadn't done anything wrong except lose a father and love unwisely. . . . How could Quinn do this to her?

Then, one day, Rio contacted her. He had not been back at the ranch, and no one mentioned his name to Marielle. It was as if he had ceased to exist. He knocked on her door one morning just before dawn and slipped in when she opened it cautiously. He seemed as lost and unwanted as she.

He was visiting her, he told her, not returning to the ranch. She was grateful even for that attention, although he seemed subdued and preoccupied. She had no idea where he had been all this time and he did not volunteer the information.

He wanted to go to San Francisco to be on his own. He didn't think he had a future on the ranch. She knew exactly how he felt.

"I'll take you with me if you want," he suggested suddenly.

"They're sending me away to school. New York," she admitted sadly. "Miss Penelope recommends it highly. I don't want to go."

"We can get away before they send you east. It'll be easy."

"I don't know. . . . You think we can get away with it?"

He nodded and gave her a sly smile.

"But no thoughts of weddings . . . or anything like that?"

"I swear. I won't be bothering you. Unless you want me to."

"It would have to be soon. Real soon."

He became tense with excitement. "I'll let you know when." He disappeared as mysteriously as he arrived.

She was left alone once more.

As time went by and Marielle did not hear from Rio, she gave up the idea of running away with him to San Francisco. At dinner one night, it was announced that Miss Penelope would accompany Marielle to New York and see that she arrived safely at Miss Cosgrove's. Trunks were brought to her room and she was instructed to start packing.

Still she did not hear from Rio.

The next evening, dinner was a dismal affair. Quinn was at the table, sitting opposite Carmel. Penelope was on his right and Marielle was on his left. No one spoke during the meal if they could help it.

Finally she was able to get away to her room with a book, but she found she could not concentrate and decided to try to sleep. The book, a gift from Catherine Sinclair on her birthday, had fallen on the floor when she finally drifted off. Before she fell into a deep slumber, she half woke to loud voices downstairs in the main parlor. It was Morgan, Rio, and Carmel. Rio had returned and his voice sounded loud and strangely agitated.

The voices continued for a long time. She could not hear what was being said. The voices became louder and more tormented. Then they stopped.

She was absolutely certain as she burrowed deeper into her warm bed that now that Rio was back he would help her run away from the Double Raven, Morgan Quinn, and Miss Cosgrove's School for Girls.

She slept soundly for the first time since she was back at the ranch.

Chapter Twenty-six

That night, a net of darkness tightened and surrounded the many wings of the Quinn mansion, forcing its way through the doors and closed windows. Leaves falling from half-stripped branches of the surrounding trees flew about in a harsh wind. The night air outside was unseasonably warm and dry.

It was past midnight when Marielle was roused from a deep, troubled sleep. She had been dreaming and was glad that something had awakened her. She was sure it had been the howling wind trying to invade the house.

But it was not the wind that had awakened her. It was an insistent tapping on her bedroom door. She waited, and when it did not go away, she padded across the floor in her nightgown and bare feet.

"Who is it?" she whispered, her ear against the massive wooden portal.

The soft tapping continued.

She bent down, removed the wrought iron key, and peered through the keyhole. She thought she knew who it was.

Her eye met another eye on the other side of the door, peering into the bedroom. Then the eye moved away and she felt someone's breath coming through the opening. "It's me. Rio . . ." he whispered through the keyhole. "Open up. Quick."

She padded back to her bed and took the dark wool robe laying there. She slipped into it, wrapping it around her before returning to the door. The wrought iron key stuck as she unlocked it, making a loud squeak.

Then Rio stood before her, dressed for riding, and with a shotgun under his arm.

"Get yourself dressed," Rio whispered. "We're leaving tonight."

"How much time do I have?"

"Minutes. Things been moving fast. It's San Francisco time. For good! For both you and me."

"No stops, Rio?"

"No stops. I promise you. You'll be far away from this hellhole by tomorrow morning."

"What about Morgan?" she asked uncertainly.

"Morgan won't be bothering us. I swear."

"How can you be so sure?" She could not believe Quinn would not come riding to wherever they were, would not try to claim her back from whoever held her. As she looked at Rio, she thought of Quinn and the dark curls of hair flying out from under his hat, his gray eyes blazing with intelligence and a mysterious righteousness she could not completely understand, but which made her heart lose all serenity.

"Rio. I know him. He won't let me go," she whimpered.

"You bet he will. You get dressed. Warm and cozylike. We got a long ride ahead. Take one small valise. Nothing more."

She nodded her head. It had to be done. She had to break the hold. No matter how.

"Meet me at the stables. You got exactly twenty minutes."

"I understand. I'll be there."

She dressed quickly in a wool serge dress, heavy llack boots, and the sheepskin jacket that once belonged to Carmel. There was no time to do more than tie her unruly hair into a red knot at her neck and cover its shimmering color with a dark, flat hat. Packing a small leather valise with underwear and one change of clothes, she slipped a long, dark woolen cape over everything. She hoped that the obscurity surrounding her and the darkness of her outfit would hide her.

As she started for the stables, she saw a sliver of moon passing through the almost naked trees.

She knew the stables would soon loom up in front of her. Soon she could hear the neighing of a horse. All the time, she wondered if Quinn was behind her, ready to pounce. But no one was following her when she turned back to look. She slowed down and caught her breath.

Just before she reached the stables where Rio was waiting with the horses, she turned around once more and saw Carmel Quinn clearly outlined by the light of the gold crescent moon. The woman stood on top of the hill, just left of the mansion, proud and straight, unhidden. As Carmel scrutinized the house, it seemed as if the new moon was resting on her shoulder.

Under her arm, Carmel carried her rifle. Her hat had fallen onto her shoulders, still held on by its tie, and for the first time, Marielle could plainly see that the dark knot of hair on Carmel's head was untidy and hastily combed. The tousled hair was a surprise. It was not Carmel Quinn, the orderly Carmel Quinn of Marielle's acquaintance. Still, she looked like a statue guarding the house.

As Marielle turned slightly, she could see what Carmel was watching. In the distance was a man. He was much farther away than Carmel, and it was difficult to see him clearly, but Marielle knew who the man was; there was no doubt in her mind that it was Rio. Every graceful movement he made as he crouched and moved swiftly in the shadow of the house confirmed his identity. He looked very much like his brother, but there was always that simple difference that Marielle had never failed to recognize.

A tug of fear passed through her. Rio was supposed to be inside the stables getting two horses ready for them to leave. Why was he still at the house? He had been very specific with his instructions.

As he ran from one dark corner of the house to the next, Marielle saw there was a large container in his hand. It was the container that held a supply of kerosene that the servants used to refill the lamps. She could no longer see his shotgun.

What was he doing? Even as the question sprang through Marielle's mind, she knew. He had set the house afire. Any doubts were dispelled as she recognized the licks of flame and then saw him torching kerosene-soaked corners where wood met dry foliage and quickly ignited into crackling blazes of combustion.

It was too late to try to stop him. It was too late for Carmel to stop him. Yellow and blue flames licked the sides of the house and leaped higher and higher, accompanied by what sounded like a roar of destruction. The wind howled and the blaze grew. Rio did not need to do more. The fire spread so rapidly it seemed now to envelop the huge house. Each time a new section went up in fiery combustion, a popping sound went off so loudly it sounded like a cannon. After the pop, there would be a blustery sigh as the wind died down momentarily and allowed the conflagration to build at its own pace.

The front door flew open. The massive wooden portals had not as yet been torched, but flames could be seen from the inside.

Ceiling beams and furniture were already on fire in various parts
of the house. Penelope Watson, her honey-colored hair in one long
braid down her back ran breathlessly out the front door. There was
terror in her chocolate eyes, and her peaches and cream complexion was a bright pink with the heat of the flames inside.

She was wearing a white nightdress and dark wool robe very
much like the nightclothes she had purchased for Marielle. When
she was far enough away from the blaze to insure her safety, she
stopped and turned back to the house. Marielle watched her bend
over and throw up, take out a sturdy white cotton handkerchief and
wipe her mouth delicately, then straighten up and start to scream.
No sounds could be heard though. She could not compete with the
noise of the wind and the laments of the burning house. At that
moment, Hu Ming appeared from the direction of the servants'
quarters and led Penelope away.

Marielle stood planted to her spot, incredulous at what she had
seen. There were two people who knew who had torched the house,
she and Carmel Quinn. She turned back once again to Carmel's
profile. The woman had not moved since Marielle had last looked
at her. At that precise moment, she turned and glanced in Marielle's general direction. There was no expression on her face and
Marielle wondered if Carmel could see her. Then she saw Hu Ming
lead a hysterical Penelope to Carmel's side.

Carmel did not touch the younger woman or extend any sort of
sympathy. She spoke to Hu Ming, and although Marielle could not
hear what was said, she saw Hu Ming lead Penelope to a small
rock close to Carmel and seat her before he ran back to the burning
ranchhouse.

At the same time, Marielle's eyes caught sight of Quinn stum-
bling from the front doors, and as she did, her breath stopped. He
was dressed in black trousers and high boots and a white woolen
shirt torn and charred by flames. One shirttail hung outside his pants
and the sleeves of his shirt had been hastily rolled up to his elbows.
His face was drained of color underneath the residue of soot and
ashes. There were several gashes on his arms where his shirt sleeves
ended and charred slashes on the exposed part of his chest. Marielle gripped her hands into fists as she watched.

Quinn looked for and spotted his mother almost immediately. She
nodded calmly at him and turned her head slightly so that his gaze
went to Penelope. He nodded back to his mother and turned again,
looking for someone whom he could not seem to find. And then,
to Marielle's horror, he ran back into the house.

Other servants began to appear from the servants' quarters carrying wooden buckets. They assembled at the well at the side of the house and tried to form a water brigade led by Hu Ming and his son. Very little water found its way to the burning house, although they kept busy. Even if there had been more water, it was too late. The fire was strong, and the wind too sharp and dry.

Then, by the sliver of moon, Marielle could plainly see Rio creep around the burning wall of one side of the mansion. He tried to make his way toward the front door, which was now surrounded by flames. Like Quinn, his handsome face was blackened with soot and his clothes were ripped and disheveled. He had lost his hat and his thick hair fell carelessly in all directions, forming a dark curly halo of insidious beauty that nevertheless could not disguise the maniacal look on his face. His eyes shone with hardness, hate, and jealousy. They frightened her more tonight than they ever had in the past. He had a crazy mission, it was quite clear, but Marielle found it impossible to guess what it was. It was the deranged expression in his eyes that made her start moving very slowly toward the house.

And, then, as surely as she felt the house was doomed, she knew that Rio planned to kill his older brother. Although the knowledge must have lain dormant in her brain for a long time, only now did it begin to make sense. Rio was a lunatic whose madness could be touched off at anytime. And now he was going to kill Morgan in order to make up for the fact that he was the second son of Carmel Quinn and not the first. He was going to kill Morgan to stop Carmel and Marielle, both, from loving his brother. He was going to kill Morgan to keep Marielle for himself.. *He was going to kill Morgan Quinn.*

She decided to skirt the spot where Carmel and Penelope were, and go around the other way to reach the front of the house. It was not easy, but she crept on until there was only open ground between her and the front door of the house. For a moment she wondered why she crept back to the danger of fire and the madness of Rio. She should be fleeing in the other direction, as far away from the Double Raven and its inhabitants as her feet could take her. San Francisco. The magic city. Lotta Crabtree was there. Lola Montez would soon be returning from Australia. The Booths would return one by one. There were theatres in San Francisco. She was considered a grown-up in San Francisco, an actress, a young lady with talent and a future.

But what about Morgan Quinn? What if he were trapped inside the house, pinned beneath a wooden beam or the ceiling of a burning room, unable to escape as the flames crept nearer and nearer. She closed her fingertips over her lips to still the fear that might escape and become screams. As she wormed her way to the house, she saw Quinn crash out of a window on one side of the front door. The broken glass splintered around him. He continued to tumble and landed almost into the arms of Rio, who was moving on hands and knees away from the front door.

Both brothers, bloodied and blackened by the fire, stood up. Marielle saw Quinn speaking to Rio; then Rio's mouth opened in a crazy laugh. It seemed even crazier to Marielle because she could not hear the laughter against the wind.

Quinn grabbed his brother and shook him hard. The open-mouthed laughter ceased. Quinn shouted; again Marielle could not hear. She looked past them at the house, now a blazing shell. If Quinn tried to reenter the house, it would be through a solid sheet of fire.

Still he tried. Could he be looking for her? Should she stand up and try to be seen?

When Morgan saw that it was impossible to get back to the house, he ran quickly to the well and doused himself from head to boots with several buckets of water, dipped a worker's long apron in another bucket and covered his arms with it as he ran back to the burning house.

Rio closed in on him as he returned. In his hand he held a heavy wooden club. When Quinn found one broken French window on the far side of the house where flames did not lick out heavily, he tried to wriggle through.

Marielle stood up. As she came closer, she saw Rio put out a long arm and shove his brother back onto the ground. He lifted the club he was holding with the other hand and smashed it down on Quinn. The club grazed Quinn's ear and hit his left shoulder with full force.

A tussle between the two men began as Marielle crawled as near as she dared. The fire was very close; soot and ashes fell on her and the fighting men.

Both men were amazingly graceful and limber as they fought. Astonishing as it was to Marielle, they were totally unhurried now that they had found each other. Rio raised his club high over his head and Marielle realized too late that it was going to smash down onto Quinn's head. She screamed, but did not know if Quinn heard her. His right hand shot out, and with one fluid movement his fist slammed into his brother's face.

Rio was surprised, but just as quick. Again he raised the club high over his head, and before Quinn could stop him, he slammed it down.

Quinn who had managed to get to his feet before the latest blow, now fell down again, his face hugging the earth, as Rio stood over him with a wild look on his bloodied face. He continued to smash the club at his brother's inert body.

Marielle dashed from her hiding place and headed straight for Rio. He looked up and saw her. "Get away from here, you crazy bitch," he screamed, and this time she was close enough to hear every word. "Get away while I finish him off."

"No!" Marielle cried and rushed at him.

He put out one large, blackened hand and pushed. She was flung aside as if she were a fly. She found herself sprawled at the base of a rock. From under her chin blood streamed and she knew the sharp boulder had left a deep cut. She was stunned, but managed to collect herself as quickly as possible and wipe away the blood.

When she looked up, she saw Rio dragging Quinn toward the French window where flames were shooting out in waves. There was so much fire it seemed like daylight.

Then things happened so fast she was never sure she had seen everything. Carmel ran past her, her rifle still under her arm. She moved with lightning speed toward her two sons. Rio heard her and turned. When he saw his mother, an expression of fear filled his face, but he turned back to the fire, dragging his unconscious brother with him.

As he reached the flaming French window, the wind shifted and an awesome lick of fire spurted from inside. A flash of yellow and orange filled the night, and then there was a burst of crackling noise. Rio's hair was on fire. There was a momentary halo of light surrounding his beautiful face. Then he dropped his brother's arms and stood up straight and unbelieving into the flames. His eyes were open wide, his mouth slightly ajar, and a look of fear and horror enveloped his handsome features. He bent quickly as the halo of fire became larger, and tugged on Quinn's arms, pulling him even closer to the flames. He succeeded in dragging him halfway inside.

At that moment, a rifle shot rang out. Rio went down on his knees, resting against his brother's body as a gory, gaping hole appeared in his middle.

He stayed on his knees, leaning heavily against Quinn, holding his belly as his hair crackled and burned. Throwing down her rifle, Carmel ran to him and started to put out the flames with her bare hands. As she did so, he turned on her and snarled. It was an inhuman sound that came from his throat. He grabbed the tiny woman around the waist and flung her straight through the French window. No sound came from her lips as she flew across the short distance and disappeared into the flames.

When the pain of fire and bullet became unbearable, Rio reeled in the direction of the burning house. His face was distorted.

"Ma . . ." he screamed, and Marielle knew she would never forget the sound. Then he crashed back into the house where he had flung his mother. The flames enveloped him quickly.

Marielle turned away from the scene of horror and went for Quinn. She tried to pull him away from the long open window where flames licked the casements. He was too heavy for her to move.

Desperately, she tried to slap his face in the hope he would regain consciousness. Nothing happened. He remained inert. She wondered if he were dead.

A noise made her turn her head away from Quinn. A beam was falling through the paneless French doors. The long, charred beam charged down heavily, coming straight at them. It was almost on top of them and there was nothing she could do to save them. She put her arms around Quinn's defenseless body and held him tightly. The last thing she remembered was shutting her eyes against what she knew would happen next.

Part III

Fame and Fortune

Chapter Twenty-seven

With lots of faith and a little help from Lola Montez and Lotta Crabtree, Marielle took San Francisco by storm. She arrived with the two diamond stickpins, the money she had received from the sale of Lady, and the clothes on her back. Selling Lady had been heart-rending—she loved the horse so much—but since the money meant survival, she forced herself to do it. She was done with Morgan Quinn and the Double Raven forever.

She had friends working in every theatre in the city, and everyone remembered the late Jeremiah Preston and his extraordinary little daughter, Marielle, who was now grown-up. Lola was back from Australia and performing her spider dance on stage. Lotta was at the new California Theatre, and a smash as *Little Nell*. Catherine Sinclair and Henry Sedley passed through the city and stayed for several weeks before returning to New York, doing *The School for Scandal*.

Marielle's first job was for Junius Booth at the San Francisco Hall, a comparatively new theater. She played *Beatrice* to her old friend Edwin Booth's *Benedick* in *Much Ado about Nothing*. She was so accomplished in the role that soon she was hailed as a dedicated and indefatigable artist. She was so beautiful now, her admirers lined up outside her dressing room every night for a close-up glimpse of her glorious pale face with the startlingly blue eyes framed by heavy, dark red hair. The engagement lasted eight weeks and broke all records up to that time.

San Francisco was a glittering city. Marielle took permanent quarters at the luxurious Palace Hotel. She could well afford it with her salary as leading lady to the famous Edwin Booth. All her waking hours were filled with performances or rehearsals. After the show each night, she chose a different admirer to take her to late supper, at which she dressed very simply, usually in white. After the midnight repast, she would be driven back to the hotel by carriage, where she would say good night to her suitors in the lobby of the hotel. She had no other life.

She never gave her admirers any encouragement. She did, however, accept tokens of their esteem such as flowers and jewelry. No matter how little she gave them of herself, though, they always returned, seeking a smile, a handshake, a nod. No matter how small the acknowledgment, her suitors considered themselves fortunate. They came to look upon her as a distant goddess.

She tried hard not to think about Morgan Quinn. Her whole life had changed once again with the destruction of the Double Raven and the deaths of Rio and Carmel. Quinn survived, just as she had. The beam of wood that threatened both their lives landed at an angle just above their heads, and stayed there only long enough for Hu Ming and the other servants to pull them out. Then it collapsed completely and burned, right on the spot where she and Quinn had been. The mansion was destroyed.

When Marielle recovered from her superficial wounds, she found Penelope Watson nursing a very disabled Quinn. He would get well, the doctor said, but it might take months, and there was even some question as to whether he would ever be able to use his right arm again. The arm had been shattered in several places.

Penelope was as cold to Marielle as ever. For a while, they all stayed together in Hu Ming's cottage, but it was very uncomfortable living in such close quarters.

And every day, Marielle was faced with watching a helpless Morgan being cared for by Penelope. He was unconscious a good deal of the time. When he came to, he was too moody to move or talk. He faced the wall of his bed, his eyes closed, and lay quietly for long periods of time. Miss Penelope took full charge.

It took many bitter tears and all of Marielle's courage and fortitude to pull herself together and force herself to think of leaving the man she loved. But he didn't need her. He didn't want her. He had Penelope Watson.

When she finally resolved to leave, she thought her heart would break. But she was determined to do it. And, she now felt she was the last person in the world who could make Quinn happy, especially after the tragedy they had both shared. So she would go away and leave him to his beautiful, cold widow. It was the right thing to do.

When Marielle told the honey-haired Penelope that she planned to leave the crowded cottage, the widow did not try in any way to stop her. In fact, she looked smugly pleased when the big day arrived and Marielle said good-bye to everyone. Marielle did not even know whether Quinn realized that she was going for good.

She took the only belongings she could claim as her own—the two stickpins and Lady, her Arabian palomino.

She sold Lady in Sacramento for a very good price, much more than she had expected the mare to bring. She cried as she hugged the horse for the last time and continued on by public stagecoach.

In the next town the stagecoach passed through, Marielle saw the renowned Joaquín Murieta's head preserved in alcohol. Next to the gruesome sight, Three-Fingered Jack's hand had been preserved in a large jar of alcohol. Both were exhibited in glass to show the public that Captain Harry Love and his Mounted Rangers had done their job. A feeling of shock and revulsion went through her body.

Before six months had passed, she was on her way to fame in San Francisco. At any rate, she was definitely no longer starving, and she had begun to have a lot more confidence in herself.

She found Madame Benét, who had opened an establishment in San Francisco. The French dressmaker was commissioned to make all her clothes, mostly in white, mostly very simple. In them, Marielle caused a sensation. Her reputation as a great beauty and fine actress preceded her everytime she went for a part at any of the theatres in San Francisco. She always got the job.

It was while she was establishing herself in the city on the bay that the sounds of war began to come closer and closer. Every day the newspapers reported that the country was on the verge of battle. Everything Quinn had predicted was coming true.

She was working with Edwin Booth in *The Taming of the Shrew* when, one night, she looked out into the audience and saw Morgan Quinn. She stopped dead in her tracks in the middle of an important speech and searched the third row audience where she thought she had seen him. His face vanished as mysteriously as it had appeared, and when she looked up into the distressed visage of Ted Booth, she was reminded to carry on.

"What happened, my darling?" Ted asked her after they had taken their bows. "I saw your beautiful face become frightened and blank, and you stopped in the middle of your lines."

"I'm sorry," Marielle murmured. "I thought I saw someone in the audience . . ."

Ted looked at her tenderly and then kissed her cheek. "Don't look too hard, dear Marielle, lest you find your nemesis."

She tried to take his words to heart. But, secretly, she was frightened at what happened. Two nights later it happened again, and once more she discovered to her dismay that she had fantasized the man in the third row to be Quinn. Morgan Quinn was not in San Francisco, and if he were, he would not be coming to see her.

The Taming of the Shrew ended, and Ted Booth made ready to leave for New York. He had a bride waiting for him there, and he did not want to be separated from her by the war. Marielle hated for their successful theatrical collaboration to end, but Ted made her promise that when she got to New York he would be the first person she would contact.

It was only a matter of days before she was hired for another production. She had become a valuable property. She knew her career was blooming faster and more brilliantly than she had a right to expect, but in San Francisco becoming illustrious was not so difficult. Would she do as well in New York City? She knew that soon she would have to make a bid for recognition in the most important city on the continent of North America. Very soon.

Lola Montez left for New York with all her trunks and a man in tow. She had changed since her return from Australia. She was not quite as beautiful as she once had been, and she was not quite so daring. She was almost thirty-six years old.

Then, little Lotta Crabtree and her mother left on a western tour. They would stop off in every large city across the nation, until they reached the East Coast and New York. Lotta was still a little girl, but she was ready for anything including, possibly, a European tour if war developed between the North and South and made traveling in America impossible. Her mother chaperoned her as closely now as when she had first started out.

Marielle was devastated to see her friends leave. To her, they were family—the only family she could count on for moments of closeness and love.

She joined another production and, this time, her name outside the theatre, and on all the billboards around the city, announced that Marielle Preston was the main attraction, the star of the show. There was no other thespian's name over hers. She had conquered San Francisco. But it was not enough. In the back of her mind, Marielle knew she had to conquer New York.

During one of her next performances, it happened again. She thought she saw Morgan Quinn in the third row center, watching her from his seat. As she stood alone in the center of the stage, ready for her monologue, she examined the audience and realized it was a man who did not, in any way, resemble Quinn. It was simply her mind that had deceived her. She was completely shaken by the incident and decided to take a short vacation after her present contract was finished.

On closing night, the theatre was overflowing. All her admirers seemed to be there at once. She was appearing as Susan in a light-hearted play called *Black-Eyed Susan*. It was one of the few frivolous roles she allowed herself because it gave her the chance to act as well as sing and dance. It also gave her the opportunity to show off her comedic skills.

As she went into the end of the first act, she looked out into the audience and the apparition was there, sitting in front of her, exactly as her mind had fantasized him during earlier performances. Morgan Quinn was in the theatre. Again, during one frightening moment, she stopped the speech she was doing. She had the feeling that Morgan Quinn knew what havoc he was causing in her as she stood on the stage, trying to continue her work and seeing his face for the first time in almost a year. But, this time, the face did not disappear. This time the face was not a figment of her imagination.

He was there, alone, as handsome as ever, sitting in the fifth row, almost beyond the reach of her vision, but not quite. She knew for sure he was real when she saw his right arm in a splint of black silk. It made him all the more mysterious and romantic. His intelligent gray eyes, alert and watchful, did not leave her for a minute. She got the definite feeling it was no accident he was in the theater that evening. His dark curly hair fell over his brow in short ringlets. He pushed his left hand through it, but it only made the curls more unruly. She remembered that Rio used to do the same thing.

When the performance was finally over, he stood up with the rest of the audience to show his appreciation, but he did not clap. Seeing his hand in the splint of black silk made him real, absolute flesh and bone. This was not what she had feared at first—it was far worse than she had feared. His reality was bolder, bigger than her fantasy. Had he come to return her to the Double Raven? How could he demand that she do his bidding after so much time had elapsed? How could he make her return to his guardianship? The only thing he had in his favor was that it would still be a long time before she was twenty-one and legally out of his grasp.

Even from her place on stage she became aware of the sensation this man could instill in her. She found it hard to breathe and make her curtsies. For the first time in a year she was not pleased that she was in full view of an overflowing theatre. Since it was closing night, she stepped forward and said a few words to the audience. She had no idea what she was saying, but it did not matter. They loved whatever she said, as they loved everything about her.

In her dressing room, he waited in line with her other admirers with remarkable patience, watching amusedly with those eagle-clear eyes of his everything the others said and did. There seemed to be a golden heat passing from him to her. He stood leaning against the doorway, memorizing every one of her moves. All the others faded into the background. He was taller, bigger, more intense. Finally, they were all gone except he.

"Dinner . . ." he said. It was not a question or a request. It was a simple statement. He made her hotel open up their dining room even though it was close to midnight. She could not remember a single thing she ate that night.

"You will have to come back," he said pleasantly, except she was sure his mind was a million miles away, thinking of something or someone else. Miss Penelope?

When the plates in front of her were removed, he leaned back with a cognac in his hand and waited for her reply.

She sat quietly in the white dress she would have worn regardless of who took her to supper. "Where to?" she asked calmly. "There is no Double Raven anymore."

"I've started building a new house. New specifications. It will be a happier house than before. It would have been my mother's wish."

She wanted to ask him how many of the specifications Miss Penelope had approved, but she did not bother.

"I've been doing quite well earning my own living," she said.

"I am still your guardian and you are still my ward. If you insist on choosing the stage after you are twenty-one, you may do so. Without my approval, of course. Today, though, you have no choices to make."

She looked up into his eyes and smiled. She was different now, but he didn't know it—even though he was the one who had caused the great changes in her.

"I understand," she said evenly. "I will not try to cross you."

"Good!"

"When are you taking me back?"

"I'm sorry, but it'll have to be early tomorrow morning. I cannot spare any more time in San Francisco."

She nodded. "I'll be ready."

His eyes searched hers. "You won't try anything foolish?"

"No," she said.

"I'll take you upstairs. You will be all packed by morning?"

"Yes," she said.

When they got to her room, they stopped and faced each other at the entranceway while he opened the door. As he handed her the key their fingers touched, and unconsciously he leaned closer to her. She stood for an instant, weighing her pride against her desperate need to feel his touch.

She closed her eyes and allowed him to draw her into her room and close the door. It was easier to do nothing than to protest. Besides, she had not the slightest inclination of turning him away. She was different now. When she opened her eyes, she found he was looking at her in a detached way.

"The feelings I have for you are such strange ones," he whispered. "There is more to all this than love, I fear." Leaning against the closed door, he continued to drink in her beauty.

"What do you mean?" Marielle felt warmth spreading through her body despite the fact that she had more control than he at the moment. She knew what she had to do in the morning, but now there were several hours before dawn. She wondered fleetingly if it was humiliating to take so much pleasure in his nearness. She looked away as if her feelings could be dissolved by avoiding his face. She was wrong. She did not have to see. She felt passion flowing from him into her.

"Strange . . . these feelings I have," Quinn repeated. "I've always loved you, Marielle, but it seems to get worse with time. Happiness does not seem possible without you. I find I want to possess you so thoroughly that you become part of me. . . ."

She listened to the sound of his voice. She loved him. No matter what he was trying to do, she could not deny the quickening of her blood or the thumping of her heart. At the same time she knew that he was the stronger of the two, that he was going to swallow her until there was nothing left of Marielle Preston. Nothing left of the woman, the actress, the human being. She could only become an unimportant appendage to Morgan Quinn, the complete man.

She felt his warm breath as he spoke into her ear. "I want you and need you so much. I know you need me in the same way," he whispered.

"Yes!" It was not a lie. She wished it were.

He reached out with his left hand, and caught her to him. As he kissed her, his lips exploring all the tender surfaces of her mouth, she unhesitatingly raised her arms and drew him even closer to her.

He continued to penetrate and explore her mouth while she kept pulling him backward toward the bed in the middle of the room. She loved this rare man called Morgan Quinn. Nothing could stop the passion springing between them. She felt his body move with hers and they sank, fully clothed, onto her bed. She pressed closer to him.

There was no denying him, or herself. They wanted each other so much there was no time for removing their clothes. He worked the buttons of his trousers with one hand. She pushed the skirt of her exquisite white evening dress over her waist and drew her pantalets down to her knees. What did it matter? It would be the last time, she told herself. One time more.

He spread his good hand over her exposed belly, moving downward, slowly and with subtlety, until he found what he was looking for. She felt his fingers enter the moist, hot, most sensitive part of her body.

Her breath came out in long, labored gasps. Then as he rubbed and probed deeper, and she groaned in rapture, his touch drifted to the upper insides of her thighs. She parted her legs so that his fingers could do the work that made her limbs tremble, her heart beat against her ribs, and her breath leave her body in gasps of ecstasy.

Why not allow herself this pleasure? She knew what was going to happen in a few hours. She knew she must carry out her plan to save her life, to ensure the existence of Miss Marielle Preston.

"Marielle!" His voice was strong as he called her to him. She felt him lift himself onto her and enter, and plunge downward as hard as he could, deeply thrusting and filling the space inside her that needed him. He kissed her again, plunging his tongue into her mouth in the same way he had plunged his majestic masculinity into the opening that was there for him alone. The bed became a moist, moving vehicle for their passion as they surged together until the tumult of their emotions slowly came to rest. Marielle's dress was ruined, but it seemed unimportant in the light of the joy that passed between them.

When it was over, he raised himself on the elbow of his good hand and said, "We should have waited. But I couldn't. Tomorrow I will take you back to the new Double Raven and you need never leave there again. Everything in the world will be brought to you to keep you happy and satisfied." He kissed her face and wiped the sweat from her breasts with his lips. "You are mine forever."

"Yes," she said.

"You will not be perverse and do anything rash?" he asked, as he had earlier in the evening.

"No."

He left her then so he could pack and make final arrangements for their journey back to the ranch in the morning. She looked at his strong back as he walked out the door.

An hour later she had packed one small bag; she stopped by the theater to fetch her coffer of jewelry, and left San Francisco. It was all done long before dawn. Half of her jewelry paid her passage through the Panama Canal to New York, the quickest route. The captain of the ship had charged her much, much more than the other passengers, but it was worth it because she'd convinced him to sail before his scheduled departure time.

In less than six weeks, she was in New York City.

Chapter Twenty-eight

Marielle sold the rest of her jewelry except for the diamond stickpins as soon as she arrived in New York, and took comfortable but modest rooms on Charles Street, not far from Washington Square. She bought a deep-blue, two piece outfit with matching plumed bonnet and set out to see everyone she knew who could help her get work. The first persons she contacted were Ted Booth and his bride, Mary.

Ted was becoming so famous throughout the country, that articles appeared frequently in the Sunday *New York Times* about his acting style and work. He was overjoyed to see Marielle and introduced her to Mary. The two young women liked each other immediately. Mary had a serious little face that was more intelligent than beautiful, but there was a sweetness in her that was charming. She was unaffected and shy, with soft brown eyes and brown hair. Edwin had been very busy with his work; he had a contract with the Winter Garden for the entire season. Mary was always busy being a good wife to her darling Ted. They knew of no work for Marielle at the present, but they would keep her in mind. They invited her to dine with them at least once a fortnight. They were very kind and loving.

The city was a seething mass of raw energy, its cobblestone streets noisy with traffic as Manhattanites dashed through their narrow thoroughfares without regard for personal safety. New York frightened many newcomers with its crowds, coldness, and seeming lack of heart. But Marielle did not consider herself a newcomer. The ways of Manhattan came back to her. She grasped at the idea of her success here and managed to keep it within her at all times, so no matter how discouraged she felt, she always had reason to keep on.

Horace Greeley, the editor of the important newspaper, the *New York Tribune*, wrote powerful editorials about an Illinois senatorial campaign in which another newcomer, a tall, skinny young man named Abraham Lincoln, debated Stephen A. Douglas on the question of slavery. Young Lincoln lost the election but won the debate. Mr. Greeley, fiercely antislavery himself, helped Lincoln gain public attention with his eloquence in his case against slavery.

Harper's Ferry, Virginia, became famous when abolitionist John Brown attacked a Federal arsenal to secure arms for a slave revolt. The surprise attack failed and John Brown was hanged. The man who captured Brown was a Colonel Robert E. Lee.

On good days, Marielle sat in the little park on Washington Square and read the daily newspapers. On rainy days, she read the papers over coffee in her cozy rooms. She was always surprised at how Quinn's words were fast coming true.

As her money dwindled and her confidence waned, her lack of success in finding theatre work caused a brief depression. But Ted and Mary urged her on, and made her feel it was only a matter of time.

She found Lola Montez, the Countess of Landsfeld. Lola had stopped acting and dancing and had become an earnest-minded lecturer on women's rights. Marielle went to see her at the Stadt Theater on the Bowery. The audience was composed mostly of men, old admirers, who were curious about what she looked like now. They cheered enthusiastically at the end of her speech, but did not come backstage after the lecture. The few women present, except for Marielle, were singularly resentful of what she had to say.

After the lecture, Marielle visited with Lola at her little house at Nineteeth Street and Third Avenue. She lived alone with her dogs and told Marielle that her health was so poor she had to spend many of her days in bed. Lola had become a fading flower. There was no man in the background, like in the old days.

Lola, like Ted and Mary, urged Marielle to have faith in her beauty and ability. "Do not give up," Lola said in her French accent, which she had never lost. "The rewards when reaped are astounding. It is worth anything and everything. And I don't mean money."

The Countess brewed herb tea for both of them. She had given up coffee and hard spirits for the sake of her health. Her regimen was spartan in comparison to what it had been in the past. "Do you know what my motto is?"

Marielle smiled and shook her head.

"Courage! And shuffle the cards well."

Marielle knew what she meant. Lola was prone to be gay when the world crashed down on her.

Just before she left, Lola gave Marielle the names of a few men who might help her find work. One of them was a prince, Grigori Aleksandrov. "I've read that Prince Grigori is en route to New York from St. Petersburg. He is interested in the theater. If you contact him, something may come of it."

Marielle promised. She also promised to visit Lola often.

Still she could not find work. New York was vastly different from the Far West. There was no dearth of beautiful women willing to go on the stage. The city was full of actresses, both talented and beautiful, who had come from all over the world to do exactly what Marielle was trying to do.

She used Lola's contacts except for Prince Grigori, whom she could not find. Nothing came of them except dinner invitations, which she declined politely.

One day, sitting in Washington Square with an open newspaper, Marielle read that the eminent old-timer, Edwin Forrest, had returned to New York to play Hamlet at Niblo's Garden.

Quickly, Edwin decided to close his *King Lear* and open with *Hamlet* at the Winter Garden before Forrest's opening. Before Marielle had a chance to go see Booth, he came to her. He needed an Ophelia who was very young, very beautiful, and, above all, could act. He also needed an actress he could direct into a performance that would enhance his.

After months of despair and fear she would never work on the stage again, Marielle was given the role of Ophelia opposite Ted Booth's Hamlet. She was in heaven, even though it meant starting from the bottom again. Her name on the playbill was in tiny letters compared to Booth's and she received all the publicity and fanfare, but Marielle did not mind. Nor did she mind the grueling weeks of rehearsal and Ted's painstaking methods. It was an opportunity other actresses would gladly have killed for, a wonderful way to start. She would never forget her dear friend for giving it to her and wondered if she would ever be able to return the favor.

She worked like she had never worked before. Edwin Booth was brilliant. The production was a sensation. Forrest played to good houses too, but the audiences clearly preferred Booth's production.

Marielle was the real winner though. The sophisticated New York public came to see Booth and left with a new name on their lips: Marielle Preston.

* * *

Surprisingly enough, it was Edwin Forrest who gave Marielle her next job. After reading her reviews in the Sunday *Times*, he insisted she be Desdemona to his Othello. Again, her reviews were extraordinary. She was launched as an upcoming young star, one of the most beautiful ones the reviewers had ever seen on the stage. The offers began to trickle in, even while she was still working with Edwin Forrest. She decided to stay with him when she was given the part of Portia opposite his Shylock. It was the right decision. The role established her, once and for all, as an actress with extraordinary talent. After that, she was able to pick and choose. Several impresarios offered her top billing above anyone else in the company in which she would work. After thinking it over, she accepted an offer. Again, it was the right one.

She bought an elegant new outfit—a white filmy dress with a long white wool cloak to match. Continuing to live modestly in her quarters on Charles Street, she accepted few invitations, except those from old friends like the Booths or Lola Montez. Her life in New York had begun to duplicate her life in San Francisco. Occasionally, she would have supper with an admirer. The admirer stayed in his carriage at Marielle's insistence when she was brought home—it was a rule of hers. Not one of her suitors ever questioned her on it.

She received a letter from Mary Ann Crabtree with a little note at the bottom in Lotta's hand. They were touring eastward, stopping in every city big enough to accommodate their production with a full house of cheering spectators who could afford to pay little Lotta well to entertain in her own inimitable way.

Once again, lines began to form outside her dressing room. After each performance she thanked each admirer personally in the remote way she had cultivated in San Francisco. One day, a man brought her a bouquet of flowers after a show. Not recognizing him as one of her regulars, she thanked him thoughtfully, and turned to someone else.

"Do you still have Snowball?" the man asked, and grinned.

She turned back to him. He had the same apple cheeks and wide cheerful grin, but now he was stocky and his hairline was beginning to recede. But it was the same Johnnie Fox, Quinn's old friend on the *Andrew Jackson*.

Marielle's eyes misted as she greeted him. How could she forget Johnnie Fox?

"I've been second mate on a merchant ship called the *Sparta-cus*. For the past few years we've sailed between Le Havre and New York. But now, I'm going to be first mate on a new ship. Going by way of Panama to San Francisco."

She had supper with Johnnie Fox that night, and told him all about giving Snowball to a fine family with three young children who could care for and love the little white cat and keep it safely from harm's way.

"Have you ever seen Morgan Quinn again?" he asked with curiosity.

"I saw him in San Francisco, just before coming to New York," she said, telling him the exact truth, but not elaborating. "He is no longer going to sea, although I understand he owns several ships."

"Always wanted to bump into him again. He was a good sailor. I think I'll try to get in touch when my ship docks there."

"I believe he owns a ranch also," she said in a noncommittal way.

"Does he now?"

They did not speak about Quinn any further. Instead, Johnnie told her about himself. He no longer was a shy boy whose face got red when he talked with a woman. He was a man now, with a French wife in Le Havre and an infant son. He was planning to bring them both to the United States once he got settled on his new ship and schedule.

It was a lovely, gentle evening, but when Marielle got home and went to bed, she took many memories of her first meetings with Morgan Quinn out of a reserved place in her thoughts and relived them. It was the first time since she had left the West, oh so long ago, that she had allowed herself to think about the man who had changed her life so wholly.

Perhaps Marielle's sweetest triumph came when she opened in a new extravaganza called *Pocahontas*. The play was semioperatic, with the leading characters interrupting their story every now and then to sing music that had been composed specifically for the play.

It was a most unusual opening; the melodies were lilting and easy to remember, and the words were simple and catchy so that the public could repeat them. The audience was enchanted. Marielle played the title role in a long, black wig and was more bewitching than ever in an authentic buckskin costume covered with tiny glass beads. Everyone in the cast acted and sang, and there was a colorful Indian war dance at the close of the second act.

The Prince of Wales, traveling as Baron Renfrew, came to a performance of *Pocahontas*. He was so taken with Marielle that he came backstage at the end of the evening. As he congratulated her, one of his emissaries stood by with a jeweler's case. When he turned to take his leave, the emissary handed a velvet case to Marielle. In it was a magnificent diamond bracelet.

The next day, a different intermediary approached Marielle with an invitation to a private party given by the supposed Baron Renfrew. Marielle refused the invitation and sent back the diamond bracelet at the same time. The so-called Baron sent the bracelet to her once more with a note saying that he hoped to see her again sometime in the future. Would she please keep the bracelet as a small token of his esteem? She threw it into the leather coffer with her other trinkets.

During the long run of *Pocahontas*, Lola Montez died. She had been ravaged by disease, and at the end her mind was wandering. Marielle could not attend the funeral because of a matinee performance, but she went out to Greenwood Cemetery the following morning to put flowers on Lola's grave.

The plot was peaceful and overlooked a small pond, but the day was icy and bleak. A tombstone had not as yet been erected over the small mound of earth that covered Lola's casket. Marielle placed her flowers on the grave. As her eyes misted, she wiped the tears away with a small, gloved hand that she took out of a white fur muff. Before she knew it, she found herself talking to her old friend.

"Thank you, Lola. Thank you for everything. I shall try and remember your courage in living your own life, no matter what. And I shall live as you did, I promise you."

A tall, serious-looking man arrived at the gravesite, smiled at Marielle tentatively, and put a huge wreath of splendid lilies next to Marielle's small offering. He stepped away politely, but did not leave. He was not handsome in the conventional way, but there was something regal about him, about the cut of his clothes, the way he held his head, the aristocratic look in his soft, dark eyes.

Just before Marielle was ready to leave, he stepped closer to her and in a soft, almost unaccented voice introduced himself. His name was Grigori Aleksandrov. He was an old friend of the Countess of Landsfeld and had heard about her death too late to come to the funeral. He was Russian, he told her gravely as he handed her an engraved calling card.

Would it be possible for an old friend of Lola Montez to take tea with another old friend of the Countess?

Marielle mulled over his offer and looked up at him from under her thick fringe of lashes. The wind blew through the long length of silken red hair left uncovered by her bonnet.

"Yes . . . of course!" she murmured in the remote way she had acquired.

When Prince Grigori offered her his arm, Marielle took it and gave him a faint smile. The dimple in each cheek deepened and accented the pink flush on her face. After dismissing Marielle's public conveyance, the prince led her to his private carriage waiting discreetly outside the gates of the cemetery. On his face was a faraway, lost look. The prince had fallen in love.

That year a tall lawyer from Illinois was elected president, and no sooner did he take office than the fighting started in earnest. Abraham Lincoln did not want war, but he would not allow the United States to be torn asunder by the secessionists.

Life in New York did not change much, except that now Marielle saw more blue uniforms in her audiences. Her life did not change much either, except that she leased a luxurious but narrow little house close to the Booths in the Gramercy Park district of the city.

She also wrote to Madame Benét and offered to sponsor her if she wished to come to New York and open up a place of business. Marielle would pay for everything and be a silent partner in the venture. She received a grateful letter of acceptance from Francine Benét. The French couturiere was leaving her shop in San Francisco with a trusted helper and would come to New York, where she and Marielle could make plans for the future. However, the loan that Madame Benét would accept from her benefactress would have to be paid back first before she would accept any share in the profits. If that was agreeable to Marielle, Francine could start almost immediately. Marielle wrote back that it was, indeed, more than acceptable. It was not just an investment she was making; she would have a trusted friend and confidante close by.

Shortly after this, President Lincoln declared a blockade of all Southern ports. Johnnie Fox returned to New York. His ship was one of the vessels the North was going to use to patrol Southern waters. The vessel was being fitted properly for the job, and Johnnie had some time on his hands. He came to the theatre and invited Marielle to supper afterwards.

Marielle had to break an engagement with Prince Grigori in order to see Johnnie, which made the prince very unhappy. "There is no reason why we can't make a threesome for dinner," she told the prince.

"Thank you, my dear," the prince said in a crestfallen voice. "But I will just have to conjure up your beauty tonight. Someone else more favored than I will be facing it in person."

"Tomorrow night, Grigori," Marielle said in a kindly way.

Prince Grigori Aleksandrov had to content himself with her promise. She swept out of the theatre with Johnnie Fox as a large crowd watched with interest and envy. She noticed nothing, but Johnnie was overwhelmed by her popularity.

"I found Morgan Quinn," Johnnie announced proudly, even before they ordered supper.

Marielle twirled a champagne glass filled with orange juice and forced herself not to say anything.

"Marielle," Johnnie leaned forward and spoke in a confidential whisper so that the waiters could not hear. "He is sending shiploads of gold to the North, all the way from California."

"He must be a very busy man." Marielle sipped her sweet drink nonchalantly.

"And a courageous one. He is outfitting one of his own ships and plans to captain it himself. He hopes President Lincoln will commission him and his ship so that he can help tighten the blockade. He feels the blockade will prove the South's undoing."

"Is he married now?"

Johnnie looked up at her in surprise. His round cheeks puffed out thoughtfully as he cut through a thick ration of mutton. "We talked about the war all evening. I never thought of asking. Nor did he ask me. He doesn't know I'm a father, nor does he know my wife and son will be arriving in New York soon."

"Congratulations. I know you will be very happy when your family is safely on American soil."

"Oh, by the way," Johnnie said as they were preparing to leave the restaurant. "Did you know there is something wrong with Morgan's right hand. Some sort of bad accident he was in a while back. They would not accept him when he tried to form his own cavalry regiment. But in the Navy, it's different."

Again, when she was alone, Marielle was left with thoughts of Quinn. This time she did not try to suppress them. Instead, she let them flow freely as she sadly gave in to the whisperings of her heart.

* * *

Prince Grigori Aleksandrov turned out to be a good friend, an ardent admirer, and a persistent suitor. "There is nothing I would not do to make you happy," the lovesick man told her. He did not mind that the world saw his love for the beautiful, young actress.

She celebrated her twenty-first birthday with him alone at a sumptuous dinner at the stylish Şt. Nicholas Hotel. She wore a white, diaphanous, silk chiffon gown purchased especially for the occasion and a cape lined with white sable. Her hair, always enhanced by the color white, shimmered in long, curling silken strands that flamed even more in the glow of the huge chandeliers hanging throughout the high-ceilinged dining room. Her face was serene, and her eyes became pools of clear blue as they reflected the dancing lights from the lamps in the middle of each table.

After the caviar and champagne was served (straight vodka in a water glass for the prince), Grigori brought out her birthday present. It was a matched set of rubies and diamonds made into a necklace and earrings; its intricate setting obviously had been crafted in Russia. She had never seen any jewels so exquisite in her life. Catching her breath at the sight, she allowed Grigori to fasten the necklace around her smooth, alabaster neck and removed her own earrings to replace them with the birthday gift.

She remembered the garnet brooch and eardrops she had worn on her eighteenth birthday when she had also worn a white dress. Now though, she had everything she had ever wanted, including what she had wanted the most—*freedom.*

Becoming twenty-one meant coming of age, at last being legally done with Morgan Quinn. She had never felt free of Quinn, even in New York. He could swoop down at any moment and return her to the Double Raven. She would search the faces in the crowds in the street, turn her head and look for someone following her, scan the audience from the peephole in the curtain in the deadly suspicion of what she might see. When she entered a room, she stopped first at the threshold. It was whispered that she did this in order to make a grand entrance, but the truth was that she was afraid Morgan Quinn would be in front of her, and that would be the end of her career, her independence, her very existence. He would take over her life and do with it as he pleased.

Now, on her birthday, she need never have that fear again. She was free; she was independent; she was supporting herself more grandly than many other thespians, and she had the adoration of everyone who watched her perform. And she wouldn't stop. She would keep on going from here. She would do it for Papa, who had never reached the pinnacle, though not for lack of talent. All he had lacked was drive. She, his daughter, not only had his talent, but her own drive and determination to reach the very top.

Still, she couldn't help wondering how badly she needed Morgan Quinn and why. Physically, she had never stopped wanting him. She had admitted that to herself a long time ago, and had decided to simply live with it. How did one conquer one's emotions, though? Unless, of course, she could replace him with someone else. Perhaps with Prince Grigori?

As she was thinking this, Prince Grigori proposed to her, as he did every week. "Have you not decided whether you would like to be a princess? I can arrange it very easily. At a moment's notice."

"Thank you, dear Grigori," she heard herself saying, and she laughed, the mirth tinkling delightfully from her throat. "But I am not ready for you. I am merely a simple, little girl who would not know what to do with the title of princess."

"Do not try to deceive me. You are not simple at all. And I will be happy to teach you anything you do not already know."

"Everybody wants to teach me," she said ruefully.

"You did not let me finish. I think the only thing I need to teach you is how to be happy . . ."

She interrupted him again. "But I am happy," she persisted, and smiled at him in her most beguiling fashion.

"I do not believe that," the prince said with a note of melancholy in his voice. He looked exceptionally regal this evening in his dress uniform of red, white, and gold. There was a saber at his side.

"You are beginning to look gloomy. Your Russian eyes will cry *for* me if I let you. Smile, Grigori. For me!"

"Tell me one thing I can do for you to make you truly happy, and I will smile forever."

A soft giggle escaped her lips. "Let's see . . ." After taking a tiny sip of champagne, she set the tall crystal glass down and pretended to mull over his proposal. "Well . . ." she said, and this time she did not giggle. "I might like to produce and direct and star in my own version of *Hamlet*."

"But you have done Ophelia many times. Why would you do the role again?" He looked bewildered. "Ask for something worthwhile."

"I do not mean to play Ophelia in my own production. I mean to play Hamlet." She was deadly serious.

Grigori let out a long breath. "Aaaah!" he said, staring at her in fascination for a long time. He lifted his glass of vodka high and saluted her silently.

Chapter Twenty-nine

Finding an Ophelia who was young enough to play opposite her was just one of the many problems Marielle encountered in the months to come. Marielle remembered all the hard work Ted Booth had put into his *Hamlet* and worked even harder to make her company as near perfect as possible. Her standards were so high, everyone else caught the fever and worked as hard as she did. Grigori insisted on being sole backer, and that it be the most opulent theatrical offering of the season.

"I will be agreeable to your terms and spare no expense," Marielle told him at tea time as they went over the many production details that came up each day. "But only if you recoup your investment completely before I draw any profits. I will, however, accept a small salary for my services as an actress." She remembered the words Francine Benét had written to her when she offered the Frenchwoman backing for her dressmaking establishment.

"It is not necessary," Grigori said stiffly, and Marielle got the feeling he was insulted. "I insist that everything be the best."

"You must agree to this financial arrangement, Grigori dear."

"Whatever you say," he said quickly, and signed the business papers she had placed before him.

Francine Benét had arrived in New York several weeks earlier and had found a suitable building on a fashionable street for her new venture. Even now she was getting ready to open for business. She was only waiting for her new seamstresses and helpers to arrive from Paris. She had written and recruited several of the women she knew who had been apprenticed at the House of Worth, where she had also been formerly employed. Marielle was happy for her and listened to her plans and helped when she could. She felt she had made a wise investment in her friend's future.

But she had outrageous plans, too. Everyone agreed that there must be secrecy about Marielle's *Hamlet* up until the last minute before the big publicity campaign. They did not want anyone else getting wind of what Marielle was attempting. She did not want some veteran actress getting there ahead of her. She remembered Edwin Booth and Edwin Forrest both doing *Hamlet* at the same time in the same city simply because Forrest could not keep his mouth closed while he was preparing his company of actors.

It was going to be the best-kept secret in Manhattan. Yet, there were whispers that something unusual was about to happen on the New York stage and that it would set tongues wagging.

As the exhausting rehearsals began Marielle committed herself to being a hard taskmaster, to creating her own unique version of Shakespeare's tragedy. She worked from early morning until late at night and even on Sunday.

She hired Madame Benét to do the costumes for the entire company, and the results were daring and beautiful. Even the old-timers in the company were impressed. Marielle's costume was left for the last. It was very simple, what she had always dreamed of when she thought of Hamlet. When she tried on Francine Benét's creation for the first time and showed it to Prince Grigori, he was speechless.

"What do you think? Will it be alright?"

"You are amazing. I have never seen you more beautiful, yet I have never seen a handsomer young Hamlet."

Marielle was pleased. "You shall see, dear Grigori, a Hamlet who is not just a character in a famous play, but an individual; everyone who watches me will see a reflection of themselves in this *Hamlet.*"

"I don't doubt it," the prince said with a twinkle in his eye.

Madame Benét had used silk, sable, and the richest black she could find to set off Marielle's red hair and pale skin. The startling blue of her eyes became even more electric as she donned the short tunic and fitted the well-made black silk stockings to her long, slender legs. Her cloak was lined with the same dark sable that trimmed the silk tunic. Her hair was a masterpiece of deception in that one of Madame Benét's ladies from Paris had been able to keep it clustering over her head in bountiful shimmering disarray without having to cut it. Yet it still looked like a style the young Hamlet might have favored. She did not try to hide her feminine attributes; she ignored them completely. The effect was ravaging. As she asked for opinions from the company, they stood dumbstruck; there was simply nothing to say.

Marielle was ready to sign the lease on the theatre and make announcements when it was discovered that the Booth brothers were performing together for one night only on the very date she had planned to open her production of *Hamlet*. They had engaged the Winter Garden for the evening and were already advertising Shakespeare's *Julius Caesar*.

"What do you intend to do about this situation?" Prince Aleksandrov asked as he accompanied Marielle to yet another grueling rehearsal.

"We shall not panic," Marielle said calmly.

"I can try and buy them off and arrange for them to perform together at some other time."

"No. We will set back our own opening exactly one week. We will continue as if nothing has happened. Edwin Booth is my dear friend, and I've waited too long to let a minor detail like this upset me. Or upset him."

The prince looked at her admiringly. "I shall make the new arrangements today, while you rehearse. Leave everything to me."

"Thank you. And, Grigori, please arrange for the best box at the Winter Garden so that we can be present at my friends' triumph. I would not want to miss it for anything."

"Naturally. That will be no problem." The prince prepared to leave. "By the way, I want to propose marriage to you again. Perhaps this is not the right time, but I cannot help myself. I have never stopped wanting you as my princess, even more so now that you will be the most famous Hamlet in the world."

Marielle leaned against him affectionately. "You have been very good to me, Grigori. And do not think I have not given your proposals my full consideration."

"Well?"

She smiled at him gently, then said, "Let us talk about it some more, right after the performance of *Julius Caesar*. Take me to supper afterwards, and remind me to speak to you of our future."

The prince leaned over and kissed her forehead with just a hint of reverence on his face.

She *had* thought about Grigori and the advantages a marriage to him would bring. It could be called an alliance more than a marriage. She would have everything money could buy, a title if she wanted to use it, and entry into every high-ranking social circle in the world. He loved her and was good to her.

She would say *yes*, she decided, next week, after *Julius Caesar*.

Chapter Thirty

It was on that fateful night of the Booths' Winter Garden appearance that Morgan Quinn came back into her life. He had found the precise moment to interrupt her when she needed him least, when he could wreck her complex plans for the future, and throw her body into a state of treacherous betrayal, her mind into confusion. They met again, backstage, when the prince and she went to pay their respects to the Booths.

Her gossamer dress, made of pure golden threads, shimmered with her every movement. As she walked to the dressing rooms backstage, people caught their breaths; she seemed to be walking in a halo of light made by both her hair and her dress. The crowds parted and let her through. She did not notice this bit of homage; she took it for granted. Her cape trailed behind her on the floor as she swept by to congratulate the Booths, and instead came face to face with Morgan Quinn.

Even before she looked up into those devastatingly sharp gray eyes, her heart thudded in her chest.

"Who is that man?" the prince asked. He was right behind her as they came closer to Quinn.

Marielle was startled that the prince asked the question, but she really did not wonder over it for long, because it was obvious that Quinn made his presence felt wherever he went. He was taller than everyone else and handsomer even than John Wilkes. He was a man whom nature had favored.

"He is my guardian," she whispered to Grigori, and then stopped awkwardly and corrected herself. "He *was* my guardian until I turned twenty-one."

"He is too young to have been your guardian."

She gave a delicious giggle. "I thought so too. That is why I have never obeyed him."

At the same time, she swept into Quinn's view, took his hand and shook it before he had a chance to protest, and kissed him on the cheek. She played it to perfection, the ex-ward greeting her ex-guardian. She could see he was visibly shaken by her sudden appearance; little did he know she was more shaken than he. But she was the actress and would never let him see.

The prince had chuckled at the answer to his question, and had not quite believed her. But the dear man did make the meeting just a little bit easier even though he accepted Morgan Quinn at face value. There was no way she would ever make him understand the dread of lack of freedom Quinn had brought into her life.

Now Quinn stood stock still, leaned back his head slightly, and looked her over, very much the same way he had done on Saturday afternoons when he reserved time to chastise her for the bad reports given her by Miss Penelope.

She hung onto Grigori's arm. Several times she was waylaid as friends and admirers sought her out. Finally, Grigori found her again and led her to the exit. She was glad they would be alone at last.

When they reached the prince's private carriage, though, she was amazed and horrified to find Quinn inside. The prince had invited him to have a drink with them, and Quinn had accepted.

She knew Grigori Aleksandrov was trying to be kind to the man he thought had been such a big influence in her early life, but she scowled in the darkness of the carriage and wished he were more discerning about just how much of Quinn she wanted to see.

They drove to the Fifth Avenue Hotel, another new and luxurious establishment built to cater to the creature comforts of the very rich. Even here, her face was well-known, and their party was given a table in a private corner of the restaurant.

She sat sipping champagne, flanked by the men. Grigori held a glass of vodka; Quinn drank whiskey. She listened to the conversation of the two men as she played with her linen napkin and the stem of her glass. It was easy to see that Grigori and Quinn liked and respected each other immediately. They talked about California and politics and the war. Quinn's ship was in New York for repairs that would take several weeks. A cannon ball had forced it out of action, but no hands had been lost and Quinn was thankful. It could have been worse, he said. His commissioned ship was part of a blockade of gunboats hemming in the Gulf of Mexico and the Atlantic Ocean.

As he talked to Grigori, he seemed to forget Marielle. Or perhaps he was trying to ignore her. But then, when the conversation slowed down, he stopped talking altogether and stared at her, his eyes drinking in every one of her features as if to memorize them in case there was no next time.

She became embarrassed by his steady and very intimate gaze and tried to look away, but his steely gray eyes impelled her to return his look, and she became lost in a spell of sweet nostalgia. She imagined she felt his touch and realized he may have brushed her knee accidentally under the table with his long, outstretched legs. A tremor ran through her, and she hugged her arms around herself. The prince tried to cover her shoulders with her cape, but she shrugged it off without thinking. She did not want the feeling to go away. Her eyes went to Quinn's hair, that wonderfully thick, dark, unruly hair falling in ringlets onto his forehead. Even now, in the spectacularly civilized setting of the lighted hotel, he looked like he was ready to draw her into his arms.

Prince Aleksandrov looked from one to the other, puzzled. Marielle felt sorry for him. Continuing to sit in her place between the two, she wanted one of them so much, she tried to forget the other was there.

"Let me see your hand. The one that was injured in your accident." She had to touch Morgan Quinn in some legitimate way or she felt she might die.

He lifted his right hand and brought it closer to her, almost in front of her pounding bosom. The heat from him came through and seemed to burn her right where the décolletage of her dress exposed her bare skin. She took his hand and turned the strong fingers palm up, and then palm down, and then she pretended to search for scars. She could not let go of his warm, vibrant fingers, and only because she remembered that Grigori was sitting on one side of her did she keep from taking his hand and placing it on the soft visible rounds of her breasts as they throbbed through the gold fabric of her gown.

"I do not see that there is anything wrong with your hand," she said finally, knowing there was a tremor in her voice that she could not control. "I was told it was shattered."

"It has healed. It took a long time. It will never be quite the same."

She continued to hold on to his hand, and he let her.

"Marielle, my dear . . ." Grigori said in alarm. She quickly released Quinn's hand, or perhaps he might have withdrawn it from her—she was not sure.

Grigori signaled hastily to the waiter for another vodka and for the others to have their drinks refilled. When she looked at Quinn again, she thought she detected a smile he could not keep hidden. But by the time Grigori turned back to them, the smile had disappeared from Quinn's face.

Somehow, that angered her. She felt he was having a private laugh at her expense. She became more infuriated the more she thought about it while the men merely went back to talking about California and the horse Quinn had found and bought back that had once been hers. He was breeding Arabian palominos now, and the mare who had started it all was Lady, the horse he had purchased for Marielle for her eighteenth birthday. The prince thought it was a charming story about a girl and a horse. Little did he know the many things the storyteller had left out of his tale. Some day she would have to tell the prince the whole truth. Somehow, that angered her even more. Now, she felt, Quinn was trying to make a fool of Grigori too.

"Morgan . . ." she said impulsively. "Prince Aleksandrov and I have an announcement. We want *you* to be the *first* to know. We are planning on getting married."

She did not know she was going to say it; even Grigori looked surprised and then very proud and pleased. Picking up her glass, she leaned back and tried to evaluate how her ex-guardian was taking the news.

Quinn picked up his glass, took a long swallow of whiskey, and then put it down very deliberately. He turned to the prince and opened his mouth to speak.

"I do not need your consent," Marielle interrupted him again with a fierceness she did not know was in her. "I am over twenty-one now."

Except for his mouth, which closed tightly against the words he was about to say, Quinn was in complete control. He turned from the prince to Marielle. "It is customary to congratulate the groom." Turning back to Grigori, he put out his hand. "Congratulations, sir. You have taken yourself a handful."

Marielle found his knee under the table and kicked him with her pointed French slipper. She was sure Grigori was aware of what she had done, but she did not care. Anything to hurt the devil, Quinn.

"What date do you think will be best, my love?" she asked, and smiled sweetly at the prince.

"Why not right after the run of your next production. Right after you finish with *Hamlet*. We can start tonight though, by becoming engaged."

"Done. I am very happy, Grigori," she said, and turned to see what effect it had on Quinn.

He had a closed, stony look on his face. She felt triumphant. "Of course, Mr. Quinn, being you're practically family, I will see that you get an invitation to the wedding." She dimpled prettily and turned to make sure he saw her happiness. "In the meantime, since you have to be in New York for a while, you are invited to my opening night next week. I will see there is a good seat for you in the third row center. I would not want my loving former guardian to miss it."

That night sleep did not come. She sat in an oversize armchair in her nightdress and a wool dressing robe in front of a smoldering fire and waited for what seemed an eternity. By four o'clock in the morning, she gave up. But something made her continue sitting in the chair just a little longer. She picked up a book of poetry and opened the pages at random without really reading. Tonight she would not sleep at all, she knew, no matter if she went to bed or not. He would come. She knew it as surely as she knew her own perfidious body and how it felt every time she thought of him.

Morgan Quinn, who had arrived in the middle of a war, thousands of miles away from where he belonged, was as handsome and as cold and cruel as always. He had sailed back into her life as if he had never been gone, merely to torment her. The sailor returned from the sea.

Restlessly she put down her book, and as she was about to close it and get up, she heard the clattering hooves and clanking wheels of a hansom cab; and then she heard the sound of boots on the cobblestones—someone was at her door.

He pounded on the heavy wooden door. When she opened it, Quinn stood before her, tall and mighty, sending a charged current between them. It was dangerous for her to be alone with him, but it was the kind of danger her body could not resist.

He came into her house as if he thought he belonged or worse, as if he felt he owned it, immediately making himself comfortable in the very armchair she had just vacated. Obviously, he had had a few drinks, not enough to make him drunk, but enough so she could detect the aroma of spirits on his breath. "Shall I start up a fire? Would you like me to put on the kettle?"

"No. A brandy will do." He seemed gloomier than usual, and spread his long legs out toward the fire, which gave out little warmth.

She poured him a small brandy, which he drank down in one long gulp while she fed more logs into the fire.

"I think we best talk," he said after he put his glass down.

"You cannot stop me from getting married this time. You have absolutely no legal hold on me."

"I do have a hold on you. Only it's not legal this time. You must not marry your Prince Charming."

"Why not, pray?"

He looked away into the orange flames as they crackled and popped. "You don't have to marry him. You can marry me."

"Oh? Whatever happened to Miss Penelope?"

He had the audacity to look amused. That slightly crooked smile that she could not resist was on his lips, but his eyes, she noticed, were watchful and arrogant.

"Why don't you tell me all about Miss Penelope?" she said more sharply than she intended.

"She has not been at the ranch for a long time. She left shortly after she finished nursing me back to health. Which, I might add, was more than you did for me. I told her the truth about you. She was shocked."

Marielle felt her face flush pink. It was true. She had left the ranch before he was well—or could stop her.

"She is in Oregon, where she teaches school," he continued, and his sense of humor got the better of him as he smiled again. "She has recently found herself a satisfactory widower who fills all her requirements. They plan to marry and have children as soon as possible."

The kettle boiled, and she poured herself a cup of tea. "And what is the truth about me? What did you tell her?"

"Everything."

"Absolutely *everything*?"

"Yes. And that I loved you and was going to marry you."

"And how did she take that?"

"She said it was about time. Believe me, she was on your side. She said that if I treat you like a child, you will act like a child. So I am treating you like a grown-up. I love you, Marielle. I am offering you marriage."

"Why didn't you offer me that from the first?"

He looked up from the fire wearily, and paused as if to think. "Oh, God! So many reasons—none of which had anything to do with your age. The most important one was Rio. There was something wrong with my brother."

"I knew there was something wrong. I think I knew almost from the beginning," she said sadly. "But you refused to tell me anything."

"You were too young . . ." He let the sentence trail off as if he did not mean to say it, and looked grim. "Rio would have gotten worse as he grew older, or so we were told by doctors in the East who specialize in his kind of sickness. It couldn't be cured, they said. It started to progress very rapidly after he turned eighteen. He could easily have become a murderer if we hadn't watched over him very closely."

Automatically, Marielle's hand went up to her throat. She remembered the time Rio had hurt her and that she had not spoken up.

"Rio was in love with you, Marielle. He really believed he was going to marry you. There was nothing I could do except withhold my consent whenever he asked for your hand. I was a torn man. I was in hell. I could not marry you myself because of the effect it would have on Rio, and I could not tell you. I did not want you to be afraid all the time."

"So you let me suffer the unknown to make it easier for you?"

He groaned. "It wasn't like that at all. There was also the war. I knew there would be one, and I felt a responsibility to offer my services to the North. It would not have been fair to you to be married to someone who was not there—maybe for years—or worse. You might have been widowed, and then you would have been alone on the ranch with Rio. Did someone as young as you need all those problems?"

"So you gave me worse problems. I never knew what was happening. Where I stood. It was very lonely. And I was afraid."

"I will make up for everything in the past. I promise you. The Double Raven is bigger and better than it ever was. It is a warm and beautiful house now. I rebuilt it myself. My mother had no part in this building. Carmel always felt it was her fault Rio was tainted because he came from her body. She was a bitter woman. In her bitterness she built a cold, unhappy house. It's not that way now."

He paused, and she left the room and returned with a small, velvet case, which she handed him. He opened it. In it were the two diamond stickpins she had never had the heart to sell, even when she needed the money the most. He closed the box with a look of gratitude and gave it back to her. "Thank you. Keep them for us."

She nodded and returned the velvet case to the other room. When she came back he pulled her down on his lap. The heady aroma of brandy assailed her nostrils. She felt his touch and that was all that mattered as he curved her into his lap.

"Hu Ming is still at the ranch, and his family oversees our entire operation while I'm away. It could be a very happy home."

"You must tell me . . . Morgan . . . say it out loud. Will you really treat me as an equal if I become your wife? As someone who can think for herself?"

He nodded and laughed. "Yes. I need you, Marielle."

"I'm not sure I believe you."

He spoke very carefully. "Oh, yes. I need you. I am a haunted man. I cannot stop remembering your touch. The taste of you is with me even when you are not. My lips thirst for the juices of our love." All the time, he stroked her as he held her and spoke.

His face glowed in the firelight and she could not take her eyes from his, those gray eyes that could say more than any words. But he was saying the right things now, and she listened and found she could not reject them. She loved him. He loved her.

"My body aches to breathe in your sweetness, to touch the softness of your skin."

He always made her breathless. All she needed to do was look at him. "Quinn," she whispered, and put her arms around him and gave him her lips as she caressed him. She gave herself up to him, unable to keep her hands from touching him. Her fingertips tingled as they caressed his face. His lips were firm and full, and she could not think of anyone in the entire world she would rather be kissing, even the Russian prince she had promised to marry. She pulled away regretfully from him. She would have to break her engagement to Grigori. It would not be pleasant. It would hurt the prince very much. But it had to be done.

"There is no reason anymore for us to deny ourselves the happiness we deserve. You will be happy and safe at the ranch. You will never have to worry about earning your living again. I have enough to make your life easy for the rest of your days."

"What about my career? What about my *Hamlet?*"

"I will take care of everything. I'll cancel for you—pay off everyone. You need never go on the stage again."

"What are you saying?"

"I am saying you need not be beholden to your prince—or to anyone else. I will buy out the entire production. You don't ever have to fight your way to success again. You will be my wife. I can take care of you."

She slid off his lap, and stood facing him. Shaking with anger, she still felt that special urgency that came when he was near, that terrible urge to touch him. But she controlled herself, as her hurt and wrath surfaced. "Do you mean to say that in order to be your wife I must leave the stage?"

Quinn smiled devilishly, that very special smile she found so hard to resist. "You don't understand. You don't *have* to be an actress. You don't *have* to subject yourself to being in the public eye."

"No. *You* do not understand. I like to act. It's part of my life."

His face became a mask of cold steel. She had never seen him look so handsome, or so angry.

"You are still a contrary child who cannot come to terms with reality."

"Your reality," she screamed. Her nerves exploded into a million tiny particles of rage. "Get out," she screamed at the top of her voice and forgot to care about the neighbors. "Get out once and for all. Get out!"

And then she started to throw things.

Chapter Thirty-one

The day of Marielle's *Hamlet* opening dawned cold and dreary. By mid-afternoon, it started to snow. The sun tried hard to push its way through, but gave up and hid so completely that the bleak sky seemed pewter in color. Marielle bundled up in warm clothes and heavy boots and was the first of the company to arrive at the theatre.

Inside, the theatre was so cold it took more than an hour before the janitor could coax heat onto the oversize stage. By the time the entire group was assembled for final rehearsal, some warmth had crept in, but not enough to keep the actors' teeth from chattering as they spoke Shakespeare's words. Marielle had every footlight on the stage and every light in the house lit. It helped, and they rehearsed right up to afternoon tea. Then she dismissed the company for two hours before they would assemble again. This was it. The next time they worked together, it would be in front of an audience.

When they all returned from their short rest period, most of them were covered with snow and looked like white ghosts until they shook themselves off and the snowflakes floated to the floor to melt in puddles around their feet. Marielle had not bothered to leave the theater.

She sat in her dressing room, drinking hot tea and waiting for the most important hours of her life. As always, the closer she came to a first-night performance, the more fear she felt and the sicker she became. Tonight, even more than on other opening nights, she felt the urge to throw up. She alone was completely responsible for success or failure. The minute she went on stage, she would have no one but herself to blame if the response was bad. Never before had she felt so vulnerable. The role of Hamlet, she had been told, had that effect on an actor.

Prince Grigori stopped by and gave her words of encouragement. She smiled wanly, but hardly listened. Then he left at her insistence for his seat. At the moment of truth she had to be alone.

The theater started to fill early. The balcony, with its cheaper seats, filled first. Rowdy, working-class devotees of the drama, who could not afford to sit in the loges or downstairs in the orchestra, sat close together, smelling of the workday they had just put in. Tonight they seemed to be a sullen crowd, although Marielle's face was not new to them, and she was one of their favorites. The weather was bad, and the word was out that something was amiss, something was going to be different, and they were intrigued, but suspicious. They shook the snow off their clothes and settled down to see what was being offered. What they needed was something to take them far away from the harsh reality of their everyday lives.

The orchestra filled up next, together with the standing room only seats in the back of the theater that were sold after every other seat had been taken. She would have more than a full house tonight. As the saying went, they were hanging from the rafters. The standees jostled each other for the best positions. There was great excitement throughout the theater, but as Marielle looked through the peephole, she thought she detected a note of hostility. She didn't know where exactly the notion had come from, and she shrugged it off.

Presently, she donned her black costume and made herself ready for her entrance. She sneaked to the peephole once more, and the entire theater was one mass of faceless humanity, coughing and hacking, chattering and moving their bodies into more comfortable positions. There was a dampness in the air; perhaps, Marielle thought, because of all the snow that had melted off the garments.

In the third row center was Morgan Quinn. After the first pulse-pounding reaction to his presence, she was not really surprised to see him. She had hoped he would have the decency to stay away after the battle of the other night, but then, his sense of decency was rather limited.

She had been dreadfully hurt by his open insensitivity the night he had come to her house. But, no, she had not been surprised. She would have been amazed if he had behaved differently. His actions were pure Morgan Quinn, the man she hated, and the same man for whom she felt a great tug of love each time he appeared. Instinctively, she knew that thinking about him now was bad, and she forced herself to think only of the performance ahead. She would deal with him afterwards. In the meantime, it would not hurt for him to see her in the glory of her finest performance, accepting the accolades of an astonished following. Now she felt as sure of her acting ability as she was unsure of the meaning of her hate and love for Morgan Quinn.

Grigori was seated in the second row; in fact, there were people she knew everywhere in the theater. The rosy cheeks of the women and the cherry noses of the men made the evening seem unreal, as if everyone had put on stage makeup and would be performing along with the cast.

Checking her Ophelia, she found the young actress waiting in her little dressing room, the beautiful white costume Francine Benét had fashioned barely covering the goosebumps on her arms. She assured the girl that she always felt that way too, kissed her on the cheek, and left her reluctantly. She remembered how Ted Booth had left her the first time she was to play Ophelia, and how she had felt.

It seemed forever before the curtain was raised and she stepped onto the stage with the applause of the entire audience ringing in her ears. They were welcoming her, telling her they were with her, that they loved her. She had to tune them out in order to give them what they wanted. A fine performance. She used her body and her voice the way she had planned; every single word, every single nuance, every motion, had been prepared and worked on till she had felt it was letter-perfect. Her trained voice and slim body in the black tunic and black silk stockings did exactly what she commanded. As she worked, she knew she was good. *Very, very good.*

Later, she could not remember at what point in the play she felt something hit her lightly on the chest. Whatever it was fell to her feet. Automatically, she looked down and saw that it was a bunch of rotten carrots. She could smell the decaying vegetables as she continued on.

Then came a cabbage, flying into one of the other actors, splitting and falling in green and yellow pieces all over the stage. A hoarse male voice was soon heard from the back of the balcony. "Yer ain't astin' us to buy yer masquerade, Marielle?" The voice was loud and somewhat inebriated, and the men around the voice laughed and started to jeer.

Her voice broke for one split second, but then she continued. She was a professional. The actors around her looked bewildered, but they, too, continued.

"Yer sure stanin' on a set of gorgeous gams for a man," another gruff voice rang out from the gallery. There were more laughs and catcalls.

"Yer daft, girl, yer know, trying to be the same as me," another voice rang out clearly, and she was assailed by the smell of a rotten egg that exploded at her feet.

Many in the audience tried to shush the troublemakers, but instead of helping they found themselves contributing to the bedlam.

Marielle persevered, wondering how long she could be heard above the dreadful uproar. It got worse every second. Would her Hamlet be doomed never to be heard to the end? She labored on, enduring all indignities as the story sped toward its closing, but she knew she could not persist much longer.

It was then she heard a voice from the front of the orchestra, powerful and strong and raised above the terrible din. It was Morgan Quinn's voice. He got up from his seat and turned around, and held up his long muscular arms for silence. "Give the lady a chance, and make your opinions known at the end, after she has finished what she is trying to do." He put his palms out toward the balcony, raising his hands higher. "Or else . . . let the man who would like to be the first to be thrown out by me, personally, speak up now." He stood tall and straight and strong. His voice was so sure, so confident of what he was saying, the clamor died down, and as it did, Marielle shivered, let out a long breath, and started again with hardly a break in her speech.

She did not know what happened after that, but she was able to finish the play in relative quiet and get off the stage. As soon as the curtain came down on the last act, the same male voices picked up where they had left off and drowned out the applause that came from other parts of the theatre. The velvet curtain became stained with the juices of squashed vegetables and malodorous eggs. There was even a small group of shrill female voices—women who were unhappy with an actress who tried to bite off more than she could chew, and who wore silk stockings and male tunics so the world could see her legs.

Escaping to her dressing room was not easy, and she was not sure she could get through the hostile mob outside the stage door. She ordered the back of the theater to be closed off to all visitors except Prince Grigori who was, after all, the financial backer and her fiancée. She was exhausted and in a state of shock, and she did not know how long she could keep the tears from flowing, letting the world know how miserable she felt. Her life was ruined. The entire New York theatre audience she respected so much had watched her grand and ambitious and very expensive fiasco. After the reviews came out in the newspapers and proved she was a complete fool and utter failure, she would never be allowed on a stage again.

Still wearing Hamlet's black tunic and black stockings, she had Grigori's carriage drive her home. "I must be alone," she pleaded with him backstage afterwards. "Promise me you will not intrude on my privacy tonight, please."

She did not relish the look of pity mingled with sad love she saw on his face. It spelled out the truth—that she had failed miserably and her career was over. Grigori's face had told her everything. Not only that, she was the laughingstock of New York. No one bothered to stop her as she dashed to the street and into the empty carriage waiting for her.

"It does not matter, my beloved, what they think," Grigori had said, but that look on his face told her it did matter. Very much. Still, as much as he commiserated with her, he honored her wish to solitude and left her alone.

As the carriage rolled through the streets she wondered whether she would have to leave New York; she knew she could never again face the jeers and catcalls she had faced tonight. She remembered the rotten vegetables coming from the cheaper gallery seats, flying through the air, landing at her feet, striking her body. She still heard the anger of the disapproving audience—the boos rang in her ears and even in the quiet of her rooms once she got home. She put her hands over her ears and tried to drown out the sounds she could never forget.

Flinging herself on the bed, she did not bother to light a fire or a lamp, and sobbed her heart out. She had never felt so alone and defeated in her life. Papa, she thought, I have sullied the name of Preston. I am sorry.

She did not know how long she lay there crying out loud when she thought she heard a knocking on her front door. It was loud and insistent, and she cried harder and hoped it would go away.

After a while, whoever was outside started pounding. She stumbled off the bed in the dark, made her way to the door, and opened it. All the time the pounding continued until she thought the heavy door would splinter.

A crisp, fresh wind blew into her face as the door opened, and by the light of a street lamp across the way, she saw Quinn standing alone, filling the doorway with his presence. There was no carriage or hansom cab in sight. He must have walked. It had stopped snowing and the night was very still.

She turned, leaving the door ajar, and left him to come in by himself if he so insisted. Flinging herself back on the bed, she left him to do what he wished in the dark rooms. She was sure he could hear her sobs, but since she could not control them, she continued on as if he were not there.

She heard him close the door. Then she heard him light a fire. The crackling of the logs as they ignited punctured the air with little sharp hisses that competed with her sobs. Finally, after taking off his coat and throwing it on the little sofa in her parlor, he came into the bedroom, gracefully lowered himself to the floor at the side of her bed, and knelt so that he could be close to her prone body.

She became very much aware of his presence, the sound of his breathing, and his voice as he talked softly to her.

"You are a fine actress, my sweet, contrary Marielle, and the most courageous woman I've ever met."

"Go away."

"I will not go away until I've had my say. I want you to know that there were many more out there who liked and understood what you did than those who did not."

She did not answer, but she listened, her face hidden in the pillows, her back to him.

"The crowds didn't expect to see a performance like yours. People are suspicious of anything new and innovative that they don't understand. They're afraid of surprise. They hate to think, and they tremble at the thought of wonder in their lives. You gave them everything, but they could not accept it. They didn't know how. You overwhelmed them. And you dumbfounded and overwhelmed me too."

He spoke so softly she had to quiet her sobs in order to hear what he had to say.

"I will never go on the stage again," she blubbered into the pillow.

"You will go on the stage again." It was not a command; it was a statement.

"Never. The hurt is not worth it."

"Yes, you will go on the stage again," he said gently. "Because it *is* worth it." He took her hand in both of his and brought it up to his lips and kissed it.

She turned her head slightly. "Hold me, Morgan. I need someone to hold me just for a little while," she whispered.

He continued to kneel beside the bed, but he turned her around and took her in his arms unhurriedly and held her, cradling her quietly with the strength of tautly muscled arms. After a while, he put his head down and rested it on the gentle swells of her breasts.

A heart-stopping wave of emotion swept through her body, just as it always did when he touched her, and she became engulfed in the pleasure of his nearness. He raised his head and kissed the long curve of her neck. Her hands reached out and brought his face up to hers until their lips met, and they began to explore and penetrate and taste each other's mouths.

The rooms were dark except for the glow of the fire, and she was reminded of the night they spent in the cabin in the wilderness, where there were only the two of them, alone in the world. It was like being in a womb, just the two of them in the security of their aloneness. She wanted him to entwine his body with hers so that she need never be only herself; she could always be part of him and the sureness and confidence he inspired. After tonight, especially, it was she who needed him much more than he needed her, no matter what he said.

His tongue teased hers and made her blood race through her body demanding more, needing more. Oh, she needed him desperately to quench the passion in her that only he seemed to know how to start. Oh, she needed him in so many different ways.

She felt him remove the short tunic she was still wearing. How strange that on the day of her most dismal failure, she still wanted him to take her.

He stripped down before her, uninhibited in his nakedness, unconscious of his splendor. And in the dim light she saw the scars on the inside of his right arm where it had been shattered. It had not been his hand at all, but his right forearm.

"Come here, Morgan . . . come to me," she said, and as he came to her she took his arm and pressed her lips to the scars, kissing them gently and with great love. From now on, every time she saw them she would remember how he got them and why. She moved the softness of her mouth over the scars and tried to taste the pain that had gone into their making. "I love you, Morgan

Quinn," she said simply. "I shall always love you, no matter what."

A smile played on his lips and there was a flash of triumph in his gray eyes as he took her in his arms. "Say it again, Marielle. Right now!"

"Why? I have said it before. I have said it more often than I care to think. If not to you, certainly to myself."

"Say it, Marielle."

"I love you, Morgan Quinn."

"It's the first time I've believed you."

"What do you mean?" she asked, her fingertips stroking the magnificent taut flesh of his chest, and her lips caressing the flatness of his belly.

"I was so wrong. After tonight, I promise you, I will never think of you as a child again. Not after what I saw you do on that stage. You were magnificent."

He kneeled over her and kissed the tight buds of satin heat curving out from the ivory swells of her breasts. With a soft moan, she pressed him closer, daring him with her enveloping arms to take every part of her most secret self. She needed him to take her in her failure, to want her when no one else did. She pressed him downward even more, and his lips and tongue went straight to the tiny round in the middle of her smooth belly, as if he knew exactly what his tongue must do to make her moan even more.

It was then, as his tongue continued to explore and probe and feast on her flesh, that it occurred to her that she was still wearing her black silk stockings. She slid her hand downward, loosened the tiny garter she was wearing, and rolled the stocking toward her ankle, trying to free herself of one stocking at a time without having to change her position. But she felt Morgan's hand close over her fingers. "Leave it be," she heard him say.

She let the stocking be, right where it was, rolled halfway down her calf. As he spread her slender legs, she saw the flash of one round white thigh and naked knee, while the other was still fitted with the black stocking almost up to the top of her thigh. It did not matter, because he was able to find her most sensitive, private places just above and beyond the thigh, and was even able to reach the smooth alabaster of the inside top of her thighs to kiss and make her drown in the blissful sensations coursing through her body.

Her body moistened as he reached for the velvet cleft in the middle of her widespread legs. Her body burned beneath his hands. Straining toward him, she made it plain that she was ready to receive him, and finally felt and accepted him as he plunged into her. They fit so well, they blended so perfectly, their bodies were so made for each other, that the moment they were completely entwined they began the rhythm that would make them rise and fall in complete, exquisite unison—until the mystic moment when he took her with him into a world no one else could enter, where their rapturous bodies dove into a maelstrom of wild, magical exultation.

It seemed to make some kind of perverse sense that their coming together tonight should be so good. She felt much better, as if her life was not at an end. Perhaps it would be just beginning. She loved every part of this man. She needed every part of him. She had just proven this by being able to put her troubles out of her head for him. She lay next to him now and touched the side of his strongly muscled thigh to make sure he was real.

Even as she ran her hand over his long, smooth muscles, he entwined her in his arms and proved he was very real. His lips were close to her mouth as he spoke. His breath was warm and familiar on her skin. She knew exactly what he looked like even though there wasn't enough light to see his face.

"My offer of marriage still stands, Marielle, if you are impractical enough to break your engagement with your rich prince. I must admit he is a good marriage prospect. Financially, I am not nearly as well-off as he. I have given most of our gold away to the North. But I am not poor by most standards."

She was lost in thought for a long while, and he allowed the easy silence to lie between them.

"I would like to accept your offer, my sweet Quinn. That is, if you promise not to be embarrassed by a wife who is a former actress. I will be a good wife and, and one thing you can be sure about, I will *never* go near a theatre again. You were absolutely right about everything."

"No. I was absolutely wrong to think that I could make you give up your acting. You would never be happy. And then, I would not be happy."

"I need you to help me, Quinn. I want to close the theatre, pay off all debts, and forget that I ever thought about the stage. I think if I sell most of my jewelry I will have enough. But, if not, I would like to borrow from you. To pay back Grigori, especially."

"You can borrow everything I have. But, do you mean to tell me you don't intend to complete your run of *Hamlet*? You intend to default on your obligations?"

"I don't intend to default. I will see that no one is owed anything. My jewelry will take care of most of it."

"I don't mean that kind of default . . . and you have to remember that you owe yourself something too."

"You saw what happened tonight. If it hadn't been for you, I can't tell what might have taken place. Do you want to put me through another night of such humiliation?"

"You were extraordinary. They were the ones who did not understand. But you must make them accept you."

"I can't, Quinn. I'm not strong enough. I can't go through it again."

He looked at her with sympathy and gave her little kisses as he held her. "I want you to marry me, Marielle. And I want you to continue to be what and who you are. How will you ever grow as a human being if you keep running away from every difficult episode in your life. I was wrong. I admit it freely. After last night, I think you can be my wife and a performer at the same time. And I think we can be happy if we work at it. Are you going to give it a try?"

"No, my darling. It's much too humiliating. I can't continue the run of the play. You're asking too much of me."

"Last week, when you refused my offer of marriage, you were right. There were too many strings attached to my offer. Now I've done a turnabout. I've seen you on the stage. I know what you can do. You belong there. Why are you refusing me now, when I have fully accepted your talents."

"I'm not refusing marriage. I'm only refusing to act."

"Marielle, my beautiful angel. You must. Not for me. For yourself. You must continue your acting career."

"No. No. No," she said very softly.

"Believe in yourself. Believe that they will accept you and they will. I promise you."

He enveloped her in his arms more closely and, as he made love to her and took her body and gave her his, he talked. He talked long into the dawn.

Chapter Thirty-two

There were crowds milling around the theater and congesting the street when Marielle and Quinn arrived two hours before the play was to begin. A line outside the box office that stretched for almost two blocks moved slowly as playgoers were turned away from an already full house. The ticket holders who waited for the theater to open were a volatile mob, and Marielle thought she saw eggs sticking out of their outer pockets and vegetables concealed in the inside pockets of their open coats. Some ticket holders hawked their more expensive reserved seats for double and triple their value.

She turned to Quinn with dismay. "I think it will be a repeat of last night. We're making a big mistake."

In answer, he took her by the arm and they pushed their way into the theater. Again, the crowd parted as she wended her way from the lobby into the dark orchestra. Quinn closed the theater doors behind them, or the mob would have followed her in.

Backstage, the company had assembled and waited for someone in charge to tell them what to do. Prince Grigori, Marielle noted, was conspicuous by his absence, which was not surprising since Marielle had earlier in the day told him the truth about herself and Quinn. Her cast gathered around her, their eyes solemn and guarded, and waited for orders for the night's performance, if there was to be one. From the expressions on their faces, it was easy to deduce that most felt there would not. On some of the faces, Marielle saw flashes of sympathy and regret.

Every review had been disastrous except for the *New York Sunday Times*, which lauded her performance as a *tour de force* for women's rights. At home, Quinn had kept the newspapers away from her, but here at the theater she read every one. She wondered what she was doing here, why she bothered to prepare herself for another night of disaster. What good would it do to fail completely two nights in a row. But, then, she looked at Quinn's face and took heart. He led her to the middle of the circle of players and waited for her to speak.

She cleared her throat and looked at the serious faces in front of her. She thought she detected tears in her Ophelia's eyes as the young girl waited along with the others.

"The audience and the first night reviewers have been unsparing in their condemnation and ridicule." She looked for strength at Quinn, but he had moved aside. No matter what he had said or done during the night, he was not going to help her now. She would have to do it herself. She was on her own. Strangely enough, she understood his reasoning.

"We have the theater for the next two weeks. I cannot say what will happen tomorrow night. But what say you to performing tonight? This house is sold out, and I am game to do my best once more. You will be paid one way or another, so don't let money influence your decision."

They stood around her silently, and then her young Ophelia spoke. "I'm ready," she said in her sweet, girlish voice.

The others, one by one, nodded in affirmation.

Marielle stood with dignity and held up her hands. "Then we'll continue."

They cheered her then, and she wondered if she was doing the right thing, and if they would be cheering her after the performance tonight. This evening could be worse than yesterday, depending on the mood of the mob. Most of the audience knew exactly what they were going to see, and might better prepared with vegetables and eggs.

She looked at Quinn, who was standing at the outside of the circle of players. He looked proud of her, his face showing his admiration. But what would it be like tonight? Would he be as proud of her when the curtain came down as he looked now? The sick feeling in the pit of her stomach returned. It was another opening night, but so much worse. . . . She had never been more afraid in her life.

If they hung off the rafters yesterday, today even more bodies squeezed into the interior of the theater. Some even sat on the floor, in the aisles along the far walls. How so many spectators had been squeezed in, Marielle did not know, but when she looked out the peephole she saw a solid mass of faces. The ticket sellers in the box office had taken advantage of every inch of space and had sold it at a profit.

It felt a little like a hanging out West. Thirty minutes before the curtain was due to be raised, everyone was seated and many in the gallery were stamping their feet.

She was overwhelmed with a sense of panic. Fear constricted her throat. She felt hot and cold by turns, and found herself trembling like a leaf.

Moving away from the peephole, she went from dressing cubicle to dressing cubicle and acted her heart out by setting the minds of her fellow players at ease. A loving pat here, a kiss there, a kind word to a grizzled veteran actor, and they believed that she was not afraid of what was to come. No matter how she felt inside. Then she went back to her own dressing room, where Quinn waited for her, and collapsed on the chair in front of her dressing table.

It was time for the curtain to go up. Putting her head down and her hands up to her face, she took a deep breath. "I can't go out there, Morgan," she managed to whisper, "I'm too afraid."

She looked up at him. There was no sympathy on his face, only his own strength and courage, and he could not hand that over.

"Come," he said. "I shall stay with you until you have to make your entrance. I cannot go on stage with you."

She nodded numbly and stood up. It was like going to her own funeral.

He led her toward the stage. She held on to the sleeve of his coat as if she could draw his full strength through the material of his clothes. He was her *raison d'être*. The strong current of his life flowed through her. Without him, nothing mattered; with him, there was purpose and direction.

On cue, she made her entrance. There was complete silence from the audience. Even the coughing had stopped. A small smattering of applause began, probably from friends, and that, too, soon died. She opened her mouth and her first speech came out, and she lost herself in the character of Hamlet—she became him, and her voice became strong and clear and confident.

Only the absence of sound from the audience kept bringing her back to reality. Normal sound. Where was it? The silence was heavy, hanging in the air, permeating the walls, eating into the velvet curtain. She dared herself to look into the audience and saw only blank stares. Not one compassionate face. They were there to hate her, and if they were doing it differently than they did the night before, it turned out to be even more devastating in the end.

She became angry as she continued. She knew exactly what she was doing. How dare they respond that way? The silence seemed more unbearable with every passing minute. Three hours. There were no coughs, no noisy turns of bodies, no spontaneous whispers between partners at some small piece of business on stage; there was only utter stillness.

Finally it was over. She had given them the best of herself. She had given them all. There was nothing left inside her to give. She was drained.

She stood on the huge stage and waited for their response. There was nothing. Silence still prevailed. There was a deep stillness that could not be broken. No one moved.

The other actors joined her on stage; she stood in the middle and they lined up on either side of her, as if to shield her from the silence in the audience.

From the distance, she saw the back door of the theatre open, and Quinn slipped into the room. He stood in the rear and started to applaud. He was the only one, and his applause echoed through the stillness like thunder. It seemed like an eternity, but he continued to applaud alone. Then they all started to applaud. In unison, with a roar, the audience stood up and cheered and applauded.

Marielle took her bow and her company of actors took theirs, and still the cheering and applause continued. The company of actors left the stage and Marielle stood alone. "Bravo," she heard all over the theater, and the cheering continued.

She left the stage and the applause went on. She returned to take bow after bow. She had never had so many curtain calls in her entire career. The exhaustion left her. She felt fresh and new. The applause was music in her ears. They had decided that they loved her again.

He was waiting for her when she got back to her dressing room with a bottle of champagne. She could see his broad shoulders and tapered back as she came through the open door. Running up to him lightly, she thew her arms around him, the side of her face resting against his strong back.

"Thank you, Quinn. I know what you did. I saw."

He put the champagne down, turned around slowly, and enfolded her in his arms. "You did it. I just helped them tell you. They were too slow for me. But it was you . . . you alone, who made them applaud."

"Still, I liked what you did."

"Don't think of it as something I've done."

"It's okay, Morgan Quinn," she said softly. "It's okay for you to do things for me. I've decided I like it. In fact, I love it. It's perfectly okay for you to take care of me. I need it."

"It's true. You do." He looked down at her and kissed the tip of her nose.

The well-wishers descended on them then, crowding them apart, kissing and congratulating Marielle, smiling, laughing, chattering nonsense. The atmosphere was festive, but insane. She was pulled away from him and the throng closed in around her. She shot him a beseeching look and put her hands out so that he might take hold and not let her be taken away. But her public was strong in number, and Quinn was pushed farther back as her adoring followers regrouped around her. It was far worse than it had ever been in the past. They surrounded her and touched her and handed her huge bunches of roses for which she had no vases.

She smiled and kissed hundreds of people and tried to work her way back to Quinn, all the time keeping him in sight. At last she was able to touch him again. He helped her inch into a corner and turned his broad back so that the advancing mob could not get at her.

"To hell with it all, Quinn," she shouted to him above the noise. "I want to go home. Back to the ranch."

He bent over her. "You've got them, Marielle. You don't have to go home. New York is at your feet. It's all yours. Everything you ever wanted."

She put her arms around his neck and got as close as she could with any sort of propriety. It did not matter that the room was filled with her friends and followers, all back in the fold now that everyone was sure she was a success. The crowd in her dressing room laughed and accepted the fact that she put her arms around a man who was not her husband, and gave her lips up to him in sweet surrender.

"Let's go back to the ranch, Quinn. If I ever want a theatre, you can build me one in San Francisco. If that's too far from home, you can build me one in Sacramento," she whispered and continued their kiss. "But remember, never build one too far away from where you are."

"I can build you one right outside your front door, if that's what you want. But are you sure you know what you want?"

She backed away playfully. "You surprise me, Mr. Quinn. You, my darling guardian, who are supposed to know me so well. Don't you know by now that you are *not* the man I *thought* I hated. You are the man I *know* I love. Yes. That's what I want. I'm sure."

"Oh, God," he said, hugging her slim body to him. "It won't be easy."

"I know," she said. "I am a very difficult person." He lifted an eyebrow and gave her that special smile she could never resist. "Wait till you see how difficult I can be."

He took her by the hand and somehow got her past the crowds surrounding them, out of the theatre, and into the street. Holding her hand tightly, he led her away and started the trek uptown to her house on foot. She had to run as fast as she could to keep up with his long strides. But she did not mind. People along the way smiled good-naturedly as they watched the tall, lean man in evening clothes and the beautiful woman with deep red hair in a strange short tunic and black stockings peeping out from an open fur cloak stride along the streets of New York. Many recognized her and shouted her name in friendly fashion and paid her homage by stopping until she had passed.

She smiled back at everyone. Let the public say what they will about her tomorrow—tomorrow there would be only one voice she would hear—Morgan Quinn's.